## Acclaim for Catherine Alliott's previous novels

'Possibly my favourite writer, and a perfect beach read. It's big, fat and funny . . . The writing is both sparkling and intelligent' Marian Keyes

'Alliott is quick, observant and on top form' *Daily Mail*

'Witty, hilarious and highly recommended' *Prima*

'I literally couldn't put this down. An addictive cocktail of wit, frivolity and madcap romance' *Time Out*

'If you're heading off on a last-minute holiday, then this is the book for you' *Sun*

'A tongue-in-cheek romance intelligently laced with humour' *Radio Times*

'Charming, clever, well written, laugh-out-loud funny with a great plot' *Irish Times*

*Also by Catherine Alliott*

The Old-Girl Network
Going Too Far
The Real Thing
Rosie Meadows regrets . . .
Olivia's Luck
A Married Man
The Wedding Day

# not that kind of girl

# catherine alliott

**headline**
review

First published in 2005 by
REVIEW

First published in paperback in 2006 by
REVIEW

An imprint of Headline Book Publishing
1

ISBN 0 7553 2321 1 (B format)
ISBN 0 7553 310 36 (A format)

Typeset in Bembo by Palimpsest Book Production Limited,
Polmont, Stirlingshire

Printed and bound in Great Britain by
Mackays of Chatham plc, Chatham, Kent

Headline's policy is to use papers that are natural, renewable and
recyclable products and made from wood grown in sustainable forests.
The logging and manufacturing processes are expected to conform
to the environmental regulations of the country of origin.

HEADLINE BOOK PUBLISHING
A division of Hodder Headline
338 Euston Road
London NW1 3BH

www.headline.co.uk
www.hodderheadline.com

For my godchildren –
James, Isobel, Eleanor, Catherine,
Sam, William and Hugo.

# chapter one

'What's up, Mum?'

Angus put his head round the playroom door and saw my face. I hastily wiped my damp eyes on my towelling dressing-gown and pulled it firmly around me as I perched on the sofa.

'Oh, nothing, darling.' I sniffed hard, turning away from him.

'What?' He came in. 'What's wrong?'

'Well, it's just . . .' I licked my lips. 'Tamsin's been caught shoplifting again.'

'Again?'

'Yes, and you know she's pregnant?'

'Is she?'

'Oh God yes – didn't you know?' I swung back to him, wide-eyed. 'Yes! She's having Jeff's baby. And when the police came to question her I thought Jeff was going to be livid,

1

but he wasn't, he was sweet. Completely sweet. Put his arm round her and everything, said he'd stand by her at the trial and – ooh, I don't know.' I pulled a tissue from my pocket. Blew hard. 'That set me off, I think.'

Angus regarded me in the doorway. 'You're sad.'

'No, I'm not, darling. I'm fine.' I got briskly to my feet and found my slippers.

'No, as in pathetic. You don't get out enough, Mum.'

'Angus, it was a particularly moving scene, all right?' I snapped, moving quickly to the television to turn it off. 'If you had an ounce of artistic sentiment in your soul you'd appreciate that kitchen-sink drama can be incredibly moving. Ask Harold Pinter.'

'What – *Home and Away*?' He snorted. 'Give me a break. Is this what you do when we're at school then? Loll around watching soaps?'

'Certainly not,' I bridled. 'I only came in to turn it off since you'd been "lolling" in front of it all morning!'

'Well, anyway, Penny's here. I just saw her car coming down the lane. She's probably parking in the drive right now.'

I stared at him in horror. 'Already?' I squeaked. I pushed past him and ran through to the kitchen, clutching my blue bathrobe to my chest as it fanned out behind me. 'She wasn't supposed to be coming until lunchtime!'

I stared out of the window in disbelief as, sure enough, Penny's shiny blue Range Rover, without a speck of London dirt, performed an immaculate three-point turn in the gravel sweep outside. It reversed under the kitchen window and parked neatly by the back door, right next to my tubs, which at this time of year should have been a riot of autumn colour, but instead, with their blank, staring earth eyes, looked more like a couple of Damien Hirst exhibits.

'It *is* practically lunchtime, Mum. It's ten past twelve.'

'Is it? God!' I glanced at the clock aghast. 'Where's the morning gone?'

'In your case, down the cathode-ray tubes – and by the way, Dad rang to ask if you'd picked up the chickenwire he ordered from the farmshop.'

'No, I haven't picked up his sodding chickenwire! When does he imagine I've got time to do that, in between feeding his goats and clipping his bantams' toenails? Now quick, out of my way. I must get dressed before Penny sees me.'

I scurried away from the window and made a dash for the back stairs, but in my haste tripped over Angus's cricket bat, cunningly propped up against the kitchen table. Staggering to stay upright I barked my shin on the table leg, swore violently and shut my eyes tight, seeing stars. When I opened them again, it was to see Penny breezing in through my back door, blonde bob shining in the low October sun, lipstick gleaming, her arms laden with flowers. She stopped in her tracks and beamed delightedly at Angus.

'Good heavens. My favourite godson! What the devil are

you doing here? Didn't expect to see you at a midweek girly luncheon. You haven't been expelled, have you, you little toad?'

He grinned as she ruffled his flicked-up fringe.

'Oops, sorry.' She hastily poked it back into place. 'Probably spent all morning petrifying that, haven't you?'

'I have actually, and no I haven't been expelled, although it was touch and go last week. Only kidding,' he added hastily, seeing my face darken. 'No, I've got an exeat.'

'An exeat! God, the more you pay, the more you get the little blighters home, don't you? Oh, and incidentally, I owe you a birthday present, and since I never know what to get you . . .' She dived into her bag and pulled out a twenty-pound note. Stuffed it in his hand. 'Quits?'

'Cool. Thanks, Penny.'

He turned on his heel and made for the back stairs, keen to squirrel it away no doubt, before his mother could get her thieving hands on it and use it to pay the daily. Rather pathetically, I made to follow him.

'Just going to change, Pen,' I warbled gaily. 'Won't be a mo!'

But Penny hadn't been her school hurdling champion for nothing, and in a trice she'd crossed the room, negotiated the cricket bat, and seized my arm.

'What the hell have you come as? Mrs Shagpile?'

I turned, cowering in the beam of my oldest friend's

critical gaze, caught in her vicelike grip. She was looking as glamorous as ever in pale blue Agnès B cashmere and black bootleg trousers.

'Golly, what's wrong?' She peered. 'You look terrible.'

'Do I?'

'Awful! You're so pale, and your hair's all lank and greasy and you're still in your dressing-gown, for heaven's sake. Are you ill?'

Spotting a convenient lie, I scurried towards it. Sniffed hard. 'I haven't been awfully well actually, but I'm feeling much better now.' I nodded bravely. 'I was just going up to shower. But how are *you*, Pen?' I deflected neatly. 'Lovely to see you.' I returned her embrace, horribly aware that I hadn't brushed my teeth and my dressing-gown was probably a bit ripe.

'Really well.' She beamed, then looked concerned. 'But you should have said you were ill, Henny – I wouldn't have come.'

'Oh, I'm not *ill* ill, just – you know. A bit under the weather.'

'Well, you look ghastly. Oh – these are for you.' She turned and tossed the flowers neatly in the sink. 'I had a feeling it might be coals to Newcastle, but obviously not, judging by the state of your pots. I passed a terrific garden centre on the edge of your village, incidentally; you should pop in. I was a bit early so I nipped in and got all my winter pansies. Only white ones, of course,' she added quickly, and I made a mental note in my taste file that pansies were fine so long as they were virginal.

'Oh, and this is for Marcus.' She tossed me something mauve and frilly.

'What is it?'

'A lavender cushion. Someone at work swears by it, says it has him sleeping like a baby in moments. You just tuck it under your pillow—'

'And Bob's your uncle. Or not, in Marcus's case,' I said wryly. 'Thanks, Penny, but we have actually been down the lavender route. The bedroom smelled like a tart's boudoir for a while, but with limited success. I think he's back on the Chinese potions at the moment.'

'Ah. Still a problem then?'

'Oh I wouldn't say that . . .'

Personally I thought my husband's obsession with insomnia was his own private fantasy. I'd been lying next to him for nigh on fourteen years, and as far as I could tell the man slept like a baby, but he was convinced he only averaged about four hours a night. Every morning I was lucky enough to receive a detailed account of precisely how many hours he'd slept and which remedy – ranging from the herbal to hard prescription drugs to be used only *in extremis* – he'd resorted to. Currently, we even had a star chart on the back of the bedroom door which he filled in assiduously with coloured pencils, thus managing to turn sleep deprivation, literally, into an art form. I tossed the cushion up and caught it.

'Thanks for this though. I'll pop it in my undies drawer instead. Do it now, while I go and get dressed.'

'I'll help myself to a drink then, shall I?' she yelled after me as I finally made it to the stairs. 'Since I've only driven about sixty miles to see you and taken a whole day off work?'

'Do!' I yelled back, ignoring her irony and taking the steps two at a time. 'It's in the fridge. Oh – Angus.' I cannoned into him at the top of the stairs. 'Get Penny a drink, would you?'

'OK. Can I have one?'

I stared. 'Don't be utterly ridiculous, of course you can't. You're fourteen!'

'So? I'd be on a bottle a day if I lived in France. Piers's mum lets him have that when they go to their château in Normandy.'

'Well, bully for Piers,' I snorted, wondering not for the first time if we'd been right to send Angus to a school where his proximity to minor aristocracy and sons of film stars gave him delusions of grandeur. Next, it wouldn't just be the wine he wanted, but the château as well.

'And find her a decent glass, Angus,' I yelled as I ran to my room. I stopped. Hurried back to the landing. 'Not one of those horrid dishwasher-stained ones,' I hissed as he mooched languidly down.

'Your poor Mum,' I heard Penny say as he went back in the kitchen. 'Not well?'

'Oh no, she's fine,' said Angus in surprise. 'She always looks like that. Never gets out of her dressing-gown unless she's going somewhere.'

I ground my teeth and gripped the banister rail tight, shutting my eyes and counting to ten as the kitchen door swung shut, muffling their next exchange. When I opened them again, I stood for a moment, gazing through the huge landing window opposite. The garden stretched away, past the hideous blue trampoline which blotted the landscape, and down to the stream at the bottom, fast-moving and fringed with ancient willows and limes, their leaves just turning russet now and dripping aesthetically in the water. On the other side of the stream the paddocks rolled up the gentle slope to the hills beyond, where cows grazed in pure Constable country. A charming pastoral scene. A perfect rural idyll. And the estate agent had said as much, as he'd proudly waved his arm at this very window.

'Look at that! You won't get a better view than that and still have your husband home in time for supper. Nothing to be seen for miles.'

This much was perfectly true. Nothing could be seen for miles; not a dicky-bird. Well, no, quite a few of those actually – but no people. A bucolic dream house in the heart of the Kentish countryside: a long, low whitewashed farm with an acre of garden, a couple of lush paddocks, a stream running through the middle, and just for good measure, a handful of ducks gratuitously thrown in by the vendor. And I'd picked it myself, this house. Plucked it from the pages of *Country Life*, not six weeks after Marcus had floated his company, when our bank balance had changed colour miraculously overnight from red to the verdant green of the hills beyond.

'That's the one!' I'd said, running in to show him as he read the *Financial Times* in the bath in our Holland Park townhouse. 'That's the one I want, Marcus!'

And I'd said it again a week later, when I saw it through the rain-spattered windows of the car as we parked at the end of the track, getting out eagerly to pick our way down the pot-holed drive, splashing through the puddles. I couldn't get to it fast enough. It was all I'd ever wanted. And I'd wanted it so badly. And now . . . I straightened up. Took a deep breath. Well, now I'd got it.

Angus was outside now. I could see him sauntering across the paddock, tall and loose limbed, hands deep in his pockets, shoulders hunched, heading for the barn where his quad bike was kept. Off to burn up a few fields, no doubt; off to roar up those hills to the woods. I smiled. Lovely for him. Lovely. And for Lily too. A wonderful fairy-tale retreat to come back to from boarding-school. No doubt she was trotting around on her pony even now. Maybe that was it, I pondered, narrowing my eyes thoughtfully at the view. The fact that they came back to it. Remembering Penny downstairs, I went off down the passage to change.

Not wanting to appear in my usual uniform of jeans and bobbly jumper, I eschewed the jumble of perpetually recycled clothes on my chair and opened my wardrobe. The door almost creaked with misuse, and mysteriously, everything inside appeared to have shrunk. I finally came down incongruously, but rather defiantly dressed, in a maroon velvet skirt and a T-shirt of Angus's proclaiming the legend FCUK.

Penny raised her eyes, but didn't comment. She was sitting primly on a stool at my recently commissioned beechwood island in the centre of my kitchen, legs crossed, chin up, looking horribly punchy. In fact, she looked for all the world as if she were about to chair *Newsnight*. As the credits rolled and the music started, she mutated into Kirsty Wark, complete with quizzical gleam and – I'd swear – a hint of a belligerent Scottish accent.

'Angus tells me you've been watching television all morning,' she said accusingly, cutting to the chase.

And I hadn't even got my foot in the door. Hadn't even crossed the terracotta threshold.

'Yes, I do occasionally,' I agreed blithely, making for the cupboard where the glasses were kept and deciding at the last minute to bluff this one out. 'Some women turn to yoga or Pilates to relieve the stress, but I find *Home and Away* does it for me. Don't you ever indulge?'

She looked horrified. 'NEVER.'

'Well actually, I only do it occasionally, Pen,' I said cravenly, caving in dramatically. 'I was only really switching it off because Angus had been watching all morning.'

'Henny, is everything all right?' she asked, ignoring my last lie.

'Yes, of course it is,' I said testily. 'What d'you mean?' I poured myself a glass of wine and perched opposite her at the island.

'Well, I've been a bit worried about you recently.'

'Recently? What d'you mean, recently, I haven't seen you recently!' I laughed.

'No, but on the phone. And actually, that's sort of why I've come down.'

'Oh?' This sounded ominous. I shifted nervously on my stool.

'You just don't seem to have the same skippy enthusiasm for this place as you did when you bought it. You were full of it last summer, and now you seem a bit – I don't know. Lukewarm. Deflated about the whole thing. I know your dad being ill has rocked you, but on the phone the other day you almost groaned when I asked you about your plans for the garden.'

'Nonsense, I'm not deflated – you just obviously caught me on a less buoyant day, Penny, that's all. Blimey, I can't be like a helium balloon all the time. I've got to get down to the nuts and bolts of living in this sodding rural idyll, haven't I?'

11

With these last, immoderate words hanging suspended in the air, I slipped off my stool and turned to take refuge in the fridge, opening the door and peering in balefully, pretending to get lunch. Half a lemon and a sweaty packet of Cheddar stared back at me, where there should have been a Waitrose cooked chicken and some Parma ham. Damn. I'd fully intended to get it.

'And it's nothing to do with Dad, incidentally,' I said quietly, finding a bag of salad. 'He's been like that for years now. It's hardly likely to hit me between the eyes just because I've moved house, is it?'

'No. Right. Sorry,' she said quickly. 'I shouldn't have said that. And I'll say no more. You're like a pig in clover here and that's the end of it.'

I sighed. Turned. 'Well, all right, if you must know, I am slightly . . .' I hesitated '. . . less euphoric about this place than I was a year ago.'

She boggled at this admission. '*Are* you? But, God – why? I mean, it *is* idyllic, and so incredibly green-making for the rest of us urbanites. Why? It was your heart's desire a year ago!'

'I know,' I said miserably, reaching up to get a cheese-grater out of the cupboard.

'You begged and bullied Marcus to move out of London. Banged on and on about how you were suffocating there and needed fresh air and space, how the children needed it—'

'Oh, the children *do* need it – they love it, there's no doubt about that. And they were the ones who said they couldn't live outside a fifty-yard radius of the video shop or the Notting Hill Odeon; said they'd get withdrawal symptoms. But no, they couldn't be happier. Angus has teamed up with some local boys who fish and roar around on hideously dangerous quad bikes, and Lily's got her pony and is deeply in love. Spends hours washing his bottom and kissing his muzzle, or vice versa. She's going to make some man very happy one day,' I added archly.

'She certainly is. And Marcus?'

I smiled. 'Ah, Marcus.' I paused in my cheese-paring. Put the grater down. 'Marcus is born again.'

'What d'you mean?'

'I mean he's embraced the countryside wholeheartedly, Pen. The same man who declared it both terrifying and pointless a year ago and came out in a rash on the approach road to Clapham Common, has truly seen the light. The same man who felt weak without carbon monoxide coursing through his bloodstream and pavements beneath his feet is an out-and-out convert.'

'Is he? Heavens. So – what does he do here?'

'Do? Oh, he never stops. Last spring he single-handedly restocked the orchard, and now he's breeding bantams. In the space of six short weeks my husband has become a leading authority on poultry. He used to take the *Spectator*. Now he takes *Feather and Fowl*.'

'No.'

13

'I swear it. And he even – get this – enjoys the commute. Relishes it, in fact. Says it gives him time to catch up on his latest deer-stalking periodicals.'

'He stalks deer?' She glanced around nervously. 'Where?'

'Oh, they come strolling out of that wood behind us.' I waved my hand airily in the general direction. 'Wander brazenly into the back garden and nibble at the fast-food outlet I've so graciously provided for them.'

'Sorry?'

'My herbaceous border,' I said grimly. 'One reason perhaps, for my lack of skippy enthusiasm about the garden. They stand there guzzling their veggie burgers all of ten feet from the back door. Too tempting for Dead Eye Dick, I'm afraid.'

'You mean . . . he shoots them?'

'One,' I corrected. 'He's shot one, Penny, and believe me, there was nothing sporting about it. He was at the bathroom window in his dressing-gown at the time and the kick from his brand new rifle knocked him flat to the ground. I had to slap his face to bring him round, and meanwhile Lily was sobbing and being sick in the other bathroom. Having a Bambi moment.'

'Oh Lord.'

'She's hardly spoken to him since.'

Penny looked stunned. Shook her head. 'Golly, I just can't imagine it. I mean – he was always a bit of a black jeans and leather jacket man in London. Bit of a dude.'

'Not any longer,' I said darkly. 'In the space of six short months he's metamorphosed from Cool Marcus riding high on his Camden Town Production Company, to Colonel Harry Llewellyn riding Foxhunter.'

Her glass froze en route to her lips. She put it down. 'He *hunts* as well?'

'Oh yes,' I said breezily, sprinkling the sweaty grated cheese over the limp salad. I put the bowl in front of her rather defiantly. 'Twice a week sometimes. We don't see him for dust around here. Him and Fabrice are at it all the time.'

'Fabrice?'

'His new squeeze.'

'Oh Lord.' Penny seized her wine glass again. 'I'm so sorry, Henny. I had no idea.'

'It's his mount, Penny,' I informed her dryly. 'He does indeed squeeze her between his thighs, but happily, she's equine.'

'Fabrice is a horse?' She took a gulp of wine. 'Well, that's a relief. Sounds like something you put down the loo.'

'I wish I could,' I said bitterly, shaking a bottle of salad dressing rather too vigorously. 'But I have a feeling this mare wouldn't flush.'

'But . . . can Marcus ride?' enquired Penny incredulously. She took the dressing from me and sprinkled some over her salad. 'God, I didn't even know he could.'

I shrugged. 'After a fashion. He's had some intensive training since we've been here, went on a six-week course. And you

15

know Marcus, he doesn't go at anything half-cocked. He has all the zeal of the recently converted.' I smiled. 'But my spies tell me that's no substitute for being born in the saddle. We're talking big fences here, Pen, galloping across some pretty rough terrain. He's locally known as Teflon.'

'Ah.' She grinned. 'He comes off.'

'Let's just say he's a keen student of the ground over which he travels. Regularly inspects it at close quarters. In fact, I'd go so far as to hazard that Marcus has eaten dirt.'

She giggled and put down her fork. 'God, I remember spilling Chardonnay on his linen suit in the Bluebird once. He couldn't get to the loo quick enough to mop it off. Can't imagine him flat on his face in cow poo.'

'Well, he's never come back with clean breeches yet,' I purred, stabbing at my salad.

'But – doesn't that worry you?' She forked up some rather sad-looking rocket. Regarded it dubiously. 'That he might hurt himself? People break their necks on the hunting field, don't they?'

I considered this, head on one side, chewing slowly. 'I wouldn't mind a *clean* break,' I admitted, 'but I couldn't be doing with pushing him round a bungalow. Up and down ramps.'

'Henny!'

'Oh, don't worry,' I sighed. 'He bounces. At least, he has done so far. And then everyone shrieks with laughter and

16

races to catch Fabrice. It's all part of the fun, apparently. And of course they're desperate for new recruits who haven't been born in the shires with a mouthful of silver.'

'Pity he's not black,' she observed. 'He could be spearheading their advertising campaign.'

'Well, quite.'

'But – what about the production company? Isn't he still going into London to do that?'

'Oh yes, a few days a week, but it's all going so well he's letting Barry take the reins more now.'

'Really? But it was his baby. He was such a workaholic!'

'Because it interested him,' I said with a sigh. I put down my fork. 'You know Marcus: he only does what interests him, and then goes at it with a passion. Mucking out is his passion now.'

'Good grief.' She blinked at me, astonished. 'He really has got the bug. Quite the country squire.'

'Shall I tell you something, Penny?' I pushed my plate aside and leaned forward confidentially. 'Marcus has planted precisely one hundred and twenty-two trees in our orchard out there.' I pointed behind me. 'Now when you consider that the average apple tree bears a hundred and twenty-three apples, that's a lot of fruit.'

'It certainly is. And does he imagine that you're going to be bottling and pickling it?'

'*Yes!*' I shrieked suddenly, making her jump. I slammed the flat of my hand down on the counter, rattling our glasses. 'That's *exactly* what he imagines, Penny – that's entirely my point!'

Penny gazed at me for a moment, eyes wide. She looked confused. 'But – hang on. That's what you wanted, isn't it? Isn't that why you came down here? I thought you wanted all that gathering in of the harvest, plucking and squeezing in your own cider press—'

'I know,' I wailed miserably, 'I did, because I thought that's what everyone else would be doing. But they're not! They're not doing that at all!' I turned anguished eyes on her.

'They? Who's they?'

'You know, all my neighbours here in Happy Valley. All my embryonic girly chums, the wives of other budding Colonel Rufty Tuftys who've cashed in their City bonuses and waved goodbye to the Northern Line – I thought they'd all be growing their own veggies and selling them at the local WI, organising barn dances, that sort of thing. But they're not!'

'So what are they doing?'

I sank my head dramatically in my hands. Pulled at my roots. 'They're captains of industry,' I muttered darkly. 'That's what.'

She stared. 'Oh, don't be ridiculous. They can't be.'

'OK.' I raised my head defiantly. 'Let's see.' I put my hand up to tick off my fingers. 'First there's Sara Cowdray who looks like a cross between Meg Ryan and Claudia Schiffer and goes to London three days a week to run her upmarket shirtshop in Jermyn Street.'

'Nice little sideline.'

'It grosses her eighty thousand a year.'

Penny shrugged. 'OK.'

'Then there's Alice Wynne-Jones who makes beautiful pots in her puke-makingly beautiful converted barn, then there's Harriet Masters who runs a mail-order clothing company – oh, and up the road there's—'

'OK, OK, I get the picture.'

'They all bloody *do* something, Penny. And I had no idea!'

'Right,' she said, picking up her glass and swirling her wine around thoughtfully. She looked at me carefully. 'And you thought you could swan down here and get away from all those people in London who so churlishly asked you what you did all day while your children were at school. Thought you could sink into a glorious rural, yahoo existence?'

'Certainly not,' I bridled, refilling my glass. I sat up primly on my stool. 'You know very well I've never had any truck with that sort of rot. I've always considered my role as a full-time mother and homemaker hugely demanding. Never had time for anything else.'

'But now that they've gone?' she persisted. 'Now that Angus and Lily are away for weeks on end, only home for exeats and holidays, and even then only pausing to borrow your make-up or block your phone line – what do you do then?'

I bit my lip and got up to put the plates in the sink. Leaned the heels of my hands on the porcelain as I narrowed my eyes out of the window at the meadow, rolling up from the stream to the hills beyond.

'This house took a lot of sorting out, you know, Penny,' I said quietly. 'It was a wreck when we took it on.'

'But it's not now!' she retorted.

'No, but there's always something to do. It's like the Forth Bridge. Heavens, there are still rugs I need for the drawing room, and only this morning I noticed Lily's curtains absolutely *shriek* at her carpet. I must change them. And these tiles need a border. They're desperately dull above the Aga.' I clattered busily in the sink. 'Harriet Masters has got a lovely cockerel motif around hers, I might ask her where she got it.'

There was an eerie silence behind me as I rinsed the plates.

'Henny, have you rung my uncle yet or not?'

I laughed. 'How could I possibly ring him when this house is still such a mess?'

She got up and stood beside me. 'This house is perfect and you know it. It took that interior designer precisely six weeks to tart it up at vast expense – Bunny Campbell-Walker or whatever she's called.'

'Campbell-Waller,' I said bitterly. 'And she lives in the next village where she runs her design showroom from a converted bothy in the garden. Her sister, Louisa, the one who designed our garden, has the top floor for her landscape-garden business.'

'Henny,' she said dangerously. 'Ring Laurence!'

'But I'm not qualified to do anything, Penny,' I wailed, dropping the plates in the suds. 'It's all right for you, you're a sodding coffee trader. He'll want someone *far* more qualified than me. He's a famous – what is he?'

'Military historian, and all he wants is someone to *org*anise him – and you've spent the best years of your life doing that. Houses, children, a husband – you're supremely qualified.'

'But he'll ask me what I've done, and I've never done anything!'

'Nonsense, you worked before you met Marcus. As a – gosh, what were you exactly?'

'A secretary,' I said dully. 'Or in my grander moments, a personal assistant.'

'Well, there you are then!'

'Yes, here I am then. Fifteen years later and qualified only to keep someone's diary and pick up suits from the dry cleaners.'

'But that's exactly what he wants,' she insisted. 'I promise you, he's so chaotic, he never knows where he's going to be next – he *needs* someone like you to look after him! I've told him you'd be perfect, and he's dying to meet you.'

I bit my lip and stared out of the window. Penny's uncle was rather famous if one knew one's military historians, which

I didn't. Apparently he'd written several weighty tomes on various battle campaigns and lectured regularly on the subject at Cambridge. He presumably shuffled around some dusty gothic pile in a mouldy corduroy jacket and carpet slippers, searching for his glasses, getting increasingly bad tempered, and scratching his beard. Or his bottom. I sighed. I wasn't convinced it was my dream job, but on the other hand, Penny was right. I *could* do it, and it would get me back into the real world. Back into London. And actually, how cool would it be, to go to lunch at Sara Cowdray's or Alice Wynne-Jones's and say, 'Yes, I'm working for Laurence De Havilland, the military historian. Yes, *very* demanding, but frightfully good to use one's brain again, you know, and heavens, you've got to do *some*thing, haven't you? Can't sit at home all day!'

Penny was watching my face. She reached in her bag and pulled out a pen. Started scribbling on the back of an envelope.

'Now I'm going to go and find my godson, and get him to show me the lie of the land,' she said quietly. 'Get him to talk me through his dad's orchard.' She snapped the biro nib back smartly. 'You, meanwhile, are going to ring Laurence.'

She pushed the envelope towards me and gave me a beady look. Then she reached for my calendar, hanging on the wall beside her and flicked through it. 'You could go and see him on Monday, actually,' she observed. 'You're not doing anything. In fact, you're not doing anything at all next week, unless you count a charity Christmas fair. In October, for heaven's sake!'

'Oh Pen . . .' I quaked.

'Do it!' she said crossly, making me jump.

She got off her stool and crossed to my bootroom, delving around for some wellies. Dilly the black Labrador began to bark excitedly, knowing a walk was in the offing. Penny took off her kitten heels, slipped some boots on, and made for the back door, Dilly running frantic circles around her legs.

'And don't forget to tell him you did history A-level.'

'I didn't,' I yelped, scurrying after her as she went outside. 'I didn't do any A-levels, I did a secretarial course instead.'

She popped her head back round the door. 'I know,' she said. 'So lie. You're good at that.'

I watched as she flung an old Barbour of mine round her shoulders and strode out confidently across the gravel, head back, blonde hair blowing in the wind, a tall, commanding figure, instantly looking the part in this rural setting, as indeed she always did in any setting. Had done no doubt at school as Head Girl, then in the City as a trader, and now, still a trader but a rather more important one. A senior partner, holding her own in a man's world, despite having a pair of demanding three-year-old twins at home. I noticed she hadn't brought them with her today. Too clever by half. No no, she'd left them behind with the nanny.

And I'd never been able to do that. Ever, I thought, moving back to the sink. I'd always had my children on my hip or around my feet, taken them wherever I went. Emotionally I

23

hadn't been able to leave them, but also . . . well, they were my passport to cosy domestic life. I'd worn them like a badge, which said proudly, *I don't go out to work because I do something far more important*. And there was no arguing with that.

But Penny was right, I couldn't hide behind them any more. They were away for weeks at a time, and when they came back, it was home they wanted, not Mummy. I was part of it, but it was the lying around on sofas they needed, the chilling, the kicking at stones in the stream, not my undivided attention. Definitely not my undivided attention. And I had to have more in my life. Had to, or I'd end up like my mother. I shivered and seized a dishcloth to scrub away at a stain on the draining board, just as she would have done. I dropped the cloth, horrified. My hand strayed to the envelope Penny had scribbled on. I stared at it.

Ten minutes later she was back, with Angus in tow, having found Lily too. Lily's face was glowing, her fair curls bouncing off her head like a halo as she came through the back door on a blast of cold wind.

'Phew!' She was struggling under the weight of her saddle. I regarded her affectionately. She glared back. 'M-um!'

'Oh. Sorry, darling.' I rushed to help. Took the tack from her arms.

'And can you put it all in the bootroom, Mummy, I'm whacked. Freckles just jumped the whole cross-country course. Two foot nine!'

'Oh, well *done*, darling,' I gushed as she went – just about managing to take her boots off – to flop in front of the television in the playroom, followed by Angus. A fight ensued about who took command of the remote control.

'Can't she do that?' enquired Penny, following me down the passage as I whipped it all away.

'Oh, she does mostly,' I assured her over my shoulder. 'But she's a bit pooped.'

'And can you give it a wipe too, Mum?' Lily called. 'I got some mud on the bridle. Oh – and wash my girth and numnah?'

'Will do,' I called back, reaching for the saddle soap and getting a J-cloth from the cupboard under the butler's sink.

Penny leaned against the wall watching me, her arms folded.

'So, did you ring him?' she asked casually as I wiped the leather before setting to with soap.

'Hmm? Oh yes, I did,' I agreed brightly, face bowed to my task.

'And?'

'And yes, you're right, he's awfully nice.' I rubbed hard. 'Very sweet.'

'So?'

'So, I'm going to see him soon. Going to pop in some time. Heavens, this is filthy.'

'On Monday.'

'Er, well probably not Monday, Pen. But you know, soon.'

'No, on Monday, Henny. At twelve o'clock.'

I glanced up.

'I rang him,' she said grimly. 'From my mobile. Because I knew you wouldn't. He's got an interview with a journalist at eleven, but he'll see you after that. Now if I were you, my friend, I'd put that cloth down and give it to your daughter. Then I'd go straight upstairs and see to your wardrobe. You might want to sort out some interview clothes since this is the first one you've had in fifteen years. Unless, of course, you think that a crushed velvet skirt and a T-shirt proclaiming you're up for some dyslexic sex is appropriate, in which case, go as you are.'

And giving me an arch look, she relieved me of the J-cloth and went to find Lily.

# chapter two

Theoretically, weekends were reserved for a spot of action under the marital duvet. No marathon sessions, you understand, nothing to threaten a middle-aged heart, but a burst of reasonable activity on a Saturday night, followed by a going-through-the-motions on a Sunday morning. On this particular weekend, however, a combination of tiredness on my part and inebriation on Marcus's – plus increasingly savvy children wandering round the house – had saved the effort. Thus it was that on Monday morning, as my husband stood at the bedroom window buttoning up his shirt and preparing to go to work, I sensed an air of deprivation about him.

'It's a sad day when a man starts envying his cockerel,' he remarked bitterly as he gazed down at his bantams in the cobbled yard below.

'Hmm,' I murmured abstractedly from the bed, deep in my *Daily Mail*.

'Look at him, the bastard. He just wakes up, struts out of his coop, and with a cock-a-doodle-doo, nails the first bird who passes. The fact that it's his sister couldn't matter less – it'll probably be his aunt next. Look at him, Henny. That's the fourth one he's had this morning.'

'I know.' I sipped my tea sleepily. 'I've been watching him. Angus has too. Hope he's not getting ideas. He's hardly a role model.'

'He's fit though, isn't he?' said Marcus enviously, his nose getting closer to the glass. 'He's a fit lad, and a happy lad, too. Christopher the cockerel is undoubtedly a happy lad.'

'Yes, but what about the poor hens? They've hardly opened their eyes and they're being rogered.'

'Trodden,' he corrected. 'Technical fowling term. Trodden.'

'Ah.' I looked up from my newspaper and narrowed my eyes thoughtfully. 'I like it,' I decided. 'Very apposite.'

'Not in your case,' he snorted, turning to me. 'You haven't been trodden in weeks.'

'Eight days, actually,' I replied crisply, licking a finger and flicking over the page. 'We did it last Sunday.'

He sighed and slung his tie resignedly round his neck. Pulled it up, like a noose. 'You see? That's so *depressing*. The fact that you know exactly how long it's been.'

'It's not depressing, Marcus, just necessary,' I said cheerfully.

'You lie. And you have far more of your quota than most married men your age. I promise you, you are not short-changed.'

'Says who?' he squealed indignantly as he sat on the end of the bed to put his socks on.

'Says the mummy mafia, that's who. One thing I have learned since coming down here is that these girls don't know how to drink. One bottle of Sancerre at lunchtime loosens tongues, and believe me, a couple of times a week for a fifteen-year-old marriage is not bad going. Some of these women haven't done it for months.'

'Like who?' He turned, interest getting the better of him.

'Like Sophie Carter for one. She hasn't let her husband near her for three months.'

'Three months!' He yelped in agony as he went back to his socks. He shook his head sadly. 'God, poor old Eddie. Poor old Eddie Carter. He comes home from the City after a ghastly commute, works his fingers to the bone to pay the mortgage and the school fees, and all the poor sod wants is a bit of *legover normalis* . . .'

'Sophie works as well, don't forget,' I remarked. 'She's probably tired.'

'Ha!' He gave a sharp bark of laughter. 'Call that work? Poncing around in a friend's antique shop?'

I didn't answer and returned to my paper as he disappeared into the bathroom to comb his hair. Two minutes later he was back. 'Still,' he observed, raising his chin as he adjusted his tie in the mirror, 'he's obviously doing something wrong. Perhaps I should set him straight? Give him a few tips next time I see him in the Fox and Firkin? Or even set Sophie straight.' He grinned at his reflection. 'She's a good-looking bird, probably just needs a refresher course. I'd soon have her back on track.'

'I'm sure Eddie would be delighted,' I drawled. 'Sophie too, come to that. I can't think why you don't offer your services to Relate, Marcus. Think of all the marriages you could save. You should be available on the National Health.'

He laughed as I slipped out of bed and made for the shower. I grabbed a towel en passant and pulled my T-shirt over my head. Suddenly I was aware of him watching me.

'Hen,' he wheedled, following me as I went to the bathroom. 'All this talking dirty has got me a bit . . . well, you know. I don't suppose you fancy a bit of—'

Oh Lord. I nipped quickly into the shower cubicle and turned the taps on full blast. Grinned at him through the steamed-up glass. 'Sorry!' I yelled as the water poured off me.

When I emerged five minutes later, padding back into the bedroom in my dressing-gown and rubbing my hair with a towel, Marcus was doing up his cufflinks and reaching for his jacket.

'Tease,' he muttered gloomily as he thrust his arms in the sleeves.

'Marcus, it's Monday morning, for heaven's sake. The children are prowling around downstairs and Linda's due any minute. Anyway, I thought you were on the seven forty-eight?'

'Could have made it the seven fifty-two,' he said huffily.

'Oh, great. You'd have allocated precisely four minutes for our love-making?'

His eyes widened. 'Who said anything about doing it twice?'

I threw the towel at him and went to brush my teeth.

A few minutes later I was back, combing my wet hair thoughtfully off my forehead. Marcus was busy filling in his star chart on the back of the bedroom door.

'So you don't think that's work then?' I asked lightly as I came through the door.

'What?'

'What Sophie does. In the antique shop.'

'What, prancing around sticking labels on rocking chairs? Hardly rocket science, is it?' He coloured four red stars in a row, his tongue poking out of the corner of his mouth.

'So you wouldn't mind if I did it?' I sat down damply on the side of the bed.

'Did what?' He turned.

'Well, you know, work. You wouldn't mind if I went back to work.'

31

'Back?' He regarded me with amusement. Controlled his mirth as he reached for his briefcase. 'As what?'

'Well, what I was before.' I hesitated. 'A sort of . . . personal assistant.'

'To whom?' he asked.

'To a military historian, as it happens.'

His face slowly lit up with delight. 'A military . . .' but it was too much. A huge snort of laughter escaped him before he could finish. He guffawed, he staggered, he dropped his briefcase, he slapped his leg, and finally, he collapsed on the bed beside me, howling.

I regarded him, lips pursed, as he wiped his eyes and made hysterical retching noises. Was he going to be sick, I wondered. Eventually his mirth subsided.

'Oh God,' he gasped, 'that's good. That's very good. A military historian, yes, splendid.' He gave a hiccup of mirth. 'A subject you're well acquainted with, your knowledge of which,' he struggled for composure, 'is extensive. Tell me, which particular battle, from our illustrious past, will you be regaling him with first? The Battle of the Bulge, perhaps? The 1854 Crimean Uprising? The Peloponnesian War?'

'It's not that funny,' I snapped, snatching up my hairbrush and stalking to open my wardrobe. 'I don't *need* to be qualified in that sense. He's Penny's uncle, and he just needs someone to organise his day, that's all. Someone to keep his diary, do some typing, that sort of thing.'

'Sorry, sorry,' he said weakly. 'Yes, quite right.' He wiped his eyes. 'I'm sure you'll be brilliant. And no, I don't mind at all. Oh God,' he gasped, getting up from the bed, 'that was funny. That was really, very funny.'

I turned, suddenly. 'You don't mind?'

'Mind what?'

'If I'm not here? At home?'

He raised his arms helplessly. Let them fall to his sides. 'Why should I mind? There's no one else here, for Christ's sake. I'm at work, the kids are at school . . .'

'And if they're not, there's always Linda,' I put in quickly.

'There's always Linda, and they're both teenagers, for crying out loud. You fuss over them too much, Hen. It's high time you did something else.' He reached down for his briefcase. I saw his shoulders start to shake again. 'But forgive me if military history wasn't the first thing I imagined you'd hit upon on your return to the workplace.'

Still giggling quietly to himself, he picked up his loose change from the chest of drawers and tottered out to the landing.

'Oh, that's made my day,' I heard him gurgle as he went downstairs. 'Really made my day.'

'Better than sex?' I called after him.

'How would I know?' he yelled back. 'I can't remember.'

With Marcus out of the way and the bedroom to myself, I continued my ministrations in earnest. First I applied my make-up with infinite care, then slid on a silk shirt, then stockings, and finally – the little black suit. I shimmied into it excitedly. Despite Penny's warning I hadn't even bothered to try it on, so sure had I been of its suitability, its timeless elegance, its mixture of cutting-edge chic and sophistication. But – horrors! What was this? I gazed at my reflection. Was the skirt really so short? I tugged at it frantically. The shoulders so padded? I whipped the foam inserts out and slipped the jacket on again. Oh no, hopeless. Like a bosomless bra. Hurriedly I shoved the pads back in. Yes, no, it was fine, I decided. Fine. Not in the least bit eighties. Not in the least bit like Joan Collins in a Martini advert.

In the mirror, pale grey eyes stared anxiously back at me in a heart-shaped face. My hair, dark and feathery, framed my high cheekbones, and my skin was clear and creamy, but – my eye travelled down – those *legs* . . . Since when had those knees become so round? So bulbous? So patently embarrassed to be out on display? Was it because I wasn't used to seeing them? Hadn't seen them for years? I tried going out of the room, stalking confidently back in – and catching a surprise glimpse of myself in the mirror. But it was no good, the knees still screamed, 'What are we *doing* here?' Hastily I ripped the black suit off and replaced it with something more matronly, more suitable for going to parents' evenings and sports days – and visiting, well, learned professors, actually. I nodded my head confidently and went downstairs.

34

Predictably, I ran the children to ground in the playroom. They were sprawled in front of the television in what passed for their pyjamas, horizontal on a sofa apiece, their heads propped up on bent elbows like a couple of Roman Emperors. In true, Epicurean style the remains of a feast – presumably gorged after Marcus and I had gone to bed last night – lay abandoned on the floor. A flotsam of banana skins, empty crisp packets and lemonade bottles rolled luxuriantly on the carpet. Muttering darkly I stepped through the midden to gather the detritus, bent double like a cotton picker, whilst my irritated offspring frowned around me, desperate not to miss a second of some crucial dating programme; desperate to know if Maria had snogged Darren.

'Breakfast,' I informed them, trying not to snap.

Angus, eyes still on the screen, silently held his hand out for a plate.

'No, in the kitchen.'

'Can't we have it in here?' whined Lily.

''Fraid not, darling, you can sit at the table today. Come on, I've made you bacon sandwiches.'

Lily dragged her eyes away from Darren and gazed up at me. 'Why are you looking so smart? What's with the skirt and pearls?'

'Come on, chop-chop!' I said, ignoring her and hastening to turn off the box. As the room went quiet, so the spell on my children was broken. No longer held in thrall to the magic lantern, they gazed blearily into space, as if they couldn't quite remember what they were doing there. Then they got wearily to their feet, swinging their legs around as if they were made of lead, and dripped after me to the kitchen.

'I've got something to tell you,' I beamed as they slid languidly into chairs at the table. I sat opposite them, clasping my hands expectantly.

'Oh God. You're not pregnant, are you?' Lily looked appalled.

'Of course I'm not pregnant.'

'Don't be silly, she's far too old,' said Angus.

'I'm not, as it happens,' I said testily.

'That would be *so-oo* embarrassing.' Lily shut her eyes.

'Anyway, darlings,' I began again, re-lacing my fingers and smiling brightly. 'You know how I've always – well, always been here for you. Always taken my role as a mother very seriously, and how I've always – well, not in a horrid way, but rather looked down on mothers who weren't around to collect their children from school, that sort of thing.'

'Are you and Dad splitting up?' enquired Angus, without much apparent grief or interest.

I stared at him, horrified. 'No, of *course* not. Of course we're not splitting up. No, it's just that I thought – well, I thought I might . . . in a very minor way, and only a few days a week, sort of . . . get a job. Thought I might go back to work.'

36

Angus frowned at his cutlery. 'Did you use this knife to spread some Marmite with?'

'What?'

'Before you cut my bacon. Did you use it for Marmite?'

'No, Angus, I didn't.'

He sniffed it. 'Smells funny.'

'So!' I smiled brightly. 'What d'you think?'

'I think I'll change it.' He got up and went to the drawer. Riffled around for another and sat down again.

'What d'you think?' I repeated evenly.

'About what?' Lily reached for *Pony Magazine* to read as she ate.

'About me getting a job!'

'Oh.' She shrugged. Flicked a page over. 'Fine.'

'You don't mind?'

'Why should we mind?'

'Well, darling, as I've just explained, I've always taken my maternal role very seriously. Always been there for you. This is quite a departure.'

'How can you be there for us when we're at boarding-school?' enquired Angus.

'Well, you're at boarding-school now, yes, but when you were younger . . . I suppose what I'm saying is, I wouldn't have dreamed of working then. Like some mothers did,' I added smugly.

Angus looked surprised. 'Oh. We always thought you probably wanted to, but couldn't do anything.'

I frowned. 'What?'

'We didn't know you chose to stay at home,' said Lily. 'We just thought – you know, that you hadn't got any qualifications and couldn't get a job.'

My mouth fell open.

'Of *course* I could have got a job!' I exploded. 'What nonsense, of course I could. I just didn't want some – some nanny bringing you up!'

Angus shrugged. 'We wouldn't have minded. Tom Fowler's got a really fit nanny.' He grinned. 'I wouldn't have minded that.'

'Oh Angus, you would. And Tom's mother worked all hours – she hardly saw her children.'

'Yeah, but she's really cool. She does all the marketing for Stella McCartney,' put in Lily. 'Gets wicked clothes and goes to all the London parties. Tom and Jessie went to one at Visage with her last week. She must be your age, Mum, but she looks loads younger.'

'So does Will Jessup's mum,' said Angus. 'She works in publishing, just published Jonny Wilkinson's autobiography. Will met him at a photo-shoot. Got a rugby ball signed by him and everything.'

'Well bully for Will Jessup!' I snapped. I regarded my children in horror. 'Are you saying you'd have *liked* it if I'd gone out to work? Had a cool job in marketing or publishing?'

'Well, obviously,' laughed Lily, getting up to put her plate in the dishwasher. 'But don't worry, Mum,' she squeezed my shoulders and ruffled my hair affectionately as she came back. 'We can't all be high achievers. We're happy with you just the way you are.' She reached for an apple and sat down again. 'These aren't Dad's, are they? Can't I have a secret Sainsbury one?' She glanced around then bit into it dubiously.

'Well, I'm – I'm staggered.' I slumped back in my chair, appalled. Stared blankly at the wall behind them. 'All these years I've sacrificed for you.'

'What d'you mean?' Angus asked, puzzled.

'For you two!' I shrieked, sitting up. 'Put my career on hold to bring you up.'

'What career?' Angus looked bewildered. 'I didn't know you did anything. I mean, I know you once worked for Dad, but—'

'Didn't know I did anything!' I exploded. 'I'll have you know I was extremely high-powered before I met your father.'

'Really? What were you?'

'I was a – a very personal assistant. To a *very* important man!'

'Oh right. Who was he?'

'He was a – an advertising man, like your father. His name escapes me, temporarily, but he was fearfully important.'

'Did you earn much money?' asked Lily.

'Certainly I did. Certainly! Loads of it.'

'How much?' asked Angus.

'Well,' I blustered, 'it won't sound much by today's standards, but seven thousand pounds a year was a lot of money in those days.'

Angus smiled kindly. 'Course it was, Mum.' He got up to put his plate in the dishwasher.

'And I could have earned a lot more if I'd carried on working.'

'Yup,' he agreed, shooting Lily a warning look.

'But anyway, the money's immaterial. I gave it all up to nurture you two. To make sure that in the holidays we – we played leap-frog. Made gingerbread men . . .'

'I don't ever remember making gingerbread men,' remarked Lily as she munched her apple.

'Well, OK, maybe not. But heavens, I always made your birthday cakes.'

'Yes, but that doesn't matter, Mum.' She smiled consolingly.

'What d'you mean, it doesn't matter?'

'Just because Jessie was allowed to choose hers every year from Tescos. I've forgotten about that.'

I stared at her, aghast. 'Don't you remember that enormous rabbit I made? With the liquorice whiskers? It took me four days!'

She blinked. 'Er, vaguely. I definitely remember Jessie's pink Barbie one though. With the necklace made of sweets. I so-oo wanted that.'

'But – d'you not remember being pleased I was at home? When some mothers didn't get in until seven o'clock? How I always helped you with your homework?'

Angus laughed. 'Come on, Mum, you were always gossiping on the phone to your friends when we were doing our homework.'

'I remember you being obsessed with cushions,' mused Lily, screwing up her face in an effort to recall. 'Holding them up to the curtains and whimpering, "But do they match?"'

'And I remember you sobbing when I got into Falcon Court,' Angus said. 'Dad thought something awful had happened when he got home, but you said they were tears of joy and it was all you'd ever wanted.' He shivered. 'Scary.'

'Oh yes! And my Common Entrance,' recalled Lily. 'I thought you were going to have a breakdown. Remember when I came out of my science exam—'

'Yes, thank you, Lily,' I snapped. I wasn't proud of that little episode. Lily had strolled out of her exam to be met by an interrogating mother at the school gates. I'd hustled her to the car and made her recite the entire paper, question by question, on the way home.

'And then there were pictures of seasons,' Lily had said, beside me in the front seat, 'and you had to name the one with the leaves on the ground, so I said spring. That was right, wasn't it, Mummy? Spring?'

41

By the time Marcus came home from work I had to have my cheeks slapped. Have brandy put to my quivering lips.

'But she's eleven!' I'd wailed. 'Where have I gone wrong?'

I regarded my children now as they faced me over the kitchen table. Slumped in their chairs, Angus, jack-knifed, he was so tall, munching their apples open-mouthed; their hair lank, their pores open, their skin greasy. Like two enormous hormones.

'Right,' I said faintly. 'Right. Well, if all you can remember of the past fourteen years is an academically ambitious mother whose only sense of personal fulfilment came from her soft furnishings, it's clearly time I moved on. Did something for myself.'

Angus shrugged. 'We're not fussed. Just, you know, whatever makes you happy. Chill.' He turned and tossed his core at the bin. It hit the swing lid and went in. '*Ye-ess*. Fancy being thrashed at table tennis, Lil?'

'Yeah, orright.' She got up. 'I'll beat you though. Anyway,' she paused in the doorway as they went out, 'what are you going to do, Mum?'

'I'm going to work for . . .' I stopped, remembering Marcus's mirth. Remembered too that Angus's last school report had said he showed an astonishing grip of the Crimean War. 'I'm going to work for an academic,' I said quickly. 'A very esteemed academic. If I'm lucky,' I added hastily, remembering, too, that I hadn't got the job yet.

'Right.'

'Well, aren't you impressed?'

Lily smiled kindly. 'It's not exactly Stella McCartney, Mum. But it's a start.'

# chapter three

'What are you wearing?' Penny barked bossily down the phone as I whirled around the kitchen, grabbing keys, tokens for the station car park, earrings from the fruit bowl.

'A tweed skirt, grey jacket and pearls. Too formal?' I asked anxiously.

'No, fine. I'm just checking you're not still in your pyjamas. Chickening out.'

'Good God, I wouldn't dream of it. The children were extraordinary, Penny, most illuminating. They've clearly had me down as a sad case for years – think the world of women like you with proper jobs.'

'And after all you've done for them?' she said dryly.

'Well . . .'

'Come on, what did you expect? A pat on the back? A medal?' She sighed. 'We none of us get it right, my friend. Don't beat yourself up too much about it. And anyway,

44

you'd have done all this a lot sooner if it hadn't been for your dad.'

I swallowed. Thought of Dad in the Home that Mum and I had finally given in to. Imagined him sitting there now, at a Formica table with six other inmates, having breakfast perhaps . . . an old man dribbling opposite him, another beside him being helped with his cornflakes. That institutional smell, a combination of cabbage and soiled clothing, an ingrained stench seemingly impervious to the efforts of the hospital laundry. A nurse, squatting brightly beside my father on her haunches: 'Come on, Gordon, eat up!' I shivered. Wondered what he'd say now if things had been different. 'Going back to work, Henny? How marvellous.' Then, mildly perhaps: 'Who's looking after the children? Not that Linda woman?'

I said goodbye to Penny, promising to ring when I got back, and as I replaced the receiver, heard a car in the drive. I glanced out of the window. Linda, cheeks pink with effort, was shifting her colossal weight carefully out of the front seat of her Escort. She made her way heavily across the front lawn, skirting the bird-table my father had made in occupational therapy last Christmas. It was a basic, rudimentary structure with jagged edges and rough nails, a tray on a stick, but one that he'd clearly been proud of. He'd presented it to us in the dayroom, wearing a paper hat from a cracker, swearing, as was his recent wont.

'There. What the fuck d'you think of that?'

There'd been an awkward silence. Five years ago, he'd have looked up from the *Observer*, peered benignly at it over his reading glasses and observed, 'Well, a blind man would be pleased to see it.'

Mum couldn't impose it on her neighbours in the communal gardens at the flat in the Finchley Road, and Benji couldn't bear to accommodate it in Chelsea it upset him so much, so it had ended up here, in my front garden in Flaxton. I thought I'd loathe it, looking at it every day from my kitchen window; reminding me of the man my father had become, but funnily enough, when I'd filled it with nuts and the birds swarmed around it regardless, I found it strangely comforting.

I hastened to the loo now, so as not to see Linda's face when she came into the kitchen and spotted last night's pans in the sink. There were only a couple, I reasoned, everything else went in the dishwasher, but she never failed to make me feel guilty. As I locked myself in, I caught sight of myself in the mirror. Fiddled nervously with my hair. It was probably too long now I was thirty-something, but Marcus liked it that way.

'Don't cut it,' he'd say crossly when I came back from the hairdresser's. 'I like it as it is.'

And I liked it too. Made me feel young even if I wasn't.

I scanned the collage of photos which decorated the walls

and spotted one of Dad holding Lily on a beach when she was about six. He was smoking a pipe, looking very calm, very still. I gazed into his clear, lucid eyes. Swallowed.

I looked like him. Everyone said so. Less so, perhaps, as I grew older. The eyes, huge and grey, and the pale skin, yes, but the mouth – which I'd always thought was his, wide and generous – seemed to be shrinking these days. Looking more like Mum's.

I sighed and went back to the kitchen. Linda was already planted firmly at the sink, ostentatiously scraping burned fat off a grill-pan. She snorted when she saw me.

'Blimey, what's this? Miss Jean Brodie?'

I glanced down at my skirt. 'Oh. No, I've got a job interview.'

'A job interview!' Her pale eyebrows shot into her crispy blonde perm. '*You?* As what?'

'As a researcher for a historian,' I replied shortly, wishing, not for the first time, that I hadn't employed such a 'character'. A 'conscious card', as my brother would say. I'd thought her fun and amusing when she'd first waddled into my kitchen, sucking her teeth and telling me my chickens had death foot, and that the whole place needed a good seeing-to, and that she was as happy with her hand up a horse's backside as she was with it down a lavatory, but now I wondered whether someone a little more servile wasn't what I needed.

She was a huge woman, with big legs that, as Angus said,

made you wonder how they met at the top they were so thick at the bottom. Marcus had replied that it didn't bear thinking about. She can only have been about fifty, but had an old woman's habit of farting gently at every step. As she rocked from side to side now to get to the table, an unfortunate smell pervaded. I skirted her and made for the back door.

'If you wouldn't mind making sure Angus doesn't watch television all day I'd be grateful,' I said obsequiously, 'and Lily could perhaps do some revision. She's got exams when she gets back.'

Linda rose magnificently to this, suddenly realising I was putting her at the helm. Her back straightened as she turned, eyes bright.

'Right. I'll get after them, shall I? Get 'em off them settees the moment I've cleaned this kitchen. They can tidy their rooms an' all.'

'Marvellous,' I said faintly, thinking that that would be a first, but that actually, Linda would probably achieve it. Might even get them to pick up those wet towels instead of side-stepping them gingerly like landmines, get them to wear socks and brush their teeth. In fact, it occurred to me as I shut the back door behind me and hurried down the gravel to the car, that this working lark was a doddle. I stopped still in my tracks. Why had I come to it so late? Why had it taken me fourteen years to get to this point? Why hadn't anyone told me – Penny, Eva, any of my other mates? No wonder so many women did it. *I Don't Know How She Does It?* Oh, I do. You just get someone else to do it. Feeling a bit light-headed with realisation, I toddled down to my car.

By the time I arrived at Laurence's house later that morning I was walking on air. Not only had I had the pleasure of walking through Covent Garden at lunchtime, pausing briefly to watch the acrobats in the Piazza, loving the crowds, being propelled by tourists and feeling as brisk and impatient as any other commuter, but now that I'd slipped down a side turning and emerged into a quiet, rarefied street, I was in heaven. Never mind that the litter rolled luxuriously in the gutter, or that two doors down, a young lad lay prone in a doorway in a sleeping bag – never mind. This was what I'd come for: a slice of old, elegant London, still visible through the detritus and the grime.

The house itself was tall, white and stuccoed. Did Laurence De Havilland own the whole thing, I wondered? My excitement mounted. Yes, he probably did. And no doubt I'd have the run of it. Whiz from floor to floor finding his hat, or locating his walking stick, and then when I'd finished transcribing his historical notes or whatever else he wanted me to do, I could swan off for lunch in the Piazza. Meet a friend in a wine-bar, whistle round Whistles – the very idea made me feel about nineteen again. It was as though a film was lifting from my life, revealing the exciting and the possible, just as the predictable and the mundane – a jumble of pots and pans and laundry – melted into the air.

I gazed up at the four storeys, almost expecting to see the great man himself at a desk in the window, peering down over his half-moon glasses as his interviewee nervously mounted the steps. How many had he seen already, I wondered? Was I the tenth this week? Had he rejected the others out of hand? Was he only seeing me as a favour to Penny? I smoothed down my skirt, clutched my shoulder bag tightly, and rang the bell.

Moments later, a light tread came down the hallway, accompanied by girlish laughter. Something hilarious was shouted back upstairs. I frowned and stepped backwards. The door was opened by a ravishing-looking girl of about twenty-five, with waist-length dark hair, slanting eyes and a wide sexy mouth. She was wearing a tiny white T-shirt, low-slung jeans, and her feet were bare. His daughter? She flashed me a perfect smile.

''Ello! You must be 'Enrietta?' Her French accent was weighty.

'H-Henny. Henrietta – that's right.'

'Emmanuelle,' she offered. 'Come, come een,' she cooed, standing aside to usher me through. ''E's waiting for you upstairs. I take you up, yes?'

'Um, thank you,' I said, flummoxed, as I followed her towards the stairs. Daughter, I decided. Must be. Or granddaughter even. But French, clearly, or Spanish, so . . . golly, was he foreign? Penny hadn't mentioned that. Could one have a foreign uncle? Was Penny secretly French?

'You 'ave come far?' she asked, flashing me another adorable smile as she twisted around on the stone staircase to look at me encouragingly.

'Um, not too far. Flaxton – in Kent. A little village.'

'Ah, pretty! I love the countryside. *Si charmants*, your *villages*, *n'est-ce pas?*'

'Um, yes. It is. *Ch . . . armant.*'

'He ees in here, in ze attic,' she trilled, as she led me further and further up, around the huge stone staircase encased in a wrought-iron balustrade, and just as I thought we could go no further – we were there. My guide breezed in through some double doors and I found myself standing in a long, billowing room. It was pale and spare, like a cool husk. The walls were white and covered in bright modern paintings, and the boards beneath our feet were wide, bleached and uncovered save for one, jewel-like rug. A bank of French windows looked out over the street, hung with simple calico curtains, and around the room were dotted modern pieces of furniture, very much in the David Linley mould. Two huge creamy sofas faced each other at the far end of the room, one with its back to me, and to the left stood a leather-topped desk covered in books. It was a beautiful room, but conspicuously empty. There was no sign of its owner, except – heavens. Was that a foot, sticking out over the end of that sofa? A stockinged foot?

'Laurie, get up!' Emmanuelle danced across and tweaked the big toe. 'She's 'ere. I told you she's 'ere!'

'Ouch!' The body attached gave a yelp, and the next minute, a dark tousled head shot over the back of the sofa.

'Oh God, sorry. I was about to reach my best score.'

He threw down a Game Boy, jumped smartly to his feet and came across the bleached boards with his hand outstretched, smiling broadly.

'Hi. Laurie De Havilland.'

I stared, horrified. This man was in his late thirties at most; tall, dark, with intense brown eyes – bedroom eyes, my mother would have called them – a gravelly voice and flashing white smile. He was devastatingly handsome but in a decidedly wicked, twinkly sort of way. As he stood beside Emmanuelle in a pink shirt, old torn jeans and his socks – was there a no shoes rule here? – I gaped back, painfully aware of my good suede boots, my ghastly tweed skirt, my pearls.

'It's Henrietta, isn't it? Penny's told me all about you. You're just as I imagined.'

'Well, you're not,' I blurted out. I couldn't help it. 'You're much too young!'

He threw back his head and laughed. 'Too young for what?'

I blushed. 'Well, I thought . . . Penny said you were her uncle. So I rather imagined . . .'

'Some crusty old geezer with a walking stick and a monocle chasing you round his desk?' He moved to a side-table where there was a tray of coffee. Poured a cup from the percolator. 'Sorry to disappoint.'

'Oh no, you haven't,' I rallied. 'It's marvellous. I mean – oh God.' I blushed even harder, vowing to kill Penny for not briefing me properly.

He laughed. 'Penny's grandfather married three times. He was a bit of a rascal, by all accounts. I'm the result of the old boy's last gasp when he was in his seventies. And it really was his last gasp, as a matter of fact, since he died on the job, having impregnated my mother. What a way to go, eh, sugar?'

Was he calling me sugar?

'In your coffee.'

'Oh. No, thank you.'

'Milk?'

'Please.'

'You know, you look awfully familiar.' He regarded me carefully as he handed me the cup. So did he, I thought as I took it nervously, the cup rattling boisterously in the saucer, but I couldn't for the life of me think why.

''E say that to all ze girls,' chided Emmanuelle, crossing to a desk where she picked up her handbag and a bundle of letters. 'I go now, Laurie, *oui*?' She went across and kissed him prettily on the cheek. Girlfriend. Definitely girlfriend, my scrambled brain decided.

53

'And I post these for you on ze way,' she went on. 'You look after 'Enny, yes?'

'Oh I will, and listen, *chérie, après le déjeuner, peux-tu . . .'* He continued in quickfire French, to which she responded even faster. I tried to look simultaneously alert and patient while this exchange was taking place. At the end, she turned to smile at me apologetically.

'So sorry, but my English is so bad, sometimes I lapse wiz Laurie.'

*'Ah oui,'* I agreed. *'Absolument.'*

They looked at me, surprised.

*'Absolument* to lapsing with Laurie, or speaking French?' he enquired.

'Oh, er . . .' God, he was wicked. 'To speaking French,' I said, seeing it as the lesser of two tiger traps.

'You speak French?' Emmanuelle said with interest.

I kept a vivacious smile going. Couldn't speak for a moment. *'Absolument,'* I said again, the palms of my hands feeling distinctly sweaty.

'Well, that helps,' observed Laurie thoughtfully, 'although you won't need it much. And incidentally,' he winked, 'Emmanuelle's never lapsed with me in any other respect, although I'd love you to think she had. Might think it was part of your job description.'

'You mean . . .' I turned to her, startled.

'You are taking over my job because I am going 'ome. I'm

54

going back to Paris to marry a decent man and get away from thees terrible one I work for, for two years.' She grinned. 'I weesh you luck, 'Enny. He flirt for England, but don't worry. 'E all mouth and no . . . 'ow you say?'

*'Pantalon?'* I offered.

They both laughed.

'*C'est bien vrai,*' said Emmanuelle.

Flushed with success at making them laugh, I kept the bright smile going. Couldn't turn it down actually, let alone off. I suddenly wanted this job so badly. Every fibre in my being wanted to be part of this glamorous, fun, flirty set-up, in this gorgeous, spacious office, sitting at – well, presumably that was my desk, I thought, eyeing a smaller, more isolated one under the window, almost scrabbling to deposit my bag underneath it, in fact – in the same room as this terribly important, but terribly attractive man. Oh, we'd swap careless banter, no doubt, but I'd also be an indispensable part of the organisation, a cog in the wheel, spinning round in my chair and calling out, 'Laurie, darling, don't forget you're at Cleopatra's Needle today!' Or, 'Elgin Marbles tomorrow, my love,' or whatever it was he did. What *did* he do, I wondered feverishly. Suddenly I wished I'd given all this a bit more thought. Done some research. I felt like Alice, stepping through the looking-glass, away from the unmade beds, the groaning laundry basket, the rows of empty jam jars awaiting their home-made crab apple jelly, into a glorious, glamorous world, but having trouble recognising it, it was so alien. Having trouble getting my bearings.

'And you tell 'er everything she needs to know, yes?' warned Emmanuelle, wagging her finger at him as she moved towards the door. 'You tell 'er you always forget your plane tickets so she needs to pack them for you, and you tell 'er you never get to ze Television Centre on time so she need to book you a cab, and—'

'Television?' I interrupted, a mite too breathlessly. 'Why on earth would you need to – oh!' I stopped. Stared at him. 'Golly, *now* I know. I knew I'd seen you before somewhere, but I couldn't think where. You do one of those history programmes, don't you? One of those Simon Schama-type things. I saw you last Sunday, in a bright yellow shirt in a cornfield in France, talking about those Shakespearean battles – "once more unto the bridge" and all that. I'm sure it was you!'

He inclined his head in benign acceptance of this. 'Or even breach, and the shirt was a mistake since it clashed with the corn, but you're right. I was indeed prowling around Agincourt's battlefields last Sunday. Although of course it was all pre-recorded, so I wasn't actually there.'

'No, no, of course not,' I agreed warmly. 'It was probably filmed months ago, but how exciting! And do you go too?' I asked, far too keenly, of Emmanuelle.

She laughed. '*De temps en temps*, but not often abroad.

Mostly because he's forgotten his script, or his glasses, so I'm just rushing across London to find him. But you'll get a few trips,' she added kindly. 'OK – I go now. *Au revoir – et bonne chance!*' She waved at me as she left. Blew Laurie a kiss.

'It's not much of a travel job, I'm afraid,' Laurie said smoothly, crossing to a sofa and indicating I should sit opposite. 'More of a stay-put-and-hold-the-fort appointment really.'

I hastened across, wishing I hadn't sounded quite so much like a vacuous Miss World contestant, keen to see the world and be on television. What, sliding into shot handing him his glasses perhaps, Henny? Waving to the family?

'Oh, and that's entirely what I expected,' I said, hitching up my skirt as I sat down so it wasn't quite so dowager-duchess. It was a bit too tight to do that though, and my descent was accompanied by the unmistakable sound of a seam splitting, as the lining of my skirt, designed to accommodate legs and not buttocks, ripped. We gazed at one another transfixed. I felt a hot flush rush up my neck.

'So,' I said quickly, clearing my throat, 'I imagine it's just as Emmanuelle said. Lots of – you know – admin.'

'Well, a fair amount,' he replied, recovering quickly. 'You don't mind that?'

'No! Love admin. Golly, I do enough at home. Well, you know,' I made a face, '*de temps en temps.*' God, do *relax*, Henny. I made an effort to compose my features and look serious.

'And of course I'm a big history fan,' I added soberly.

He smiled. 'I've never heard it put quite like that before, but that's marvellous. I don't know what Penny told you, but I'm a military historian. I was in the Army for a while.' He scratched his head sheepishly. 'Got a bit of a thing about battles, I'm afraid.'

'Oh, *battles*. God, me too. Don't get me on the Peloponnesian War, or we'll be here all night!'

His eyebrows shot up. 'Really? Is that your subject?'

I licked my lips. 'Er, not just that one,' I said quickly, wishing Marcus hadn't mentioned it so very recently. I shifted nervously in my buckling sea of tweed. 'Lots of battles, really. You know, the Battle of – of . . .' I glanced down at my ballooning lap '. . . the Bulge, the Battle of Pearl Harbor, the Battle of Potemkin—'

'Battle . . . ship, *Potemkin*?' he enquired, eyebrows raised.

'That's the one. Probably my favourite, but they're all good, aren't they? And of course we've got our very own battleground close to home that we're so proud of.'

He looked surprised. 'In Kent?'

'Well no, Sussex. Hastings. But it's not far, is it?'

He got up quickly, mouth twitching perceptibly, and turned his back on me. Clearing his throat, he rustled some papers on his desk. 'No, it certainly isn't,' he agreed. 'But to be honest, Henny, an in-depth knowledge of military history is not strictly necessary. Can you type?'

'Oh, *absolument.* Drrrrr!!' I drummed all ten fingers on his coffee-table to demonstrate.

'Excellent. Only Penny said you hadn't worked for a while, so I wondered—'

'Ah, but I kept up my skills. You've got to, haven't you? And frankly, it's about the only thing that impresses my children these days, the fact that I'm faster on the computer than they are. Well, obviously, a few other things impress them too, but—'

'Obviously.' He smiled. Perched on the edge of his desk, he folded his arms and regarded me kindly. 'Look. All I really need, Henny, is someone relatively flexible to field my calls, keep my diary and reply to letters and faxes. Oh,' he grimaced, 'and sometimes keep the journalists at bay.'

'Journalists!' I gasped. Suddenly I saw myself opening the door to hordes of paparazzi, camera bulbs flashing wildly in my face, like that guy in Notting Hill in his underpants. Except I wouldn't be in my underpants. I'd be in a sexy little black dress with a row of seed pearls. Or maybe a chic Chanel suit. Pale pink. Bouclé wool. Very short. Have to diet, the legs weren't great at the moment.

'Henny?'

I came to. 'Oh yes, I can do that,' I assured him. 'I'm frightfully cool under fire.' I was dimly aware that battle analogies were tumbling *ad nauseam* from my mouth. 'Marvellous at fighting the flak.'

'Good. It's really not that difficult, and Emmanuelle seems to manage it fairly effortlessly, so we'll just play it by ear, shall we?'

He turned and shuffled a few more papers and I took it as my cue that the interview was over. I jumped up.

'So. This is you,' he said, crossing the room athletically and disappearing back out to the landing. 'In here.'

I snatched up my handbag and after a quick glance over my shoulder to check my skirt was still intact even if the lining had gone, followed him across the hallway into a little office.

'It's a bit cramped, I'm afraid,' he was saying.

Ah. Right. So not together in the billowing drawing room. Still, this was an awfully pretty room, I decided, glancing around at the spriggy blue wallpaper and the pot plants. Emmanuelle had made it very feminine. Very homey. I spotted a photo of a chiselled dude, presumably her fiancé, on the pinboard above the desk. And actually, I could relax a bit more if I wasn't in the same room as Laurie. Wouldn't make so many gaffes. And naturally I'd be popping in to lighten his historical load, take through coffee, insist he take a break and flop down on the squashy sofa when I felt he'd been working too hard. Yes, I'd be a sort of protector to this great man. And indispensable, of course. People would say, 'Yes, he's marvellous, but I don't know where he'd be without Henny. She's his right arm. He can't *move* without her.'

'Emmanuelle will clear some of her stuff away,' he was saying, glancing around. 'But what d'you think?' He turned to me. Quite close now, his eyes intent on mine. Gosh, he was tall.

'Oh, yes. Lovely. But – d'you mean – that you'd like me to take the job?'

'Yes. If that's all right with you?'

'You don't want me to . . . I don't know, take a typing test or something?' I seemed to remember doing that when I started in the advertising racket. But that had been years ago.

Laurie scratched his head. 'To be honest, how fast you type is not really an issue. You can do it with two fingers for all I care, as long as it gets done.'

'Oh no, all of them!' I waggled them, grinning.

'Good.' He put his hand on my shoulder to guide me out and down the stairs – a light, friendly touch, much as he'd touched Emmanuelle – but it turned me to jelly. But then Emmanuelle had that gorgeous hunk on her pinboard, didn't she, so it wouldn't affect her equilibrium. And, of course, I had Marcus, I thought guiltily.

'You're married to an adman, I gather?' Laurie remarked, reading my thoughts as he went ahead of me down the stair-case. 'Penny said.'

'Yes, that's right. Except that Marcus has got his own production company now. But he was the creative director of an ad agency in London. That's how we met.'

'You worked for him?'

'Yes, I was his secretary. Fell in love with the boss. Usual story.' Oh *no*, Henny. I went hot behind him. 'I – I mean,' I stuttered, wondering what on earth I did mean, but he'd already stopped. Turned to look at me on the stairs.

He gazed at me intently. What, I wondered nervously. Had I got lipstick on my teeth? Lost an earring? I put a hand up tentatively.

'Of course,' he said slowly. 'I knew I'd seen you some-where before. I was at your wedding.'

I blanched, taken aback. 'Were you? Heavens, I don't remember that. How awful of me. But . . . well, you must have known Marcus then, because I don't—'

'No, no, I'm sorry.' He looked embarrassed. 'Not that wedding. It was – you know. To Rupert.'

I felt the blood leave my face. 'Oh. Right. You know Rupert?'

'Yes.' He turned quickly and walked on. I followed dumbly down the stairs. We reached the front door.

'I'm sorry, Henny, I shouldn't have—'

'No, no, it's fine,' I said quickly, and laughed nervously. 'Well, obviously it's fine. I've been married for fifteen years now. Got two children. S-so how come . . . I mean—'

'We were in the Army together,' he said simply. 'Household Cavalry.'

'Of course.' I stared. Of course. 'You said you were in the

Army.' Somehow I'd thought the Paras though, or the Marines. Something a bit more meaty. More battle-scarred. But no, he'd been in the Guards. A cavalry officer, like Rupert. A gin and tonic officer, I used to tease. A ceremonial soldier who changed the guard at Buckingham Palace, rode out in Hyde Park on a gleaming charger, bits and buckles jangling, entertained in the Officers' Mess at St James's Palace. Or Jimmy's, to the cognoscenti. Looking glamorous in mess-kit, toasting Queen and Country, smiling at his girlfriend over the silver and the crystal . . .

I tried to keep a bright smile going. Tried to come up with some merry banter as Laurie opened the door. I remembered agreeing that I'd see him later on in the week, that I'd start at nine thirty, and that I'd look forward to getting the details of my contract in the post. Then I left, and Laurie shut the door. But as I walked down the street, I had a strange sensation in my legs. Had to stop at some railings. Not to hold onto them or anything, just – to touch them briefly. Steady myself.

My head spun. So Laurie had been at my wedding. At the church in Hanover Square. In the congregation in his morning-coat, or perhaps even in a professional capacity, in the Guard of Honour. Swords raised, Rupert's comrades had formed an arch at the door for me, the bride, to pass through. I remembered their crimson tunics, their helmets and silken head-dresses. And how they'd melted away, embarrassed, when

I'd run up the church steps, hitching up my ivory silk gown, my veil flying. But I'd had to see for myself. Been unable to believe it. But then – I'd had to believe it. Had had to allow myself to be gently led away, to be passed, like a piece of delicate china, hand over hand, from brother, to uncle, to father, down the steps, back into the bridal car at the kerb.

Then, with my father beside me, I, the unmarried bride, had been driven away. Driven home.

# chapter four

I first met Rupert through Penny, when I was nineteen. Actually, that's not strictly true. It wasn't *directly* through Penny, because she didn't know him, but through her boyfriend at the time, the lovely Philip Berrington. Philip was a cavalry officer, and by virtue of that, had invitations to a ball his Battalion was throwing at Wellington Barracks that summer. Penny was his guest and I, as her flatmate, had been tossed a double ticket if I could find someone to stump up the cash and escort me. I could – happily, since I couldn't possibly afford it myself – and I was in heaven.

It was to be a grand, black-tie affair to celebrate the safe return of Philip's troop – or company or whatever it was called – from Cyprus, where as far as I could tell, he and his mates had spent a jolly six weeks water-skiing, scuba-diving and passing out in beach tavernas, coming round only to lob the restaurant chairs in the sea and be chased away by the outraged Cypriot owners. Philip would tell these tales of laddish derring-do with tears of mirth running down his cheeks, and Penny and I would laugh along with him. But I do remember asking him, as the three of us sat nursing our warm lagers in the Admiral Codrington one night, what his company was actually doing on the island. He'd looked a bit vague, but eventually scratched his head and muttered something about important garrison work that could only be carried out by highly trained security forces, so no doubt these high jinks were a smokescreen for some terribly dangerous, covert operation. I never quite got to the bottom of it.

Anyway, the ball was to be held in June, and Penny and I were in an agony of anticipation. Penny would go with Philip, and I . . . well, I would probably go with Hughie Fullerton. Hughie was my supposed boyfriend at the time, and another friend of Penny's. (All my friends, in those days, came courtesy of Penny who was far more socially savvy than I was and collected friends rather as some people collect stamps. It helped that she came from a rather grand, if slightly impoverished family, whose lack of funds had not, so far, impeded their connections.)

Hughie was a friend of her brother's and he took me out on a fairly casual basis. Casual in the sense that our dates were infrequent, and although we'd snogged a bit, we hadn't done much more. I was, however, bracing myself for more, because Hughie had recently indicated that if he was stumping up eighty quid for the double ball tickets, he expected some collateral. And actually, I was resigned to that. There are only so many gin and tonics a girl can accept without incurring the quid pro quo, and apart from that, there simply wasn't anyone else on the horizon.

So Hughie it was. And he was fine. Fine. So what if he was a touch pink and blond for my tastes and slightly overweight with unfortunate pale eyelashes which put one in mind of a pig? So what? He didn't make me heave, and I'd learned to keep my eyes tightly shut when I kissed him. That seemed to work. Why, only the other night when he'd put his hand on my thigh in the cinema I'd definitely felt something stirring deep within me. OK, I'd had my eyes firmly on Hugh Grant at the time, but still, I reckoned it was progress.

So, from our tiny ground-floor flat in Wandsworth, Operation Battalion Ball began. Penny and I spent many happy hours making big, hand-rubbing plans as we deliberated and dithered over what to wear in Hughie and Philip's honour. In a weak moment we even rang our respective mothers for advice, or even money. A wise move on Penny's part, who got the latter, but not so smart on mine. Penny's mother, although strapped for cash, instantly lobbed her an advance on her wages, which enabled her to go straight to Monsoon and secure a strapless gold lamé number which she hustled home delightedly in a carrier bag. My mother, however, ticked the advice box. She never did anything long-distance either, which was why, that same Saturday, when Penny returned to try the dress on in the flat, my mother was in the audience.

As Penny let the shimmering fabric fall over her bronzed shoulders and skinny hips, there was a stunned and admiring silence.

'What d'you think?' she asked, looking at her reflection, then twisting around to see the back in the mirror.

My mother sniffed. She shifted her weight meaningfully beside me on Penny's bed, her face pained.

'Well, it's very grown-up, dear,' she opined eventually. That, I knew, meant fast. How I longed to be fast.

'You look fantastic, Penny,' I breathed in awe.

'And so will you,' said Mum firmly. 'Here.'

She handed me a package. It was large, soft and squashy, and somehow I just knew it didn't contain a hefty cheque or a Monsoon voucher. As I shook the fabric from the folds of tissue, it dawned. Out tumbled her old ballgown from the 1950s: a shiny white Norman Hartnell number which had been stuffed at the back of her wardrobe for about a hundred years and which, Mum informed me in sepulchral tones, she'd be honoured if I'd wear. I swallowed.

'But . . . Mum, I can't. It's ancient. It won't be fashionable.'

'It's timeless,' she insisted. 'And it's a ball, Henrietta.' She leaned closer to me, the better to hiss in my ear. 'You don't wear gold lamé to a ball, for heaven's sake. You wear taffeta!'

She shook it out and bullied me into standing up as she

held it against me, head on one side, eyes narrowed.

'Perfect,' she decided. 'Don't you think, dear?' She turned to Penny, whom she admired hugely for her impressive background, even if she did have some unusual fashion ideas. Penny bent to smooth the skirt fabric down thoughtfully.

'Well, it's in good condition,' she observed kindly, ignoring the fact that the white silk was greying slightly and the whalebones were almost protruding at the top of the strapless bodice. 'And it looks as if it would fit you. Try it on.'

'Of course it'll fit her,' declared my mother roundly, and in no time at all had me out of my jeans and T-shirt and stepping into it in my pants. She zipped it up smartly at the back. 'Like a second skin – look!'

Gallingly, it did fit well. Horribly well, and I gazed in the mirror appalled. I didn't see the hourglass figure shown off by the tight corseting to the waist. Didn't see the ample bosom spilling seductively over the bodice, or my long dark hair falling in swirling pools on my pale shoulders. All I saw was – my mother. Twirling around the Hammersmith Palais in the fifties, in my father's arms, red lipstick smile fixed, hair permed, eyes bright, intent on her man. I felt sick. Clawed frantically between my shoulderblades at the zip, but Penny stayed my hand.

'Dye it,' she said sensibly. 'You can't afford to buy anything like this, Henny – dye it black. And take the petticoats out.'

I saw my mother flinch at the suggestion, suck her teeth

in horror, but she kept quiet and I, in turn, stopped scrabbling. Penny had a point. It was a classic design, just too
virginal and meringue-like at present. But after a soak
overnight in a bath of black Dylon, and with its nets removed
and nine inches taken off the hem to make it calf-length, like
so . . . the pair of them dropped to their knees to demonstrate, hoiking it up for me to see in the mirror . . . it might
just work. I sighed.

'OK.'

Mum sat back on her heels and nearly purred with pleasure.
I smiled grudgingly back at her in the mirror. Everyone has
their saturation point, and in those days I could be bullied or
coerced into most things pretty successfully, particularly by
my mother. Partly it was my upbringing, and partly that was
just the way I was. Coercible.

And so it was that two weeks later on the allotted Saturday
night, Philip, Penny, Hughie and I piled out of a taxi into
the parade ground at Wellington Barracks, laughing and
joking excitedly. And actually, that was the best bit, as is so
often the case. The preamble. The before, rather than the
event. The getting dressed in the flat with Penny, music
blaring as we put on our make-up; the glass of champagne
with the boys when they turned up to collect us; the light-
hearted taxi drive over. I wouldn't say it was all downhill
after that, but the next few hours certainly contrived to be
something of a disappointment.

# not that kind of girl

I couldn't help noticing, for instance, as we walked up a flight of concrete steps, that the Officers' Mess was supremely ugly. It was modern and tasteless with patterned carpets and glaring overhead lights, where I'd hoped for Doric columns, marble floors and high, ornate ceilings to dance under by lamplight. Instead, we drank warm champagne in a bright, overcrowded room where, to be heard above the noise, ruddy-faced boys raised imaginary chins and brayed loudly at hugely confident girls with very white shoulders, their throats encased in vast pearl chokers handed down from doting grandmothers. Penny wafted off with Philip, and Hughie and I stood and looked awkward together.

Later, we ate at tables of ten, but aside from Penny and Philip, I knew no one, and the rest of my table, including Hughie, got drunk very quickly in order to get down to the serious business of throwing food. The fixed smile on my face never wavered, and I told myself it was such fun as a bread roll whizzed past my ear and Hughie tipped a glass of water down his neighbour's neck. I told myself the same thing when Hughie pulled me roughly from my chair and onto the dance floor in a separate room, to gyrate around to 'Nutbush City Limits'. A disco, I thought in horror. Then I pulled myself together. Well, of *course* it was a disco. What did you expect, Henny – a band? A string quartet in the corner?

Well, perhaps. You see, somewhere in the dark, furry recesses of my mind I'd imagined just that. That this would

71

be a real ball. Something out of a Georgette Heyer novel, something I'd read about and seen in TV period dramas, something that I'd supposed, ridiculously, could be transported through time, to a night in 1989. To a night in my life.

Hughie's eyes were glinting dangerously in the coloured disco bulbs, and the moment the mood changed and we lurched moodily into 'Lady in Red', I knew I was sunk. A clinch and a grope were the only things on his mind. He pulled me to him possessively and his hands roved across my bare back and further down the matriarchal taffeta. I wished I was the sort of girl who could laugh and remove his hand firmly, but instead, I held my breath and hoped the song would end soon. Encouraged, Hughie plunged his face eagerly into my cleavage as if he were bobbing for apples. I gritted my teeth but suddenly – his head shot back and he gave a cry of pain. He clutched his eye.

'Shit! What was that?' he yelped, rearing away from me in horror.

I peered down. A sharp piece of whalebone was protruding from the top of my bodice.

'Oh. Sorry, Hughie. It's rather an old dress. I think a bit of the corset's worked free.'

'Nearly had my bloody eye out! Think I'll have to go and bathe it.' He glared at me, incensed.

'I should,' I soothed, possibly too quickly. 'And I'll wait for you back at the table.'

# not that kind of girl

He shuffled off huffily and I made to go back, but instead, feeling hot and flustered, took a right turn, and wandered out of the French windows onto the balcony for some air.

The balcony stretched the length of the dining room and overlooked the parade ground where one or two fairground attractions – dodgems, a bucking bronco – had been hired for the night. Quite a few people had gathered to hang over it and shriek encouragement to their friends below, but I worked my way to the end where there was a dark corner, and where I knew that Hughie would be too pissed to find me.

It was late now, and most people were either snogging furiously – almost as if there were a prize involved, I decided, eyeing a couple beside me going at it with a vengeance – or swaying to the deafening music, champagne bottles held aloft. I found a chair at the far end where I had a bird's-eye view of the action below. A very glamorous girl in a shocking-pink dress was being urged onto the electronic bucking bronco by a group of hearty friends. I watched in awe as she climbed astride the horse, her skirt hitched up high around her thighs. The machine started: slowly at first, and she swayed rather sexily along with it, then more vigorously, back and forth, up and down, as it tried to buck her off. One arm held high above her head, she rode it rodeo-style, her brown legs flashing, roared on by the crowd. I watched, spellbound. For all that I wouldn't want to be on that thing, I envied her confidence, her bravado, the way she shrieked with laughter as she finally bailed out, falling into her admiring boyfriend's arms with a flourish.

The horse shuddered to a standstill, and as it did, someone else clambered eagerly aboard. A man, minus his dinner-jacket, in shirtsleeves and loud braces. As he eased his considerable bulk into the Western saddle, I realised it was Hughie. I leaned forward, resting my chin on my hands on the balustrade. This should be interesting. Clearly the eye had recovered.

His face was very pink against his white shirt and pale blond hair, and it was getting pinker by the minute as the machine threw him about. With none of the style of the previous rider, he hunched his shoulders, tucked his head in, and held onto the pommel for grim death. I laughed quietly to myself as he was tossed about like a sack of potatoes, dimly aware that someone had sat down beside me, but too gripped to turn. Finally he was thrown from the saddle, and landed with a mighty 'Oomph!' in an undignified heap on the ground.

I chuckled quietly.

'Poor old Hoggie,' said a voice beside me. 'Hasn't exactly got a jockey's physique, has he?'

I turned to find a very tanned, tawny-haired boy beside me in mess dress. His hair was cut short in the Army style, but a long fringe flopped into piercing blue eyes. I wondered how he got away with that.

'Hoggie?'

'That's what he was known as at school. Bit cruel probably, but these things stick. You can see why it was irresistible though, can't you?'

I giggled, imagining a porcine Hughie with snout and trotters, snuffling along in school uniform, a curly tail protruding from his ample behind. Suddenly I felt disloyal.

'He's lost quite a bit of weight, actually,' I said defensively.

'Oh. Sorry. I didn't realise . . . Is he, I mean, are you two . . . ?'

I flushed. 'Oh no. Well – yes and no,' I finished lamely, feeling even more disloyal. I looked down and picked at a taffeta seam. 'I suppose we were a bit,' I admitted. 'I mean, I came with him tonight, and he probably thinks we are, but my heart isn't really in it.'

'So where is your heart?' His blue eyes challenged mine, goading me.

'Nowhere yet.' I raised my chin. 'It hasn't found anywhere worth lodging.'

He smiled. 'I know that feeling. It's like having a wallet full of money and nowhere to spend it, isn't it? The great thing is though, not to fritter it. Not to blow it on rubbish.'

I gazed at him. It seemed to me he'd cut right to the heart of my craven, cowardly soul.

'I wasn't about to,' I lied brazenly.

'Excellent,' he said softly. Our eyes locked for a moment. He held out his hand. 'Rupert Ferguson.'

I took it. 'Henrietta Tate.'

He sat back in his seat. 'So is Hog— sorry Hughie, all that brings you to this God-awful ball tonight?'

I smiled. 'No, actually I came with a friend. Penny Trevelyon.'

'Ah, the lovely Penny. Lovely Penny and Pyrrhic Philip.'

I frowned, startled. 'Why d'you say that?'

'Because she's still in love with that chap Tommy Rutlin who dumped her last summer. Old Philip's got her on his arm, sure, but it's a bit of a pyrrhic victory for him, isn't it?'

I bit my lip. It was true. Penny was still mad about Tommy, but Philip was very decorative and there was always a chance Tommy might be watching . . . wondering why he'd let her go. Eating his heart out. I turned to look at this boy beside me. Wondered at him. At his insights.

'Well if this ball's so God-awful,' I asked, 'why did you come yourself?'

He sighed. Slipped further down in his chair and thrust his hands deep in his pockets.

'Oh, I don't know. A sense of dreary obligation, I suppose. It is my Regiment's party, after all, and one always assumes these things are going to be better than they are. Where I come from though, a ball's a ball, with everyone in dresses like yours, dancing time-honoured steps with military precision.'

'Where's that?' I asked stupidly, wondering for a crazy moment if I'd hit upon a time-traveller.

'Scotland.'

# not that kind of girl

'Oh.'

'It's all this hopping around on the spot and wondering what sort of expression you should have on your face that I find taxing.'

I giggled. 'I know that feeling. And then you wonder if you should join in with the chorus.'

'Heaven forbid,' he shuddered. 'Never join in. And never punch the air to "Hi Ho Silver Lining". Please tell me you don't do that.'

'Do I look as if I do that?'

He smiled. 'No.'

'And even if I did, you can be sure I'd pick the moment that everyone else had decided *not* to, and there I'd be, mid-punch, mid-shriek, feeling like an idiot.' I laughed.

He watched me with a sideways look. Didn't say anything for a second. Then: 'How about some breakfast?'

I glanced over my shoulder into the dining room, where a couple of uniformed guardsmen were stationed behind a long white table, lifting silver domes from dishes to reveal soggy scrambled egg and greasy bacon. A raucous, staggering queue was already forming to hoover up the blotting paper.

'Won't it be as bad as supper?' I asked dubiously.

Supper had been the usual mass-catering disaster. Smoked salmon with all the consistency of tennis balls, followed by lamb that was surely sheep.

'Oh, much worse,' he said cheerfully, getting to his feet.

'No no, I meant breakfast somewhere else. Where they can cook.'

I glanced up, surprised. 'You mean . . . go out?'

'Why not?'

'Nowhere will be open, will it? It's one o'clock in the morning.'

'I know somewhere we can go.' He grinned down at me.

'Ah.' I nodded back knowingly. 'Your place.'

He looked surprised. 'No, I didn't mean that, actually.'

'Oh. Sorry.' I felt stupid. Smutty too. I got to my feet and felt my face burn. Pretended to smooth down my dress to hide it. 'Sure, we could go out,' I heard myself saying. 'Why not? I could do with something to eat.'

I followed him as he pushed through the scrum on the balcony, then walked back across the crowded dining room, making for the stairs. My heart was pounding. As I caught up with him, we passed the door into the throbbing disco and I saw Penny dancing with Philip. I hesitated. Was I just going to go? Without saying goodbye? I knew she'd be going back to Philip's, but still, we usually spoke. Touched base. And what about Hughie?

'It's only round the corner,' Rupert promised, reading my mind. 'We'll be back before this lot get turfed out.'

Somehow, I knew we wouldn't, but I wanted to believe it. Wanted to go along with it, to trip lightly down the steps and out into the parade ground with this attractive, willowy boy, muscle through the throng around the dodgems and the bucking bronco, pass through the vast wrought-iron gates and slip away unnoticed, into the night.

And it was a beautiful night. The stars looked like diamonds tossed carelessly on black velvet in the sky above us, and the air was warm and enveloping. I felt it wrap around my shoulders like a shawl. As we crossed the Mall outside Buckingham Palace, dodging the traffic and pausing in the middle to dash across to the other side – I suddenly felt I could breathe again.

'You going to be all right in those shoes?' Rupert asked, glancing down as I tottered along the pavement beside him. 'It's just around the corner, but they look lethal. We could take a taxi.'

'Fine,' I lied, wobbling furiously. 'And anyway, I want to walk.'

I did. Strolling along past Clarence House and up towards St James's under the rustling plane trees, I felt, for the first time that evening, calm and soothed. I didn't want to rush off in a taxi. I wanted to dawdle, to savour every moment.

In the event though, I wasn't fine. It wasn't just around the corner, and when we arrived at Maria's Café at the other end of Jermyn Street, I was barefoot, clutching my shoes, and with Rupert's jacket around my shoulders as the velvety night had turned nippy.

'Not far!' I squeaked as he pushed through the steamy café door. 'Bloody miles!' I fell panting inside.

'Sorry. Poetic licence.' He grinned. 'Didn't want to put you off.'

The place was tiny and crowded: full of men slurping bright red tea from mugs and eating great plates of bacon, eggs and chips, intent on copies of the *Sun*. I glanced around, surprised.

'Gosh, what's this? An insomniacs' retreat?'

'It's for taxi drivers, mostly,' he explained, going quickly down an aisle and easing into the only available table. 'Sit, quick. And spread out, or Maria will squeeze another brace of cabbies in here.'

Too late, a couple of elderly men came in behind us.

'Room for a little one, luv?' One of them squeezed in on the bench beside me, looking tired. He did a double-take. 'Blimey, look at you two. All dressed up and nowhere to go? This the best he can offer you, luv? You should be round at the Ritz!'

Rupert grinned and described the execrable food at the party we'd just been to, and how we were in need of Maria's cooking. I remember sitting there, watching him, and thinking how Hughie would have brushed these old men off with an arrogant remark. Well, let's face it, Hughie wouldn't be seen dead somewhere like this in the first place.

'Might give that place a swerve then, Ron, when they pour out of there later on,' observed one cabbie to the other. 'Can't take their drink, them toffs. Specially the officers.' He winked indiscriminately at Rupert. 'Most of it ends up rollin' around in the back of my cab. Tuck in, luv,' he nudged me. 'It'll get cold.'

Rupert had ordered a fry-up for both of us, but for the first time in my life, I couldn't eat. As I toyed with my bacon and gazed at him across a steaming mug of tea, listening as he chatted to the cabbies, answering questions about the Guards, letting them tell their own stories about life in the Forces, I couldn't help feeling, with some certainty, that this was a moment for which I'd waited a very long time. And it didn't matter that such a moment had been ambushed by two elderly men either; I was content to listen. To observe. To have this particular mess coat around my shoulders, and that particular knee half an inch from mine under the table. I nestled contentedly back into the jacket, savouring its warmth, its smell.

After I'd managed to rearrange my plate a bit and Rupert had cleaned his, we went outside into the night. The door shut behind us and the cool air hit my flushed cheeks. I glanced at my watch. Half past two. The ball would surely be over by now; no point going back. I hesitated, wondering what would happen next. Here I was, in an unfamiliar part of London, miles from home, and everything told me I should be hailing a cab back to Wandsworth. Rupert and I glanced at each other on the pavement, and there was a tremulous moment when, if a move was to be made, it would have been now. But Rupert sensed my indecision and misinterpreted it. His arm shot in the air.

'I'll get you a taxi.' He hailed one without difficulty. 'Where is home, incidentally?' He glanced back over his shoulder at me as the cab purred towards us.

'Wandsworth,' I said miserably, wondering where his was and why we couldn't go together. 'Which way are you going?' I asked. Perhaps he lived in Clapham. Perhaps we could share.

'Oh, I only live round the corner,' he said airily.

Round the corner? We were in the middle of St James's. How on earth could he live round the corner?

'Sorry, mate, I'm not goin' sarf of the river.' The cabbie shook his head and shifted into first again. 'Not at this time of night.'

And off he drove, only half to my regret. Rupert shrugged and tried again, but it was the same story. No one wanted to go that far with an empty cab on the way back.

'Looks like you'll have to come back to my place after all,' he announced cheerfully, as cabbie number three declined our fare.

Suddenly my nerve deserted me. What – just like that? I mean, I was pretty sure he was absolutely gorgeous and everything, but I had only just met him. And the thought of some smooth bachelor pad in SW1, with a couple of aristocratic flatmates padding around in Paisley dressing-gowns whilst their model girlfriends hogged the bathroom, suddenly filled me with dread.

'Oh, it's OK,' he said, seeing my face. 'Don't look so

worried, I live with my father. It'll be separate rooms, and since the spare room is connected to his I'm *fairly* sure I can resist the temptation to corridor creep. His other faculties may be failing, but his hearing is excellent.'

'Oh right,' I said, relieved. I fell in beside him as he walked. 'Are you sure that's OK? I mean, it looks pretty much as though I'm not going to get back tonight,' I twittered nervously. 'Unless I walk. But if you mean home as in your parents' home . . .'

'As opposed to a bachelor pad complete with sleigh bed and black sheets? Is that what you were expecting?'

I grinned sheepishly. 'Something like that. Although I never got as far as the black sheets.'

Rupert, it transpired, lived in Albany, a place I'd hitherto never come across, let alone knew existed. It had all the appearance of a large country house, although Rupert quickly assured me it was full of apartments, and was set incongruously behind the Royal Academy, just off Piccadilly. The main entrance, a vast oak door, was locked.

'Damn.' Rupert frowned. 'I've only got my set key. We'll have to go up the back passage – if you'll excuse the expression.'

I giggled, and he led me around to a side entrance, and then through a covered walkway around a courtyard garden. There were various staircases leading off it, and the place had a hushed, collegiate feel to it.

'Gosh, what is this?' I gazed about as we went. 'An exclusive gentlemen's club?'

'That's not so wide of the mark. Entry is by recommendation only, and you generally have to wait for someone else to snuff it to get some rooms. This place is full of dying Generals. Come on, up here. This is Dad's set.'

Happily there was no sign of his father as Rupert let us in. The place was in darkness, and the paternal bedroom door firmly shut as we tiptoed past it down the corridor. We stopped at the next one and Rupert opened it.

'There's a bathroom off it,' he whispered, pointing, 'but it's only fair to warn you it's also Dad's. Cough loudly if you need to pee in the night.' He grinned at me in the gloom.

I made a mental note to hold onto a full bladder if it killed me.

'Right.'

We gazed at each other in the doorway.

'Good night, Henrietta.'

'Henny. Usually.'

'Good night, Henny Usually.'

He lifted his hand, and with his finger faintly traced a line down my cheek. I could feel my heart picking up speed. Then he leaned forward and kissed me softly on the lips.

'Night.'

'Night.'

He turned to go, and I went in and shut the door behind

me. I leaned back on it, listening to him pad off down the corridor. Shut my eyes. My heart was still pounding, banging away against my whalebone corset. Moments later, when I opened my eyes, I was still holding on very tightly to the doorknob behind me.

# chapter five

Breakfast the following morning was an interesting affair. Rupert's father was a more distinguished, and far more forbidding version of his son: very tall and slim, his now greying, but obviously once fair hair swept back off a high brow, his eyes still a vivid blue. He instantly got up from the breakfast-table as I came into the kitchen, held out his hand and introduced himself as Andrew Ferguson, but I felt there was a frostiness behind the excessive courtesy. Hardly surprising, I thought, slipping into a seat opposite him, when a young floozy emerges from your spare room, not only unannounced, but wearing the most extraordinary clothes.

Obviously I couldn't have appeared in a vintage Hartnell ballgown – although with hindsight, he might have preferred that – so Rupert had lent me a black T-shirt that was too small for him and a pair of khaki shorts which I'd dragged in at the waist with an Army belt. He'd assured me the effect was very fetching as I'd met him in the passageway, but I wasn't convinced.

'But what about my shoes?' I'd whispered, slipping on last night's high heels and casting anxious eyes towards the kitchen.

Rupert scratched the back of his neck. 'Probably not. He might think you've strolled in from Shepherd's Market.'

'Shepherd's Market? Where's that?'

'A few blocks down. It's where the hookers hang out.' He grinned.

I whipped them off in horror. Consequently, my feet were bare as I slid into my seat. I felt like a street urchin.

'Rupert tells me the taxi cabs were reluctant to convey you to Wandsworth,' Andrew said meticulously, offering me some toast from a silver rack.

'Um, yes, otherwise I'd have gone home. But it was too late to get a train, and much too far to walk.'

'Of course.' He inclined his head graciously in recognition of this, but I felt his disapproval. Felt I should have had a magic carpet tucked handily in my evening bag.

'And you're very welcome, my dear. As all Rupert's friends are.'

Now why did I get the impression he was letting me know I was one of many? He reminded me of a tall, pale daffodil, his elegant head bowed, but not blowing in the breeze. In a Ming vase perhaps, in a grand conservatory.

'But won't anyone worry about you?' he asked lightly, using

an apostle spoon to scoop the Frank Cooper's from a china pot and not just sticking his knife in as we did at home.

'Well, obviously I'll ring my flatmate in a minute,' I prattled nervously. 'But she probably won't be there either. I mean, she may have stayed at a friend's. A girlfriend's.'

I blushed guiltily and could feel Rupert grinning at me as I dug deeper holes, but in the world I inhabited – which might well be fast and loose but was the real one – if a flatmate didn't appear there was no need to call the emergency services. I wondered how Rupert managed his social life with such a vigilant father.

It was quite an unusual set-up, I thought, glancing around surreptitiously as we munched our toast in silence. Despite the embossed linen tablecloth, silver napkin rings, toast-rack and milk jug, and despite this very dapper man in his moleskin trousers, Oxford shirt and gold cufflinks, it all looked slightly incongruous in this small, shabby kitchen. There was no natural light as the window overlooked another building, and the strip lighting above us cruelly illuminated the warped Formica work surfaces, the floor tiles erupting in places, and the tired magnolia paintwork. I had the impression of standards being maintained in reduced circumstances. The rest of the flat, I'd noticed, was in a similar condition. The bedroom I'd slept in had had a threadbare carpet, a thin candlewick bedspread, and the mirror above the basin was cracked. Likewise, the wardrobe and bedside table – the only pieces of furniture in the room – were scuffed and worn. I wondered how long these men had been fending for themselves.

Rupert seemed keen not to prolong the meal.

'Finished?' he said, getting to his feet, having downed a bowl of Sugar Puffs in record time.

'Oh. Yes. Sure.' I made to get up, leaving half my toast, but Andrew put a finger on my arm.

'Let her finish, Rupert.'

It was said lightly, but it was the lightness of steel. This was a man who was used to being obeyed. I sat down again, and as another silence threatened to prevail, decided prattling was preferable.

'Are you in the Army too, Mr Ferguson? Like Rupert?' Golly, Mr? Or Major? Or even Colonel perhaps?

He smiled thinly. 'I might have put it the other way round, but yes. Rupert followed me into the Life Guards.'

I had a sudden, ridiculous vision of father and son as swimming-pool attendants, in tight vests and shorts, blowing whistles furiously, Rupert running behind his father.

'Dad commanded his Battalion at Goose Green,' put in Rupert helpfully.

'Ah.' I nodded, and a farmyard scene complete with duck-pond sprang inconveniently to mind. Goose Green?

'I don't think there's any danger of me doing that,' he added. 'I mean, commanding my Battalion, rather than going to the Falklands.'

Ah, right. The Falklands.

'That's not what I hear at Regimental Headquarters,' put in his father smoothly. 'Paddy Faulkner thinks there's every chance. So long as you stick with C Company.'

There was a silence and I had a feeling of tension in the air. Of high hopes upon him.

'I'm sure he'd do it brilliantly,' I said staunchly, without the faintest idea what I was talking about, but I earned a smile from Rupert. His father looked surprised, but I detected a glimmer of something human around the mouth, too. He cleared his throat.

'Are you from an Army background, Henrietta?'

'No, my father's an engineer.'

'Ah.'

I found the monosyllable hard to interpret. Was that OK, I wondered, an engineer? Or not great?

'We travelled quite a lot though,' I added wildly.

'Ah.' This was a more encouraging 'Ah', and was accompanied by a knowing inclination of the head. Presumably Andrew now imagined I'd lived a similar ex-pat life to theirs; upping sticks every few years to go abroad, adapting to different cultures, being the new girl on the block, whereas in fact Dad had been posted to Hull for six months and Mum had stayed in London, refusing to accompany him. We were only widely travelled in the sense that we went to Puerto Banus for our holidays.

Hoping he wasn't going to quiz me further, I folded my napkin carefully and glanced at Rupert. He got to his feet decisively. Andrew also stood.

'Are you away?' He proffered his hand again. 'Very good to have met you.'

'And you,' I agreed, thinking how extraordinary to have shaken hands with someone twice over breakfast, a meal I normally took in bed, or on the hoof.

Outside in Piccadilly, we walked down towards Knights-bridge in silence, digesting the last ten minutes. I was shuffling along in a pair of huge flip-flops Rupert had found me, and he was wearing an old felt hat, jeans and a red T-shirt with a rip at the back where he'd yanked a particularly tickly label out.

'He's nice,' I ventured shyly.

'Dad?' Rupert smiled. 'He's fine when you get to know him. Bit frosty when you first meet him.'

'And your mother?' I glanced up nervously. His profile beside me was calm and relaxed though.

'Oh, Mother left years ago. Went off with Dad's best friend, a Brigadier in the Blues and Royals. They live in America now.'

'Oh. How awful.'

He shrugged. 'It was at the time, but we were both away at school. Boarding-school rather softens the blow. You create your own world.'

'Both?'

'I've got a younger brother. He lives in Australia now.'

'Oh, right. Quite young to have emigrated?'

'He wants to be a cameraman. Natural history, that sort of thing, and that's where the work is. He knew from an early age what he wanted to do. My father thinks he's dropped out.'

'So . . . you were the one to conform. Toe the party line?'

He smiled. 'That may be the way it looks, but I like the Army. I like the way of life, the people. Gives me a sense of belonging. Like a great big family, I suppose.' He glanced down at me as we dodged the crowds. 'And I know what you're thinking. As a substitute for mine?'

I laughed. 'Well, is it?'

He shrugged. 'Who knows? I just enjoy it. It's what I've always wanted to do.'

'You're lucky to have a plan.'

He smiled. 'Don't you know what you want to do?'

'I haven't the faintest idea.'

I had, actually, but I couldn't tell him. Couldn't tell him I found work desperately overrated and what I really wanted to do was meet a lovely man and get married one day. That in my shallower moments I saw myself, sunglasses perched on head, Gucci carrier bag swinging, pausing in a hotel lobby to ask if my husband had left any messages. How could I admit that? I couldn't even admit it to myself.

'And you've always lived with your father?' I went on.

'Never wanted to move out, live with other guys in a flat?'

'Of course.' He jumped on a 137 bus which had stopped at the lights beside us, grabbed my hand to pull me aboard. 'Come on, this'll do us.' He steadied me as the bus lurched away. 'But you can't always do what you want, can you?'

I stared up at him as we wobbled, and wondered what he meant by that. Then realised, and felt humbled. Personally I couldn't wait to get away from home. I'd been overjoyed to leave my overbearing mother who argued and bickered with my father, and felt no shame in leaving Benji, my younger brother, with the pair of them. Fond as I was of Dad and knowing he'd miss me, when Penny, my new best friend at secretarial college, had casually mentioned that her parents owned a flat in Wandsworth and would I like to share it with her, I'd jumped at it. As Mum had too, actually. She was nothing if not ambitious for her children and wanted some of Penny's kudos to rub off on me. Wanted to say to her neighbours in our Finchley Road block, 'Oh yes, Henny shares with Archibald Trevelyon's daughter, you know. An old Cornish family. Goes to masses of parties, Henley, Ascot . . .' I felt ashamed, and wondered how much of her *had* rubbed off on me. How thin the membrane was between us. God, I even had similar aspirations.

'What are you thinking?'

He'd followed me upstairs and down to the front of the bus. The front seats were empty so we took one.

'That you're a much nicer person than I am,' I said glumly as I sat down.

He laughed. 'How can you say that? You've only known me two minutes. And anyway, I might be painting a much glossier picture of myself just to impress you. You might otherwise consider it pretty sad of me to still be living at home at twenty.'

I regarded the aquiline profile beside me: the straight nose, the felt hat tipped rakishly over gleaming blue eyes. 'Sad' was not a word that sprang instantly to mind. Suddenly, his face changed.

'Shit. It's not supposed to turn left here. Come on.'

He grabbed my hand and we flew down the gangway, pounding down the steps again and jumping off at some lights on Queenstown Road.

'I thought you were in the Army?' I panted. 'Whatever happened to navigational skills?'

'Could have sworn the one-three-seven went over Wandsworth Bridge. Oh well, never mind. Let's walk.'

He still had my hand and my heart soared. We hadn't even discussed whether or not he'd see me home, he'd just naturally assumed he would. A good sign, surely?

We walked back through Battersea Park, kicking up the cherry blossom on the gravel paths, and then wound our way through a maze of Victorian terraced streets, oblivious of our surroundings and taking a very convoluted route home. As we went we chatted and teased one other, and made each other laugh quite a lot too. Two young people alone in a big city, with world enough and time, to enjoy. The girl, to the casual observer – that old man perhaps, walking his Cairn terrier – was laughing immoderately in outsized flip-flops, as the boy, encouraged by her laughter, performed even more comical facial gymnastics and threw a felt hat in the air. If he were feeling mellow, this passer-by, and not too embittered by the world, he might even have smiled to himself. Recognised the signs. Because I suppose we were falling in love.

We finally made it back to the flat at about lunchtime, starving and exhausted, but elated too. I have to say I was embarrassed to open the door and find the place in the same chaotic state as Penny and I had left it last night. The flat faced south and all the windows were shut, so the first breath one took was a bit like inhaling deeply in a barman's trouser pocket. Ashtrays flourished in the sitting room, overflowing with cigarette butts and tissues, and lipstick-stained glasses and an empty bottle of champagne stood sentry on the mantel-piece. A bowl of crisps had apparently been tipped over and trodden into the carpet.

'Oh, er, sorry. We left in a bit of a hurry last night.'

I flew around like a mine-sweeper, tipping ashtrays in the grate, opening windows and tucking bottles under my arm as I headed for the kitchen. The kitchen was worse. It looked as if we'd been burgled. But as I slammed cupboard doors shut and threw bottles in the bin, I couldn't help feeling pleased. I'd left this flat with such a sense of resignation last night, with Hughie, and now here I was, back with this lovely man. This 'catch' as my mother would have put it. I shuddered at the thought.

As I darted around, I flicked the answer machine on, then hurriedly turned it off as Hughie's voice roared, 'Where the hell did *you* get to last night!' Clearly miffed at missing his rumpy-pumpy. I took a quick peek in my bedroom as I flew by. Clothes, hairdryer, tongs, hangers and tissues littered the floor. I gathered them all up in my arms and shoved them under the bed. Why, Henny? Any particular reason?

I found Rupert back in the kitchen, with his head in the fridge. 'Food?' he enquired, balefully.

'Ah, no. Not always.'

'What's this? Taramasalata?' He brought out a bowl of pink goo and sniffed.

'That's Penny's face-pack,' I said, taking it from him quickly. 'But we've got a few eggs and a bit of cheese. Maybe we could do something with that?'

Well, I couldn't, naturally, but Rupert created a very fine omelette, and even found an ancient tin of anchovies to crisscross along the top, something I wouldn't have dreamed of doing. For one who aspired to a domestic role I was aware of the paucity of my knowledge and how much I had to learn. Right now, though, I was keen to learn more about him, and as we sat side by side on the sunny back step, over-looking a patch of tired London lawn, our plates balanced on our knees, I quizzed him about his life in the Army.

He told me about Northern Ireland where he'd just been for six months. About the frustrations and the bravery of the people who lived there, and about his own frustrations as a soldier. He told me how he regularly stopped terrorists at border patrols but was unable to arrest them even though they were known to be killers. He told me about the booby-trapped cars, the snipers still at large, and about the time he and his men had stumbled upon a barn which had turned out to be wired, full of explosives. How his mouth had dried as he'd wondered if he was being watched, if these were his final moments, and how, when they'd successfully detonated the explosives without any casualties, he'd felt a rush of adren-aline – similar, he realised, to how his father must have felt on marching to liberate Port Stanley. That was the moment, he said, that he'd realised this was important. Something he wanted to do.

I was fascinated and sobered by his tales, which differed dramatically from Philip's, and also quietly pleased to discover that he was back in London for a long stretch now.

'So what about you?' he said eventually, cleaning his eggy plate with the back of his fork. He looked at me quizzically from under his hat. 'You know all about me, what do you do?'

'Me?' I flushed. 'Oh, I'm just a secretary. I work in an ad agency, in the creative department. But I'm not creative myself,' I said hurriedly. 'The people I work for are, though. They write brilliant commercials and things. I just type them.'

He smiled. 'I'm sure you do more than that. What's your boss like?'

'Marcus?' I shrugged. 'Nice. I mean, he's always been kind to me.'

'Probably fancies you.'

I laughed, pleased that he imagined other men fancying me. 'I doubt it. Anyway, he's not remotely my type. Older, Jewish – not that that matters,' I said quickly. 'But very dark and thick-set. He's quite amusing, though.' I shrugged. 'Anyway, he's fine. Doesn't shout too much when I'm late or accidentally pour coffee over clients. He's quite important, actually,' I added quickly, trying to beef my job up a bit. 'I mean, we're one of the biggest ad agencies in London.'

'I know,' he nodded. 'You're in Berkeley Square, a stone's throw from me now that I'm stuck at St James's doing tedious ceremonials. Maybe we could meet halfway? In the park?'

My empty plate wobbled precariously on my knees and I judiciously removed it. Cleared the decks, as it were. For surely, if we were to meet halfway, some sort of meeting might have to take place here, first? I think I said as much with my eyes, and certainly I read it in his, because the next thing I knew, he'd taken me in his arms and was kissing me on that sunny back step. His hat tipped off, and tumbled down his back.

Predictably, and rather wonderfully, we spent the rest of the afternoon in bed. In fact, that day pretty much set a precedent for the next few weeks. We spent a lot of time walking around London – through the parks, along the river, exploring great swathes of the city I never knew existed – a fair amount of time with Rupert teaching me to cook, and a great deal of time in bed. Penny was desperately trying to make a go of it with Philip and had more or less moved into his salubrious Chelsea pad, so we pretty much had the flat to ourselves.

I didn't ask what his father thought about him spending so much time away, and he didn't volunteer. We popped over to Albany occasionally for Rupert to pick up more clothes and I always wanted to wait outside, sensing his disapproval, but Rupert made me come in. Andrew was civil to me but cold, and privately I thought he thumped the walls in anguish when I'd gone.

My mother, of course, nearly thumped the walls with joy. The first time I took Rupert home, she opened the door to our third-floor flat just off the Finchley Road and yelled, 'Darling, how marvellous!'

I wasn't sure whether it was me who was marvellous, or Rupert, but it soon became clear. She gave me a brief kiss, then lunged to shake Rupert's hand, taking it in both of hers, like a vicar. Her eyes were unnervingly bright, and since it was too early for her to have been at the sherry, I feared the worst. We'd arrived for tea, but instead of the usual tray in the sitting room, Mum had laid a white cloth in the dining room and piled it high with sandwiches, scones and cakes, all on doilies and all on the best china. I regarded the scene in horror. As Dad and Benji slipped obediently into their places at the table, Dad's mouth twitched. I wanted to scream, 'But we don't do this. Honestly!'

Grudgingly though, some of my heart slipped in Mum's direction. She'd tried so hard to make Rupert welcome, and Andrew had tried so little to do the same for me.

And Rupert was charming. He admired my mother's collection of *Sunday Times* colour supplement ornaments on the sideboard behind him, agreed that scones could be dry but these definitely weren't, and politely ate himself to a standstill. My heart nearly burst with pride. He looked so tall and handsome in our tiny dining room, had had to fold himself up, practically, to sit on the spindly chair, and was now cracking jokes with Benji and telling Dad about Army life.

My mother, at the head of the table, seemed to glow and expand with pleasure, until I thought she'd explode. Every few minutes she'd interrupt to spray crumbs and squeak, 'Sandhurst!' or 'The Life Guards!' or 'Your grandfather was a General!'

Dad winked at me at one point, and I tried to see the funny side but when Rupert ran out of material and Mum felt it was her turn, it was hard.

'You know, Rupert, we haven't always lived in a flat like this,' she said, as she bustled back from the kitchen with a fresh pot. 'We used to have a much larger one, but Gordon rubbed his boss up the wrong way and we had to cut our cloth. I've always been the dutiful corporate wife, of course – gave cocktail parties for clients and what have you – but I'm afraid Gordon's a bit of a maverick.' She gave a tinkly laugh as she sat down to pour. 'Anyhow, we manage, and we always put a bit aside so that Henrietta and Benjamin could go to private schools – so important, don't you think? And of course I've always had help in the house. We've got a Filipina at the moment, a lovely girl, and nothing's gone missing yet, although Mrs Greenburg downstairs had one and said hers wasn't entirely honest so we shall see. Mind you, Bertha Greenburg would notice if the poor girl took an extra biscuit with her coffee, well let's face it all our neighbours round here would, if you know what I mean. Another flap-jack, dear?'

I dug my nails deep into the palm of my hand and glanced at Dad, but he was munching his cake solemnly, silent as usual. Suddenly I felt angry with him. If only he'd take control, rein her in occasionally, cut her off with a curt, 'That'll do, Audrey.' But he never did. She was almost encouraged by his silence. She was becoming more of a loose cannon, and sounding more and more like Alf Garnett by the day.

As I hurried Rupert along, up from the table and across

to the door, I noticed Benji, who was then eleven, reach up and whisper something in his ear. Rupert gave a snort of laughter, then covered it as he turned to shake Dad's hand and say goodbye. I had an awful feeling Mum was going to curtsey as she took his hand – she certainly did something horribly deferential with her head – and said she'd been honoured to meet him.

'Honoured!' I hissed at her, when I went back a moment later to recover a scarf I'd left behind.

'Well, darling, I am. It's not often we get a visitor like that, and to think you're going out with him!'

'Oh, why are you such a terrible old snob?' I spluttered, my eyes stinging.

'Snob?' Her eyes widened. 'No no, Henny. I told you, I thought he was delightful.'

'What did Benji say to you?' I asked Rupert, when I'd clattered to join him at the bottom of the stairs.

'He wanted to know if I'd slipped you one yet.'

I stopped in my tracks, shocked. Shook my head and walked on. 'God, my *family*,' I groaned. 'What must you think of us?'

'I liked them,' he grinned.

'Liar,' I snarled.

'Well, they're more entertaining than mine.'

I grimaced, but actually, he had a point.

*　　*　　*

Time passed, quickly and blissfully. Over the next few months, Rupert and I, having gone through the heart-fluttering motions of heady new love, settled into a – well, definitely still heady, but steady relationship. He rang me every day and we'd arrange assignations in Green Park, munching sandwiches together on deck chairs, then meeting in wine-bars after work. Occasionally we'd eat in cheap bistros, finances permitting, before repairing to bed. Even my mother, given time, simmered down a bit and managed not to shriek and genuflect in his presence, Dad quietly approved, and Andrew . . . well, Andrew was just Andrew. I, however, was in heaven. Even though we were well and truly an item now and people would say our names in the same breath, invite us to the same parties and send us joint invitations, I still found myself stopping still occasionally. Just . . . stopping still. I'd stare out of windows in the flat, pause at my computer at work as my heart gave an exultant kick and I wondered if it was all true.

In no time at all, it seemed, Christmas was upon us. Amazingly, Rupert was to spend it with us, whilst his father went to visit Rupert's brother, Peter, in Australia. I remember the pair of us marvelling at this turn of events, while carrying a Christmas tree – one of us posted at each end like paper-hangers with a table – up the Finchley Road to my parents' flat.

'I thought he'd decided Peter had dropped out?' I yelled, stationed as I was at the front, or as Rupert would have it, the fairy end. It was beginning to sleet and the ice was stinging my face. I paused to turn my back on it, to wrap my scarf more firmly around my neck.

Rupert, at the roots end, shrugged. 'He does, but I guess he thinks he has a duty to go. He hasn't seen him for two years and Peter can't afford to come back. My father does have a heart somewhere, it just takes a bit of finding.'

I grimaced. 'Tell me about it.'

We bent our heads and walked on through the sludge.

'Christmas in the southern hemisphere can't be bad,' I remarked at length. 'I quite fancy a turkey sandwich on a sun-drenched beach for a change. I don't mind snow, but I can't be doing with this wretched horizontal ice.' I ducked down into the collar of my coat.

'Well, quite. I could certainly hack it. Anyway, I'll be there myself next year.' It was said lightly, but his voice was strained.

I stopped. Turned. 'You'll be in Australia?'

'No, but the Far East. Hong Kong. That's where my Battalion's being sent in the spring.'

I stared at him, slack-jawed. 'Your Battalion? You mean – and you're going with it?'

He looked miserable. 'Of course, if that's where we're sent. For three years, so we've been told.'

'Three years!' I dropped my end of the tree, so shocked that I couldn't speak for a moment. We stood there in the icy wind, facing each other.

'When?' I said eventually.

'End of March.'

'Oh.'

After a minute I picked up the netted bundle of pine again. I turned round and we resumed our trudge. I stared at the ground.

'But I'll be back often,' he said from behind me, trying to be cheerful. 'And you'll come and visit.'

'Of course.' But I couldn't keep the misery from my voice. Three years. 'But . . . we'll be apart, Rupert. Nevertheless, we'll be apart.' I stopped again and turned to face him. Hating him suddenly. Hating his job, which came before me.

His shoulders drooped miserably. 'I know.' Suddenly he looked up from the slushy pavement. 'Unless we get married.'

I stared. 'What?'

He glanced away, embarrassed. 'I just meant . . . Oh, I don't know,' he mumbled.

I looked at him, trying to gauge his seriousness.

'D'you mean it?'

He gazed back at me. Did a flash of fear cross his eyes? Or did he just square his shoulders?

'Of course I mean it, otherwise I wouldn't have said it, would I?'

A foolish grin spread over my face. Over his, too. We dropped the tree in the street and I flew into his arms.

'If you mean it, I'll answer you,' I whispered as I hugged his neck hard. 'Yes. I will.'

Elated, we lugged the heavy tree back to the flat, full of plans, full of euphoria, full of the notion of being in Hong Kong together, with a place of our own – married quarters. If my voice was slightly louder and shriller than his, I didn't stop to consider it.

My mother, naturally, nearly cried for joy when I told her, clutching a tea-towel to her breast when I burst into the kitchen, ice still clinging to my hat and scarf, Rupert behind me, grinning sheepishly. Dad was delighted too, everyone was – all the friends and relations Mum instantly got on the phone and rang. Well, why wouldn't they be? After all, we'd been going out for nearly eight months, we were madly in love – OK, we were both only twenty-one – but what the heck? As my mother said repeatedly, we knew what we wanted, which was to be together for the rest of our lives, and what was the point of going through three years of hell to achieve it? What was the point of a long-distance relationship conducted via letters and phone calls with the occasional precious visit, when I could be with him all the time, setting up home, like I'd always dreamed of?

And so the wedding machine roared into action with my mother firmly at the helm. I wasn't there when Rupert told his father on his return from Australia, but his congratulations to me when we visited him later in Albany were tight-lipped and restrained.

'Congratulations, Henrietta. Marvellous news. Couldn't be more thrilled.'

I swallowed.

The wedding was to be in early March, in the Guards Chapel, with 150 friends and family – mostly Rupert's, it has to be said – and a reception afterwards in the Officers' Mess. But suddenly, I got cold feet about the venue and changed it to the church in Hanover Square where I'd been christened. I felt desperate, suddenly, for some associations of my own. And Rupert agreed. Looking back, he agreed with most things I said during those frenetic, slightly blurred three months.

The banns were read, the dress was made, fittings were done for me and Penny, my maid-of-honour, and for some adorable little attendants I'd never seen in my life before and whom my mother had probably plucked off the street, adorable attendants being necessary. My excitement grew.

A hen-party was held, a stag-party for Rupert, and at work, at the agency, a great fuss was made. Champagne corks popped in the boardroom, because of course, I wasn't just getting married, I was leaving. I remember my boss, Marcus, looking at me fondly – strangely, even – as he gave the speech. Said how much they'd all miss me, and then handed me a present and a funny card – a drawing of me in a Life Guard's helmet and not much else – whilst I, skippy with excitement, was just dying to be out of there, to be gone. I remember kissing everyone goodbye and thinking how lucky I was. How they'd all still be here next week, on the familiar third floor, whilst I, Mrs Rupert Ferguson, would be flying to Hong Kong to start a new life.

Well, the rest you know. But perhaps for form's sake, it should be touched on briefly. Perhaps the painful, streaky little home movie should be re-run one last time.

The day dawned bright and sunny, and everyone went ahead to the church, save my father and I. I remember my mother kissing me goodbye in her bedroom where I'd changed; adjusting my floral head-dress, beaming at me in her pale lilac suit, lipstick on her teeth, whilst Benji, in a ridiculous morning-coat and top hat, pulled a face. Then it was just Dad and me. I was dry-mouthed with excitement, but Dad chatted beautifully, squeezing my hand as we got into the back of the car, not too emotional, keeping calm. I remember driving through London, then up to the church, and being told casually by an usher that Rupert was late.

Thinking no more of it, we drove around the Square. Paused again at the steps, then drove on a bit more. Down Bond Street, past Russell & Bromley where I'd bought some shoes for my honeymoon, before we drew up again at the church. Dad got out to check. A few minutes later he was back, worry etched on his brow. He told the driver to drive on, and we parked a little way down the road this time, a bride and her father, in the back of a huge black car. Dad murmured encouragingly to me the while, but after a bit, he

108

got out. I was alone with the chauffeur for what seemed like hours, but was probably only a few minutes. Out of the car window I saw Dad having a whispered discussion with my uncle on the church steps. Then finally – a decision. He came back, sat down beside me, and told me gently. We'd have to go home. Back to the flat. Forty-five minutes had gone by. It was beyond all reasonable hope.

'I'm so sorry, darling.'

I remember his eyes, full of tears, and my own shocked disbelief. It wasn't true. It *couldn't* be true. Despite his gentle protestations, I had to get out. Had to hitch up my skirts and run, veil flying, up that flight of steps to the open door – to see for myself. The congregation had been murmuring avidly but there was a deathly hush as I appeared. All heads turned as I stood in the doorway. I stared past them, horrified, to the spot at the top of the aisle where he should have been. Andrew, expressionless, met my gaze. My mother, her face crumpled, was dabbing at her eyes in her Dickins & Jones suit. She started clumsily towards me. I took one last wild look around – then turned and fled.

I don't remember much about the rest of the day, because nature, conveniently, has a way of numbing these things. Of blurring the unbearably sharp edges. I do remember – vaguely – the drive back home. The hushed whisperings in the flat, the comings and goings of relatives, the piles of unopened presents, and I remember being put to bed, perhaps with one of my mother's pills, like a Jane Austen heroine with the vapours.

The days went by and I stayed at home, like a convalescent. Penny visited, other friends too, and I remember the pain, the disbelief, but more than that, more than any of that, the terrible, terrible shame. I longed for Rupert, missed him dreadfully, but the shame drenched everything. Great waves of it would wash over me as I stood brushing my teeth, or as I sat blankly watching television. I became physically hunched by it. I remember, as I went out for the first time, just down the road to the shops, feeling I couldn't walk upright because of it. And all the time, I had an awful nagging feeling. Had I pushed him? Had I pushed him too hard? Had I run home and told my mother too precipitately, giving him no time to consider, no way out? My breathing became shallow at the thought. I was shrinking by the day.

It was only when my mother actually became ill herself and took to her bed, that I realised how like her I could be. Within days, I'd straightened my back, and my resolve, and gone back to work.

They all knew, of course: the copywriters, the art directors, the secretaries, and some of them had even been there at the wedding. Marcus certainly had. But they took me back like a shot, the temp dismissed in seconds. And they were sweet. All of them. Nevertheless, as I tapped away at my computer, hiding in my familiar cubby-hole on the third floor,

# not that kind of girl

I felt my shame like a red letter, burning into my back. I felt as if those in the know were whispering to the uninitiated, 'Oh, that's Henrietta Tate. She was jilted.'

'*No!* Not at the altar?'

'Practically. At the church door.'

'God – how awful!'

And Marcus was particularly kind. Gentle. No questions. Just a cup of coffee perhaps, placed on my desk at lunchtime if he was working in his office, and – did I want to talk? No? Fine. No pressure.

I didn't hear from Rupert. I knew his Battalion had gone to Hong Kong, because Penny told me Philip was there and that suddenly, she wasn't too sorry. I knew that Andrew went to see my parents, because Benji told me. Just Dad, he'd asked to speak to apparently, not Mum. Alone, please, in the study. I'm not sure what was said, but Benji said that when Andrew came out, he looked as if he'd been crying, and that minutes earlier, when Benji had pressed his ear to the study door, he'd heard him talk of the terrible, needless shame heaped on his boy. Of *prepotary* women.

'No, Benji. Predatory.'

Eventually, Marcus and I did talk, in the pub across the road after work, or sometimes he'd take me for a meal. Occasionally he'd cook for us at his house in Holland Park. Nothing happened, but he was kind and understanding, and after a while, he made me laugh. He was funny, as I think I've said.

111

A year later, in the spring, Penny moved in with Tommy Rutlin and her parents decided to sell the flat. I moved in with Marcus, with a lot less fuss from my mother than I'd anticipated, considering his background, but then an awful lot of water had flowed under various bridges, and to be honest, I think she was almost pathetically grateful to him. I hope I wasn't, too.

Marcus couldn't have been more different than Rupert. Physically, of course, being dark-eyed and stocky, but temperamentally too, being older and wiser and knowing exactly what he was doing. Whom he was marrying. Where he was going in life.

He set up an independent production company in the autumn and, being well-known and respected within the industry, was instantly successful. We were married, quietly, in a North London register office in November, and there was a small gathering afterwards in a restaurant near my parents' home. Angus was born the following year.

# chapter six

'So! My first day.' I took a muffin out of the bread bin, split it efficiently, and popped it under the Aga lid. 'Wonder what it'll be like?' I turned, beaming.

'Bit early, isn't it?' Angus wandered into the kitchen yawning sleepily in boxer shorts and a T-shirt. He looked absently round the room, scratching the pit of his chest. 'What's the time, for God's sake?'

'Early,' grunted Marcus from behind his newspaper at the table. 'But your mother is re-entering the field of employment today, and feels the need to share the experience with us.'

'Can you drop me at Tom's on the way to the station?' Angus yawned again and sat down, rubbing one eye with the heel of his hand.

'If you're ready in two minutes, yes. Good heavens. It's Lily.' Marcus clattered his cup in its saucer in mock horror.

'A face I thought I'd never see at this hour of the morning. Welcome.'

'Why's everyone up?' she whispered, clutching her dressing-gown to her possessively and looking pale as she lowered herself into a chair. 'Oh God, I feel sick.'

'Do you?' I froze, mid-bite of muffin, and rushed anxiously across. 'Oh well, then I won't go, my darling.' I felt her head, crouching down beside her. 'You are a little hot – maybe you should hop back to bed and I'll bring you a nice cup of tea. I'll ring in and say I'll be—'

'She's fine, for God's sake,' snapped Marcus, folding up his paper with a flourish. 'She only feels sick because she's never seen seven o'clock before, and if you're going to cry off every time one of your children whinges, you'll never keep a job. God, I remember now why I hate employing women. They're either pregnant or lactating or administering to offspring. Bloody liability.'

'Certainly I'm going in.' I straightened up hastily from Lily's brow. 'You'll be fine, darling,' I muttered. 'Just don't – you know – overdo it. Linda will be in soon.'

Lily slumped further down in her chair, until she was forced to sit bolt upright. 'You're wearing my shirt!' she exclaimed.

'Oh yes. I thought – well, if you don't mind.' I smoothed it down caressingly. 'Only mine are all so baggy and old-fashioned.'

'Looks cool on you,' said Angus admiringly and I glowed

with pleasure. One of the bonuses of having a strapping thir-teen-year-old daughter was that I could just about borrow her clothes. This black stretchy number was a winner, if a little snug.

'It's practically indecent,' Marcus said darkly into his coffee. 'Come on, we're going to be late.'

He threw the remains of his cup down his throat and moments later, was marching out of the back door towards the Range Rover, clutching his briefcase. I hurled some final instructions to Lily about unloading the dishwasher and not answering the door to anyone until Linda arrived, for which I received a withering look, then ran outside to get in the front seat beside my husband. Angus, trainers in one hand, grabbed a pair of jeans from the laundry basket and hopped into them as he ran across the gravel, wincing in his bare feet. He opened the boot and crawled in behind us.

'Quite fun, this commuting together, don't you think?' I said brightly, reaching for my seat belt.

Marcus grunted.

'And we can do this most days, can't we? You drive us to the station, and we'll get the train together. Saves taking two cars.'

'Unless I've got an early meeting,' he muttered. 'This is late for me.'

'Oh, well yes. Of course, I might have an early meeting too. Might have to – you know, take Minutes. That kind of thing.'

'I think you'll find things have moved on a bit since your day, Henny. Not many Minutes are taken. A lot of business is done via email.'

'Is it?' I clutched my handbag nervously. 'Only my short-hand's pretty rusty, Marcus. If I have to do it, d'you think I can ask him to go slowly?'

He shrugged. 'Personally I use a Dictaphone.'

'Why don't you use your finger like everyone else?' Angus quipped, then sniggered dirtily.

'Thank you, Angus,' I snapped. 'I don't need smut on my first day.'

'Go-*lly*, sorry. Just making light commuter talk. Someone's nervous. This'll do, Dad. Drop me at the corner and I'll walk to Tom's. Not sure I can bear the tension.'

We disgorged Angus in a jumble of ripped jeans, the T-shirt I knew he'd slept in, and no doubt the boxers as well. Now if I'd been at home I'd have noticed that. Made him change. First black mark against my mothering skills.

'Trainers!' I yelled, as he made to lope across the field to Tom's farm in bare feet.

'Oh.' He loped back and took them from the boot, still not bothering to put them on, I noticed, as he sauntered off.

As we approached the little country station I spotted other, smartly dressed souls hurrying to the entrance, looking purposeful and efficient as they strode out. Just like me, I thought excitedly. Close up though, I couldn't help noticing they didn't look entirely happy; rather grim and washed-out, in fact, but then again it was still early, and they were probably busy running through their presentations in their heads. So much better than wondering how full Waitrose was going to be.

'If I drop you here, you can get a *Telegraph* and some Polos for me while I park.' Marcus came to halt outside a kiosk.

'But you've already read *The Times*. And why Polos?'

'Because I like to read the *Telegraph* on the train and occasionally, I masticate a mint. Is that all right with you?' he said evenly.

'Oh. Yes,' I said humbly, altogether new to this side of my husband. To his morning rituals.

'And get me some cigarettes, would you?' He roared off in the car.

I knew better than to remind him he was trying to give up, and meekly joined the queue at the kiosk. It occurred to me, whilst I waited, that I too could develop rituals. I could get the *Daily Mail*. Yes, how different would that be, not to spend the usual half hour over it with a cup of coffee in my dressing-gown, before getting on the telephone for a chat. Which actually, was wherein the problem had lain. Because just as I was settling down for a protracted gossip with say, Laura down the road, she was likely to stop midflow and say, 'Damn. I must go, Henny, that blasted Hickey woman's arrived to look at her fabric.' Or Camilla, when I tried her next and raised the possibility of a coffee later, 'Oh God, I'd love to, but I've got a client coming at ten. I'm designing a knot garden for her, must dash.' But now, I too had to dash, I thought happily.

'Yes, luv?'

'The *Telegraph*, a packet of Polos and the *Mail*, please. Oh, and twenty Silk Cut.'

'Which ones?'

Oh Lord. Which did he have? Silver, blue or purple, I could never remember.

'Um . . .'

The vendor turned to read the packets. 'D'you want *Smoking Kills*? Or *Causes Heart Disease*?'

'Oh. Gracious. Well, not kills, obviously . . .'

'*Serious Damage to Arteries*?' His hand hovered over a packet.

'Er, less drastic, I suppose, or . . . no, that one.' I pointed eagerly.

'*Impotence*?'

'Please. Marvellous.'

He grinned. 'Doesn't come with a guarantee, you know.'

'More's the pity!'

He laughed. 'Let me know, eh, luv?' He winked.

'I will indeed,' I chuckled.

Pocketing my goodies, I felt decidedly perky. Nothing like a little light banter with the paper-seller every morning. Why, I'd be calling him Bob soon, or Ron. My, this was entertaining.

'Here, darling!' I waved extravagantly as Marcus marched up. He didn't stop and strode briskly past me. I blinked, then dashed after him.

'You're in a hurry!'

'Because the train is due in precisely forty-five seconds.'

'Oh.' I quickened my pace. 'Cut it a bit fine, haven't we?'

'That is entirely the point, Henny,' he said as we clattered at breakneck speed down the flight of steps to the platform. 'One does cut it fine. It's so that one can breeze into one's office and exclaim airily to one's colleagues, "Oh yes, a delightful rural idyll and not another house in sight, but only forty-five minutes door to door".' He handed me my ticket. 'There are two things men lie about in life. One is the length of their dick, and the other is the length of their commute.'

'I see. Rather childish and pointless?'

He nodded. 'Correct. For that is what we are.'

This silenced me somewhat. The train arrived and we barged our way onto what seemed to me an unnecessarily crowded carriage. We only just got a seat beside each other.

'Phew!' I sat down with relief. 'Morning.' I smiled at my other neighbour who glanced at me in nervous horror. Everyone looked so gloomy and tetchy. Marcus instantly opened his *Telegraph* and folded it efficiently. I opened my newspaper.

'Elbows,' he barked.

'Oh, sorry.' I tucked them in like a petrified chicken. It

was desperately uncomfortable, and terribly difficult to read. By Orpington I'd given up and instead, engaged Marcus in bright conversation about the various back gardens we were passing as we went through the suburbs and how, as a child, I'd loved train journeys and always fantasised about the occupants of the houses, wondering what their lives were like.

'This isn't going to work,' he growled as we got off together at Charing Cross.

'What? What isn't?' I scurried to catch up. God, he went so *fast*. I was sure he didn't move like this at home.

'This commuting together. It's a mistake. We'll talk about it tonight. I'm thinking separate carriages.'

And with that, he disappeared down the escalator towards the Northern Line and Camden Town, and into the bowels of the earth. I stood at the top, shocked. Separate carriages? Heavens, it sounded like separate beds. A turning-point in our marriage, perhaps. And why so grumpy? I walked on. Was it because I'd had a headache last night? Hadn't indulged in nookie? I seemed to recall him sarcastically apologising for attempting to inconvenience me as he rolled back to his side of the bed, and then knocking back a handful of Chinese herbal sleep remedies. Perhaps they hadn't worked, and he'd had a bad night. Or maybe he was still feeling short-changed. Hmm. I might have to tick a certain box tonight.

I sauntered off across the Strand and up into the labyrinth of streets around Covent Garden, enjoying the morning sunshine. When I reached the grand white-stuccoed frontage of number 42, I hesitated, wondering whether to ring the bell or just push on through, trilling, 'Morning!' confidently. After all, I reasoned, I was arriving for work. Couldn't ring the doorbell every day, surely? But on the other hand, this was Laurence's private house, and it would be awful to blunder in and find him in his boxers, spoon poised over a cereal bowl in front of breakfast television. In the end I gave an apologetic little half-ring – pathetic, worst of both worlds – and Laurence opened the door. He was wearing an old checked shirt over a white T-shirt and jeans, and looked even more disreputably handsome than I remembered. He ran a hand through his dark locks.

'Henny! Welcome. Do just barge in, no need to knock.' He stood aside to let me in. 'I've been having a frantic tidy-up knowing your approach was imminent, and you've caught me mid bin-run.' He reached behind him for a black sack and dumped it on the front step. 'Didn't want you to recoil in horror at the mess on day one, it's a bit like *Life of Grime* in there.'

'Oh, I'm sure it's not. And you shouldn't have bothered,' I twittered as I followed him upstairs, secretly delighted he'd made an effort for me and wondering if I could still leap steps two at a time like he did. Definitely younger than me, but not much, I hazarded. I made a mental note to try it at home.

He ushered me into the long white drawing room, which

admittedly didn't look nearly as pristine as when Emmanuelle had been *in situ*. 'Now the awful thing is,' he admitted as he lunged about the floor, snatching up books and cushions as he talked, 'I'm going to have to dash. I've got a breakfast meeting with a producer about my new series in about ten minutes, so I shall have to leave you in the lurch. I'm really sorry, Henny.'

'Don't worry,' I said. 'I'll cope.'

Actually, that was fine, I thought as I gazed about. I preferred to get my bearings on my own, feel my way around, poke through a few filing cabinets – if they still existed – without him standing over me, pleasant though that would be later, I thought as he straightened up from his tidying and regarded me anxiously. God, he was attractive. Like a modern-day swashbuckler. A pirate chief with dark curls and flashing eyes.

'Sure?' His eyes cleared with relief. 'Oh well, that's great, because although I'll be in and out today, it'll mostly be out. It's just sod's law that you're starting on a particularly frantic day.'

'Best way though, don't you think? In at the deep end. What would you like me to do?'

'What I'd *love* you to do is field all my ghastly calls.' He started gathering up papers and books. 'They mostly want interviews – unpaid, of course, the bastards – so unless it's the BBC or anyone interesting like Parky, say no. Politely, of course.'

# not that kind of girl

'Of course. Although I'm afraid my telephone manner won't be quite as sexy as Emmanuelle's.'

'Ah yes.' He flashed me a wicked grin. 'She gives good telephone.'

I giggled.

'More prosaically though,' he went on, 'I'm afraid there's a monumentally dreary manuscript waiting to be typed up. It's my script for the next series which I like to write myself, and if I wasn't so computer illiterate, I'd type too. It's all on these wretched little tapes.' He indicated a bundle on his desk. 'I gabble away into a machine when I'm in the bath, and the thing is, I need to be able to read it back. Usually in the bath again where I get it wet, and then have to beg you to print it out for me all over again.' He grinned at me disarmingly from under his floppy fringe, like a small boy admitting to a penchant for catapults. 'It used to drive Emmanuelle up the pole. She'd say, "Why can't you read it on-screen like everyone else?" But I'm afraid I'm desperately old-fashioned.'

'Oh, me too,' I agreed eagerly, hoping he'd never discover quite how old-fashioned and trying not to imagine him in the bath. Very bubbly, of course, so nothing showing, script propped up on tanned knees. A cigarette going maybe, in an ashtray on the side. Bathroom chaotic, towels everywhere, papers all over the floor, needing a woman's touch to sort it out. Not that I'd be clearing up around him in the bathroom, stooping round the tub as he read and puffed away, but in

123

here perhaps? Would this have been Emmanuelle's domain? My fingers itched to plump those cushions.

'Great,' he said cheerfully. 'Right – I'll shoot off now if you don't mind. Oh, and work where you like, by the way. Emmanuelle preferred that little room, but this is all set up for you, too.' He indicated the desk in the window I'd originally imagined was mine. 'It's got a better view, but it is less priva—'

'Oh, I think I'll stay here.' I scurried eagerly across, dumping my bag firmly on the chair like a German bagging a sunbed.

As I wriggled out of my jacket I felt him look at my tight black shirt approvingly. I pulled in my tummy, thinking that at least my waist wasn't too bad, even if my bottom was a bit big. God, he didn't mess about, did he? I smoothed down my shirt as his eyes frazzled me.

'And what I thought was,' he went on, breaking the moment and reaching suddenly for his coat, 'tomorrow, since I've got a slightly clearer schedule, we could have lunch together and I could run you through a normal day.' He shrugged on his coat and gave me a wide smile. 'How does that sound?'

'Wonderful,' I glowed, hopefully not too pinkly. Golly, lunch with my boss already. Couldn't wait to tell Penny.

'Now if you want to type in peace, just switch the answer machine on and ring everyone back when you've finished. Oh, and if someone called Jessica rings, could you tell her I'm . . . um . . . away. For a bit.'

# not that kind of girl

'Away from your desk, or away away?'

'Er . . . away away would be great.' He smiled sheepishly. 'If you don't mind telling a tiny white lie.' He held his thumb and forefinger a fraction apart.

I didn't mind in the slightest, and assured him as much. I also had a feeling it might be the first of many. Poor Jessica. I smiled. Oh well.

When he'd gone I sauntered around the room for a bit. I ran my hand lightly over the bronze on the mantelpiece, a dancer in the dying swan position, and peered at the abstract picture above her. Great splurges of colour on a huge canvas. Quite jolly, but I was pretty sure I could have done it. I could already hear Marcus snorting at it in derision. I scanned the bookshelves, head on one side, but the titles meant nothing to me, so I went to the window and gazed down at the scene below, my forehead pressed to the glass. It was quieter now, the working day well under way, but occasionally, a suited executive would scurry into a building along the street, barking into a mobile, or a motorcycle messenger would draw up and leap off his bike with a package. Business as usual, and I was part of it. I wasn't a housewife up from the sticks on a shopping spree, or a tourist seeking diversions in the Piazza, gawping aimlessly at the juggler on stilts, I was part of the make-up of the city; a cog in this huge metropolitan wheel, a worker ant. I sat down happily at my desk, my heart racing. Oh, I'd been so lucky to find this job. *So* lucky.

Tentatively, I put on the headphones and snapped a tape into the machine. I hadn't done this for years. Used to loathe it, actually, at the agency – all us secretaries did. We'd groan with dismay if anyone waved a tape at us, hating to be shut off from the world and preferring to take dictation so we could chat and make phone calls, but actually, I was alone here so it didn't matter. Also, I knew I could do it. I snapped the answer machine on and typed away, listening to Laurence's incredibly deep, sexy tones.

And it was rather informative, actually. I didn't know much about Eleanor of Aquitaine, but she was clearly a bit of a goer. Had firm views on warfare and plenty of firm young lovers too, judging by . . . ooh, I say. As another knight's garter twanged and her wimple bit the dust, I decided Laurence was obviously of the opinion that combative history was psychosexual, and that the outcome of most battles boiled down to whether or not one General was better in bed than the other. I rattled away furiously, keen to keep up with the plot, delighted I could still go at breakneck speed, and paused, only at twelve o'clock, to ring Penny.

She was in a meeting. Ah. Yes. Hadn't been to one of those yet. Oh well, Laura then. Probably picking her toddler up from nursery school. She was, and nearly drove into a ditch.

'Laurence De Havilland!' she squealed. 'Hang on, I've got to stop. But Henny, he's gorgeous! D'you mean the one *I* mean? The one on the telly? With the twinkly eyes and the billowing corduroys, striding around ruined castles looking moody?'

'The very same,' I agreed happily. 'Although he's in tight black jeans today, but still, heaven. He's taking me to lunch tomorrow.'

'No! God, and all I've got is a meeting with stuffy old Marjorie Clarkeson who's messing me about with her Colefax fabric. Says it's too blue, silly tart. What does she expect when it's called *Blue Floribunda*? So what does Marcus think about all this?'

'Marcus? Oh, he's dead relaxed.'

'Really? I always thought he was the jealous type. I remember Hugo Sergeant chatting you up like nobody's business at Sally Thwaite's fortieth – you were wearing that tight red number and he dragged you onto the dance floor, remember – and Marcus was fuming! I thought he was going to take him outside.'

It was true, Marcus was quite protective. But I'd always rather liked that. Liked the fact that he was still as besotted with me as ever. I felt the need to defend him.

'Yes, but Hugo's such a groper, everyone knows that. Marcus is quite happy for me to be chatted up at a dinner-party but he does draw the line at me being pawed.'

Perhaps though, I thought privately as I put the phone down, I wouldn't introduce him to Laurence immediately. Laurence was decidedly tactile – I remembered him touching my shoulder as he'd said goodbye at my interview – and had a roving eye which Marcus would spot immediately. Of course, it was just his cosmopolitan, luvvie way, but Marcus was neither of those things. Found them rather contemptible, in fact. I stared out of the window and wondered how many girlfriends he had. Laurence, not Marcus. Loads, probably. Well, Jessica, for starters.

I sighed and picked up the headphones again. Still, no harm in a little light fantasising, was there? Or even a bit of harmless flirtation. After all, I was married, so perfectly safe. I snapped in my next tape, hoping that lunch tomorrow would be somewhere small and cosy, somewhere dimly lit – so flattering for the over-thirties – and not one of those fashionable eateries with chrome seats and overhead lighting that Marcus had mistakenly booked for our wedding anniversary: we'd taken one look at it, shuddered, then dived into a taxi back to the candle-lit gloom of our usual haunt, the deep-buttoned Italian near the flat in Kensington. Yes, with luck we'd be somewhere very dim indeed tomorrow, and I'd listen intently as he told me all about Anne of Cleves or Catherine of Aragon or – I narrowed my eyes out of the window – yes, I probably *could* name all of Henry VIII's wives, if I had to. I ran through them in my head. Divorced beheaded died, divorced beheaded survived. It was all coming back to me. Perhaps I could offer to do some research? I'd have my head cocked to one side – in the restaurant, this is – in an alert, but not too agog manner, wearing that pink top I'd bought in the Ralph Lauren sale at Bluewater. The lacy one. It was very fitted and I *had* thought it too low-cut for work, but I didn't now. Oh no. Not at all.

I typed away joyfully, but after a while even my nimble fingers ran out of steam, and I turned off the tape, exhausted. I played back the answer machine and began ringing all the people who'd called, introducing myself as Laurence's new assistant and apologising for his unavailability, but promising the man at the *Guardian* that I would indeed get Laurence to ring back in person, since he assured me he intended to write a very flattering profile which would give him great publicity for his new series. This was where my talents really lay, I thought excitedly, as I scribbled the journalist's name and number down on a pad. Sorting the wheat from the chaff. Having the nous to know which calls Laurence would want to take and which he wouldn't, and of course a lot more would come with practice. But even after one morning I felt I could tell who the time-wasters were.

I was just about to ring back one such opportunist from *Chat Up* magazine who'd rung twice already and wanted to know if Laurence would pose naked but for a fig leaf with Cheryl from *Big Brother* in a feature on breasts through the ages – I was pretty sure he wouldn't and intended to tell the journalist as much – when the phone rang again.

'Laurence De Havilland's office,' I purred professionally.

'Could I speak to Laurie, please?'

I went cold. In fact, my heart all but stopped. Then it beat on again, unnaturally fast. Quick as a flash, I pitched my voice an octave higher.

'I'm afraid Laurie isn't here at the moment. Can I get him to ring you?'

'No, it's OK, I'm moving about a bit. I'll ring him later. Will he be back this evening?'

'Yes, should be.'

'OK, thanks. Bye.'

I put the phone down. My heart was hammering now, against my ribs. I'd know that voice anywhere. I looked at my hand, still clutching the telephone. Drew it back quickly, as if the receiver were molten lava. I knew it after fifteen years and I dare say I'd know it in another fifteen. I pressed my fingers to my lips, which, unaccountably, were trembling slightly. What I didn't know was the effect it would have on me after all this time.

# chapter seven

After a few minutes of sitting stock-still in my chair, I lowered my hand from my mouth. Stupid of me not to consider it, I thought, my mind racing. Not to consider Rupert ringing here. After all, Laurie had told me at the interview he knew him, why didn't I imagine he'd be on the phone? Why didn't I *think*?

But I had, I reasoned as I pushed my chair back and got up to pace the room. That night, after my interview, after I'd hugged a lamp-post in the street, I'd gone home and sat on the end of my bed, gazed out of the window at the sheep-flecked fields, and thought through the implications of working for a man who knew Rupert, but decided I was overreacting. After all, it was years ago, in the Army, and that connection was long gone. And anyway, I was happily married to Marcus, what difference would it make? What difference could it make, working for a man who once knew Rupert?

But I hadn't actually considered speaking to him, had I? Hadn't envisaged *that* little scenario. Hadn't asked myself how it would feel to hear his voice on the end of the phone. I stopped pacing and gripped the tops of my arms hard. I certainly hadn't anticipated the rush of blood through my body, nor the bucketful of adrenaline that had shot precipitously up the back of my legs.

I swallowed and sat down again, staring at the phone. Right. Well, I could deal with this now, now it had happened, and thank heavens it *had* happened while I was alone, without Laurie glancing across from his desk, watching my face go white, seeing my hands tremble. I looked down at them in my lap. Clenched them hard.

After a moment, I picked up my headphones and clamped them to my head. Without stopping for lunch – I couldn't eat – I worked solidly. I transcribed piles of tapes, printed them out on reams of paper, and stacked them high in neat piles. I knew Laurie would be delighted, but that wasn't my motivation. I wanted to keep those keys tapping relentlessly, wanted to lose myself in the monotony of the task, to have to think just enough to forget myself, but not enough to really use my brain. To wipe it clean to a blank sheet, just as I had fifteen years ago, on the third floor of an advertising agency, in a little cubby-hole, surrounded by spider plants and pictures of the office party: turning my back on the busy corridor behind me, the outside world.

When the street outside began to fill up, I looked at my watch. Five o'clock, and the homeward rush had started. I pushed back my chair and wondered what to do. Did I stay and wait for Laurie? Or simply shut up shop and go home? Hours hadn't exactly been discussed, but he knew I had a family and wouldn't want to stay late. In the event, just as I was putting on my jacket, he rang.

'Oh God, yes – go! Sorry, I meant to say, do leave before the rush, and just shut the front door behind you. I'm sorry I haven't made it back, I got completely tied up – but go.'

I did, and walked to the station along with a sea of people, all stony-faced and focused. Feeling numb, I found my own features setting accordingly. Charing Cross was heaving, and naturally someone trod on my heel and broke my sling-back, and since it's virtually impossible to walk in a sling-back minus its sling, I had to sort of drag it, like the medieval village idiot with a club foot, all the way to the crowded terminus, one hand pulling Lily's shirt down as it rode up with the exertion, the other clenched in battle. I arrived cursing under my breath, just as the top button of Lily's shirt, unable to take the strain any longer, popped off.

Squinting up at the board, I discovered my train was in, and shuffled to the gate, letting go of the shirt to wave frantically at the guard and thereby losing my modesty and my shoe, and by the time I'd retrieved it – the shoe, not my modesty – the whistle had gone and the doors had shut.

'Oh, thanks very much!' I stormed, furious.

'Sorry, luv, but if I held it up for everyone, I'd be here all day. Yer shoe's broke, by the way.'

Half an hour later, squashed in the gangway of a crowded train, my toes pinched, a briefcase jammed into my back, my nose buried in someone's armpit, an *Evening Standard* slowly lowered in front of me.

'Good *evening*!' beamed its owner, giving me an unnaturally bright and knowing smile. It took me a moment to recognise my neighbour from this morning's commute. Ah. Point taken.

Marcus was at the kitchen table when I hobbled in through the back door; he had a can of beer in one hand, and a fork spearing a pickled onion straight from the jar in the other. His own copy of the *Standard* was propped up on a Rice Krispies packet, and cereal bowls and milk bottles decorated the table.

I regarded the scene in horror. Through the playroom door I could see Lily, prone on the floor on her tummy watching *The Simpsons*, surrounded by plates and mugs from breakfast, her pyjamas and dressing-gown still on the floor where she'd let them fall. It took a moment to find my voice.

'Oh God!' I gripped the doorframe. 'Didn't Linda come?'

Marcus glanced up absently. 'Hm? Oh hello, love.' He went back to his paper. 'I don't know.'

'Lily!' I hastened to the playroom. Came between her and the screen. 'Didn't Linda come?'

'Oh. Yeah.' She raised her eyes briefly up my legs, then

peered around them to see Bart again. 'But her mum was ill, so she only got as far as the stables.'

'Hope she mucked Fabrice out,' muttered Marcus from the kitchen.

'Yeah, she did.'

'Never mind the bloody horses, what about my house!' I shot back to the kitchen and still in my coat, grabbed cereal packets and threw them in the larder. Hurled bowls at the dishwasher.

'God, *look* at this place – and oh! Lily darling, did you have any lunch? Lily?' There was a terrible thumping noise coming from upstairs, from Angus's bedroom. 'LILY!'

'Wha'?' She turned, annoyed.

'Did you have any lunch?'

'Yeah, I had some peanut butter.'

'Peanut butter! Were you here on your own all day?'

'Um,' she rolled over to face me, to consider this. Her brow wrinkled with the effort of concentration. 'No, not all day. Angus and Tom were here a bit.' She grinned. 'Raiding the drinks cupboard, mainly. How was your day, Mum?'

'Raiding the – oh God, were they *drinking*? Angus!' I ran to the bottom of the stairs. 'ANGUS! HAVE YOU BEEN DRINKING?'

The music was deafening. I ran to the cupboard, seized a broom and thumped the handle on the ceiling. After a moment he came to the top of the stairs.

135

'What?' Like his sister, annoyed.

'Have you been drinking?' I yelled.

'Oh God, Mum, just a couple of Bacardi Breezers. Chill. Bloody Lily, stirring as usual, just 'cos we wouldn't let her have one. I was being responsible.'

'Responsible!' I shot my hands through my hair and swung around to survey my kitchen; my children wallowing in squalor, my husband in the midst of it, eating pickled onions from a jar. He glanced up.

'What's for supper?'

'Oh God,' I breathed, sinking into a chair. 'This isn't going to work.'

'It'll be fine,' Marcus yawned later, beside me in bed.

'It won't be fine.' I moaned, eyes wide to the ceiling in the dark. 'The children clearly aren't old enough to be left, they behave like savages when I'm not around. The whole thing's a disaster!'

'Not a disaster,' he mumbled sleepily. 'And shush. I'm dropping off. Under Karen's orders. Seems to be working.'

'Karen?'

'My sleep therapist. Hypnotherapist, actually. I'm supposed to imagine a pleasant scenario, then work with it. I'm imagining her firm young breasts at the moment, do you mind?'

'Not in the slightest,' I muttered. Oh God, my babies! I was deserting them, and they still needed me.

'And then work with it?'

'What?'

'Well, obviously I'll have to fondle them?'

'Yes, fine. Whatever.'

'Undo her bra and let them drop gently into my hands like two soft little bundles?'

'It's hopeless,' I sighed.

'No, no. Seems to be working.'

And not only was it hopeless on the home front, there was Rupert too, on the work front. I heard his voice in my ear. 'Don't worry, I'll call later.' Those lovely deep, modulated tones . . .

'Oh God, it's a mistake!' I sat bolt upright in horror.

'Fine – I won't!' Marcus yelped in terror, sitting up beside me.

'I'll hand in my notice tomorrow.'

'Oh, don't be silly.' Marcus flopped back on his pillows again. 'This is what you wanted! Don't give up just because Linda didn't come, she'll be back tomorrow and the children will be at school the next day. For God's sake, get a grip. You said you loved your day.'

'I did,' I admitted guiltily, lying down again. 'Most of it.'

'And your boss is all right?'

'Yes, he's . . . fine. He's taking me to lunch tomorrow. To – you know. Chat things over.'

There was a pause. 'Well, there you are then,' he said gruffly.

137

We were silent for a moment, in the dark.

'Lunch,' he grunted, at length. He turned over onto his side, facing the wall. 'Never have time, myself.'

'Of course not, you're far too busy,' I cajoled quickly. 'And that bloody awful journey . . .' I said, changing the subject but glad I'd cleared lunch with him. 'Honestly, I don't know how you do it every day, and you never complain.' There. Toss him a brownie point. He grunted again.

'Don't know why you don't use the flat more,' I went on. 'It occurred to me, Marcus, you never use it, and it's just sitting there. If it was me and I had a late meeting like you sometimes do, I'm sure I would.'

It was true: our lovely pied-à-terre just off Kensington Church Street mouldered elegantly, unoccupied. We'd bought it when we sold the London house, faintly scared about leaving Town completely and thinking we'd always be up, popping to the theatre or to restaurants, but of course, we never were.

Marcus grunted again, but Karen's hypnotic charms, fleshly or otherwise, were clearly doing the trick, and rhythmic breathing began to emanate beside me. I knew better than to disrupt it.

I, however, had a ghastly night, tossing and turning and having extraordinary dreams, which culminated in a nightmare vision of being chased down the street, naked but for a dirty bra, by Rupert, Laurie and Marcus, who were galloping after me on horseback in Life Guard uniforms waving sabres, followed by Lily and Angus, wearing rags and clutching a begging bowl, crying, 'Where's our food? Our clothes? Oh, you *naughty* mummy!'

Christopher crowed at what felt like dawn, and I vaguely remember Marcus mumbling something about going in early and why didn't I take his MG, and then I turned over and went back to sleep. I drifted into a much nicer dream about rescuing Prince Harry from a gang of terrorists and Prince Charles becoming my best friend, and when I awoke, it was eight-fifteen.

I stared at the clock in disbelief. Eight-fifteen. Eight-fifteen? Oh God, I was going to be so *late*! Shit!

I flew out of bed and dashed to the shower, tripping over the step into the cubicle in my haste, and bashing my head on the tiled wall opposite. The pain was excruciating and I saw stars. Real stars. Gripping my head as it began to throb madly, I groped my way, moaning, to the bathroom cabinet. With eyes half-shut, I rummaged around and found some paracetamol. I threw two down, gulping water straight from the tap – oh, and one more for luck. Never did any harm. Ooh, my head! But as I swallowed the third pill, I looked at the bottle. It was small, and made of brown glass, just like the extra-strong paracetamols I got on prescription, except that this bottle was not mine. It was Marcus's. And it was full of Temazepam.

I sat down heavily on the side of the bath and clutched my mouth in horror. Oh . . . my . . . God. I'd just taken not two, but *three* of Marcus's sleeping pills! Jumping up again, I gazed at my reflection over the basin in dismay, almost expecting fangs. I'd never even taken one, not ever, and these were . . . oh dear Lord . . . I trembled as I read the bottle. These were 20 mg jobbies, which I knew were strong. What would happen to me? Had I overdosed? Would I fall into a coma? Should I make myself sick?

Feverishly, I stuffed my fingers down my throat and leaned over the loo. Couldn't do it. Couldn't reach the nodules. Toothbrush perhaps, much longer reach . . . I tried but – oh God no, dis*gus*ting! I removed it and spat saliva in the basin. How did bulimics do it, I wondered? I stared at my reflection again, eyes wide. Right then. I squared my shoulders. Only one thing for it. I'd have to soldier on as if nothing had happened. Golly, they were only little pills, and some nights they didn't even knock Marcus out, although three, I thought nervously, three might do something.

But if I was quick, I reasoned, throwing my clothes on, they wouldn't kick in for a bit. And heavens, when they did, I could fight it. Hadn't the Nazis used sleep deprivation as a form of torture, and who was that frightfully brave Resistance girl who fought sleep for days in that film – wassisname – *Carve Her Name with Pride*? Well, I'd fight it too. Easy. Just hope I won, I thought nervously, and it wasn't a case of *Carve*

# not that kind of girl

*Her Name with Shame* as I was found snoring on the tarmac at Flaxton station.

I tore downstairs in my race against time, to find Linda already filling up the kitchen sink. She turned as she heard me, Marigolds raised as if about to perform an operation.

'Oh Henny, I'm awfully sorry about yesterday, love, only me mum's been having ever such funny turns recently and I really didn't think I could—'

'Fine. Fine,' I gasped. 'Not to worry. Here all day, Linda?'

'Yes, all day. Except I might nip to McKay's later. Only they've got a sale on and I could do with some new duvet covers. I've got my eye on some fitted sheets and—'

'Splendid, marvellous. Children still asleep?'

'Er, yes, I think—'

'Super. Must fly,' and I did, out of the back door, failing to shut it and leaving her still talking. But then, that wasn't unusual.

I ran to the little black MG parked around the side of the house and unlocked it with trembling hands. What if the police stopped me? Was it worse than driving with alcohol in my blood? And if I had an accident, would I go to prison? No, I'd be fine, I reasoned. I was only going down the road, and the pills weren't even kicking in yet. Or *were* they? I sat down, with a jolt remembering – too late – that I needed a plastic bag to sit on. The canvas roof leaked and, as usual, rain had soaked the driver's seat. Cursing my luck, I drove

141

furiously to the station and parked eccentrically in the car park. There. That was the worst bit. Now if I collapsed, at least I wouldn't kill anyone.

I tottered from the car, eyelids feeling decidedly heavy now, legs a bit wobbly. The back of my skirt was sopping wet and stuck to my legs as I staggered on. I felt like an exhausted Saga holiday maker whose colostomy bag had burst. Never mind. It would be dry by the time I got to work. I made my way gingerly down the flight of steps to the platform, where as luck would have it, the train was in.

I got a seat next to a rather cosy-looking fat man and looked longingly at his lap. If I could just rest my head for a second . . . He crossed his legs, terrified as I eyed his groin. Thirty minutes later I awoke at Charing Cross, to find, happily, I'd only made use of his shoulder. Looking askance, he shook me off — something he'd presumably been trying to do for a while as I'd lolled all over him, watched, no doubt, by an amused carriage of commuters, many of whom I was sure I'd meet again. No matter. I'd had my kip, and I was certain that would revive me. I stepped off the train and yawned widely. Oh yes, that would do the trick. All I'd needed was forty winks and — oh *God*. I staggered. Felt my head. Was I going to collapse? Somehow I made it outside and emerged on the Strand.

'Taxi!' I tapped on the window of one parked in the station forecourt.

'That's just down the road, luv,' the driver said when I gave him the address. 'Be quicker to walk.'

'Humour me,' I muttered, clambering aboard.

'Ah, right.' He grinned. 'Morning after the night before, eh?'

'Well quite,' I agreed politely, hoping I could keep my eyes open until I got there.

Luckily the door was ajar when I got to number 42, and even more fortuitously, when I'd crawled up the mountain of stairs and arrived at my desk, I found a note on my computer from Laurie.

*Had to dash to a meeting at the BBC, damn it, but should be away by 12.00. Meet you at 12.30 in Kensington Place. Many many thanks for the transcripts – marvellous! Still wet from the bath!*
*Laurie*

I gave a shaky smile and thanked my lucky stars. By some small miracle he a) wasn't here to know I'd arrived at ten o'clock, and b) wasn't to know I was going to put the answer machine on and have a kip on that yummy-looking sofa for a couple of hours before lunch. What luck. I tottered towards its creamy depths, my eyes closing now like a baby's, and was on the point of prostrating myself, shoes kicked off – when a head popped around the door.

143

'Laurie not in today?' A middle-aged woman with corrugated grey curls and a hooked nose regarded me beadily.

'Um, no. He's got a meeting at the BBC.'

'Ooh, lovely. Just my luck.' She sidled in dragging a mop and a bucket. 'I'll do this room now, then, before I start downstairs. You don't mind, do you, duck? Only he much prefers me to do it when he's out, and I don't like to disturb him.'

'Oh. No, fine.' I found my shoes and clutching the furniture, felt my way back to my desk.

'Only I thought I'd get all them books out today and dust 'em.' She gazed greedily up at the shelves. 'Filthy, they are. Ruby, by the way.'

'Henny,' I croaked.

'You carry on, luv, don't mind me.'

Well, I could hardly do that, could I? I eyed the sofa longingly and lowered myself into my chair.

When it became clear that Ruby was going to keep up a running commentary about the state of the place, and how Laurie never bothered to take his dirty mugs and plates out, bless him – ooh, and you wouldn't believe what she sometimes found down the back of the sofa, I gave a shaky smile, clamped on the headphones, and tapped away. At approximately two words a minute.

At twelve o'clock, Ruby lit a post-cleaning cigarette and slumped back in that covetable sofa to admire her gleaming spines. I, meanwhile, picked up my jacket, bade her farewell, tottered downstairs, and poured myself into the first passing taxi. If anything, I decided as I gripped the seat hard, I was feeling worse. My legs felt completely boneless, and something had happened to the muscles in my eyelids. They didn't seem to be working. The effects should wear off soon though, surely, I thought in panic?

Thanking the driver profusely for waking me up, I weaved inside the restaurant. I'd beaten Laurie to it, and as I took my seat – just managing not to hang on to the waiter's arm as he showed me to it – I fumbled in my pocket for my mobile. I'd ring Marcus. He'd know. He'd know how long it took for the bloody things to wear off. His answer machine was on, and his PA's too. Damn. Penny then. She'd know, of course she would. She was eminently sensible. She answered immediately, in cool, efficient tones.

'Penny Trevelyon.'

'Penny!' I gasped, my voice sounding unnaturally loud suddenly. I couldn't seem to gauge its volume. It rang around the restaurant. 'What d'you know about drugs?'

A couple at the next table glanced at me quickly, then back at one another, eyebrows raised.

'Drugs? Not a thing. You know I've never indulged. Why?'

'No, no, not the psychedelic kind,' I muttered, blushing and turning my back on the couple. 'Proper ones. Medicinal ones. Sleeping pills, for example.'

She paused. 'Why?'

'Because I took three of Marcus's by mistake this morning. I thought they were paracetamol. And Penny,' I yelped, 'they were double strength!'

There was a silence on the other end. Then, quietly: 'Where are you now, Henny?'

'I'm in Kensington Place waiting for Laurie, but I think I'm going to pass out.'

'Well, for heaven's sake get up right now and go straight home to bed,' she said forcibly. 'If you've taken three double-strength sleeping tablets, you're in no fit state to be anywhere other than flat on your back! Either that or in hospital.'

'I can't, Penny,' I wailed. 'What'll he think?'

'Just tell him what's happened,' she hissed. 'He'll under-stand, he's human, but you can't sit there nodding off over lunch! Go to the flat, for God's sake. If you're in Kensington Place, it's only round the corner.'

'Yes, but Penny, it's only my second day. I can't just— Oh hi, Laurie.' I cut her off brutally, switching the phone off too. I threw it in my bag.

'Hi there.' He swooped low to kiss my cheek, fringe flopping fetchingly. Golly. That woke me up a bit. Quite close to the mouth, too.

'Sorry I'm late, but the wretched wardrobe woman wanted to go through a tatty old collection of corduroy suits at the last minute. Droned on about how they'd give me gravitas, an academic air. You all right?' His dark eyes scanned my face as he sat down. 'Look a bit peaky.'

'Fine! Fine,' I rallied, taking my chin out of my hands. 'Just a bit – you know – tired.'

'God, me too, I'm knackered. Let's get a drink, shall we? That'll perk us up. Waiter!'

Would it? A drink? A lightbulb went on in my head. Yes, of course, I thought feverishly. A stiff drink *would* wake me up.

'A gin and tonic for me,' he was saying to the waiter, 'and Henny?'

'Same.' I grinned. I never drank spirits. 'And make it a double.'

Laurie looked surprised. Surprised, but encouraged, too. He smiled. 'Yes, OK. I'll have a double too. And we may as well order some food, while we're at it. The mushroom risotto's frightfully good in here but—'

'Fine, I'll have that.'

'D'you want a starter?'

'No, and no pudding either.'

Let's get this show on the road, I thought grimly. Let's get it over and done with. In fact, why bother with food? Surely the gin would do nicely. And make it snappy, I willed to the waiter's departing back.

Moments later, our drinks appeared. As Laurie leaned back in his chair and launched into a monologue about his volatile

catherine alliott

relationship with his producer, I gulped mine down quickly. It was extremely strong and I practically had to hold my nose. I was also aware that, although Laurie was chatting, he was watching me with interest. Was he wondering if he'd employed an alcoholic, perhaps? No, just a narcotic, I thought, sniggering foolishly to myself.

Laurie talked on. His producer, it transpired, was of the opinion that all history could be traced back to sex, and his sole aim in this series was to get as many shots as possible of Mary Tudor in bed with William of Orange. Laurie was just explaining to me the pitfalls of such a strategy, given Mary's well-documented frigidity and William's predilection for small boys, when inexplicably, he ground to a halt.

'Henny, am I boring you?'

'No, why?' I murmured.

'Well it's just you've got your head on the tablecloth and your eyes are shut.'

I jerked upright. 'Sorry. No, not boring at all. Jolly interesting actually. Especially the bit about the iron chastity belt. But – oh God, I'm sorry. I think the drink's gone to my head.'

It was a mistake, I realised that now. Especially a double. I was beginning to feel not just tired, but very peculiar. And pissed. Very, very pissed. I had a feeling I might pass out.

'Now that's encouraging,' Laurie murmured, fixing me with dark, smouldering eyes. 'I like a girl who lets a bit of liquor go to her head.'

I leaned across the table and seized his hand. 'Laurie, it's no good. I have to go to bed.'

He looked around, startled. The couple on the next table were agog, albeit behind their menus. Laurie coughed. Straightened his tie.

'Henny, I'm thrilled, naturally,' he murmured nervously. 'And frankly I'm with you all the way. I thought to myself the moment I saw you, Now there's a very attractive woman. If I'm not careful I can see myself getting entangled with her . . . but don't you think we should at least sample the risotto?'

'No, no.' I shook my head vigorously. Another mistake. I held it, lest it topple from my neck onto Kensington Place's tasteful wooden flooring. 'Not that sort of bed. I mean to sleep. You see, Laurie,' I lowered my voice. 'I've taken an overdose.'

Within minutes Laurie had paid the bill, unordered the risottos and was ushering me out of the front door.

'You're an addict?' he squeaked, looking white and appalled as he flagged down a passing taxi. 'Jesus, Henny, I had no idea! Penny didn't say, and God, I didn't think to check your arms. You certainly don't *look* like a—'

'No, sleeping pills,' I insisted, the cool air at least having some effect on my vocal cords. 'I took Marcus's sleeping pills thinking they were paracetamol. Took three. I've just got to lie down, Laurie.'

'Oh!' He stared at me as I stumbled into the back of the taxi. As he got in beside me and sat down, his mouth twitched. 'Right. So, we're not off to the nearest hospital to have your stomach pumped, then?'

'God, I hope not. No, just to twenty-four Campden Hill Grove for a little lie-down.'

Luckily there was no traffic, our driver was swift, and we were there in moments. Laurie chuckled as he helped me out of the cab, and I have to say, by now, I was feeling a little less drugged-up and much more ginned-up. Beginning to see the funny side.

'So,' he reflected in amusement as he helped me up the path to the elegant cream Georgian house – if the neighbouring Nina Campbell curtains twitched, I didn't notice. 'Day two, and my new PA pops a handful of pills, sinks a double gin, and drags me back to her place.'

Suddenly, this struck me as terribly funny. I lost the use of my legs and doubled up weakly on his arm, wheezing hysterically.

'Key?' he hazarded, as I swayed violently.

I opened my handbag wide. 'Take it!' I gasped wantonly. 'Go on, ferret around all you want.'

'Jesus,' I thought I heard him mutter, but I was probably mistaken.

As he found the key and helped me through the door to the hall, I continued the commentary.

'Yes,' I agreed, weak with laughter now. 'Your new PA, a woman of uncertain years, with questionable motives, two teenage children, stretchmarks and her first grey pube, drags her gorgeous young boss up to her lair . . .' at this I playfully seized his tie as we mounted the stairs, pulling him along behind me, '. . . assaults him on an empty stomach – doesn't even let him get his hands on a bread roll—'

'Or even a ciabatta,' he commented as he put the key in the flat door, 'since we were going smart Italian and not greasy spoon. Bedroom?'

'Down the end. Or even a ciabatta,' I agreed drunkenly as he propelled me down the hall. I lurched into a doorway en route. Swayed. 'Ooh, Laurie. This looks nice.'

The bath suddenly looked terribly inviting. I put one leg over the side.

'No, no.' He heaved me out bodily. 'Not in there. Bed. This way.'

'Bed,' I repeated seductively, rolling my eyes lasciviously as I leaned against his shoulder. 'B.E.D.' I licked my lips. 'Mmmm . . .'

'Now, you lie down here and – ooh Christ, Henny!'

I'd obeyed orders and flopped back on the double bed, but still had hold of his tie, pulling him down on top of me. I lay there, giggling under his weight, still holding on tight, his nose to mine, whilst behind him, the elaborate ceiling rose was spinning in a curious manner, like a demented Ferris wheel.

'You're a very naughty girl,' he admonished, tapping my nose lightly. 'With a very pretty face, and if you weren't so catastrophically slaughtered I'd be sorely tempted to take advantage of this situation and indulge in a little afternoon delight. As it is though . . .' He untangled my fingers one by one and eased himself gently away.

'Spoilsport!' I grabbed the back of his head with both hands and pulled his lips down to mine.

At that point, puzzlingly, I saw double. Two heads. Laurie's, obviously, clamped in my hands, but another, more familiar one, framed in the doorway. I frowned, confused.

'Marcus?'

Laurie was off me in a trice. Standing to attention by the bed, frantically smoothing down his hair, his tie.

I sat up, frowning. 'Marcus. What on earth are you doing here?'

He looked terribly pale, my husband, standing there squarely in the doorway, in his pinstripe suit, briefcase in hand. And rather temporary. Why didn't he come in, I wondered?

'I'll leave you,' muttered Laurie, sliding away and somehow sliding past Marcus, which was no mean feat, because my husband was a big man. Not desperately tall, but wide. Solid. Broad shoulders. I'd always rather liked that. Found it comforting. I lay down again as Marcus advanced towards me. I wasn't finding him terribly comforting now, though; his face looked fuzzy against the horribly mobile ceiling. Not very restful. I shut my eyes again. And actually, I thought blearily, if he was here for what I thought he was here for, he could forget it. I really wasn't up for it. If he was hoping for a bit of gratuitous leg-over with his wife on a Tuesday lunchtime, he was out of luck. In fact, the very idea of doing anything untoward with him, or Laurie, or just about anyone, for that matter, suddenly made me feel decidedly ill. I didn't open my eyes again, but let my limbs, which felt like lead weights, sink into the bed. Possibly right through it.

'Not now, darling,' I murmured. 'Got a bit of a headache.' And with that, I passed out.

# chapter eight

When I awoke, the flat seemed very quiet. Very still. The light had changed too. Well, let's face it, it had disappeared. It was October, so the days were getting shorter, but not that short, surely? I gazed blankly at the dark, opaque windows, then down at my watch. Six o'clock. Six o'*clock*? I sat bolt upright. Had I really been asleep that long? I frowned into the gloom in an effort to remember how long that was, exactly. When had I arrived? I had absolutely no idea, and frankly, not the slightest idea what I was doing here, either.

I flicked on the bedside lamp, swung my legs over the side of the bed and frowned down at the cream carpet. Not a very practical colour, but chosen on the grounds that it would get only very occasional use in our smart London flat. I rubbed the soft pile with my toe, puzzled. Odd. I didn't remember taking my shoes off. Perhaps Marcus had taken them off? I seemed to remember him being here, and Laurie too. I shook my head, bemused. What was that all about? Had we all had lunch together? Here? And had I cooked it? I wracked my brains. No, too weird. Just Laurie and me then, I decided. Out somewhere, in a restaurant. Yes – a mushroom risotto, that was it. Well, it had to be out, I was pretty sure I couldn't cook that.

I went to the bathroom and brushed my teeth, feeling a bit better now. That little sleep had done me the world of good. Ah yes, *sleep*. I paused, mid-brush. Gazed at my reflection in the mirror. Gracious, it was all coming back to me. I'd taken those wretched sleeping pills. Then I must have had a nasty turn in the restaurant and Laurie must have deposited me back here. That was good of him, if a little embarrassing, I thought with a squirm. I tried vainly to remember arriving, coming up the stairs, but . . . no. Shook my head. Couldn't. Anyway, having deposited me, he must have rung Marcus to tell him I was here in case – well, in case I passed out or something, I thought, colouring up. Yes, that was it.

I found my shoes and wandered into the drawing room. And Marcus had clearly waited until I was asleep and then gone back to work. He could have left me a note, I thought, glancing around, but then he was always very economical with the written word. I smiled. Why bother with a pen when you could email, fax or text, was his theory, but unfortunately I'd never got to grips with technology, so it was no good checking my mobile. Unlike my offspring, whose little thumbs moved faster than the speed of light, and who'd insisted I should learn, as their friends' mothers had.

'You must, Mummy, you must!' Lily would urge. 'It's *so-oo* embarrassing, and you're *so-oo* missing out!' She was right, I was. And I should. So that when I received a message from her saying *Just off to geography*, I could respond with *Splendid. Just off to Waitrose.* How on earth was I managing without it?

So had Laurie come inside, I wondered, right into the flat? No, probably not. He'd probably just dropped me at the door, in a taxi. I wouldn't have minded him coming up though, I reflected, moving around the room admiringly. I'd forgotten how nice this place was. I fingered the Osborne & Little curtains at the window. It *was* nice, having money, I thought guiltily, although sometimes I felt we had too much. When we'd bought the farm and then this place, both of which needed doing up, I'd left the décor of the farm to a friend but had done the flat myself. I'd found it both cringe-making and exhilarating to breeze into designer showrooms in Chelsea and pick out sumptuous fabrics, before sauntering up the King's Road to look at antiques with prohibitively expensive price tags swinging from them, enquiring casually of the haughty assistant, 'That sofa-table in the window. When would you be able to deliver?' That had them dropping their supercilious sneers and scurrying across in their Gucci loafers, I can tell you.

And I had gone a bit over the top here, I admitted, strolling around, speculatively, head on one side. But Marcus had been thrilled. Delighted. He'd made the money and wanted to spend it, or me to spend it. He didn't want it lolling around in the bank, or in trust funds for the children; in fact, the very idea brought him out in a rash. 'No child of mine,' he'd fume, in a Victorian, bewhiskered Papa sort of way, 'is going to think they don't have to work for a living. Not when I've done it all myself.'

'Oh aye, oop mill and down pit,' Angus would say sardonically, but it was true – Marcus had pulled himself up by his bootstraps from the little draper's shop his father had had on Kilburn High Road, and although he didn't bang on about it, he wasn't inclined to forget it, either.

I remembered Marcus taking me there when we got engaged. To the shop, *Levin's*. He'd embraced his father warmly at the till behind the counter, a tiny, spare man in shabby trousers, an ancient brown cardigan – a skullcap, too – speaking English with a Viennese inflection. I'd been surprised. Not by the clothes or the foreign accent, but no one kissed in my family, let alone hugged. We'd mounted the back stairs to the little flat above, where Joseph Levin lived alone, Marcus's mother having died some years back. We'd sat at a tiny table in the front room drinking lemon tea and eating mundel bread and streusel. A radio had played fuzzily in the background, a foreign station, as I recall. There was an electric fire burning, but no central heating, and every few minutes, a train would rumble by and we'd hang onto the cups as they rattled. All around the room were piles and piles of newspapers, which Joseph never threw away. He never threw anything away.

As we got up to go, Marcus tried covertly to press money on his father, but Joseph refused, smiling proudly at his son in his smart clothes, admiring with his eyes the BMW at the kerb below. I'd felt uncomfortable because I wasn't Jewish, but Marcus had said his father wouldn't mind, that Joseph just wanted him to be happy. He'd walked us downstairs and when we'd got to the shop, Marcus had moved through the aisles, amongst the rolls of cloth, packed tightly from floor to ceiling, fingering them lovingly – reverently, almost. He told me how he'd helped in here as a child, grown up in here. Then he'd pulled a roll of fabric from the wall and thrown it expertly at the counter, the blue-grey silk shooting out like a shining, rippling sea. He'd cut a length with a flash of scissors, laughing, and popped it in a paper bag, showing me what he'd done as a boy. Joseph, half his son's weight and height, was quiet and watchful beside us. I'd laughed too, but I'd treasured that piece of silk, and when we were married a few months later, I'd had it made into a little bolero jacket to wear over the short cream dress I'd worn to the register office. I remember the flash of surprise, recognition and then love in Marcus's eyes as he saw me, and then his father's face at our reception at a local restaurant, nodding as he touched it, smiling. His eyes swimming.

I moved on around the flat, holding the tops of my arms, looking at the luxurious furnishings. The heavy drapes in the dining room puddled fashionably on the floor, and I thought how Joseph would have sucked his teeth at that, at the flagrant waste. And I did try not to be wasteful. Had deliberately chosen a modest farmhouse with a pretty garden and a couple of acres, not the zonking great Lipton Hall on the other side of the village which was also for sale and which Marcus would have been happy with. But he was also happy with the farm. As long as I was, he was, and that had always been the way. He loved me to distraction, I was so lucky in that. So this extravagant flat had been my concession to him. My way of letting him say, *Look where I came from, where I began. Look where I am now, what I've done.* And why not? Why not have a flat in leafy W8 and throw money at it, if you could?

Yet somehow, it made me uncomfortable. Because lots of people worked hard, and not everyone was so amply rewarded. I thought of Penny, Penny who *had* to work, despite her protestations that she'd never be without her job. She could have married the gorgeous Philip, complete with family brewery business to stroll into after the Army, but had clung on for dear life for lovely penniless, prospectless Tommy Rutlin, who managed an art gallery and brought in about enough to feed the cat. So Penny had worked her socks off.

She'd put down the deposit on the house in Clapham, waited until she was a partner before she had children so she could afford their education, and generally kept the show on the road. And that made me feel guilty. I'd once said to Marcus that I'd like to—

'What?' He'd regarded me in amusement over the menu in The Ivy. 'Give her some money?'

'Well . . .' I'd shrugged helplessly.

'You can't just hand people a cheque, Henny. It embarrasses them. Emasculates them, even.'

But there were ways, and he knew how.

When Tommy took a deep breath and bought the art gallery from the owner, then looked around wildly for backers, I know Marcus waded in. He didn't tell me, but I saw the relief on Penny's face when they came to lunch one Sunday. I remember her getting a bit pissed and attempting to thank him, Marcus brushing it off, embarrassed.

And that had always been his way. If you had money, you spent it, you helped people, you didn't hoard it, as Joseph had done. I remember the look of horror and distress on my husband's face when Joseph died. All that money under the mattress – a terrible, thin old mattress, with terrible, tatty bedlinen. His ancient pyjamas – rags, almost – folded neatly on the pillow. Marcus, with his head in his hands.

Joseph had died in the shop, serving a customer, working to the end. At the funeral in Kilburn, the synagogue had been packed – *packed* – with people of all ages, colours and religions, for Joseph, a strict Jew, had embraced everyone. So many people had come up to us – women, mostly – a lot of them Indian, in saris – pressing our hands, telling us how Joseph had sold them fabric on the never-never, and sometimes the absolutely never. How they'd made clothes for themselves, their families, hung curtains, thanks to his kindness. And Marcus had inherited that streak. That generous spirit. I sometimes wondered how many more Tommy Rutlins there were. You never completely knew the person to whom you were married. As I stood now, looking out over the Kensington rooftops, I felt a rush of love for him.

More recently, he'd been great about Dad. But he'd felt so helpless, too. When Dad had finally gone into hospital, it had had to be National Health and not private, because however much Marcus had wanted to pay, that was where Dad was going to get the best treatment. Senile dementia, or one of its variants, they'd called it. Not Alzheimer's, but a very acute form. At seventy-two, my father had suddenly become a child again. He threw tantrums, wet the bed, became more and more abusive and unpredictable, until Mum – who I have to say had lived with it for a long time without letting on, shielding him in her proud way from the world and even from Benji and me for a while – finally had to give in.

I remembered so vividly that day, three years ago, when Mum had phoned us, and we'd dashed up to London. I remembered her following Dad's ambulance in the car on her own – she'd insisted – to the hospital. Benji and I had gone in later that evening, while Marcus and Francis, Benji's boyfriend, waited in reception. Dad was sitting up in bed in stripy pyjamas, very bright-eyed and alert – provocative, even – Mum beside him, ashen-faced but very relieved.

'Someone's taken one of my cards,' Dad had said accusingly, as Benji and I sat down. 'I had forty-two yesterday, and look. Forty-one.'

On the bedspread were the Players cards he'd collected as a boy and now kept in his pocket, along with his penknife and a conker on a string.

'I'm sure it'll turn up,' I soothed, leaning forward on a grey plastic chair by his bed. 'Don't fuss.'

'I wouldn't mind, but it was my cricketing one,' he grumbled, lifting up the bedclothes and peering to check it hadn't gone down there. 'One of my best.'

'How are you finding it, Dad?' asked Benji. 'Food all right?'

'Well, it's better than hers, at least I can eat it,' he said, glaring at Mum. 'And I don't have to listen to her voice all day, either. Whoever she is.'

We cringed, and Mum bowed her head in shame, but this was par for the course. A facet of Dad's condition. He had no idea who Mum was, or Benji and I for that matter. He thought like a child, and spoke like a child. He was not a cruel man, in fact a very kind man, but right now, he had no brakes.

'And I don't want to be married to her any more, I want to be married to Beverly,' he declared, matter-of-factly, as if he were merely changing his best friend at school. He picked up his cards and carefully stacked them together, his face petulant. 'I've told her that, but she won't listen. Hey, Beverly.' He sat up straight and waved excitedly as a large black nurse languidly pushed a trolley full of instruments past. 'What's the difference between a man's willy and a chicken leg?'

'No idea, Gordon,' she said resignedly in her sing-song Caribbean accent.

Dad flushed, delightedly. 'D'you want to come on a picnic?'

As she grinned and moved on, unperturbed, he roared with laughter, flopping back on his pillows and hooting at the ceiling. As his mirth subsided abruptly, he sat bolt upright.

'Hey, d'you think he's got it?' he hissed, glaring suspiciously at his neighbour, a dribbling ninety year old, ga-ga and open-mouthed in the bed beside him, incapable of even having a pee on his own, let alone taking one of Dad's cards.

And that was really what was so awful, as I said to Marcus on the way home, the windscreen wipers swiping away torrential rain. Yes, it was undignified for Dad, but actually, he was happy. He wasn't aware of his condition, just busy wondering if it would be baked jam roll for lunch and if he'd be allowed to play in the garden afterwards. Whereas Mum . . . Well, Mum was in pieces.

My mother was a strong, domineering woman, but little

by little her strength was being eroded by her family's fortunes, and that, in the end, was all she cared about. Which surely is only another expression of love? And as far as she was concerned, our fortunes had plummeted. After my disastrous non-wedding to Rupert, her dream son-in-law, I'd then married a Jew, the son of a Kilburn draper. She probably didn't think it could get much worse, until Benji, whom she'd hoped would become a doctor and marry a female doctor – she fondly imagined their hands brushing as they passed scalpels to each other during operations (Mum could so easily out-Finchley Road her neighbours) – appeared to be gay, and living with a boy called Francis. Having picked herself up off her scrubbed kitchen floor after that life-shattering revelation, she was making the bed one morning, only to find a turd, lying thick and solid, steaming on the bottom sheet. When she confronted her husband who was up a tree at the time, throwing stones at next door's greenhouse, he thrust his lower lip out defiantly and said, 'No, I didn't. *You* did it. In your sleep. I saw you.' I think that was the last straw for Mum.

Marcus had reached out and squeezed my hand in the car. 'There's nothing you can do, sweetheart. He's where he is, and it's the best place for him. And don't worry about your mother, she's as tough as old boots. She'll recover.'

She was tough, and eventually she did recover, but only after she'd been to stay with us at the farm for a long while. One day I'd popped up to London to see her, unannounced, and as I'd parked the car outside the block of flats, I'd seen her come out of the front door and almost didn't recognise her. My mum, who wouldn't have been seen dead walking to the shops at Swiss Cottage without high heels, a cashmere coat and full make-up, was in an old green cardigan, her hair in a headscarf, white face bowed. A neighbour greeted her and she fleetingly raised a hand, but she was crushed. Defeated. And I recognised her condition. Remembered of old the feeling that the weight of the world truly was on one's shoulders, and that it was physically impossible to hold one's head up.

I persuaded her to come and stay at the farm, which she did. She was quiet and withdrawn for a long while, but gradually, she picked up speed. Rapidly, actually. And nearly drove Marcus to distraction. He bit his lip stoically as she sterilised all the eggs he brought in from the henhouse which had 'chicken's business' on them, was uncomplaining when she insisted we wash the Christmas turkey inside and out with soap – we didn't, but I think we got away with it – and only drew the line at her forcing poor Dilly the Labrador to have a bath every day. When she put a Clear Glade air-freshener in the downstairs loo, from which Marcus emerged, informing her that he preferred the smell of shit, we decided that in the interests of family relations, she was better and should go home. She did, feeling much happier, and with her recently coiffed head held high. The entire family, including Dilly, spilled out into the yard to wave a cheery and heartfelt goodbye.

It had taken six months, though — *six months*, I thought with a jolt as I gathered up my handbag and had a last look around the flat, before she was better. Not many husbands would have put up with their mother-in-law for six months, but then again, Marcus was a bit of a saint. My saintly husband, I thought with a smile as I shut the front door behind me. Don't suppose many wives could say the same of their spouses without a hint of sarcasm.

When I got back to the farm an hour and a half later, night had well and truly fallen. I turned the MG's engine off and gazed around, letting the soft night air and the wonderful quiet wash over me. One of the reasons I'd fallen in love with this place was that you couldn't hear a sound. No noise, no traffic, unlike Lipton Hall up the road, which had the A41 on its doorstep. As I got out of the car, a plane flew overhead, en route to Gatwick. I smiled. Teach me to be smug.

On the other side of the yard, Bill the gardener, whom we'd inherited from the previous owners and who lived in the tiny cottage on the edge of our land, was shutting up the chickens for the night. His bent stance was illuminated in the outside light. I tried to make a dash for the back door, but:

'Orright then, Henny?'

Damn. Too late. He'd seen me.

'Yes, thanks, Bill.' I turned and forced a smile.

When I'd originally heard that a gardener came with the house and would we please keep him on in the cottage, I'd been enchanted. Of *course* we would, how heavenly. A lovely, sweet, authentic old retainer! And so he had seemed. Weather-beaten and widowed, and with nothing he didn't know about gardening and farming, Bill was the salt of the earth. And Marcus, who really did know absolutely nothing about country living but was keen to learn, was beside himself with joy.

'He knows the name of every single plant in the garden, Henny. Imagine, he's been digging it for forty-five years!'

'Great,' I agreed, relieved. A born and bred townie, I was happy to pop a few pansies in here and there and fiddle with the hanging baskets, but I didn't relish the thought of digging over that huge herbaceous border at the back.

And Bill proved to be a treasure. He worked hard, and I'd have long chats with him at the kitchen table when he popped in for a cuppa, and I'd pick his brains as I tried to learn a bit about flora and fauna. But then the chats got longer and longer, and I needed to get on, and when he *finally* got up to go – he'd wink.

At first I'd winked back, thinking – sweet. Then one day when he winked, he leered and rubbed his balls. I nearly dropped the teapot.

When I told Marcus, he said, 'Don't be ridiculous. He's a rough country chap, he was just having a scratch.'

'Marcus, he *winked* as he did it!'

'Coincidence,' he scoffed. 'And no, we're not getting rid of him, Henny, he's invaluable. You know how impossible it is to get a good gardener round here – you told me so yourself.'

This much was true. I'd rashly told him how Laura Montague – a great local mate and another recent evacuee from London – whilst lunching at a rather grand house belonging to a born-and-bred called Belinda, had seen a gardener out of the window and casually stuck her head out and asked if he had time to work in her garden, too. Belinda nearly threw the salad bowl at her.

'Never,' she'd roared, incandescent with rage, '*ever*,' she screeched, steam pouring from her nostrils, 'try to poach my gardener again!' Laura had broken a cardinal rule of country life and had scuttled away chastened, her tail between her legs.

Yes, Marcus had a point. Good gardeners *were* thin on the ground, and I certainly didn't want to clean out the chicken-house or give the horses hay while Marcus was at work. I bit my lip.

'And don't flirt with him,' my husband added.

'Flirt!'

'You go all smiley and twinkly. People get the wrong idea.'

I couldn't *speak* I was so angry. The man was repulsive! Warty, whiffy, chicken shitty. Flirt!

But then there'd been the knicker-drawer incident. A

couple of months back, I'd reached for some pants one morning to find my knicker drawer – usually a riot of untidy, winding garments – completely transformed. Bras and pants had been neatly folded, and arranged in tidy rows. I'd stared, astonished. Then ran downstairs to quiz Marcus.

'Don't be ridiculous, of course I didn't.'

The children, then. I was met with withering stares. 'Why would we, Mum?'

Linda, perhaps. She'd turned off the hoover. Leaned on it and sighed. 'Henny, I never even put your jumpers away, just dump 'em all in the airing cupboard. I don't go anywhere near your drawers.'

'Then who,' I'd shrieked to Marcus, 'who would do it! Who, in God's name, would tidy my knicker drawer!'

'Your mother?' Marcus had hazarded, eyes still firmly on the golf. Ah, Mum. I rang her.

'No, dear, I wouldn't dream of it. Might get ticked off,' she added huffily. 'It was bad enough when I threw all those things that were past their sell-by dates out of the larder.'

'It's got to be *him*,' I'd hissed in terror to Marcus, glancing fearfully out of the window to see if Bill was listening. 'He's the only one with a key, for God's sake, and recently when he's left a note for me about watering the greenhouse or something, he's put a little kiss at the bottom!'

I nearly passed out with horror. The thought of his gnarled old hands riffling through my underwear, folding my knickers lovingly – sniffing them, perhaps? I clutched the breakfast-table.

'At least they were clean,' remarked Marcus, calmly getting up to switch the television off as the last putt went in.

'Marcus!'

'Henny, it was you, I'm sure of it,' he sighed as he made for the back door. 'Remember when you ordered another leg of lamb, forgetting you'd already ordered one? And that time when we went to the Hammonds' party and you realised you'd got odd shoes on? You're just getting a bit ditzy in your old age, tidying up and forgetting you've done it.'

'Oh, don't be ridiculous! It would take half an hour to tidy that drawer. I'd remember doing that.'

'Clearly not,' he'd said blithely, and off he'd gone to the stables, unconcerned. Convinced he was right. But I *was* concerned, bloody concerned. And recently, I'd been cold-shouldering Bill, to see if I could get the message across that way.

'There's no one in,' he informed me with a sly grin as I made for the back door, eyes front. I gave a tight little smile.

'So I see.'

The gravel drive, I'd noticed, was conspicuously free of cars, which was surprising really, because it was now half past eight and I'd assumed Marcus would be back before me. Must be working late.

'They was in,' he went on, leaning in an alarmingly

permanent manner on the five-bar gate. 'But they've popped out, see.'

'Ah. Thank you, Bill.'

Probably popped out for a pizza, I thought as I put the key in the door. Or a curry in town, realising I was going to be late and there wouldn't be any supper. I let myself in quickly and shut the door behind me, turning on the lights. The long, low, heavily beamed kitchen with its cheery yellow walls came to life. It was tidy too. Incredibly tidy, so Linda must have stayed all day. No sign of the children, as Bill had said. Ah yes, it was their last night at home, I realised, putting my handbag on the island, so Marcus might well have taken them out. Where, I wondered. Oscars? Yes, probably Oscars. Perhaps I could join them? I glanced at my watch and made for the phone to ring and check they were there, when I noticed the note on the table. I picked it up. Unfolded it.

*Henny,*

*Clemmie rang to see if Lily could stay the night, and Angus is at Tom's. I'll pick them up and take them back to their respective schools in the morning. I'm at the Rose and Crown, and will be here for as long as it takes you to clear your things and move out. By all means live in the London flat until we sort everything out.*

*Marcus*

I stared down at the piece of paper in my hands. Realised I didn't understand the last two lines. I read them again. Then I felt the blood leave my face. My legs felt strange, so I lowered myself into a chair at the kitchen table. Outside, Christopher gave a last, sorrowful crow before he was shut up for the night. As Bill raised his head from securing the latch on the coop, I looked up and caught his eye. It was hard and knowing.

# chapter nine

I sat there for a moment, staring blankly at the note in my hands. Suddenly I dropped it, as though it were white-hot, burning me. It spiralled to the ground and came to rest on the terracotta floor. I felt quite light-headed. Quite weak and woozy, as I did when I hadn't eaten for some time. For one surreal moment, I wondered if I'd stepped into someone else's life by mistake. Someone else's kitchen, someone else's marriage. I sat there, staring dumbly at the yellow walls, at the little hanging blackboard we used as a shopping list. It stared back at me. Marcus had chalked up *shoe polish* and *loo paper* and someone else – Angus, probably – had added *Pringles and stuff*. Abruptly, I came to. No, this was my kitchen, my marriage. I felt the blood surge back to my cheeks, anger mounting. In a trice, I was on my feet. Snatching up the car keys and ignoring Dilly who was scratching and whining at the bootroom door, I flung open the back door and slammed out of the house to the car, fully aware that Bill was watching.

Ridiculous man, I fumed as I got back in the driving seat and slammed that door behind me too. Ridiculous! What the hell was he up to? What was he – chucking me out? Out of my own house? For what? Oh stupid, *stupid* man!

I roared off down the drive, leaving a cloud of dust in my wake and possibly in Bill's face, and hurtled off through the narrow country lanes. Hawthorn and blackberry bushes brushed the side of the MG as I squeezed past cars I'd normally pull in and wait for, and I got some astonished glances as wing mirrors clashed noisily. As I shot through the village touching fifty, I spotted Val Parsons, parish councillor and pillar of the community, coming out of her house. Only the other day I'd met her in the lanes and spongily agreed that people drove *far* too fast through our village. I cravenly hit the brakes as I caught her shocked face out of the corner of my eye. Stupid, *stupid* man, I seethed as I rounded the bend, checking in my rearview mirror that she was out of sight. I picked up speed. What was he thinking of? And what on earth had possessed him to go to the Rose and Crown, our local hotel, in our very small market town, where everyone knew us, and where word would be round in seconds! *Oh, Marcus is at the Rose and Crown, didn't you know? His wife has* – well what? What had I done, for crying out loud? I pursed my lips and increased the pressure on the accelerator.

The lanes became broader as I roared on towards town. I

mean, yes, all right, presumably something *had* happened at the flat, I thought, wiping a bead of sweat from my upper lip, otherwise he wouldn't be in such a state. Something to do with Laurie, I thought uncomfortably, glancing quickly at my reflection in the rearview mirror. And the more I thought about it, the more I realised that at some stage, the three of us *had* all been there in that flat together, which was odd. I racked my brains furiously. No, no it *wasn't* odd, because Laurie had taken me back there to sleep off those pills. Was that what was bugging Marcus? Was he so insanely jealous that he couldn't cope with my boss doing me a good turn? A friendly favour? Oh, the man was barking. He'd gone mad! Was he having a breakdown, I wondered. A midlife nervy thing, like Tessa Parker's husband, who was found wandering through Flaxton in his jim-jams looking for chocolate? I shot a despairing hand through my hair. Christ, that was *all* I needed.

And then to hole up here, I thought, careering around the picturesque market square and screeching to a halt in the hotel forecourt, for all the world to see, sneakily arranging for the children to be out for the night so I couldn't say goodbye to them before they went back after their exeats – ooh, it was outrageous. The man had a screw loose. Needed a good slap.

I hastened up the stone steps and through the wooden doors to the reception of this quaint, olde worlde Elizabethan inn that was now a hotel. I remembered having a drink here, in that very bar, I thought as I dashed past it, with Marcus, when we'd first arrived. We'd had a meal, too, in the dining room, and been surprised at how good it was, having rather looked down our London noses at the over-elaborate menu – guinea fowl in a juniper jalouse with fresh young spinach leaves. As opposed to stale old ones, we'd giggled. I wasn't giggling now.

'Excuse me, can you tell me which room Mr Levin's in?' I gripped the front desk breathlessly.

'Mr Levin?' The receptionist, who was about nineteen, put down her novel and stifled a yawn. She scanned her register. 'Yes, he's on the second floor. Room twelve.'

'Thank you.' I headed for the stairs.

'Oh. Er, shall I ring him and—'

'No, I'm his wife,' I said firmly. 'I'll surprise him.'

I took the flight of stairs two at a time, my jaw set, and stalked off down the second-floor corridor. I rapped hard on the door of number twelve. Then – God, why on earth was I knocking? – I barged in.

The room was spare and functional with hectic orange curtains and a matching bedcover. Marcus was lying on the double bed in his suit trousers and shirtsleeves, arms locked behind his head, a whisky at his side, watching the football on television. I set my hands on my hips and planted my feet apart.

'What the *hell* d'you think you're playing at?' I demanded angrily.

He looked up at me. Then calmly, he swung his legs around, got off the bed and turned off the television. He found his shoes and came over to stand in front of me. He also put his hands on his hips and cocked his head to one side. His eyes had a dangerous gleam.

'I'm sorry?' he said softly.

'What the hell are you doing,' I fumed, 'here? Walking out, leaving me nasty little notes, telling me to clear out, whisking the children away! What's going on, Marcus?'

'I was rather hoping you might be able to tell me that.'

'What d'you mean?'

'Well, what am I supposed to think, when I pop back to the flat to collect the earrings you left behind when we last stayed there, and which you'd been banging on about, to find the door already unlocked. And, as I follow the sounds of lust and hilarity down the passage to the bedroom, to find you, my wife, lying on the double bed, underneath Mr Laurence De Havilland, your arms and legs wrapped wantonly around him, kissing him passionately, and presumably on the brink of hot sex?'

I stared. My mouth fell open. 'I was not!' I stormed. But not quite so vehemently.

'What? Kissing him, or on the brink of sex?'

'Either!'

'Oh, you were most certainly *kissing* him, Henny, I saw that with my own eyes. Really – you know – going for it.

And enjoying it, too. Your mind on the job. Not, I'd hazard, contemplating what you were going to serve at your next dinner-party, or wondering whether the bedroom curtains were too short – in fact, not even looking at the curtains. Shutting your eyes, something we haven't seen round these parts in a while, and looking quite turned on. In fact, I'd go so far as to say you were the most turned on I've seen you in a long while. Really joining in. I expect he liked that.'

I stared at him blankly. After a moment, I fumbled for the bed behind me. Sat down slowly.

'Kissing him?' I breathed.

'Snogging,' he corrected. His face was white. Set. 'And lots of hip thrusting. Like this.' He seized a standard lamp and gave it a forceful, simulated rogering.

I stared in horror. 'All right!' I shrieked, my hands flying up. He let it go. The light from the shaking bulb swung crazily around the room. I let my hands fall limply into my lap. Stared at him, aghast.

'Marcus, how awful! I . . . don't remember. I mean – if you say I did, I know you wouldn't lie, but the thing is, I took three of your sleeping pills that morning by mistake. Then I had a gin and tonic—'

'At lunchtime?' he said incredulously. 'You've never had more than a spritzer with me, but out with the boss – oh hell, let's make it a double!'

'I – thought it would perk me up.'

'Oh, it did.' He paced angrily up and down in front of the window like a prowling animal, hands thrust in his pockets. 'Perked you up a treat!'

'Marcus.' I twisted my hands in my lap, knowing I had to get this right. Knowing this was crucial. 'I'm so sorry. Really sorry. But I was quite clearly under the influence of drugs, and then the alcohol on top which I'm not used to – well, I know it's no excuse, but I wasn't *compos mentis*. Wasn't in my right mind.'

He didn't say anything. Continued his pacing.

'And – and it was only a kiss, for God's sake! It wouldn't have been anything more.'

'Oh, so that's all right then, is it?' He swung around, furious. 'A kiss?'

'No, no of *course* it's not all right, but—'

'D'you know, Henny, that many whores stipulate to clients, "anything you like, but no kissing". Sex is fine, it's a basic animal instinct. A human need. But kissing – uh huh. Too intimate. Even for prostitutes. I think I know what they mean.'

I hung my head. Then raised it suddenly. 'So what you're saying is, you wouldn't have minded if I'd done it with him, so long as I didn't kiss him?'

'I'm saying,' he hissed through clenched teeth, 'that it's a very intimate thing to do, *in* your flat, *after* a boozy lunch, *with* a man you've been working with for two days! And what would have happened if I hadn't arrived, hm? Talk me through

179

that little scenario – or – or if I'd timed my arrival for twenty minutes later? Would that still have been *kissing interruptus*, or *coitus interruptus*?'

'Of *course* it wouldn't have been *coitus interruptus*. Of *course* not. You *know* me, Marcus, I—'

'I do not know you, Henny,' he said in a strange, strangled voice I didn't recognise. 'I thought I did, but let me tell you, it was a very rude awakening to walk into my flat and find my wife clearly having more pleasure with another man than she's had in a long time with me.'

'Oh, so that's what's really bugging you, isn't it, Marcus?' I got up off the bed. 'That's your real agenda here, isn't it? Not the fact that I had a drunken kiss with some man, which I admit,' I held up my hands to staunch his flow of invective, 'was a terrible thing to do, a dreadful, shameful thing, and I'd be livid if the tables were turned and I'd caught you at it, but what's *really* bugging you is that I might have been enjoying it!'

He took a step towards me. His face was deathly white. 'You're my wife, Henny. Of course it would bloody bug me!'

I swallowed. Hung my head again, ashamed. Of course. Of *course*. I had no moral high ground here whatsoever. Whatever had made me think I had? Whatever had made me come storming in, in high dudgeon, telling him to grow up and be reasonable? I should be on my knees. I'd ruined everything. Everything. We'd been faithful to each other for fifteen years, I knew we had. Knew he had, with a certainty I'd stake my life on, and which would doubtless make other people smile. 'How can you be so sure?' they'd say. 'An attractive, successful man like Marcus? A handy flat in London?' But I *was* sure. Knew in my bones he'd never strayed. No, it was me who'd blown it. My first job in fifteen years. My first foray into London life, first taste of another world, one that didn't involve cooking and dog-walking and school runs — and I'd blown it. I'd tasted heaven and gulped it. I gazed at my hands in my lap.

'I'm sorry, Marcus. I'm truly, truly sorry.'

At length I lifted my head. His back was to me, and he was staring out of the window. The bedroom overlooked the market square, dimly lit now with old-fashioned street-lamps, their posts hung with hanging baskets, the efforts of some town councillor, no doubt, to evoke some country charm. Rain began to fall steadily in the empty street, spattering on the windowpanes.

'You asked me, the other day, why I didn't use the flat more,' he said quietly, his back still to me, stiff and broad. 'Why I didn't, after a late meeting, for instance, stay there more often. I smiled to myself when you said that. Thought, My darling Henny. So sweet. So naive. She doesn't even know what the slippery slope looks like. Has no idea she could be pushing me down it. Has no idea of the sexual pressure I'm under.'

I looked up. 'What?'

'You don't, do you? Have any idea?'

I stared, uncomprehending.

'Henny, I run a successful film production company. I used to run a successful creative department in an advertising agency. I have always been the boss. I have always had a young team, because that is the nature of my business. And unless you're at the top of the tree, forget it, it's a young man's game or, more pertinent to this conversation, a young girl's game.' He turned. 'Henny, I am surrounded by beautiful young women. Girls who would gladly sleep their way to the top. Would happily sleep with the boss.'

I blanched, taken aback. Then I laughed nervously. 'Well, Marcus, you *say* that, but I've seen the girls in your office. Susie, Pippa – they're twenty years younger than you. I mean, you're nearly forty-two and I hardly think— oh!'

I jumped as he slammed the flat of his hand down hard on the desk beside him. His eyes were narrow and flinty.

'I say it because it's true. You have no idea of the sexual tension in offices, no idea what pressure some men are under!'

I gaped at him, astonished. 'Men? Oh come on,' I scoffed. 'Do me a favour. It's the men who always do the harassing. The bottom-pinching in lifts, the—'

'NO!' His hand came down again. 'Not true! It's the other way around, Henny. I spend my day surrounded by leggy blondes in mini-skirts offering me coffee, breezing through my office, desperate to become a production assistant or a producer if they're already an assistant, pandering to my every whim. "Would you like to look at my portfolio, Marcus? Can I show you my show-reel, Marcus? Can I please sit on your face, Marcus?" I'm up to HERE in fanny!' he roared.

I blinked. Shifted nervously on the bed. 'Well. Not literally, I hope.'

'No, not literally, because I turn it down. And you've no idea how gorgeous these girls are, Henny, with their flowing locks and their gleaming mouths, and their pert little bosoms, flicking their long hair over their shoulders and tugging down their tiny skirts – God, I can practically see their pants as they put the latte and Danish pastry in front of me! And I turn it down time after time. Not on a daily basis, I grant you, but often enough to think – bloody hell!'

'Oh, so that's what's pissing you off,' I flared. 'All those missed opportunities.' Stupid. A *stupid* mistake. But I hadn't been able to resist it. I'd felt cornered, small and had lashed out childishly.

He advanced towards me. 'No. What's pissing me off is that I resisted because of you. Because I love you. Because I thought that fifteen years of marriage and two lovely children were worth more than a quick roll in the sack, and that actually, I'd rather roll in the sack with you. I didn't want the aggro of an office affair and all the lies that go with it. Oh, I'm quite sure it would have turned me on, I'm as red-blooded as the next man, but the deceit and the duplicity wouldn't. Tell me, what were you planning on saying when you came home tonight, Henny? Me – "Good day at the office, darling?" You – "Yes, but all that typing. My poor little fingers are worn to the—" bullshit!' He broke off furiously. His eyes were hard and black, like two pieces of coal. 'All my working life,' he breathed. 'All my working life, Henny, I've been in the sweetie shop. And you go in for two seconds, and your hand's in one of the jars.' He snapped his fingers. 'Just like that.'

His eyes glittered at me across the room. In the silence, the rain tapped a tattoo on the window behind him.

'And I notice it was our flat you repaired to, incidentally, not his,' he breathed bitterly. 'You didn't even wait to be propositioned. You turned into one of those predatory, manipulative women overnight. It was *your* hand tugging his neck down, *your* mouth finding his, *your* hands in his hair . . .' He broke off, in difficulties now. Tears of rage and emotion swam in his eyes as he swallowed.

'You disgust me, Henny,' he quavered. 'I thought I could rely on you. Trust you. I encouraged you to take that job. I knew you were working for an attractive man but it never, ever occurred to me that you might be planning on getting into his trousers.'

'I wasn't,' I whispered, appalled. 'That's the God's honest truth, Marcus.' I struggled, suddenly, with what *was* the truth. 'I – I mean yes,' I faltered. 'I *was* relieved to find I wasn't

184

working for a stuffy old professor, just as I'm sure you prefer your Danish delivered by a pouting blonde and not a wizened old crow in carpet slippers, and if I'm honest, a little light flirtation *was* on my mind, since the only man I talk to all day is the postman and his repartee isn't up to much, and don't tell me you don't laugh and share a joke with Susie and Pippa and notice their pretty eyes and lovely legs even if you don't touch?'

'But that's the difference. You did touch.'

'I – I know.' I swallowed. 'I did. And I'm sorry.'

There was a silence. Marcus turned around and contemplated the wet street again. A lorry rumbled past laden with rattling beer barrels, drove around the square, and then on into the distance. After a moment, he reached for his whisky glass on the desk beside him. He drained it in one quick movement, his head jerking back sharply. His voice, when it came, was thick and low.

'Go on,' he said addressing his empty glass. 'Get out. Leave me now.'

I stared at his broad back, at the resolute set of his shoulders, at his familiar, usually comforting solidity. I opened my mouth. Shut it again. After a moment, I shakily picked up my keys from the bedspread beside me, and got to my feet. I took one last look at him, framed there in the dark window, and then I left the room.

# chapter ten

I didn't go down the hotel stairs in quite the same forthright way as I'd come up them. In fact, I was shaking. I noticed the receptionist look up from her novel as I reappeared, but I didn't return her interested, pale-blue stare. Instead, I kept my eyes firmly down as I went out to the car. I sat in it for a moment, staring blankly at the darkness through the rain-spattered windscreen. This isn't happening to me, I thought dumbly. Marcus and I are not one of those couples. Marcus and I do not split up. After a while, a car drew up beside me, and out got a couple of about my age. They didn't have an umbrella, and there was a lot of squealing from the wife about her hair getting soaked. Eventually her husband threw his coat over her head and they ran into the hotel laughing, dodging the puddles. Just a normal Thursday night out in the pub. Everyone else is having a normal Thursday, I thought. No one knows what is happening to me.

I drove home and immediately went upstairs to see what he'd taken. Several workshirts had gone, a suit, his cords and a couple of jumpers, but he hadn't cleared out his entire wardrobe, I thought with relief. But then, it was me who was going, wasn't it, I realised with a jolt. Me who was going to the London flat. Banished. Sent to Coventry. I sat down unsteadily on the edge of the bed and reached for the phone. It was too late to ring Penny, but I rang her anyway.

'Sorry,' I gulped, when she came on, drowsily. 'Were you in bed?'

'No, just watching the news. What's wrong?'

I burst into tears, and of course, once I'd started crying, couldn't stop. Poor Penny had to hang on at the other end for quite a few moments listening to great shoulder-heaving sobs before I could finally control my voice. When I could, I revealed all, in little staccato sentences punctuated by broken gasps. 'I can't believe it, Penny, can't believe he's done this. Can't believe he means it. What the hell am I going to do!'

She was silent for a while. 'Oh God,' she muttered eventually. 'What a nightmare.'

'I know!' I wailed, wiping my sopping wet face with the back of my hand. It was shaking visibly. 'I know, Penny, so what am I going to do?'

'Well, nothing, for the moment,' she said firmly. 'He's at boiling point and you need to let him cool down. And he will, in time.'

'D'you think?'

'Well eventually, but—'

'But what?'

'Well, he's a proud man, Henny. *I* know that, and I'm not married to him. You surely know that.'

'I do,' I cried. 'Of course I do, a very proud man, but – but so's Tommy. So are most men, surely?'

'Yes, but it's different for Marcus.'

'Is it?' I said appalled. 'Why?'

'Well, that incredibly humble background. All that clogs and shawls bit. And his father and everything.'

'What's Joseph got to do with anything?'

'Well nothing, directly,' she said uneasily. 'It's just . . . well I adore Marcus, you know I do, but I wouldn't want to cross him.'

'Wouldn't you?' I yelped.

'No. He has a vision. A life-plan. Has done since he was about three, I should imagine, and he's not about to compromise. Marcus doesn't do compromise.'

'No,' I agreed humbly. 'He doesn't.' Then I rallied. 'But he's not a cruel man, Penny. Not unkind.'

'Oh God no, quite the reverse. But he has very firm views, doesn't he? Very strong principles. And he's principled, I think, because he knows the alternative.'

'Well yes, he knows poverty, knows hardship. But what's that got to do with it?'

'So he knows the value of things. Knows how hard it is to build something up, how long it takes, how many years, and how quickly it can be knocked down.'

'Like a business,' I said. 'Or a marriage.'

'Exactly.'

We were quiet for a moment.

'But I still think he's being utterly ridiculous,' she said staunchly.

'You do?'

'Oh *God*, yes! Christ – I spoke to you in that restaurant, Henny, I know how out of it you were, and I shall tell him so.'

'Will you?' I said eagerly. 'Oh, thank you, Pen. He'll listen to you, he respects you!'

It was true, he did. Marcus had always liked Penny. He admired the way she'd waited quietly in the wings for Tommy, hadn't gone for second-best, and then, on realising she hadn't picked the brightest pixie in the forest, had squared her shoulders and got on with making a decent living for the pair of them.

'And I'll talk to Laurie too. Find out what really happened. Ask him if he assaulted you,' she said grimly.

'Oh no! Oh please don't, Penn,' I gasped, horrified. 'I'm quite sure he didn't. I'm quite sure it was all my fault,' I said miserably. 'And – and what am I going to do about him? I can't go back, can I?'

'Why not?' she said warmly. 'You can't just *not* go back, either.'

'But surely Marcus would completely disown me if I carried on working there? File divorce proceedings immediately!'

'But on the other hand, if you don't go back, you look so guilty. As if there really *is* something going on between you and Laurie. If you ring Marcus and say, "It's all right, darling, I've resigned," he'll say, "Ah ha! Guilty conscience!"'

'And if I carry on working, he'll say "brazen hussy",' I said miserably.

'Oh I agree,' she said cheerfully. 'You can't win. It's what's known as a cleft stick. You're damned if you do and damned if you don't, but on balance, I'd at least go in tomorrow. Just to find out what happened.'

I slid my bottom off the edge of the bed and crouched, cowering on the carpet. 'And face him as well?' I whispered, appalled. 'Laurie?'

'Well, I think some sort of explanation is in order, don't you? Otherwise he'll go to his grave wondering what the hell he employed for two days.'

'That's where I'd like to go,' I said darkly. 'My grave.'

She laughed. 'Cheer up. In a few weeks' time Marcus will have forgiven you and we'll all be laughing like drains at this little episode. Seeing the funny side.'

'I doubt it,' I said gloomily, but nevertheless, I put the phone down feeling slightly encouraged. Unless she was a very good actress, Penny clearly thought it was a storm in a teacup and that all would be well if I played along with Marcus for a while. Well, I can do that, I thought as I peeled off my clothes and climbed wretchedly into bed, pulling the covers over me. I can play along, just so long as I know it's only a game, and that the frivolity will end eventually.

The following morning, at seven o'clock, I sat downstairs having a cup of coffee, my suitcase by my side. I felt like a stranger in my own home. Here I was in my dark city suit, my toes squeezed into hideously uncomfortable high heels, no husband crashing around looking for a clean shirt, no Radio Four blaring, no James Naughtie informing us about Iraqi weapons programmes, no arguments about whose turn it was to feed the ducks or take Dilly for a walk – no husband. My eyes filled with tears. I could, of course, turn Terry Wogan on out of spite, but since Marcus wasn't here to witness it, it would be a hollow victory.

Taking a quick gulp of coffee, I looked longingly at an invitation on the dresser. It was for a charity lunch at Belinda's house today, in her beautiful timbered barn. A Save the Children thing, which Laura and Camilla would no doubt be going to, as I normally would too. Camilla would pick us up in her filthy old Discovery, full of saddles and dog hair – Laura and I shrieking at the state of it – and we'd charge off down cowpat-encrusted lanes (the scenic route, Camilla would insist, showing off that she grew up here) to rock up at Belinda's, late as usual. Into the barn we'd creep, where about a hundred women would be sitting at round tables in hushed silence, the guest speaker already in full flow. We'd slide in amongst them, grimacing as one or two raised their eyebrows and tapped their watches in mock horror. It was that rather quirky vicar's wife speaking today, I remembered, the one I'd heard at the NSPCC thing, who gave an amusing talk on the history of underwear, holding up huge Edwardian bloomers and ending up with a teeny tiny thong. Everyone would get frightfully giggly as we knocked back the white wine, and then afterwards, we'd sit around having a gossip, before glancing at watches and shrieking that we had to fly – to schools, to appointments – getting in cars with flushed cheeks and calling out a cheery toodle-oo! Camilla would drop us back and then, realising I hadn't got a thing for supper, I'd dash to Waitrose – and bang into Laura again at the meat counter. We'd roar with laughter, and agree that it was *al*ways bloody pork chops in a crisis, and what did one *do* with them? Oh really? In a Gruyère sauce? Wasn't that a bit of a faff? Oh, just grate it on top . . . and then finish it off under the grill . . . marvellous. Oh, and don't forget tennis tomorrow – or 'Pat and Shriek' as we called it. Just one set, we'd agree, nothing too strenuous. See you!

Yes, that was my life, I thought miserably as I picked the car keys up from the table. The one I knew, the one I could do. The one I liked. Not this one. Whatever had possessed me to do this one? To throw it all away?

I patted Dilly, knowing that Linda would look after her, then went out to the car. I carefully arranged a plastic bag over the seat of the MG and drove to the station. Now that paying to leave my car didn't come as such a blinding shock, I had a clutch of pound coins ready for the attendant. I didn't express naked astonishment at the transaction, nor riffle frantically in my bag apologising profusely, nor write him an IOU on the back of a vet's bill. I took it all in my stride, seasoned commuter that I was, and swept under the barrier. I knew the best place to park too, closest to the platform. Knew all the tricks. Could turn them, too, Marcus would no doubt rejoinder sourly. I hung my head in shame and walked doggedly to the train, catching it, casually, by seconds as Marcus had taught me. I had a quick look around the carriage just in case . . . no. No sign of him. That was probably a good thing, I reasoned, leaning my head back as I sat down, shutting my eyes. Unless of course I was going for the sympathy vote, in which case looking and feeling like death might well swing it for me.

Once in London, I made a quick detour to the flat with my suitcase, then went back to Covent Garden. Laurie was extremely surprised to see me. In fact, he nearly choked on his *pain au chocolat.*

'Henny!' He stood up quickly from his desk, spraying

crumbs everywhere and knocking his chair over backwards in his confusion. 'I wasn't sure – I mean, I didn't expect—'

'No, you didn't expect me to come in, Laurie, and I can quite see why. If I had any sense, I wouldn't be here.' I flopped down wearily on one of the creamy sofas, misery making me casual. 'My own cowardly inclination was simply not to pitch up at all, but your niece persuaded me otherwise. She felt I owed it to you to explain my outrageous behaviour yesterday. To explain why, when you offered me a mushroom risotto, I interpreted it as an invitation to ravage your body. She thought I should apologise, which I do, unreservedly. And now, please feel free to fire me.'

I rested my head back on the cream damask and shut my eyes. Yes, fire me. Marvellous. I couldn't resign for fear of looking culpable according to Penny the Sage, but the sack – oh, splendid. What a relief. God, I'd be so grateful. Then I could just go home. Except I couldn't. My eyes filled with tears under my lids. I blinked them back, and through the haze, saw Laurie sit down opposite me. He perched on the edge of the sofa and leaned forward with a smile, forearms resting on his knees, hands clasped.

'I'm not going to fire you, Henny.'

'Damn!' I moaned, thumping the cushions with both fists.

'I've never had so many manuscripts transcribed so quickly and so accurately. It took Emmanuelle weeks to do what you did in a day, so no. No dice, I'm afraid. As for your behaviour,' he shrugged, 'surely it's easily explained away by the amount of narcotics and alcohol in your bloodstream. My only reservation about you staying on here, though . . .'

'Yes?' I sat up eagerly.

'Is what Marcus will think.' His eyes sidled nervously out of the window, as if half expecting to see Marcus pounding across the Piazza in his shirtsleeves and braces, dodging and weaving like a prize-fighter, fists balled in preparation for Laurie's teeth.

'Won't he mind?' he quaked.

I sank back into the cushions again, defeated. 'Oh no, Marcus won't mind,' I said blithely. 'He's chucked me out.'

'Oh!' Laurie looked astonished. Then horrified, as he considered the implications of this. 'But Henny, where will you go?' His face paled, nearing the colour of his biscuit linen jacket. He looked like a man on the receiving end of a paternity suit. 'I mean—'

'I've got the flat in Kensington, remember?'

'Ah yes.' His face cleared dramatically. 'Of course.'

I smiled ruefully. 'Relax, Laurie. One kiss places you under no obligation. You are not The Other Man. Rest assured, I have no plans to get into your distressed corduroys, nor to go around Peter Jones looking at toasters with you. Your body, and your desirable townhouse, are safe with me.' I heaved myself to my feet. 'And now, since you're determined to drag this thing out and extend my contract beyond two days – and frankly, beyond all reasonable limits – just point me in the direction of the box of tapes, there's a good chap. I'll go and chain myself to the computer. I hope you've got a truckload for me, incidentally. I want to type myself senseless. Wednesday's performance will pale into insignificance compared to what I've got in store for you today.' I flexed my fingers. 'Lead me to Anne of Cleves and her saucy philandering, I'll soon show her the error of her ways.'

He smiled up at me. 'Brave words, Henny, but you look like a prisoner going to the gallows. Don't you want to talk about it? Tell me what Marcus said?'

I shook my head, willing the tears not to fall. Not to soak his exquisite Turkish carpet until the colours ran.

'No thanks,' I muttered. 'He's just a very angry man at the moment, Laurie. But hopefully he'll calm down. Hopefully he'll get over it.'

'I'm sure he will,' he said warmly. He hesitated. 'Um, would it help if *I* spoke to him? Reassured him that nothing . . . you know?' He tailed off.

I focused on him properly for the first time, truly grateful. 'No, but thank you. Thank you for that. I consider that the true hand of friendship.'

Relief flooded his face, clearly overjoyed he didn't have to make that call. He got smartly to his feet.

'Right,' he rubbed his hands together with brisk finality. 'Well I'll get on then, if you don't mind. Got a load of correspondence and admin to do today, so I'll be here at my desk, scribbling.'

'And would it be all right if I went in there?' I nodded my head towards Emmanuelle's old room. 'I just think I might be able to concentrate better.'

'Sure! No, do. Absolutely.' He grinned. *'Absolument!'*

I tried to grin back, but my mouth wasn't having it. That all seemed so long ago now, that jolly banter of yesterday.

Soulfully, I shifted my few belongings: my box of tapes, my notebook, my little packet of paperclips, from one room to another. I seemed to be moving rather a lot recently, I observed. And it wasn't Laurie's presence that had prompted the relocation. I wasn't distracted by his beauty or anything like that – no, far from it. Now that I'd bitten into that particular poisoned apple and spat it out, it no longer held any charms for me. No, I just wanted to be on my own in case I needed to . . . well, howl. Or puke. I'm sure Laurie understood.

As I rearranged my new office, I heard him moving around. Making calls, then a cup of coffee. He kindly brought one in for me. Set it down beside me.

'If it's any consolation,' he whispered, 'I was terribly flattered to be ravaged by you yesterday. Enjoyed it immensely.'

I blushed and raised a smile. 'Couldn't ravage a paper bag today, Laurie. Look at me. Actually, don't.'

I peered into a tiny mirror Emmanuelle had thoughtfully

hung over her computer, the better to apply her pre-lunch lipstick, no doubt. Bags and lines blazed back. Laurie patted my shoulder, rather as one might pat a smelly old retriever. 'You look fine to me,' he said kindly.

I tapped away for an hour or two, and then I sent Marcus an email. We always contacted each other at some point during the day, usually with a phone call, but recently, with Angus's help, I'd got the hang of this more modern, and certainly today, more appropriate, form of communication. I hesitated before I sent it, but – no. I wasn't about to change the polite habits of a lifetime, I thought staunchly.

Dear Marcus,
    I've come to work today purely to explain my extraordinary behaviour to Laurie. I will resign now, if you want me to.
Henny

Half an hour later, I got one winging back.

Certainly not. Now that we are running two households, we will need two incomes.
Marcus

I stared at it, dumbfounded. Two households? After a single kiss? A single trifling, piffling indiscretion? Oh, the man was insane!

Furious, I typed up a storm, sending the keys skipping and dancing, frankly amazed that steam didn't pour from the keyboard. I transcribed reams and reams of manuscript tapes, some dating back as long ago as 1998, I noticed, since Laurie always dated them, and at length, exhausted, I took a pause for breath. As I removed the headphones and sank back in my chair, the telephone rang. I answered, but no one spoke. Odd, I thought, replacing the receiver. That had happened yesterday, before I went to lunch with Laurie. *Before Lunch with Laurie* – oh God! I rested my elbows on my desk and put my head in my hands. Was everything going to be *Before Lunch with Laurie* or *After Lunch with Laurie*? BLWL or ALWL for the rest of my life? Was it such a defining moment?

At five o'clock, I put my head around his door. 'I'm going now, Laurie.'

He looked up from his writing, pen poised. Gave a sad smile. 'You've been in there all day.'

I shrugged. Made a face. Couldn't speak.

'You all right?'

I nodded, but I was very tired now. Very emotional.

He smiled gently. 'See you Monday, then. If you feel up to it.'

I gulped. 'Bye,' I managed. 'See you Monday.'

Yes, of course, it was Friday. And I had the whole weekend ahead of me. The whole weekend in that flat. Alone. At least the children weren't around to witness all this, I thought with a shiver. At least they were safely back at school. Before I went down the stairs, I popped back to my desk and sent them both an email.

Hiya!
How's it all going? Miss you lots and love you loads,
M.xxxxx

Lily, I knew, would write back immediately, a gushing message with an eagerness that made my heart lurch and wonder if we'd done the right thing by sending her to boarding-school, even though she swore she loved it.

'You know all those *Mallory Towers* books, Mummy,' she'd said to me, her eyes shining as we'd picked her up from her first half-term, 'when the girls are all jumping on the beds in the dorm and using their hairbrushes as microphones? Well, that's just how it is! Every day!'

And I'd been so relieved. Angus had been more taciturn.

'Do you like it?' I'd asked anxiously in the school quad, piling his stuff in the boot at his respective half-term.

'Yeah, it's fine.' He went round and got in the front seat.

'Really? You really love it?' I shut the boot and ran around to the driving seat.

He gave me a withering look as he reached for his seat belt. 'Love it? Mum, it's school.'

And he'd take his time to respond to the email, too. Be

more considered, more cool, but actually, no less loving.

My eyes filled as I walked down the stairs to the front door. As I closed it softly behind me and walked towards the Tube, I thought of them both; in prep now perhaps, or maybe lining up for tea: Lily, giggling with her girlfriends at the salad bar, Angus, coming in from football covered in mud without a care in the world, laughing with his mates, his voice at that unpredictable half-man–half-boy stage. I smiled, in spite of myself. But as I crossed the Piazza, deep in thought . . . it was strange. I glanced around at the crowds. I had the oddest feeling. I couldn't quite put my finger on it, but . . . it was almost as if I was being watched.

# chapter eleven

I couldn't go straight back to the flat, just couldn't. It would be cold and empty and I'd feel very alone there on a Friday night. Oh, we'd used the place a bit, Marcus and I, had one or two drinks parties even, but I don't think I'd ever put my feet up and watched television there. It wasn't a home in that sense and I shivered at the thought of making it one. Instead, on an impulse, I took the Circle Line from Embankment to Sloane Square and walked a long way down the King's Road. Eventually I turned into Limerston Street and passed the Sporting Page on the corner. Tables and chairs had been set up outside the pub on this mild October evening, and a few people had already gathered for a drink after work. Two roads further on, my feet becoming weary now, I halted outside some pretty white mews houses. I gazed up at number eleven, then walked up the black and white chequered steps, noting with a smile the elegant lead window-boxes and the Versailles pots frothing over with a charming white flower I'd never seen before and couldn't begin to identify. It would doubtless be unavailable anyway to the likes of me, and sourced only through word of mouth by the cognoscenti from some obscure nursery in Gloucestershire. No common-or-garden geraniums here.

I rang the bell and after a moment Benji opened the door. He took a theatrical stagger backwards, then beamed at me, clasping his hands in delight, like a small boy regarding a new bicycle.

'What a *treat*! We were just saying we craved company tonight but couldn't be bothered to go out and find any, and you would have been *right* at the top of our list.' He held out his arms, and I walked into them. 'What a surprise! What the devil are you doing up in The Smoke, Hens?'

'It's a long story.'

'Well, tell Uncle Benji then. Come, come!' He released me and tugged playfully at my arm, pulling me bossily inside, but maddeningly – and it was probably the hug that had done it – my eyes filled with tears. He stopped, his hand on my arm. 'Oh Lord. What is it, dear heart? What?'

Emotion, at this point, got the better of me, so much so that however much my brother coaxed and cajoled, he had to wait, as Penny had had to, until the sobbing and catchy-breath routine had been gone through. Once the shuddering had subsided he managed to manoeuvre me down the hall and into the sitting room – a pretty, chintzy room with botanical prints on every conceivable fabric, brimming with tasteful trinkets – hustling me to a sofa in the window piped to within an inch of its life in shocking pink, and made a space for me amongst the tapestry cushions and the West Highland terriers. Falteringly and gaspingly, I told my tale. When I'd finished, he passed me a tissue from an embroidered box beside him and held my hand as I wiped my face with the other.

'Lordy,' he said finally, with feeling.

'Quite,' I muttered miserably, clutching my wet tissue. 'Lordy.'

'What a cock-up.'

'I thought you didn't like that expression,' I sniffed, blowing my nose.

'I don't, as a rule, accompanied by the usual heterosexual titter in our direction, but *in extremis*, I'll make an exception. And speaking of cock-ups, you don't think Marcus thinks . . .'

'No!' I gasped, horrified. 'No, Benji, he was there! He saw us with his own eyes and we were both fully clothed.'

'I know, but he might think it had happened before, mightn't he?'

'When?' I squeaked. 'I'd only been working there for two days, only *known* him two days!'

'Well, you managed to get him in a fairly compromising position in that short space of time,' he reasoned. 'Marcus

204

might well be wondering what went on on Day One, don't you think?'

'Oh, you mean, as I arrived for work on my first day? Panting up the stairs in my coat, running into his office and launching myself at Laurence De Havilland in a headlong dive, surfing over his desk and sticking my tongue down his throat?'

He shrugged. 'I'm just trying to put myself in Marcus's shoes.'

'Well, don't,' I snapped. 'No one can wear Marcus's size nines and stay reasonable. Oh, it's all such a nonsense.' I got to my feet and paced about the room clutching the tops of my arms. 'Such a huge overreaction, it's not true.'

Benji sighed. 'It is a reaction, though. A natural reaction. You've got to accept it as such, my love. Let him get over it. And given time, he will.'

Through the French windows at the far end of the room, I could see a tall figure out in the leafy enclosure tying overblown dahlias to canes in the fading light. His blond head was bent to his task.

'As you would if it were Francis? You'd get over it?'

I felt Benji hesitate behind me. 'It's never happened, to my knowledge, so I don't know. But . . . it's almost harder for us. So we're more careful.'

I turned. 'Harder? Why?'

'Because men are naturally more promiscuous. And there

happen to be two of them in this relationship. We don't have the glue, either.'

'The glue?'

'Marriage, children. That's your safety net. No one wants to wreck all of that. No, we have to rely on love.' He smiled fondly. 'Boring old love.'

I turned back to the garden and watched as Francis worked. Well, they certainly had a surfeit of that, I thought, as I considered what he'd said.

I think I'd always suspected that Benji was gay, but my parents certainly hadn't. They'd nearly died on the spot when, walking back up the Finchley Road one night after a meal out with friends in their local Italian, they'd discovered their son kissing a boy in a car outside their block of flats. Both boys were seventeen, and the other lad was the son of some friends of theirs.

Two sets of parents quivered and shook and shouted and blamed – and in my mother's case collapsed sobbing, forearm to brow, for weeks on end – but it didn't change a thing. In fact, Benji said later that it was actually a relief. It spared him the years of secrecy some gay friends of his later endured, wondering when to come out, if at all, to their parents, conducting secret affairs for years.

'And anyway, what did they expect?' he'd grumbled. 'With a name like Benji I either had to be gay or a dog on *Blue Peter*.'

Privately though, I wondered if it didn't force him to adopt a position – to be openly gay, and rather camp with it, whereas before, he was just a mixed-up kid who'd had girlfriends as well as boyfriends, and who knows what he'd have plumped for in the end? I knew he'd hankered for children, and I wondered if coming out so early hadn't scuppered this. I voiced as much to my mother a few years down the line, and to my surprise, she'd had pertinent views on the subject.

'Oh yes, in our day plenty of gay men chose to get married and have children. They weighed it up. Knew what they were, but chose what they'd prefer to be, instead. Made rather good husbands, actually. Very domestic and kindly, on the whole. Of course it's always a bit of a ticking time-bomb though, isn't it? Imagine, just when the children have left home and you're preparing to prune the roses and be all Darby and Joan together, and suddenly Darby goes off with Gary from Blockbuster Video, announcing that he's found his soulmate. No, maybe it's better this way round.'

I never knew my mother could be so wise. And actually, despite her early amateur dramatics, it was Mum who came around to Benji's sexuality quicker than Dad. Dad couldn't speak – and wouldn't speak about it – he was so angry. And sad. Still is, I think. Whereas Mum, who'd originally thought the world was coming to an end, finally rallied. It took a while though. When the news first broke, I'd been married to Marcus for about six months, and whilst she'd originally been pathetically grateful to her new son-in-law for plucking her daughter like a stale bun from the shelf, now that the ink was dry on the marriage certificate, she couldn't help but revert to her true colours and regard both her children as severe disappointments. I popped round once to see her at the flat, only to find her playing Tiddlywinks by herself, using her blood-pressure pills as counters.

'What on earth are you doing?' I'd whispered, horrified.

'Contemplating suicide,' she'd responded dreamily. 'You've married a Jew, and my son's gay. What have I got to live for?'

I sighed and sat down beside her. 'Mum, you like Marcus. You told me so yourself, what does it matter what religion he is?'

'Oh, it doesn't.' She turned frank hazel eyes on me. 'But it matters to everyone else. And what everyone else thinks, matters a great deal to me.'

'But . . . everyone else – who is everyone else? None of *my* friends, no one *I* know!'

'Everyone else around here.' She swept an arm expansively down the road. '*My* friends.'

'But everyone else around here *is* Jewish. Your friends are all Jewish! We live in the heart of North London, Mum.'

'Exactly.' She leaned forward and touched my arm with her fingertips, her eyes steely. 'Ex*act*ly.'

Her logic was warped, but I knew where she was coming from. She'd lost what she perceived was the high ground, that was the problem. Having occupied it – in her eyes – for years, she'd suddenly felt it crumble beneath her. She felt the joke was firmly on her and everyone was laughing at her.

Likewise, I suspect she didn't really mind that Benji was gay, but was worried about what the neighbours would say. I think she was sad he wouldn't have children, but sadder still, that in twenty years' time, she wouldn't be able to say to Mrs Greenburg downstairs: 'My grandson's studying to be a doctor, you know. At Imperial College.' Although Benji's happiness concerned her, her own reputation – immediately, at any rate – concerned her more. Which is why I think she came round quicker. She didn't have the same visceral scarring that Dad did; the grief for his only son. His boy. The guilt, too. The where-did-I-go-wrongs. Mum never went wrong. Hers was a superficial wound.

Francis had appeared on the scene relatively quickly, and for most people at least, it was a relief all round. It certainly helped Mum's healing process, her wound healed up like billyo. Francis was – *is* – heaven. The day he stepped over the threshold of the Finchley Road flat, tall, tanned, tawny-haired and jaw-droppingly handsome, Mum and I clutched each other. Just – clutched each other. And then we instantly christened him The Waste.

'What a waste!' Mum wailed to me in the kitchen as she flustered around making tea for him with shaking hands, nervously checking the tin for flap-jacks. 'He's God's gift to women, not to *Benji*,' she said in disgust.

But Francis appeared besotted by Benji, who was small, dark, darting and funny. Always an amusing child, he'd developed a dry adult wit, and quickfire repartee would crackle from his lips – beneath what my father described as his very homosexual moustache – at the slightest opportunity. Benji made Francis laugh, and when he laughed, boy did the room light up. He'd throw back his head, clutch his sides and literally shake. We couldn't help but smile. We'd grown up with Benji and were used to him, but felt absurdly proud to see someone else rolling in the aisles, delighting in him. And Francis was delighted by everything that day: Mum's cooking, the curtains, the view across the Finchley Road to the Heath – his enthusiasm was boundless, and his joy at being amongst us, tangible. Nothing was too much trouble. He jumped up eagerly to help Mum back to the kitchen with the tray, and not once seemed the slightest bit aware that his gender might be something of an issue. In short, he acted like Benji's new girlfriend, and Mum fell for it.

'He's so lovely and gay!' she whispered excitedly to me in the kitchen.

'Er . . . yes, Mum.'

'No, but really. In the real sense of the word. Such fun!'

I wasn't quite sure where I stood vis-à-vis the original or hi-jacked sense of that word in 1998, but I let it pass. As she happily unwrapped yet another Dundee cake from its grease-proof paper she hissed, 'And did you see his hair? Those darling highlights! *Must* ask him where he got it done.'

Dad, however, sat tightlipped throughout the entire proceedings, but at least he sat there, damn it, with a grim look on his face. You had to hand it to him, he saw these things through. When Francis had gone, he rose from his chair and declared that there was only one good thing about the whole sorry mess, and that was the blasted chap's name. At least he could tell his poor widowed mother that Benji was going out with a Frances, and she'd be none the wiser. Wouldn't spot the subtle letter substitution. And none of us, he warned gravely, were to let on. The shock, he was convinced, would kill her. Mum's lips twitched convulsively at this, sorely tempted.

And so Gran was none the wiser. Well, let's face it, at eighty-three and with one or two faculties fading, including her eyesight, she wasn't wise to anything much. In fact, she probably could have met Francis and still not realised anything was amiss – perhaps pausing only to wonder why this very tall girl with the American accent didn't grow her hair a bit? Wear skirts more? As it was though, they didn't meet, and she heard about him/her only by repute. Every Wednesday afternoon, in fact, when, having picked up her pension, she stopped by for tea. Ridiculous conversations then ensued as Gran, bowed and arthritic, took her place at the head of the table covered with the Swiss embroidered cloth complete with edelweiss motif, and the best china with doilies.

'Benji still with Frances?' Gran would ask, lifting her head from her hunched back like a tortoise and peering under her tight white perm at Mum. Even though Benji was at the table, she always asked indirectly, through another party, as though not quite believing the subject of her enquiry capable of speech. It was the same for everyone. 'Audrey still playing bridge, dear?' she'd ask Dad, even though she was sitting right next to Mum. Ordinarily it made us want to scream, 'Ask her yourself, you silly old bat!' but on these occasions we were grateful, since a grinning Benji would surely have given the game away.

'Yes, Gran. Benji's still with Francis,' Mum said coolly, taking the tea cosy off the pot to pour.

'Ooh, she sounds like a lovely girl. Runs a little restaurant, I gather? Across the river?'

'That's it.'

'That's nice. She must be ever such a good cook then, Audrey, don't you think?'

'Er . . . I believe so,' Mum replied carefully.

It was rather like that childhood game when you weren't allowed to reply 'yes' or 'no', and if you did, you were out. Except in this case it was 'he' or 'she' and if you did, Benji was out. In more ways than one.

'She'll turn out to be a proper little home-maker, you mark my words, Audrey.'

'I expect she . . .' A moment's pause for thought. 'I expect you're right, Gran.'

'Her father gave her that restaurant, your mum tells me.' (This, confusingly, directed not at Benji, but me.)

I nodded animatedly. 'Mmm.' (Always safe).

'Nice to have a rich daddy. I bet she's worth a bob or two, eh?'

Cringe, and another moment's thought. 'I believe you're right.'

It was taxing, and we were all more relieved than usual when she went, Mum pressing an oversized black handbag and rain hat into her mother-in-law's hands, and sweeping her out of the door into the car for the drive back to her sheltered flat in Cricklewood.

All that seemed such a long time ago now, I thought, as I looked out through the fading autumn light across the poppy-seed heads and the swaying grasses at Francis in the garden. Gran was long dead, and Benji and Francis were about the happiest couple I knew.

'Don't tell him,' I said quickly, as he looked up from his dahlias. He saw me and waved delightedly.

'Or at least,' I saw Benji's doubtful face. Knew they shared everything. 'Tell him, but after I've gone.'

He nodded quickly and we watched as Francis came loping elegantly up the garden towards us, secateurs in hand. He'd be shocked, I thought, as I opened the French window for him. Not with Marcus, but with me.

'Darling! How lovely,' he greeted me in his Boston drawl,

swooping from his great height and kissing me on both cheeks. 'Benji and I were just saying it was ages since we'd seen you, and now here you are! No Marcus?'

'No, he's . . . still at work,' I said quickly. This much was probably true. 'And I'm just here for some shopping.'

'Excellent.' But then he stopped. Peered suspiciously. 'Hey, what's up?'

'Nothing,' I smiled. 'Just a touch of hay-fever. Speaking of which, Francis, your garden is a picture! Even at this time of year. I don't know how you do it. I probably shouldn't go out there without some anti-histamine, but try stopping me.'

'Ah yes,' he admitted as he followed me outside, easily distracted where horticulture was involved. He ushered me down the passage, brimming with terracotta pots. 'I must say, I'm pleased with it this year.'

'Well, I'm not surprised.'

It was quite a large garden by London standards, but aside from a small patch of terrace by the kitchen for Benji and Francis to sit in, the entire thing was given over to flowers. We plunged into the beds and waded through a riot of colour, courtesy of stepping stones dotted handily about. Blowsy dahlia heads brushed our waists and Michaelmas daisies nodded in the breeze. It was, in effect, a cottage garden, which by definition was an oddity in London and very different from the neighbouring patches, whose tasteful all-white leafy enclosures tended to be the norm, but then this garden served a purpose. This was a working garden, where Francis grew copious flowers and herbs – and then picked them to decorate his restaurant and flavour the dishes.

The restaurant, originally a failing enterprise in an unfashionable part of Balham, had been tossed to him in disgust by a very rich and very disappointed father, who owned a chain of successful restaurants over in his native Boston, run by Francis's less disappointing brothers and sisters. When Francis inherited the restaurant – an unsuccessful 'toe dip' by his father in the London market – it had just been given a makeover of the kind all fashionable restaurants in London receive these days. Shiny wooden flooring – the sort to send kitten heels skidding – ran throughout, bright white tablecloths stared, and uncomfortable retro chairs reminiscent of the one Christine Keeler straddled in the sixties beckoned uninvitingly. A vast chrome bar adorned with a single jar of funereal lilies skulked coldly in the corner, and behind it, a couple of intimidating Latin waiters pretended to polish glasses. An overhead lighting scheme of the sort favoured by the Gestapo glared down. No doubt it appealed to some, but not many, because tellingly, it was empty.

Francis, having caught this hospital pass with an 'Oomph' to the solar plexus, set about rescuing it. Bucking the trend, he carpeted the place in a rich red Wilton and put heavy chintz drapes at the windows; in fact, he Nina Campbell-ed the place from top to bottom. He filled it with fresh flowers from his garden, found distressed leather armchairs, scattered cushions, added lamps, made sure the cook could actually cook and the waiters smile – and then watched as the women flocked in. For Francis knew what they wanted. He knew their faces looked better in candlelight, he knew they'd been on their feet all day pushing buggies and wanted comfortable chairs, he knew they needed spoiling and cosseting. The fact that their husbands came too and paid the bill was incidental. He knew who wore the trousers in residential Balham, which by now had well and truly up and come, ensuring that money was no object.

Within a year, The Country Garden was a roaring success. People crossed the river the wrong way to get to it and food critics gushed admiringly. On the strength of it, together with Benji's not inconsiderable earnings as a City fund manager, Francis and Benji bought the extremely smart townhouse they lived in today.

They'd worked hard to get here though, I thought, as I leaned forward to smell a late-flowering rose. They deserved it. I gazed around in the gathering gloom. I was alone now, Francis having taken a moment to pop back and make sure Benji was getting the right champagne out of the fridge – 'Not the Moët, sweets, it's not cold enough' – but now he returned and handed me a glass. We wandered back to the terrace together and sat down.

'So. You're on your own.'

I glanced up to meet his eyes, afraid. 'Benji told you?'

'He did, briefly, while I got the drinks.' He smiled. 'It was unavoidable, Henny. You look like you've been hit by a truck.'

I smiled weakly. 'Thanks. I *feel* like I've been hit by a truck.'

'So Marcus is pretty mad, huh?' he said thoughtfully.

I nodded miserably. 'Pretty white-faced, stony-eyed, whisky-swirling, livid.' I shivered as I remembered him pacing that hotel room.

Francis was silent. I glanced anxiously at him as Benji approached with a bowl of nibbles. 'I think it's at this point,' I tried to joke, 'that you say, He'll Come Round. Benji did.'

Francis flashed a fond smile at my brother. 'Benji would. Benji was born minus a tough outer layer. He can't bear not to be liked, for people *not* to come round. He would have been the first one in the schoolyard to say, "I'm sorry, I'm sorry! Have *all* my conkers – don't just take one! Be my best friend again?"'

Benji snorted derisively. 'Oh, I don't know.'

But I did know. Knew it was true. I'd grown up with him. Knew, if he'd been in my room fiddling with my things and we'd had a bust-up, he'd be the first to say, 'OK, so I *was* reading your *Jackie*, but listen, d'you want to watch *Top Cat*?'

'So I'm cringing and obsequious?' Benji hung his head in a mock sulk.

'No, but you always think the best of everyone. Think everyone can make up and be friends again. Believe the milk of human kindness flows from everyone's orifices.'

217

'What a horrible thought.' Benji squirmed.

'I didn't necessarily mean the particular orifice you're—'

'Don't go there!' Benji yelped, palms up, head averted. 'Just don't go there, Francis, you'll regret it. It'll be the Mr Thomas-next-door-but-one episode all over again. Remember when he asked for advice on his garden and you kept going on about the integrity of his back passage?' He shuddered. 'The poor man was limp with nerves.'

Francis laughed good-naturedly. Then he turned to me. 'I think what I'm trying to say, if Benji would let me get a word in edgeways and refrain from mobbing me up, is that I wonder if Marcus is so easily won over as your brother here. He's a proud man.'

'That's what Penny said!' I squeaked. 'What is all this proud bollocks, and why is it referred to in such reverential terms? I thought it was one of the Seven Deadly Sins!'

'It is, but we dress it up and mistake it for principles. See my father on this score,' he added soberly.

We were silent a moment. I knew from Benji that Arthur J. Steadman III didn't speak to his son – his eldest child, and hitherto the apple of his eye – for fourteen years on discovering the truth about his sexuality, but had asked, on his deathbed in a Boston hospital, to see him. Exiled by this time to London, Francis had moved heaven and earth to get there. Unfortunately, heaven had moved faster and his father was dead before he reached him.

'Marcus will get over it. Eventually,' Francis said now. 'I just think it might take a bit longer than you think.' He paused reflectively. 'In the meantime,' he went on in a more upbeat tone, twinkling at me over the rim of his champagne glass, 'why not enjoy yourself? No point wandering around with a face like wet washing – go out and have some fun, Henny. You've got time on your hands now, so why not meet up with all your single girlfriends, go shopping, take in a play, an exhibition – all the things you don't do in the country and never did when you lived in London. Nothing will bring Marcus round more than you looking like you're having a good time without him, believe me.'

I blinked. 'Francis, you're surely not suggesting . . .'

'No, of *course* I'm not suggesting anything untoward. I think that's what's known as shooting yourself squarely in the foot. I'm just saying try – and I know it's hard – not to mope. Not to sit in that Kensington flat all weekend staring out at the rain and crying yourself to sleep. There's no point. What will be will be, and other helpful clichés.'

'And for starters,' Benji got up and put his hands firmly on my shoulders, 'you're staying put for an early supper with us. It's a stir-fry, all chopped and prepared, and it'll be in that kitchen at a table laid for three in just a jiffy. I, Benji,' he wiggled his bottom, 'am your waiter for this evening.'

I tried to get up. 'Oh, but Benji, I wasn't going to stay. I said—'

'I know what you said,' he pushed me back down, 'but I've chopped enough chicken and ginger to feed the whole of Chelsea. Got carried away with my new set of Sabatiers. And the dogs can't have it – makes them flatulent – so you're having some, and the hell with your noxious gases.' He minced off determinedly.

In the event, of course, I did stay, and despite everything it was really very pleasant to sit in their cosy pink kitchen, laughing at Benji who, for his sister's benefit, was pulling out all the stops tonight. The jokes flowed thick and fast and the moment he sensed my spirits were flagging, out would come another outrageous anecdote. Most of them, Francis and I were convinced, were apocryphal, Benji's maxim being why tell the boring truth when you can tell a good lie. However, Benji swore blind he really *had* heard their neighbour through the bedroom wall saying to his wife, 'You be the horse, Clarissa, and I'll be the groom. We'll play Pony Won't Load' – as clearly as he could hear me now.

When I left at about ten o'clock they waved me off from the front step together, making me promise to call in the morning, to come for lunch on Sunday if I wanted to, and to be sure to get a taxi and not take the Tube. I thought how blessed I was with the pair of them, even if their togetherness did bring a lump to my throat. They watched me to the corner of the street and when they shut the door, I imagined them discussing me as they went back to the kitchen to clear the plates and stack the dishwasher. Benji, worried now, no longer the clown, Francis reassuring him.

'But she looked so *drawn*, Francis. So terrible.'

'Of course she did, it's the shock. But she'll recover. *He'll* recover.'

I walked on past the pub, teeming now with people, all well oiled and loitering, pints clutched to chests, swaying slightly in the dark. As I passed on, the laughter and chatter faded. I went further down the quiet residential street, the only sound being my heels tapping on the pavement. Except . . . I stopped. Listened. Then I walked on, a bit faster this time. I wanted to get close to the busy King's Road, closer to the steady flow of people, but as I was about to join it – I couldn't help myself. I turned.

He made no attempt to hide himself, to step back into the shadows, but stood still, facing me, with twenty feet or so between us. The headlights of a passing car lit up his face momentarily, but there was no need. I'd know that tall, spare frame anywhere: that stance, that way of holding his head slightly to one side, elegantly, enquiringly. I'd know him anywhere. It was Rupert.

# chapter twelve

'Rupert.' I said his name, and as I did, a great wave of adrenaline washed through me, rocking me almost. Instinctively, I clutched at the strap of my shoulder bag for support.

'Henny.' He said mine, and we stood there, staring at each other in the phosphorescent darkness. After a moment, he walked towards me. Stopped in front of me. We looked some more: feasted almost.

'You've been following me,' I said eventually, not quite trusting myself to let go of the leather strap. How odd. He hadn't changed, not really: the same flop of blond hair over his forehead, the same clear blue eyes. His face was a little fuller, perhaps, and very tanned, and his figure had filled out a bit too, but I felt the years roll back frighteningly; it was like watching the sea retreat from a beach in a speeded-up film. The last fifteen years of my life were being sucked back off that shore into the ocean, leaving this man, this man I knew so well, standing before me.

'Yes, I've been following you,' he said, after a moment. 'I'm sorry. I didn't mean to frighten you.'

I raised my chin. 'You didn't.' He hadn't. In a weird way, I'd sort of known. Hadn't admitted it to myself, but had known it was him: outside Laurie's house, on the Tube to Sloane Square, and again, in the street just now. And as I'd sat talking to Benji and Francis in the kitchen, a very small part of me had been wondering how far away he was. Wondering if he was in the pub I had passed.

'Were you in the Sporting Page?'

'Not in, but standing outside. Waiting with a drink on the pavement. While you were in that house.'

I nodded. 'Benji's'

'I know. I saw him come to the door. Almost didn't recognise him.'

Ah. So had he also seen me collapse on his shoulder? Burst into tears? Of course. Must have done. I straightened up.

'How did you find me?' I knew, but wanted to hear him say it.

'When I rang Laurie the other day, At first I didn't recognise you, you deliberately changed your voice, but when I put the phone down I thought – Yes, it must be her. *Must*

223

be. I couldn't move. Just sat there, staring at the telephone. I'd know your voice anywhere, Henny. Anywhere.'

I swallowed. His own voice was low and intent as he repeated the last word. I looked down at the pavement. Then up, abruptly.

'What do you want, Rupert?'

He lifted his arms from his sides, then let them fall in a hopeless gesture. 'So many things. To talk, to explain, to apologise . . . so many things, Henny.'

I gave a cracked little laugh. 'You've had fifteen years to do that. Why now?'

He made another impotent gesture, this time with his shoulders. 'Of course. And I should have done. And in the early days I nearly did, many times. But – well, I was so ashamed. And then later on, when I came back from Hong Kong, I heard you'd got married.'

'Still am married,' I said, slightly too defiantly, perhaps.

He looked surprised. 'Of course.' There was a silence. I saw him hesitate. 'I vaguely knew of your whereabouts, actually. Your situation. Army dinners, that sort of thing . . .' he tailed off.

I nodded. Tommy Rutlin, Penny's husband, was what he meant. Tommy had left the Army long ago, but I knew he still went to regimental dinners, knew he occasionally bumped into Rupert. And if Rupert had just been an ex-boyfriend, I'd probably have asked after him, in a light-hearted way, over supper with Tommy and Penny perhaps, in front of Marcus even. 'How's Rupert? What's he up to these days? Give him my love when you see him.'

But the manner of our parting had been so traumatic, so . . . brutal, it was impossible. Even after all these years everyone still felt embarrassed for me. Awkward. It wasn't discussed. Tommy certainly would have felt uncomfortable if the subject had been brought up, so all that I knew, I'd gleaned secretly from Penny. And even then, I knew very little. Just that Rupert was still in the Army. Had gone to Hong Kong, as planned, straight after our wedding, as I should have done, and that life had gone on for him as normal. Without so much as skipping a beat, just – minus a wife. Single quarters, rather than married quarters. Smaller bed. Single, rather than double. No sweat.

I squared my shoulders. 'I have to be going now,' I said stiffly. 'It's late.'

He reached out, touched my sleeve. I felt his touch like a burn. 'Don't go yet, have a drink. Just for half an hour or so. Please.' His eyes were raw, pleading. I turned away so as not to see them. Willed myself to move off and walk the last few feet up to the King's Road. As luck would have it, I flagged down a taxi almost immediately.

'I'm sorry, I have to get back,' I muttered as the taxi purred to a halt beside me. 'Twenty-four Campden Hill Grove, please,' I said quietly through the window, but I knew Rupert, right by my elbow, had heard.

225

'Then meet me tomorrow,' he urged. 'At lunchtime. Please, Henny, I can't let you go like this, not when I've just found you. Please, just for an hour or so.'

I inhaled sharply. *Not when I've just found you.* My heart was pounding high up in my ribcage now, all my pulses racing. I found I couldn't speak. I shook my head mutely and got inside the cab. Rupert pushed down the window. Stuck his head in.

'Twelve o'clock at the Peter Pan statue,' he shouted as the cab pulled away. He ran a few yards with it. 'Twelve o'clock!' His face broke into a hopeful smile.

I didn't look at him, just stared straight ahead as the taxi trundled down the road. Then I sat back in the seat, willing myself not to turn round. After a moment I shut my eyes, covering them with the palm of my hand. Oh God. Oh my *God*. Rupert.

The taxi purred on as my thoughts scrambled for position, spinning around in my head like a child's top. My heart wouldn't let up, either, hammering away relentlessly near the base of my throat. Seeing him again, after all these years . . . God, it was so strange, and yet, even stranger – I let my hand fall limply into my lap – it felt like yesterday. It was true what they said, I thought with a jolt. It was as if we'd been carrying on a conversation we'd had a few days ago, not fifteen years ago. Standing on the pavement like that, Rupert, as ever rather shabbily dressed in faded jeans and an old checked shirt – why,

# not that kind of girl

I could almost see that old felt hat on his head! And that smile as the cab had pulled away . . . starting at the corners of his mouth and slowly reaching his eyes. Splitting his face in two, lighting it up. I licked my lips. Clutched the handrail hard.

And there was so much I wanted to ask him, so much. It was too tempting to meet him – why shouldn't I? My heart lurched crazily again. Plenty of people in my position – married, so security in that, but conveniently with no actual husband around at this precise moment to complicate things – would have said, 'Yes, all right. A quick drink at lunchtime tomorrow, just to catch up.' Just to see what cards life had dealt us in the intervening years. And even though the manner of our parting had been so extraordinary, that made meeting even more pressing, in a way. Made it even more of an imperative. Because of *course* it had nagged away at me all these years. Of *course* I'd wanted to know where he was when I'd been at the church door, frantically looking around in my white dress. Of *course* I'd wondered what he'd been thinking, what had happened to him in the short space of time since I'd seen him two days before, when we'd parted in my parents' flat, a happy betrothed couple, kissing goodbye at the flat door, laughing – 'See you in church!' Rupert, pretending to dart down the corridor into my parents' bedroom and peek at my dress, me shrieking with mock alarm, pulling him back. It was a huge chunk of my life to dismiss, to blank, to expect me not to want to know the answers to.

I shifted position as the cab rumbled on. But I couldn't go. Of course I couldn't. I was in enough trouble with Marcus as it was, and if he ever found out . . . well, that would be it, no two ways about it. Curtains. *Finito.* Good morning. No. It was out of the question.

The following morning as I kicked through the crispy leaves towards the statue of Peter Pan in Kensington Gardens, the sky was a clear blue above me. It was more like a summer's day than an October one, not a wisp of cloud and very still, the only clue to the season being the rich golden hues of the chestnut trees. The sun was much lower too, and right in my eyes, nearly blinding me. Despite that, I saw him almost immediately. There were a few children playing around the statue as there often were – fascinated by the ragged iron boy, touching him, copying his pose, one arm and one leg outstretched in flight, laughing as they over-balanced – and then a few yards away, on a bench, Rupert.

He got up immediately and came towards me, his face clearing with relief: smiling, but anxious.

I couldn't give him a social kiss. Just couldn't. And I was grateful he didn't attempt to deliver one. He walked me back to the bench and I sat down beside him, quite relieved by that arrangement. By the fact that I could look straight ahead into the trees, and not at him.

'I can only stay for half an hour,' I said firmly. 'I promised

Marcus I'd go to Harrods and look at light fittings for our house in the country.'

'Ah. Right.'

'That's why I'm here. I mean, in London. I'm trying to get our country place organised. Finish the decorating, that sort of thing.'

'I see.'

I had a feeling he was smiling at me. I flushed and looked at my hands.

'So . . . Marcus isn't with you?' he asked.

'No, he's away on business. I thought I'd come to London for a week or two while he's away.' I'd practised this on the way over, but it sounded rather jumbled and foolish now. 'It's quite quiet in the country with the children both away at school,' I gabbled, 'so I thought I'd come up to Town. Stay in our flat, see a few girlfriends, go the theatre maybe, do some shopping. I've got to—'

'Decorate your country house – yes, you said.'

I felt the blood pump through my veins.

'You don't seem surprised to see me,' I said in a low voice.

'Well, I hoped . . . obviously I hoped you'd change your mind.' He turned to look at me. Smiled gently. 'I'm so pleased you did.'

I glanced down at my watch. 'Quarter to one. I'm forty-five minutes late. How long would you have waited?'

He shrugged. 'As long as it took, I suppose.' He stretched

his arms out along the back of the bench, eyes narrowed into the distance. 'I imagine by sundown I might have given up hope.'

I nodded. 'This was as long as I waited. Was allowed to wait. Forty-five minutes. Then Dad said we should call it a day.'

There was a silence. The park went very still, very quiet. The children had gone now, and there was just the faint rustling of a breeze in the trees. Rupert's arms came down off the bench. I heard him exhale beside me.

'Henny, I'm so sorry. So terribly sorry. And so terribly ashamed, too. Have been so excruciatingly ashamed all these years, and have lived with that shame, but I always felt that just saying sorry could never be enough. Was just so pathetically inadequate. So I didn't. Which was worse, perhaps. But I hoped . . . that by my silence, by leaving you alone, I was letting you get on with your life in peace.'

I considered this for a moment. 'You were right,' I murmured eventually. 'It wouldn't have been enough. Wouldn't have done the trick.'

So many people had said afterwards, 'Didn't he even apologise? Say sorry? Write you a letter?' And I'd always thought, How could he? I gazed straight ahead into the distance. The sun was warm on my face. I lowered my eyelashes, filtering it through them.

'Appropriate, don't you think,' he murmured at length, 'that we meet here?'

I smiled, knowing instantly what he meant. 'You mean at the shrine of the little boy who didn't grow up? Is that what you're telling me, Rupert?'

He sighed. 'I suppose if I have any excuse at all, it's that. That I suddenly – didn't feel ready. Didn't feel grown-up enough. As I sat there in that taxi drivers' café in Jermyn Street . . .'

'Maria's?' I turned. 'Is that where you were?'

'Yes. Maria's.'

My heart lurched as I remembered sitting there too, in my ballgown, excitement dancing in every vein. Falling in love with him, all those years ago.

'Why there?'

'Because in a fuddled sort of way, I thought that maybe food would help. That maybe the reason I was feeling so panicky, so peculiar, was because I was hungry, and maybe breakfast and coffee would be a good idea. After all, I'd been up since five, walking the streets, I must be starving. So I went there. I remember Maria putting a plateful down in front of me, looking at me anxiously. I must have been a pretty incongruous sight in my morning coat, surrounded by cabbies – and I remember my hands shaking as I picked up my knife and fork, having to put them down again.'

He frowned in an effort, I felt, to remember honestly. 'My overwhelming feeling,' he went on carefully, picking his words, 'no, my all consuming feeling was . . . *I can't do this. I don't feel ready*. It rose up within me, this – this ghastly wave of panic, rocking me, making me feel physically sick. But then I thought, Don't be ridiculous. It's Henny. You love her. You're in love. Of *course* you can do it. Will do it. And I remember watching the clock on the wall, with its thin black hands, watching it tick on, get closer to eleven o'clock when you were arriving at the church. Twenty to. Ten to. Five to. And then – well, obviously then I had to get up and go, otherwise I really *would* be late, but – I felt welded to that seat. As if I'd taken root. And a little voice in my head said, "What if you don't go? What if you just stay here? Let the hands tick on?" And it seemed like such an extraordinarily simple thing to do. Like changing the course of history, just by staying still. By being inert. And the more I watched the clock tick on past the hour, the more rooted to the spot I became. It was fear, I suppose. A terrible fear that gripped me. Froze me.'

He bowed his head. Rubbed a worn patch on the thigh of his jeans with his fingertip. 'That's my shame,' he said softly.

'Yes.' I nodded. 'And mine is that I knew.'

He looked up. 'What d'you mean?'

'I knew. Knew you were frightened, and ignored it. Pretended I didn't know. Pushed on. Forced your hand.'

'No, Henny—'

'It's true,' I went on in a low quavering voice. 'You asked me to marry you in a crazy, desperate moment. You hadn't thought about it, hadn't considered it, just blurted it out impetuously. I should never have said yes. Or – having said yes, I should have given you an exit route later on. Should have said, when the dust had settled and I knew you were wavering, "D'you really want to do this, Rupert? You don't think we're too young? Why don't I come and visit you in Hong Kong as your girlfriend? Why don't we write? See if our love stays the course?" But I didn't. I clung on. When I knew you were unsure.'

I thought of him sitting alone in Maria's café, his father and brother already in church, very young, very frightened. Rigid with fear, watching the hands on the clock get closer to the hour. I wondered if he'd missed his mother in those moments. Someone soft and maternal, to watch over him.

'Who found you?'

'Dad, eventually. He knew I went there sometimes, and came storming through the door in his morning-coat, fuming. There was an almighty row, a lot of shouting about honour and family name and how I'd dragged it through the mud, and quite an agog audience as you can imagine. Forkfuls of chips and beans frozen halfway to lips.'

I smiled. 'Street theatre at its very best. Although I'm surprised your father was so upset. I was never entirely convinced he approved of me.'

'He didn't approve of cowardice or desertion either. Didn't speak to me for four years.'

I turned, shocked. 'I'm sorry.'

233

# catherine alliott

He shrugged. 'I deserved it.' He paused. 'And anyway, we're fine now.'

A silence ensued as I considered the repercussions on his life. I'd only ever considered the devastation it had wrought on mine.

'So then you went to Hong Kong?'

'Then I went to Hong Kong. And threw myself into Army life. Set about getting myself a crack platoon and putting us forward for every conceivable hairy operation that came our way. We didn't stay in Hong Kong, we were just based there. We were sent all over the place, mostly where no one else wanted to go. Tehran, Nigeria, Botswana – any third-world dive where there was a bit of flak going on, we took it. I didn't really care what happened to me, you see. I just wanted to blank what had passed. Draw a veil. Put all my energy into commanding my unit and making them the best in the regiment. The toughest. And we built ourselves quite a reputation. I took them with me to Northern Ireland for four years, and then the Gulf War broke out and we were in the right place at the right time . . .'

'And you went behind enemy lines, located the Iraqi foreign minister's hide-out, destroyed it and were mentioned in dispatches and decorated for bravery. Then you joined the Special Forces.'

His blue eyes flickered up at me, surprised. 'How did you—'

234

'Tommy, as far as the SAS bit goes. But also courtesy of a fair amount of media coverage. I do read the newspapers, Brigadier Ferguson.'

He smiled. 'Ah.' He narrowed his eyes thoughtfully into the shimmering sun. When he went on, his voice was low. 'Yes, I've enjoyed a very distinguished Army life. And a very miserable private one.' He turned to face me, his blue eyes vivid in his sun-browned face. 'I've never stopped thinking about you, Henny. Never. Never stopped regretting what I'd done. Regretting that you weren't with me, as my wife, my other half, beside me all those years, in those foreign lands. Making a home with me in Ireland, Cyprus, Korea – all the different places I was posted to. Everywhere I went, when I opened the door to my new accommodation I'd ask myself, What would Henny think? What would she say? "My God, look at the cockroaches, Rupert! And the dust. Never mind, come on!"'

I felt a huge lump rise in my throat. 'I was making a home elsewhere.'

He nodded. 'With Marcus Levin. Your old boss.'

There was something bitterly implicit in that last comment. As if I'd settled for something, and he hadn't.

'With Marcus, and our two children,' I went on doggedly. 'Angus and Lily. They're thirteen and fifteen now.'

He looked surprised, as I knew he would. 'Oh. I'd thought . . .'

'That they'd be much younger?'

'Well, I just imagined . . .' He hesitated. 'So you got married—'

'The following year. And no, I wasn't pregnant. I fell in love.' I looked directly at him.

'Of course,' he said politely. Crushed. Then he recovered. 'And it's been happy ever after?' He looked at me equally directly. Challenged me with his eyes. I felt my own flit away for a moment.

'Yes.' I nodded. 'Happy ever after.'

But he'd seen my hesitation. Logged it. I got up quickly from the bench.

'And now I must go.' I fumbled beside me for the strap of my bag. Swung it over my shoulder. 'I've got so much shopping to do, and if I don't go now—'

'The Lighting Department will be clean out of fittings – yeah, I know.' He grinned and got to his feet beside me. 'I'll walk you there.'

I was flustered now, but it seemed impossible to say, 'No, don't,' and anyway, by that time he'd already fallen into step beside me.

As we walked along the paths, our shoes crunching on the gravel underfoot, through the fading flowerbeds encased with low wrought-iron railings and strewn with curling yellow leaves which no amount of assiduous park-keeping could control, I thought of all the London parks we'd ever walked through together: Battersea, St James's, Hyde Park – halfway across London sometimes, when we didn't have the money, or simply the inclination, to get a bus; happy just to be walking together, talking. And although it felt strange to be beside him now, it also felt . . . as natural as anything.

I watched our feet as we kicked up the flaming sycamore leaves that spiralled down like bright jewels in our path. His shoes – brogues, now, brown and solid – next to my expensive black suede boots, no longer two pairs of trainers together, but a familiar sight nonetheless. I remembered the way his heel came down quite decisively, the way he deliberately slowed his swinging gait to accommodate my shorter step.

'So, your father's still in London?' I asked conversationally, not wanting to get back onto Marcus, or my happy-ever-after family life.

'Still in London, yes. But not at Albany. I live there now.'

'Do you?' I looked up, surprised.

'He got tired of living so centrally. Wanted to see some trees, a bit of sky, or so he claimed. He's moved out to Richmond, near the park.'

'On his own?'

'On his own at present, but he met someone recently, so who knows. I'm not allowed to meet her yet.' He smiled. 'Her identity is still under wraps.'

'Nice for him,' I commented. I'd always thought Andrew

237

was a lonely man. That his sharp edges would soften if he met someone. 'I imagine he feels rather shy about introducing you.'

'He met her in Annabel's,' he replied sardonically. 'I imagine the reason he hasn't introduced me is because she's probably about nineteen.'

'Ah.' I was surprised, but not altogether astonished. Andrew was a very attractive man, although I somehow couldn't see him in Annabel's picking up young girls.

'And you're happy being back at that flat?' I glanced up at him. 'It must be weird.'

He shrugged. 'Not really. It's central, it's convenient, it's familiar – it suits me.' He hesitated. 'And I've got a cottage in Ireland. I was working over there for four years at one point, and when it came up for sale, I thought, Why not? I might as well buy a bolt-hole here. It's a beautiful country. I go back quite a lot. Fishing, walking, that sort of thing.'

We'd reached the railings now, where the park met the street. A natural point for me to peel off into the stream of people going in the direction of Harrods, and for him to turn left, back to Piccadilly. I looked up at him; at the lean, handsome face beside me, a face that nevertheless had a slightly ravaged look to it. A look of someone who's been slightly further down the road in life. Seen some action. Not just physically, but emotionally too.

'And you never found anyone to share your life with, Rupert?'

He held my eyes. His were clear, blue and steady. 'I never found anyone, Henny. Never found anyone to match up. You see, I always compared them to you.'

I looked down at my feet. Embarrassed, but not too embarrassed. Not altogether hating it, exactly. In fact, if I'm honest, it's what I'd always rather hoped. That he knew he'd bogged it. Missed his chance.

'But I guess there's plenty of time,' he said easily, knowing he'd got too heavy. 'I'm not entirely decrepit yet, so no doubt I'll meet someone, someday. Perhaps I should pop along to Annabel's? See if Dad's latest squeeze has got a sister?'

I laughed, relieved that he'd lightened the atmosphere. 'Perhaps you could meet her mother? Go for the older woman?'

'It would certainly make for interesting family gatherings, wouldn't it? Imagine Christmas – "Darling, shall we give the children their presents?" "Yes – here, Dad, matching leather jackets for you and Trixie, hot-water bottle covers for me and Doris . . ."'

We both laughed, and as our laughter faded, I stopped uncertainly by the gate to the street. Rupert rubbed the top of the wrought iron thoughtfully with his fingertip.

'How long did you say you were in London for, Henny?'

I hadn't. Had deliberately kept it vague. 'Oh, until Marcus gets back. He's – in Spain. On a shoot. He makes commercials, you see. Often has to go abroad.' This much was true, but why did I feel he knew it wasn't the case? Could he read me? I looked away, up the high street. Concentrated on the ebb and flow of the crowd beyond.

'Well, if you ever need an escort for all those solitary theatre trips or art galleries,' he said lightly.

I glanced back quickly. 'Oh Rupert, I don't think . . .'

'No,' he agreed, with a curt nod. 'No, of course not. Stupid of me. I wasn't thinking. Or if I was, I only meant as old friends. For, you know, old times' sake.'

I didn't answer. Knew that wasn't possible. Knew we couldn't put that particular gloss on things.

He bent and softly kissed my cheek. 'Anyway, you know where I am. Should you change your mind.'

And with that he turned left and walked away. I watched as he moved gracefully along the pavement towards Hyde Park Corner; a tall, distinct figure, then just a blond head bobbing in a sea of people. Finally, though, I lost him. He disappeared.

## chapter thirteen

When I got back to the flat I went straight to the bathroom and ran a hot bath. I don't often bathe at three o'clock on a clement Saturday afternoon, but it's where I go to think, and right now, I needed to think. I filled it to the top, watching as the bubbles rose in a shimmering cloud, bursting on the surface. It wasn't the first time I'd done some concentrated thinking in the last twenty-four hours; last night I'd been at it till two in the morning. Pacing the flat, pausing at blackened windows, looking out over the Kensington rooftops, glass of wine in one hand, uncharacteristic cigarette in the other – really giving it what for, and coming down, inevitably, on the side of meeting Rupert. Deciding this was something I had to do. Calling it unfinished business – an unresolved chapter in my life to which I had to know the ending. Yes. For sure. The trouble was, I thought guiltily as I dipped a toe into the crisp white bubbles and let myself down into the piping hot water, now that I knew the ending, I was horribly aware I'd known it all along.

In my heart I'd known Rupert had truly loved me, but simply wasn't ready to become a husband. That was why he'd left me in the lurch. And at twenty-one with no previous form for serious girlfriends, no married mates and a shotgun to his head in the form of a three-year overseas posting, who could blame him? But I'd wanted to hear him say it. Not the bit about not being ready, the bit about loving me; and about no one else matching up. Trouble was, now that he had, it didn't resolve a thing. Didn't close any chapter. In fact, I decided, sinking slowly into the steaming water, it just opened another.

Because how much easier would it have been, for instance, if Rupert had met me today and said, 'Look, I'm sorry, Henny. I simply didn't feel strongly enough for you all those years ago. Didn't feel the requisite passion. Happily for me though, I did feel that passion five years later, when I met the girl of my dreams. She's called Anna and she's a mobile chiropodist, and we live in Godalming. Look, here she is in my wallet – see? And here's one of the children, Margot and Sally, eight and six. Have you got one of yours? Oh, *so* grown-up!'

But no. I lifted an arm and slowly soaped it. It wasn't like that. And if I'm honest, I'd known it wouldn't be. I'd seen it in his face last night in the Chelsea street-lights. There'd been no need to pace the flat and wave cigarettes and posture about unfinished business, there'd been no need to go and meet him in the park today, it had been there, all along, in his eyes. This wasn't a happily married man with a Volvo in the garage and a climbing frame in the garden, this was a single man, a free spirit. A handsome, brave, distinguished man, one who, moreover, was not only all of these things, but also, still madly in love with me.

At this heady thought, I slid my bottom down the bath and went right under the water, submerging my face and hair completely. Moments later I came up for air, gasping and hoping I'd cooled down a bit. Naturally I was even hotter. I smoothed back my wet hair and surveyed the backs of my hands; fiddled with my engagement ring. It was an emerald, surrounded by some fairly serious diamonds. Not my first engagement ring, of course, my first had been a tiny moonstone, which Rupert and I had found in an antique shop in Swiss Cottage. Or so the shop had grandly described itself, but Rupert and I, nosing around in the boxes of old jewellery, had laughingly decided a Second-hand Rose Emporium was nearer the mark. I'd loved that ring. Cherished it.

Later on, I hadn't known quite what to do with it. I couldn't send it back, because that would have meant making contact, and if anyone was going to do that, I'd wanted it to be him. So for years it stayed where I'd hastily stuffed it: wrapped in tissue paper at the back of my dressing-table drawer, mouldering peacefully with old lipsticks and cracked compact mirrors. Until one day, I spotted Whoopy-Doo wearing it. Whoopy-Doo was our guinea pig, our dog substitute in London. He normally lived in a hutch in the garden, but on this particular Sunday he'd been allowed the freedom of our Holland Park kitchen, since apparently he was going to a ball in the doll's house. Lily, who must have been about six at the time, had put red nail polish on his claws, a chiffon scarf around his neck, and dangled the ring on a ribbon around one of his ears, for all the world like the piggy-wig in *The Owl and the Pussy-cat*.

'Where did you get that?' I gasped, as I turned from wrestling the Sunday roast out of the oven. I stared, transfixed.

'In your dressing-table drawer. It wasn't in your precious things, Mummy. Not in your jewellery box, so I knew it was allowed.'

'Best place for it,' sniffed Marcus over the Sunday papers. 'Round a pig's ear. Since that's what he made of things.'

'Who?' demanded Angus from under the table with his Lego. At eight he was getting rather too sharp.

'Never mind,' I muttered, putting the leg of lamb to one side and hastening across the room in my oven gloves to rescue it. But Lily was beside herself.

'No!' she wailed, clutching Whoopy-Doo to her breast. 'It's his jewel! He's going to give it to Cinders at the ball as a token of his manhood!'

This had Marcus guffawing into the Sports section. 'Token?

# not that kind of girl

I'll say it's a token, and tell her not to hold her breath for the rest of his manhood, either. She could be there all night.'

'Is manhood a willy?' enquired Angus brightly.

'Only when it's attached to a man,' replied Marcus dourly, but then, catching my eye, shrank cravenly behind his paper, knowing he was on thin ice.

I gave in with the ring, but kept an eye on it as it moved from Whoopy-Doo's ear to the top of Cinders's thigh (aka Hula-Hula Barbie), and was even mildly diverted when Lily asked me why I didn't wear mine like that. When it eventually came to rest in the dressing-up box, I told myself that was the best place for it. I persuaded myself it amused me to see Lily in my high heels and my mother's old ballgown – the very same gown that I'd worn when I'd first met Rupert, which added a certain piquancy – the moonstone sparkling on her finger. Eventually though, I lost track of the ring as it drifted around Lily's bedroom, alternately in and out of favour. But then, one day, it turned up: on the day we were moving to the country, in fact, at the bottom of a packing case. I swooped on it like a magpie, and after a furtive glance around to make sure no one was watching, wrapped it carefully in loo paper and popped it back in my dressing-table, hoping Marcus wouldn't notice. It was part of my history, I reasoned, pushing the drawer shut. My past. Heavens, he had pictures of old girlfriends squirreled away somewhere, didn't he? Actually, I was pretty sure he didn't.

245

I got out of the bath and dried myself with the fabulously soft, white towels we kept in London, which were quite unlike the thin, worn green ones at home. When I'd finished, I let the towel drop to the floor and stared at my reflection in the full-length mirror. My tummy was a bit bigger, I thought, smoothing it reflectively with the palm of my hand, and my bottom too . . . I turned round, the better to peer over my shoulder at the cellulite. But my boobs hadn't dropped, I decided, turning back and cupping them underneath with my hands. They were still full and round and just as he'd . . . just as he'd what?

Horrified, I whipped the towel around me again and picked up my hair brush, sweeping it through my wet hair with long, strong strokes, and keeping an eye on myself in . . . damn. That mirror again. I stopped brushing and leaned towards it. A few crow's feet had definitely appeared around my eyes . . . laughter lines perhaps. I tried a smile – yes, definitely laughter lines. But no grey hairs yet, thankfully. Huge grey eyes gazed back at me. Doe eyes, he used to say. And he'd shown me too, one day, in Richmond Park.

'There, see?' He'd gripped my wrist, and pointed delightedly at a rustling coming from the undergrowth. A neat fawn head appeared. 'Look, a fallow deer. See its eyes? Who does that remind you of?'

Eyes like lakes had stared back – huge, limpid and frightened – but I could see what he meant.

'I wouldn't mind her legs,' I'd commented as she'd startled away, leaping back into the woods on long, elegant limbs, following the call of her buck.

'Neither would I, but a guy can't have everything, can he?'

I'd thumped his back in mock outrage and then we'd wandered off the beaten track. Found a place to lie down in the bracken, in the middle of a thicket. We'd made love there, thrillingly, dangerously, in broad daylight where anyone could see us, and I remember, as I got up afterwards, pulling down my skirt, brushing myself free of leaves, my cheeks flushed – thinking that I'd never felt so alive. Never had so many nerve-endings been tingling at once. And there were quite a few nerve-endings tingling now, I thought, as I hastily reached for my dressing-gown and put it on. Well, I'd just had a hot bath, I reasoned, tying the cord up tight. Clearly that's why I was feeling . . . you know. Flushed.

Happily the telephone cut short any further speculation on my rising temperature, and I went to the bedroom to pick it up.

'I've just heard,' said a familiar voice tinged with an un-mistakable note of triumph. 'Benji told me.'

'Mum.' I sat down quickly on the side of the bed. 'What have you heard?'

'About your supposed lover, of course. Ridiculous!'

I froze, horrified. Thought-processes whirred. 'Oh!' I gasped finally. 'Oh, you mean Laurie. My boss.'

247

'Of course I mean Laurie your boss. How many other supposed lovers have you got?'

'Er, none. Naturally.' I crossed my legs, tucking my dressing-gown around them nervously. 'And anyway, the whole thing's a complete nonsense, I hope Benji told you that too.'

'Certainly he did,' she replied warmly. 'Although I'd have worked that one out for myself. Fancy Marcus getting in a state just because someone took you out to lunch and gave you a peck on the cheek – ridiculous. But I have to say, Henny, I saw this coming. This is what happens when girls like you go back to work. They don't like it, these husbands. Get very jealous and imagine all sorts of high jinks. "Lunch" to them is the thin end of the wedge. Marcus probably thinks you dragged this Laurie chap back to your flat afterwards!'

I gave a hollow laugh. Licked my lips. 'Right.'

'I told you, Henny, they like to know where you are, and that means in the home, with the children, with the meat and two veg ready and waiting when they walk through the door at seven. You should never have taken that job, never!'

'Mum, Marcus encouraged me to take it. It's got nothing to do with him not wanting me to work. He's not old-fashioned like that.'

'Well, he's old-fashioned enough not to like his wife mixing with attractive single men, isn't he? Now you listen to me, young lady, we need to talk. I want to have a little chat with you about how to rectify this situation and I want to do it sooner rather than later. Time is of the essence here, believe me. I'm visiting your father this afternoon, meet me at the Nursing Home in half an hour. I'll see you there.'

There was a decisive click on the other end as she hung up. I replaced the receiver. Great. Thanks, Benji. That was all I needed – Mum's trenchant views on the subject at Dad's bedside. I grimly punched out my brother's number.

'Oh sorry, dear heart, but she rang, you see. She'd already called the farm and been told in no uncertain terms by Marcus that you were living in London due to a fracas, so she was firmly on the case. He's the one spilling the adultery beans, I'm afraid.'

'What!' I got to my feet in agitation. 'Oh for God's sake,' I exploded, 'what the hell's he up to? No doubt it's all round the country by now. I expect he's sent emails to all our friends!'

'I'm sure he hasn't, sweets, but you can see how I had to say something to Mum. She'd tried to get you at the flat this morning and couldn't, and by then of course Marcus had put the wind up her. She had you in a love-nest with your rampant historian, biting a pillow whilst he thrust away behind you, naked but for his spectacles, his white, academic body quivering as he paused to whip you with an ancient manuscript or quote from the Doomsday Book, or—'

'Thank you, Benji,' I cut in acidly. 'I was out shopping if you must know. And anyway, Mum said she didn't believe a word of it.'

'Neither she did, and I'm glad you were shopping, dear heart. I thought when I tried you myself that you were ignoring the phone and lying prostrate with your head under the pillow. But no, you were up and about. Taking Uncle Benji's advice.'

'Yes, I . . . went to Kensington,' I finished shortly. 'And I feel much better now. Thanks.'

'Well, it'll soon wear off,' he warned. 'If you're meeting Mum at Dad's place as threatened, your retail-therapy glow will fade faster than a Saint Tropez tan. I should know. I went last week and I've only just recovered. I don't know what they're giving him for breakfast in there, but I'd hazard it's got rocket fuel in it.'

'Thanks for the warning,' I said grimly. 'Bit punchy, is he?'

'Just a bit. But as happy as Larry, even if Larry is away with the fairies. But I fear for our dear old mum, Hens. She's taking quite a battering. And she may be as tough as old boots, but even the sturdiest footwear wears out sooner or later. We must revisit this topic, my love, when you're feeling stronger, and a mite more up to it.'

'We will,' I told him. 'I'll give it some thought, Benji, I promise.'

It was odd, I reflected as I put the phone down, how close Benji was to Mum, and how protective, considering they'd fought so much in his youth. But then again, they were very similar in many ways. Both sharp, vibrant, tricky – often funny but never boring. Whilst Dad . . . well, Dad had always been a soothing influence on our family. A balm. Our still small voice of calm on what were often turbulent seas.

Not so now though, I thought, as I smoothed down the bedcover where I'd been sitting. Now he was the one creating the turbulence. The one kicking up the storm.

An hour later, having caught a bus and made my way obediently across to North London, I was pushing through the swing doors of the little Nursing Home. As I walked through the overheated reception, I had that same sinking feeling in the pit of my stomach that I always got when I visited Dad – only more so today, knowing I was in for a little homily from Mum.

My mother was already in the day room when I got there. She was sitting beside Dad in a circle of other inmates, all in orange leatherette armchairs, and all grouped soporifically around a television which no one appeared to be watching. It was on twenty-four hours a day as far as I could make out. Dad, dressed in jeans, a sweatshirt and blinding white trainers, was reading a magazine and steadfastly ignoring Mum as she chatted in a low voice to him. I approached the huge trainers. At home, he'd always worn grey flannels, brown brogues, and a shirt and tie – always a tie, even under a jumper – and he didn't leave the house in winter without a felt hat which he touched to people in the street. But the nurses had said it was easier to deal with him in casual clothes, so Mum had bought them, horrified. As I leaned down to kiss Mum, I noted the adult magazine he was reading. *Nuts.* My father, who used to read the British Legion magazine, had his eyes, rapt and intent, on a scantily clad nymphet dressed in rubber and wielding a whip.

'Sorry I'm late.'

'You're not late,' murmured Mum.

I took the chair on the other side of Dad, whereupon my other neighbour, a snowy-haired old lady with milky blue eyes, instantly took my handbag off my lap. She opened it with interest, peering inside whilst I watched nervously. I was fairly used to this sort of behaviour. Once, in the early days of visiting Dad, I'd been stopped by a doctor in the corridor, who'd taken me to one side and explained that Dad was improving, but must be prevailed upon to take his medication, which he didn't always do. I'd listened intently, unaware that Dad was even on medication. It was only when the conversation took a surreal turn and the doctor asked if I could give him a lift to the pub, that I was rescued by a nurse who explained I'd been talking to a patient.

I forced an indulgent smile at my neighbour who was going through my belongings with all the thoroughness of the Drugs Squad, and made a mental note to check its contents later.

'How is he?' I asked Mum over Dad's head, then realised I was resorting to Gran's old trick. 'How are you?' I asked him, leaning in to peck his cheek and catching that sweet, sickly smell I associated with him being in hospital, so different to his home smell of tweed and tobacco.

'I'm fine,' he said, wiping his cheek where I'd kissed him with his shoulder in disgust, like a child. 'But I wish you'd tell this woman to stop bothering me. I've told her countless times that even if I was married to her once as she claims, I don't want to be now. But she insists on visiting me.'

I glanced at Mum. This was a well-worn theme and as usual, she stoically ignored it. She sat implacably beside him in her best camel coat, a silk scarf tied at her neck, her legs, still good and unknotted, encased in 10-denier stockings and crossed at the ankle, her heart-shaped face beautifully made-up. Only the initiated would spot that her cheeks were slightly flushed and her eyes over-bright.

'He doesn't mean it,' I muttered for form's sake.

'I know,' she muttered, equally mechanically, back.

'I do,' he retorted loudly. Several people in the circle, all elderly and slumped in chairs, jumped perceptively at this, as if they'd been touched by a tiny electric current. They momentarily directed their opaque eyes our way, before realising it was just Gordon again, and resumed the contemplation of their laps.

'I do mean it. How many times do I have to tell her?' His voice rose belligerently, and a middle-aged Indian nurse bustled over to soothe him.

'There now, Gordon, don't take on so.'

'I'm going to marry Grace, aren't I, Grace?' he demanded of the nurse, gazing up at her like a petulant child. She chuckled.

'Oh, Gordon honey, it was Barbara last week. It's me now, is it?'

'I haven't decided,' he declared importantly, folding his arms across his chest. 'But it will be one of you. It certainly won't be *her*.' He glared at Mum and I felt her shrivel. I reached across his lap to squeeze her hand.

She raised her chin. 'Gordon, you don't know what you're saying.'

'Course he doesn't,' soothed Grace, wiping dribble from his mouth with a hanky. 'Now, Gordon, honey,' she raised her voice and put her face close to his, 'WHAT ABOUT A NICE BOWL OF SOUP? YOU DIDN'T HAVE YOUR BREAKFAST TODAY, DID YOU?'

'What about a nice big kiss?' demanded Dad.

'And how about eating it at the table for once, hm?' she went on, ignoring him. 'Like everybody else, hm?'

A few silent souls were shuffling to a long Formica table by a hatch to obediently await supper. It was only five o'clock, but everything happened early in here. Like school.

'No.' Dad pursed his lips stubbornly and looked away. He never sat at the table, but they always asked.

'All right then, I'll get you a tray. Now sit forward while I put this cushion behind you . . . that's it. It's cream of mushroom today, you like that, don't you?'

'I don't like it,' grumbled Dad as she moved away. 'I poured it down the lavatory last week, when she wasn't looking. So did he,' he pointed a finger accusingly at an old man opposite, who looked like he'd died in his chair, jaw slack, head lolling. Dad sat up excitedly.

'Hey! Malcolm! Remember we tipped that soup down the lav last week? When Grace wasn't looking?'

Malcolm retained his comatose state, but just as I looked away, I'd swear he winked.

'He does, he does remember,' chortled Dad. 'And then we put all the plugs in the basins and turned the taps on full blast! Flooded it, didn't we, Malc?'

Malcolm didn't seem to remember this though, and simulated death again. But Dad was on a roll. There was some other, highly amusing jape to recount, involving sitting under tables and peeking up nurses' skirts, and the colour rose in his cheeks as he giggled and shifted about in his seat excitedly. Eventually his giggling subsided into coughing, and then he did some faintly surprised blinking as if he couldn't quite remember what had amused him. He picked up *Nuts* again and flicked through it absently, until he found his favourite, scantily clad maiden. He beamed at her fondly, stroking her blonde hair with his finger, then turned wide, knowing eyes on Mum.

'Did you know, Audrey, that there are more calories in a blow job than in a ham sandwich?'

'Well, I know which I'd rather have,' said Mum tartly, and rather spiritedly, I thought. She got to her feet. 'Come on, Henny. He's in one of his moods today. We'll go and get a cup of coffee and leave him to simmer down.'

I walked silently with her out of the room and down the long corridor, our feet squeaking on the lino. The walls were hung with jazzy, modern prints, chosen no doubt for their bright, optimistic colours, but all the more depressing somehow, because of it. We made our way to the canteen at the other side of the building, and Mum sat at a table by the window while I got her a coffee. I glanced across at her as I collected the tray: her hands were clenched in her lap and her lips compressed as she stared out at the traffic. Composed, but broken, really. Hating it. Hating her life. Wishing her husband didn't have senile dementia. Wishing things could go back to normal. If only he knew what he was doing to her, I thought as I came back and sat down opposite her, silently dealing out cups of coffee, little pots of milk. It would kill him.

Theirs had always been a volatile marriage, and she'd always had the upper hand, her voice shriller and louder than his, but he'd loved her, I was sure of that. And he would never have wanted to redress the balance like this. And it didn't matter what he threw at her, still she came, every day except Sunday, and that was only because Benji had recently put his foot down and persuaded her to have a day off, to have lunch with him and Francis. They always took her out somewhere, encouraging her to try Thai, or Japanese, which she enjoyed: the lunches were a welcome break from the barrage of constant abuse from Dad. But I knew she came here not just because she loved him, but because she felt guilty about not having him at home. She'd been able to cope with his incontinence, even his rages and his tantrums, but him not knowing who she was had been the last straw. Now that he was in here though, I knew she felt she'd failed him.

'How are the girls, Mum?' I asked brightly, handing her the sugar. The girls were the other three in her bridge four, all neighbours, and all well over fifty. My mother came back from far away.

'They're fine, my love,' she smiled. 'And yes, before you ask, I am still playing every Tuesday. And I'm going to tapestry on a Monday, and I've joined a book club on a Friday, so if you're about to tell me I should get out more and spend less time in here – "get a life", as Benji puts it, you'll be pleased to hear I am.'

'I'm sorry. We bully you, I know. It's just . . .' I struggled for the words. 'Well, Mum, you're still young and attractive, and Benji and I don't think you should devote the rest of your life to Dad. You've given him four years now and he's not getting any better. Worse, if anything. I just think you owe it to yourself not to make him so much the pivot of your world.' I gazed blankly into my coffee. It was hard. So hard. And I'd put that badly.

She was quiet for a moment. 'I know what you and Benji think, and I'm grateful, my love.'

I looked up, surprised by her gentle tone. She met my eye. 'I am. I know what it means, particularly for you, to give me that advice.'

She meant because Dad and I were so close. She knew I wasn't advocating abandoning him and making a new life for herself lightly. And I wasn't. I loved him very much. But I also knew there was only so much a person could take.

She set down her cup carefully in its saucer. 'I . . . went to the cinema the other day, actually. Haven't been for years. It was rather a novel experience. Someone took me.'

I smiled, delighted. In point of fact I already knew because Benji had told me someone had taken her out, and I was pretty sure it was Mr Greenburg, downstairs. But I was pleased she'd told me. Howard Greenburg was an old family friend, a widower, whose wife Bertha had been Mum's best friend and sparring partner for years. Up until Bertha's death a couple of years ago, the two women had had coffee most mornings, competing about their children's achievements, bickering and laughing over the Battenburg cake.

'We saw that new Richard Curtis film. Rather amusing.'

'Good.' I grinned, and tried to catch her eye under her beautifully coiffed fringe. 'Anyone I know?'

She patted her lips with a napkin. 'Someone I've known for years.' She looked directly at me. 'And yes, someone you know, too.' Her smile faded and her eyes drifted to the window. 'But you know, Henny, it's not that simple. Particularly at my age, and in my situation. It's tricky.'

I nodded. 'I know.'

It was. Of course it was. Dad was in here and Bertha had been her best friend. Ironically, Howard's religion wouldn't even register on Mum's radar these days, too much water had gone under too many bridges for that to be an issue, but – oh, all sorts of other things would.

Mum's eyes came back from the window. She straightened up and shifted in her seat. A regrouping gesture. Always a bad sign. Her eyes lost their wistful quality and she looked directly at me. 'Anyway, enough about me, that's not why we're here. It's you I'm worried about, Henny. What on earth's going on? What's all this nonsense about you and Marcus having a row and you ending up here, in London?'

'It was a bit more than a row, Mum,' I said nervously, squirming under her probing gaze. 'Marcus thinks I'm a fallen woman.'

'Oh, what rubbish.' She put her coffee cup down with a clatter. 'Honestly, these men. Their brains are between their legs and they think ours are too.'

'Well quite. But you know Marcus, he's never wrong, and in this case he's convinced he's absolutely right. He thinks I deliberately set out to get my boss into bed. The fact that it didn't happen is immaterial. In his book it's all about intent.'

'Ridiculous,' she scoffed. 'As if you've got time for "intent" with two growing children and a big house to run and all those animals to look after – or even the inclination! I mean, look at you! Do you *look* like a woman on the brink of an affair?'

I flinched.

'You've got no make-up on, and your hair looks as if you just dunked it in the bath before you came out – you really must try that new conditioner I told you about, Henny. I'll get you some from my hairdresser in St John's Wood. It'll give you much more bounce.'

'Thanks,' I muttered, sinking into my cup. 'Bounce is high on my list of priorities at the moment. You're doing wonders for my ego, incidentally.'

'Now if *he* was the one having the affair, I wouldn't be at all surprised. An attractive, successful man, surrounded by pretty young things all day – but you!' She pulled a face. 'Now you listen to me, my girl.' She folded her cashmere arms on the table and leaned forward. 'You go straight back where you belong, before this situation gets out of hand.'

'I can't do that, Mum. He's told me in no uncertain terms to stay away.'

'*So what!*' she shrilled. A few people in the canteen glanced around. 'And how dare he, anyway? If he wants to leave, let him, but how dare he throw you out!'

I hesitated, realising both Benji and I had been slightly

economical with the truth when it came to equipping her with the full story.

'Well, he kind of believes he has just cause. And the thing is, Mum, he's absolutely livid. Hopping mad. Don't you think I should leave it a week or two? Let him cool down?'

'And let this thing gather steam and get swept away on its own momentum? Absolutely not. You go straight back now, my girl. Gather your things and get on the next train home. Walk back into your kitchen with your head held high – golly, it's as much your house as his!'

'Well, I haven't exactly contributed—'

'Financially no, but you're a wife and a mother, that's your contribution. You have just as much right to be there as he has – *more* right, in fact, as any court of law will tell you. And if you don't look to your laurels, that's where you'll end up. In the divorce courts. Good heavens, if Gordon had ever tried anything like this with me I'd have boxed his ears! You've got too much of your father in you, Henny, and not enough of me. Don't just roll over and take it, get up and have a stand-up-knock-down-ding-dong if needs be. Throw some china, get trifle on the walls, shout and scream, but get back where you belong!'

'You think?' I said doubtfully.

'Certainly I think! And what would have happened if you hadn't had a convenient flat to go to, hm? Where would you have gone then? To me? To Penny? Oh, I don't think so. Nor would Marcus have suggested it. No, you'd have fought your corner a bit more, and he'd have backed down a bit. OK, he might have banished you to the spare room, but he'd have capitulated in the end. All this is just about teaching you a lesson, Henny. I don't believe he has any intention of chucking you out permanently, he's just giving you a nasty little shock in case you ever think of doing it again. You mark my words, just before those children of yours come back from boarding-school, he'll snap his fingers and say, "Right, you can come back now," just in time for them never to have known you've been away.'

'I did wonder if he'd told the children . . .'

'Of course he hasn't. It's a great big bluff. Now you listen to me, Henny. It may be a bluff, but if this situation is left to drift it could be very dangerous. You nip it in the bud now. Go back home and make it work. Good gracious, *all* marriages need a little work occasionally. D'you not think your father and I had our sticky patches? And where would we have been if we'd just thrown in the towel? You've had it too easy so far, the pair of you, blessed with money, good health and lovely children. This is the first little hiccup you've come up against. Well, don't just cave in, fight back! Where's your backbone, for heaven's sake!'

By this stage any tiny details relating to the truth of the matter had been forgotten and my backbone was making a dramatic comeback. My vertebrae were positively rippling and popping like the Bionic Woman, gumption fairly coursing through my veins.

'You're right,' I breathed, gripping my coffee cup hard.

'Of course I'm right. This has Alpha Male Domination written all over it – I can spot it a mile off. It reeks of macho conceit and it's not good enough, Henny. You can tell him so from me.'

She paused for a moment, and I saw a metaphorical light bulb go on in her head. 'Maybe I should come with you,' she mused, and then sat up alarmingly straight. 'You've never been very good at this sort of confrontational stuff, have you? Yes. Maybe I should—'

'No, Mum,' I interrupted nervously. 'I'll be fine.' God, I could just imagine *that* little scene playing out . . . imagine the blood on the terracotta tiles, the body parts I'd find for ever afterwards: Oops, what's this in the dog basket? Oh, it's Mum's eyeball, attached to Marcus's finger. No, I'd decline that kind offer. However . . .

'You're right,' I said slowly. 'I'll go this evening. Go back home. How dare he throw me out, actually.' I looked at her directly. 'How dare he!'

We gazed at each other over our cooling cappuccinos, our eyes locked in silent assent. For once in our lives, in complete agreement.

# chapter fourteen

In the event, I went the following morning. I cooled down a bit as I rumbled back from the home on the bus, and realised that actually, I stood a better chance with Marcus if I at least arrived in daylight, rather than barging in last thing on a Saturday night. I could just see his face if I stormed in through the back door in the middle of the ten o'clock news, marching into the darkened sitting room where he was probably comfortably horizontal in front of the cathode rays, empty pizza box and beer cans beside him. He'd be at a distinct disadvantage with his wife glowering over him, and therefore, all the more unpredictable. It might bounce him into saying something he didn't actually mean, like, 'Bugger off.' No, I decided, I'd go tomorrow. And actually, another night without me would do him the world of good. Let him wonder, for instance, when he woke up on Sunday morning, why there were no croissants in the bread bin? No fresh orange juice in the fridge? Let him wonder if his shirts for next week would throw themselves into the washing machine of their own accord, the sheets whip off the bed and change themselves? He might decide he'd been rather hasty in dismissing the little woman just like that.

And so it was that I stepped off the train in Flaxton the next morning feeling much more optimistic. More . . . upbeat. I gazed around appreciatively. Even though I'd only been away a couple of days it felt like weeks, and I thought how sweet and provincial the little station looked, with its white picket fencing and neat flowerbeds. Being a Sunday morning, all was quiet, and the place basked sleepily in bosky autumn sunshine. It was one of those clear-blue-sky mornings when you could almost hear the air squeak it was so clean and crisp, and as I walked onto the empty forecourt, the birds were singing, a sound I realised I'd missed in London.

Actually, the forecourt wasn't entirely empty. A solitary taxi sat in the rank, with Simon at the wheel. An unfortunate name, as Simon was a simple soul. 'Not quite like other budgerigars,' as my mother would have put it. Years ago, he'd have walked around our village in small circles, but these days, he drove them, in a Ford Mondeo. In fact, when you took his taxi, you had to be reasonably on the ball not to have him drive straight past your destination and deliver you back to the station again. When we'd first moved here, I'd wondered if he was entirely safe.

265

'Oh yes,' the chap in the village shop had assured me. 'Totally safe. Just very slow. You'd be quicker to walk.'

'White Cross Farm?' Simon said eagerly, winding down the window as I approached. Walking was clearly not an option today.

'That's it, Simon,' I smiled.

'Thought so,' he beamed. Simon prided himself on knowing exactly where everyone in the village lived. He got out and scurried round to put my case in the boot. 'I take your husband sometimes, don't I? When the car's being serviced?'

'Quite right, you do.'

We set off at a snail's pace, giving me plenty of time to gaze out of the window and wonder at the vibrant colours that seemed to have exploded over the last couple of days, the glorious hues of red and ochre against the sapphire sky.

'Been away?' Simon hazarded conversationally, over his shoulder.

'Um, yes. On business.'

He nodded, pleased. 'Thought as much. It was the case, you see. Gave it away.'

'Ah.' I smiled.

'Expect he's missed you then, has he? Your husband?'

'Er, yes. Probably.'

'Marcus, isn't it?'

'That's right.'

He nodded. 'I dropped him off last night, as it happens. Didn't want to drive home from a dinner-party, so he called me out. Had too much to drink, I expect.' He chuckled. 'Early hours, it was.'

My head snapped back from the glorious tints and hues, etc. I stared at the back of his neck.

'Right,' I breathed.

I badly wanted to ask *which* dinner-party, *whose* house, for crying out loud, and how *dare* he go out alone without me, but I knew it would be all round the village if I showed the slightest interest.

I managed to stop Simon at the bottom of the drive before he tootled on past, and paid him, seething quietly. I waited in the lane as he drove slowly away. Out at a party, I fumed. Too drunk to drive home. Bloody hell! And who the dickens had invited him? One of my mates? She could consider herself right off my Christmas card list.

I picked up my case and made my way up the pot-holed drive, but as the house came into view, my anger dissipated. In fact, I began to feel less gung-ho by the minute. What was the plan then, Henny? What little speech have you rehearsed for him, hm? I hadn't, in point of fact, never having rehearsed anything in my life for Marcus, but then I'd never returned like the prodigal wife, either. God, this drive seemed to go on for ever. Had he had it stretched while I'd been away, to make it even more 'sod off'? I gripped the handle of my suitcase hard.

So what was the worst that could happen, I reasoned, raising my chin as I approached the front door. I turned sideways and shoved it with my shoulder. Ouch. That normally worked. Usually it was on the latch, but clearly not today. It was locked, and Marcus's car wasn't in the drive either, but then he often put it in the barn at the weekends. He might still be in. I went round the back, my heart pounding. The worst that could happen, I reasoned, was not so terrible. He couldn't hit me, could he? Hadn't done so yet in fifteen years, so that left verbal abuse, and actually, that wasn't Marcus's style either. He wasn't the shouting and swearing type. No, he'd just go very quiet. Very cold and disdainful, like he had in that hotel room. I shivered. Much worse. If only the bloody man would throw something, a gin bottle perhaps, which could catch me on the temple, and he'd rush to me, horrified, and I'd assure him weakly that I was OK, and sobbing with relief he'd clutch me to his breast and carry me upstairs for some hot sex. I stopped short of the back door. Oh yes. Sex. I rocked in my trainers. Golly, how stupid of me. That had always been the way to Marcus's heart. Had always been his Achilles heel. Why hadn't I thought of it before?

I glanced down at the jeans and pink shirt I'd rather carelessly thrown on for this encounter and wished I'd given it more thought. I wasn't used to dressing up for my husband on a Sunday. I sniffed my armpits cautiously, then delved in my bag for a lipstick and applied lashings. On an impulse, I

undid the top button of my shirt. Oh, and another. Oh –
and actually, while we're at it – I reached up my back and
deftly undid my bra through my shirt, then, hooking the straps
round each arm, produced it, like a conjurer, from the bottom
of a sleeve. As I stuffed it hastily in my handbag, I looked up
to see Bill, grinning delightedly at me across the stableyard.
I went hot.

'He's not in!' he yelled cheerily, leaning on his pitchfork,
as if perhaps wondering if the show would go on and I'd
produce my knickers from my trouser leg. Wave them with
a flourish. Da–dah!

'I can see that,' I snapped, my cheeks burning as I fished
in my bag for the key. Damn. Bloody bra fell out. I snatched
it up from the gravel, puce.

'No, 'e's not been in a while. 'E's gone—'

'*Thank* you, Bill, I am perfectly *aware* of my husband's
whereabouts!' I stormed, finally finding the key and letting
myself in.

I slammed the door behind me. The glass pane rattled
perilously, but thankfully, didn't smash. Bloody man, I seethed,
glaring at him as he grinned back. Always bloody spying on
me! God, the first thing I'd do when I came back was bloody
sack him. I don't care how good he was with foot-rot on
Muscovy ducks, he could flaming well sling his pitchfork. I
threw my handbag angrily on the kitchen table and stared
round the kitchen.

All was quiet, all was still. Just the familiar hum of the refrigerator in the background. No Dilly. She must be in the bootroom. Ah yes, there she was, scratching to be let out. And tidy, I thought in surprise, moving around. Even more so than the last time I was here. And Marcus was not a tidy man. But then, there was only one of him, wasn't there? It wasn't like having a family of four creating mayhem, was it? But all my messy piles had been cleared away, I realised with a start. On the edge of the island, there was always an unruly pile of correspondence pending attention – term dates to be put in the calendar, notification of school plays to attend . . . what had he done with all that? Swept it in the bin? Just one solitary oil bill remained. And there was something else, too. I swung about. It looked . . . brighter in here, somehow. Oh, of course. My enormous trailing jasmine on the windowsill that Marcus always claimed was dead and I maintained was merely sleeping, had gone. Disappeared. Consequently, light streamed in through the window, and only an empty blue pot remained, its usually grubby inside scrubbed out efficiently. How satisfying had he found *that* little exercise, I wondered crossly. I noticed too the gleaming sink, and the J-cloth – blue, I always bought pink – neatly folded over the taps, not slung in a soggy heap as usual. What a little marvel he'd turned into, I thought sourly. Then I saw a note addressed to Linda on the side. I snatched it up.

# not that kind of girl

*Linda,*

*Thanks for coming in this morning. I'd be grateful if you could come in every Saturday or Sunday from now on, as discussed. I've left your extra money on the side. Many thanks,*
*Marcus*

I was stunned. *Every* Saturday, or Sunday? Good God. It was as much as I could do to get her to come in during the week! How had he managed that? Well, he'd thrown money at the situation, clearly. I'd tried that in the past, but obviously not enough. And 'as discussed'? What had he discussed? Henny's appalling behaviour, Linda? Her adultery, for which I'm divorcing her? So, if I up your wages, could you see your way clear to replacing her domestically? Coming in at the weekends, sticking a casserole in the oven? I screwed up the note and flung it at the bin. Oh, the man was out of his mind. Had a screw loose!

Seething, I went to let Dilly out of the bootroom. She was scratching wildly now, having smelled me. She whimpered with delight and prostrated herself on her back, shivering with pleasure and waving her paws in the air as I made a fuss of her. Well, at least someone was pleased to see me, I thought. I straightened up. And where was Marcus, anyway, on a Sunday morning? I fervently wished I'd listened to Bill. Could hardly ask now though, could I.

I bit my thumbnail and gazed around the room, looking

for clues. After a bit, I wandered into the unnaturally tidy playroom, then on through the rest of the house. Sitting room, drawing room, dining room and front hall were all equally pristine, and reeking of Mr Sheen which I forbade Linda to use in favour of beeswax. While the cat's away . . . I wandered back to the kitchen, then suddenly had a thought. I snatched up the phone and punched out a familiar number. She answered immediately.

'Linda? Hi, it's Henny here.'

'Henny? Oh! Where are you? In London?' She sounded embarrassed. Nervous. I could almost feel her blushing.

'No, I'm at home, of course.' I laughed gaily. There was a pause. I swept on. 'Um, Linda, I'm just wondering where Marcus is. Any ideas?'

There was an even longer pause. 'Er . . . no. Sorry, Henny. I don't know.'

Well, she clearly *did* know, but wasn't saying. Or was too scared to say. The back of my neck felt hot. Prickly.

'Oh well, never mind,' I said airily. 'I expect he's around somewhere. Probably in the orchard or something. I'll go and take a look.'

'Yes. Yes, probably. Sorry, Henny . . .' She tailed off, sounding genuinely upset. I didn't want to put her on the spot any more, so I said goodbye and put down the phone.

I stared at it blankly for a moment, then absently picked up the solitary oil bill beside it. Actually, it wasn't so solitary, because underneath was a large buff envelope, addressed to me at the flat, in Marcus's hand. I tore it open. It was full of redirected mail. How very efficient of him, I thought dryly. A Boden catalogue, a drinks invitation – oh, and another envelope addressed to me, also in my husband's hand. I ripped out the letter inside.

> *Dear Henny,*
>
> *I've worked out the children's exeats, and it seems they have two more this term. I suggest you have them for the first one in London, and I'll have them for the second. I also think it would be a good idea to tell them the situation as soon as possible, so I'll meet you with them in London on the first Saturday. Let me know if that's a problem. I suggest the Savoy Grill.*
> *Marcus.*

I stared at the paper in my hands. Sat down slowly on a stool. An exeat in London? With Daddy meeting us for lunch? In some hushed restaurant where I could be relied on not to make a scene, while he gently explained that Mummy and Daddy were no longer going to live together? And yes, of course it was sad, but actually, it wouldn't make much difference to their lives now they were at boarding-school, would it? What, Lily? Yes, of course you can see Mummy as much as you like. Well, alternate weekends, naturally. Oh, and by the way, Angus, that diver's watch you wanted? I found it in

273

Harrods this morning. And that new rug for your pony, Lily? Broad wink. Take a look in the tackroom next time you're home. That's, home at the farm, obviously. Not home in London. Although of course you will have your own rooms in London. Yes, perhaps the flat *is* a bit small. Maybe we should buy Mummy a new one, hm? Throw money at it.

My heart began to thump high up in my chest. He was trying to scare me. That's what Mum had said. He was trying to scare me, and he was bloody well succeeding. I was terrified. This wasn't the Marcus I knew, the kind, loving family man I'd been married to for fifteen years. This wasn't my husband at all!

I put the letter down. Stared abstractedly at a grease spot on the wall for a moment – then came to. I slid off the stool and tore up the stairs, my mind racing. I had to look for clues. Not clues as to his whereabouts, clues to his mental state. Something that might tell me what was going on in his head, why he'd changed so dramatically, so abruptly, and actually, I knew just where to look. I swept along the corridor, still with hoover marks where Linda had been, and across the landing, but as I passed the children's empty bedrooms, I stopped. Their doors were wide open, and as I gazed into Angus's room, a lump came to my throat.

It was a sparsely decorated and rather formal room, as if any adornment had been put there with a degree of embarrassment. A couple of Chelsea posters hung on the walls, one or two cups he'd won at prep school were on his desk, and a token Bond girl hung above his bed. There was a bookcase, his music system, and a rack full of CDs, but that was it on the entertainment front. All Scalextric, soldiers, forts and trains that had once run riot in this room had been packed away, ready for me to pass onto godchildren. Only a token teddy remained on a chair. For this occupant had put away childish things.

I moved on to clutch the next doorframe, the one to his sister's room. Conversely, this oozed its occupant's personality. Puppy pictures, pony posters and rosettes abounded, so that you could hardly see the Cath Kidston roses. A pink mosquito net hung from the ceiling, shrouding the bed like a Bedouin princess's. Soft toys were everywhere, squashed onto shelves, on top of the wardrobe, on her pillows; and in a basket at the end of her bed, an orgy of naked Barbies and one solitary naked Ken – woefully under-equipped for the job – lay in a tangled heap. Lily's house mistress had said that Lily might sleep better at school if she could at least get into her bed, but Lily couldn't bear not to have her things around her. She counted them religiously every night, wouldn't let them out of her sight. How was she going to feel then, about letting her mummy out of her sight? About me not being here when she got home?

A lump the size of an Elgin marble rose in my throat, and with tears threatening, I moved smartly on down the corridor.

275

I passed the two spare rooms complete with en suite bathrooms – very grand and lovely to have but hardly used – and on to our room. It was light, creamy and sumptuous, and I gave it a cursory glance but I wasn't really interested. There'd be nothing of note in here. In *here*, however . . . I opened the door to Marcus's dressing room where an altogether different feel prevailed.

It was a small dark room with green walls: cosy and masculine, with heavy russet curtains and a single bed for those nights when his insomnia became too much. All his clothes were in here: his suits in a huge Victorian wardrobe which I found depressing and had been dying to get rid of, and his shirts in a bow-fronted chest of drawers. His studbox and loose change were on top of the chest, together with a framed photograph of the four of us the day we'd moved into White Cross Farm. The whole family grinned at me over a five-bar gate. Although nominally his dressing room, Marcus never used it as such, preferring instead to collect his clothes from here and get dressed in our bedroom, chatting to me as I woke up. One of the more curious rituals of our marriage was that he offered me his wrists every morning so I could fix his cufflinks, waking me if necessary. Penny found this hilarious.

'He wakes you up to get you to do his cufflinks?'

'Yes, why?'

'I think that's outrageous. If Tommy woke me up to offer me his wrists I'd bloody well cuff them together!'

I tried that one morning. It didn't go down particularly well.

I stood, glancing uncertainly around the room for a moment, then got to work. First I rummaged through the pockets of his suit hanging on the trouser press . . . nothing. Well, nothing unusual anyway – chequebook, pens, driving licence and loose change in the trousers. Then I looked in his sock drawer. The keys to the safe were there where naturally every burglar would look first, and some pills for heartburn. There was nothing tucked amongst his boxer shorts, or in the shirt drawer, or the jumper drawer further down. I straightened up and frowned. I wasn't even sure what I was looking for, but nonetheless I kept going. Opening the wardrobe, I riffled through the other suit he currently used to go to the office. Nothing. I went through his overcoat, not used yet because we were having such a glorious Indian summer – but again, the pockets were empty. Then I spotted his briefcase, sticking out from under the bed. I crouched down and snapped it open. Everything you'd expect to find in a busy producer's case was there – scripts, budgets, documents – and his desk diary too, kept purely for business. I opened it. Most weekends were blank, as he deferred to my calendar in the kitchen, but on this particular Sunday, today, he'd put a red line through it and written *P*.

I frowned. *P*? What was *P*? Or *who* was *P*? I flicked on, looking for more *P*s, but no. Suddenly I had a thought. Inside the lid of the case was a leather pouch, where he often stuffed letters and bills to pay at work. Marcus did all the paperwork. Another thing that astonished Penny was the fact that I'd never paid a bill in my married life.

'Not even a milk bill?'

'Not even a milk bill.'

Sure enough, the pouch was stuffed with bills and receipts. The children's school fees were there, water rates, oil bills, and a few printed out emails. They were mostly in a sheaf, and to do with work, but one was separate, and folded into four. I unfolded it, and spread it out on my knee.

Dear Marcus,

I loved your last missive, just loved it. And I agree, why shouldn't I be the mistress? What's sauce for the goose, etc . . .

We meet again on Thursday and I can't wait. I anticipate lots of action! Incidentally, why shouldn't we meet at your place now? Surely the coast is clear? Think on it.

LOL, Perdita

I sat down hard on the edge of the bed. The house seemed very quiet, very still. It was one of those peculiar moments when the world tilts on its axis. Changes colour. Darkens. And you realise nothing's ever going to be quite the same again.

I'm not sure how long I sat there. I wasn't really thinking

coherently, just listening to my heart pumping the blood around my body, like listening to a completely separate machine. After a while, I stared down at the paper in my hands. I knew I'd been looking for something, anything. But nothing as blatant as *this*. I didn't have to rack my brains too hard either. I knew who Perdita was. My breathing became shallow. Laboured. I got up from the bed, one hand at my throat. She was the riding instructor at the local stables. Perdita had taught Marcus to ride. She was tall, blonde, and in her early thirties. A divorcée. Not gorgeous, necessarily, but attractive, fit. And very, very sexy.

I fumbled for the bed behind me, realising my legs were shaky, and lowered myself to a sitting position again. Right. So. The story so far. Perdita was the mistress. My husband's mistress. My husband was having an affair. I pressed both hands to my cheeks and stared straight ahead. How long had it been going on, I wondered? I felt numb. Sick. But whilst my stomach was nauseous, my mind was feverishly putting the pieces together. What's sauce for the . . . yes, of course. Finding me with Laurie had actually been very convenient, hadn't it? I remembered how swiftly Marcus had moved, how quickly he'd got me out of the farm and into London. How pious and wronged and high-minded he'd been in that hotel room; how scornful, how disgusted, when all the time . . . the gander was getting the sauce, too.

I tried to control my breathing. Tried to slow it down.

Where, I wondered? Not here, obviously, although that was clearly what she was suggesting, now that I'd conveniently cleared out – so, where? At the riding stables? My mind flew over there. No. No, not at the stables, *in her cottage*, which was behind the yard. It went with the job, and I'd commented on how pretty it was one day as I'd dropped Marcus off for his lesson; a sweet little bow-fronted affair, with roses round the door, gables in the roof . . . Which was where they lay, presumably. Under the eaves in that bedroom, overlooking the fields, lying in a post-coital glow, what – every Saturday? After his lesson? That was how often he saw her, every Saturday morning for the last . . . well, it must be over a year now.

I bent my head forward and clasped the back of my neck with both hands. A year! How stupid of me, so *stupid*! God, it was a classic scenario. Women fell for their tennis coaches and their personal trainers, didn't they, so why should it be any different for men? And here was Marcus, being taught to ride by a willowy, sensuous blonde, every bleeding week!

And of course this woman was very much his type, I thought feverishly, jerking my head up. For Perdita was definitely a woman, not a girl; experienced, worldly, not a silly little Sloane sticking a Danish pastry under his nose every morning but a sophisticated thirty-something who knew her way round a bedroom. And what's more, who knew more than he did – for once – about another passion of his. Riding. It came to me in a flash. Oh, that would be very attractive to Marcus, very. Someone who could crack the whip – literally – and stand, legs astride, in the middle of an indoor school, tight-jodhpured and leather-booted, as he trotted around her (a private lesson, of course, no pony clubbing for Marcus), yelling all manner of sexy instructions at him.

'Grip with your knees, Marcus!'

'OK, Perdita.'

'Tighten those buttocks!'

'Will do!' (Pant.)

'I want to see you really thrusting forward now . . . thrust!'

(Marcus, speechless with desire.)

'Go deep, Marcus, deep!'

(Marcus, nearly falling off his horse with excitement.)

'*Rise*, Marcus, don't bounce. *Up* down, *up* down – buttocks clenched – CLENCHED!'

Oh, he'd be in a positive lather. He'd *love* all that. Particularly having recently vacated a bed in which a cross-looking woman with vertical hair and a Gap T-shirt had swatted away his Saturday-morning advances like a dirty fly. And now, here was a woman, clad in leather, encouraging him to thrust!

I remembered him saying, one Saturday morning after his lesson as he watched me cook lunch at the Aga, 'Perdita says the muscles we use for the rising trot are the same ones that we use to make love.'

'Does she,' I'd replied tartly. 'Well, do you think the same ones could be employed to strain the sprouts? Make yourself useful, Marcus, and take that pan to the sink.' And he'd disappeared obediently, in a cloud of steam.

I hadn't batted an eyelid. My heart hadn't even missed a beat. God, I'd practically thrown him at her. Practically said, 'Here, take him. He's in the way on a Saturday and I haven't the energy for sex, so if you could service him, that would be great.'

And even if he'd said right then, 'Look, Henny, I'm shagging my riding instructor, is that all right?' I'd probably have snapped, 'I don't care what you're doing, just get those children out from in front of the television and lay the table. *Now*, please!'

That's how distracted I'd been. How comprehensively I'd taken my eye off the ball. Because I was so sure of him, you see. So sure.

A tear rolled down my cheek and onto the letter in my hands. Then another, and another. They plopped splashily down, wetting the paper. I remembered bumping into her in Waitrose once, stopping to say hello. We'd laughed at my groaning trolley and her jaunty basket. A bottle of Chardonnay and a couple of fillet steaks. For him, I wondered now. A little candlelit supper? And then, after supper . . . Oh God, I tried not to think. Tried not to picture Marcus, his eyes shining with excitement as she writhed on top of him . . . *ohmygod ohmygod*.

I stood up sharply, trembling all over. Now what, I wondered, smoothing down my shirt with fluttery hands.

What should I do? Should I go back to London, or should I stay here and confront him? Be downstairs waiting for him, waving the letter in his face when he came home? 'Well Marcus? Well?'

A friend of Penny's had done just that. Confronted her husband with his infidelity, waved the shirt with the lipstick on the collar, or the equivalent.

'Can you deny it?' she'd cried.

'No, I can't,' he'd admitted sheepishly.

'And do you love her?' she'd screamed.

'Yes, I do actually.'

'Well, then you'd better get out, hadn't you?'

'Right. Will do. Thanks very much.'

And he had. He'd gone, and never come back. Probably couldn't believe his luck. Couldn't believe he'd been handed his mistress and his brand-new life on a plate like that. He'd been shacked up in a cosy Maida Vale love-nest ever since, whilst Lucinda, the wife, struggled on in the country – tiles falling off the roof, garden up to her armpits – trying to cope. I dried my wet face on my sleeve and took a deep breath. No, I would not do that. I would not confront him. Would not corner him. I would not wait by the back door with a rolling-pin. This called for cunning. For boxing clever. I would not drive Marcus away. Nor would I make Marcus come back to me, simply because I told him to. I would certainly, however, I thought, putting one foot in front of the other and going unsteadily out of the dressing room, I would certainly make him wish it had never happened.

In the bedroom I opened a drawer and pulled out some clothes, throwing them in a suitcase. I filled it quickly, snapping it shut. But I left the drawer hanging open, because . . . yes. My mind was buzzing now. Let him see I'd been. Let him see I'd taken more clothes. Let him know I meant business. *Oh Marcus,* I picked up my case, staring wide-eyed and unseeing out of the window, *you will regret this. You will surely live to regret this.*

I went downstairs, put Dilly away in the bootroom, then went out of the back door, a suitcase in each hand. It was a half-mile walk back to the station, something I'd never normally contemplate, particularly with luggage, but I didn't care. In fact, I almost welcomed it. My hand was still trembling, I noticed, as I locked the back door, but strangely . . . I felt energised, too. I stood a moment on the step, assessing this. Yes, I felt oddly elated. I lifted my chin and narrowed my eyes into the sun. Could it be that for all that I was shattered, for all that it felt as if someone had reached inside and squeezed my heart tight, for once I was not the guilty party here. For once, I thought, as I set off down the pot-holed drive, the moral boot was on the other foot.

# chapter fifteen

The following day, I rang Penny from work.

'Meet me for lunch,' I ordered. 'It's important.'

'Tricky, Henny. I've got a client coming in at two. Tomorrow would be better.'

'Please, Pen,' I implored her. 'I need to speak to you.'

Hearing the tremor in my voice and sensing the urgency, she was there, in the Pitcher and Piano, the Covent Garden wine-bar I'd selected, on the dot of one.

She came in on a rush of cold air, clutching her face. 'Bloody juggler in the Piazza lost one of his balls. Hit me in the eye!'

'Poor you,' I managed, thinking a ball in the eye would be the least of my worries.

She touched her cheekbone tenderly with her fingertips. 'Ouch! Anyway, what is it? What's happened?'

I handed her the piece of paper and she read it as she

shrugged out of her coat, passing it from one hand to the other as she wriggled free of the arms. Her face darkened.

'Oh shit.' She sat down heavily.

'Fairly damning, don't you think?' I said tremulously, pouring her a glass of wine and noticing that my hand was shaking too.

'Who the hell's Perdita?' she said, still staring at it incredulously.

'His riding instructor. A lithe, over-sexed divorcée who lives and works in the next village.'

'How d'you know she's over-sexed?'

'If she's servicing Marcus,' I said darkly, 'take it from me, she's over-sexed.'

'Right. So . . . have you not been servicing him, recently?'

'Penny!'

'I'm just wondering,' she said hurriedly. 'I'm not making excuses for him or anything, but you know, we all go off the boil sometimes what with children and tiredness and plain lack of interest, and I'm just wondering if he isn't feeling a bit – you know. Deprived. Whether it isn't just a quick roll in the sack and nothing serious.'

'Oh, so that's all right then, is it?' I said angrily.

'No, of *course* it's not. And if it were Tommy I'd go insane, even if I *had* been off-games. God, I'd be bloody furious. It's just . . . well, it just seems so un*like* Marcus. Infidelity. It's so tacky. So not him.'

'I know,' I said in a cracked little voice, taking the note back and gazing at it. 'So not him.' Tears filled my eyes. I'd had a bad night, and despite my brief flash of bravado yesterday as I'd marched off down the drive, I was feeling much less gung-ho this morning. My Dunkirk spirit seemed to have deserted me.

Penny leaned across the table and gripped my hand. 'Henny, it's a flash in the pan, that's all. A nonsense. It'll be fine.'

I gave a little nod to show I believed her. Willed back the tears. She let me recover, then regarded me over the rim of her wine glass.

'How long d'you think it's been going on?'

'I've no idea,' I said bitterly, 'but he's been having lessons with her for over a year now, so no doubt he's been having a bunk-up in her cottage afterwards for about as long.'

'So why don't you confront him? God, you're holding all the trump cards now – why didn't you stay there when you found it? Wave it in his face?'

'What, like Lucinda Cavendish did?' I looked up quickly.

She paused. 'Ah. Right.'

'How is Lucinda, by the way?' I said tersely.

'You don't want to know.' She sank into her drink.

'So tell me anyway.'

Penny cleared her throat. 'Living in a flat in Balham.'

'Balham? I thought she was in the country? You told me

she was tearing her hair out down there. Pipes freezing over, sheep escaping, and a nasty smell at the bottom of the garden.'

'Nasty smell?'

'Yes, you said whenever the children used the trampoline there was a horrible farty smell. Lucinda carted them off to the doctor's in the end, thought they were unusually flatulent.'

'Ah yes, that turned out to be the septic tank. It was under the trampoline, you see, and had burst with all the jumping. Lucinda didn't even know it was there and had bought the trampoline to make up for Daddy leaving. It was all rather unpleasant, actually.'

'What, Daddy leaving or the smell?'

'The smell! She found poos in the flowerbeds.'

'Oh Christ!'

'But she's in Balham now. With the two younger children.'

'Two? I thought she had four?'

'She has, but the elder two chose to live with Daddy. He somehow managed to wangle keeping the house in the country. Well, Lucinda couldn't cope with it, and the elder ones . . .' She tailed off nervously. 'I suppose all their friends were there, the ponies, the swimming pool and what have you, so they decided to stay with their father,' she finished miserably. 'Plus Daddy's got a pad in Barbados which must be quite fun in the holidays.'

'Bloody hell! How come he's got all that and Lucinda's got nothing?'

She shrugged. 'He could afford to buy her out, I suppose. And Kara – that's the mistress by the way, except he's married her now so second wife – had a bit of cash put away, so that helped. She'd worked for years and was divorced, I think. No children.'

'Sounds horribly familiar,' I breathed. I thought of Perdita's smart little cottage, her shiny Discovery jeep and designer clothes. Oh yes, she'd built up quite a nest-egg there.

'So they live with the two older children in the family home while Lucinda's in Balham?'

'Four, actually.'

'What?'

'There's four children. Kara gave birth to twins last year.' She saw my face. 'Henny, you are absolutely thinking the worst now and there is no way – Henny!'

But it was no good, I'd gone. To the loo, to either puke or howl, I wasn't sure which, and in the end, I did a mixture of both, much to the alarm of a couple of girls applying their make-up. They left in something of a hurry. By the time I'd finished and was recovering, clutching the basin and shivering, Penny came running in. She took one look at my grey face, got me a glass of water, then took my arm and led me firmly back to the table. She topped up my glass and handed me a napkin to blow my nose on. I blew noisily, like a cow bellowing for its calf, making most of the bar jump, but I didn't care.

Penny leaned across the table. 'It is not going to happen,'

she hissed vehemently. 'You are imagining the very worst scenario, now get a grip!'

I nodded bravely. Stuffed the napkin up my sleeve and raised brimming eyes to the ceiling. I swallowed. 'Bastard.'

'That's better.'

'Cunt.'

'Steady.' Penny glanced around nervously.

I blinked, surprised. 'I've never said that word before.'

'No, me neither. How did it feel?'

'Pretty good, actually.'

We were silent a moment. I gave a mighty sniff, then licked my lips, swollen from crying.

'He used what happened the other day, Penny, I realise that now. Used that nonsense with Laurie as a convenient smoke-screen to get me out of the house and hustle his mistress in. You see that, don't you?'

Penny shifted unhappily in her seat. 'Perhaps,' she admitted.

'What d'you mean perhaps? Of course! Oh, it all worked out very well for him, worked beautifully, in fact. And I played right into his hands. I've been so *stupid*, Penny. Taking the job, scampering up to London . . .' I dug my nails hard into the palm of my hand. 'I should have sussed something was up at home long ago. Should have dug my heels in and got rid of her. Stayed put and made sure he never bloody well rode a horse again. Chopped the legs off his mare – hers too. This job was a big mistake,' I said unhappily.

'Nonsense,' she said warmly. 'Think where you'd be now if you didn't have it? At least there's dignity in doing something for yourself, Henny. Not just moping around and waiting for him to come back.'

'I don't want dignity,' I said sadly, looking down at my hands. 'I want my home. My kitchen. My children. My dog. My friends.' I looked up, appealing. 'I don't want dignity, Penny.'

She made a sad face. Reached across and squeezed my hand again. 'I know.'

We were silent for a while. At length I looked at my watch. 'You ought to go, Pen. You've got your client at two.'

She nodded. 'I have. But I don't like to leave you like this.'

I shook my head, tears welling again. 'I'll be fine.'

She shot me little anxious looks as we left the bar together. We walked silently through the Piazza, dodging the crowds, hands in our coat-pockets, shoulders hunched. The juggler was on stilts now, juggling his socks off. He winked at Penny. She glared back.

'Come and have supper on Friday night,' she said as we paused at the top of Laurie's street. 'I've got Benji and Francis coming and some people Tommy used to work with. They're a bit dry, but I thought Benji might liven them up a bit. I shouldn't think they've met a gay couple in their lives, I'm hoping he's going to be on flying form. Come.'

I smiled weakly. Dear Pen. She adored Benji. Always had done.

'Thanks, but I don't want to go out. I want to be on my own for a bit.' I hesitated. 'But Penny, you couldn't – tell Benji for me, could you?'

'About Marcus?'

I nodded. 'I don't want to go through it all again, and I know he'll be . . . well . . . he'll be shocked.'

She nodded. 'Sure. I'll ring him this afternoon. I can do that.'

'Not Mum though,' I added quickly. 'Not yet.'

She looked horrified. 'Henny, there was no *way* I was going to ring your mother!'

'No, but I meant, tell Benji not to.'

'Oh. OK.'

We parted: she to catch a cab back down Fleet Street to the City, and I to go back to the office.

When I got there, Laurie was tearing his hair out. All morning he'd been worried about some TV contract that should have been sent weeks ago and still hadn't arrived (I think he was wondering if they really *were* going to renew his contract, or ditch him in favour of some glamorous Oxford graduate who'd been making quite a name for herself in the history world recently, albeit on a rival channel). The Beeb had promised to bike it round that morning, but there was still no sign of it, so I sat down at my desk and spent the rest of the afternoon making a series of frantic phone calls: chatting up other PAs at the BBC, getting them to chase their executives, emails flying back and forth. I finally organised a three-way telephone meeting with Laurie, his producer and his director. It took most of the afternoon to set up, and funnily enough, the day passed quickly. I was surprised when it was five o'clock. Laurie, so grateful that I'd managed to jack up the meeting *and* procure the contract, which was now sitting on his desk, came into my room, running his hands through his dark curls, his eyes wide with relief.

'I don't know how I ever managed without you,' he said. 'Honestly, Henny, you're a life-saver. Emmanuelle was sweet in her way, but she didn't pull her finger out like you do.'

If I hadn't been so miserable, I'd have glowed with pleasure.

All right, Penny, I thought grudgingly as I trudged back to the flat that evening, getting off the Tube at High Street Ken then walking slowly up Church Street. A small amount of dignity doesn't hurt. Just a smidgen. I'll give you that.

The next couple of days passed grey and miserable, the Indian summer having disappeared as abruptly as it had arrived. The crisp golden leaves turned to brown slime underfoot, and the skies were leaden and cold. But that was fine. That suited my mood. I didn't want sunshine.

I worked hard and saw no one, answering Benji's sympathetic emails and entreaties to come and have lunch with polite refusals, and leaving the answer machine on when he called. I didn't feel like talking. Wasn't up to it. There was a

293

certain comfort in hearing his voice though, and I think he probably guessed I was in the flat, listening. He always signed off with a sigh and an, '*Au revoir*, dear heart. Love you lots.'

I sat at the pretty Georgian desk in the window of the drawing room overlooking the walled garden, and wrote long chatty letters to Lily and Angus at school. I got sweet ones back, via Marcus of course, at the farm. Naturally he'd read them first as they were addressed to the both of us, and I hoped they brought a lump to his throat. Caused a chill to settle on his heart.

*Dear Mummy and Daddy* (wrote Lily)

*We've had a brilliant day today because exams have finished and we were allowed to wear any clothes we liked! I wore my new patchy jeans and that purple top you bought me in Top Shop with my dolphin necklace. Yesterday we were allowed to go into Oxford with Miss Barker, but I've spent all my money. Already! Can I have some more?! PLEASE!! Also my mobile's run out! Annabel Bagshaw is going skiing in Wengen for New Year and I said we might go too. CAN we?! You said we might, Daddy. Give Freckles a big kiss for me AND Dilly, and tell them I miss them loads.*

*LOTS of love and hugs,*
*Lily XXXXXXXXX*

Angus was more prosaic. More chilled.

# not that kind of girl

*Dear Mum and Dad,*

*We won four nil on Saturday which was pretty good considering we're supposed to be a crap side. They had a retard for a goalkeeper which helped.*

*Food here revolting as usual, so any Red Cross parcels appreciated.*

*Have you decided about skiing yet? Ed Palmer's going to Wengen, and he's got a really fit sister. No pressure.*
*Love, Angus*

Christmas. New Year. I gazed out of the window at the swirling leaves being torn off the trees by the wind. They spiralled down to the garden below and were whipped around the base of a sycamore tree. I leaned back in my chair and folded my arms tightly, watching them dance. No, darlings. Your father hasn't decided. He hasn't got that far yet.

That night I dreamed that Marcus and I and the children were skiing down a mountain in Wengen together, schussing merrily along in bright primary colours with wide beaming smiles, like something out of a Ski yoghurt advert. Then suddenly, at the bottom of the slope, instead of our favourite restaurant, there was Perdita, naked on a horse.

'Come on, Marcus!' she urged.

Marcus shot me a look of sheer delight. 'Look who's here!' he cried.

'Yes,' I growled. 'Look.'

Marcus skied down and leapfrogged up behind her in the saddle. From nowhere appeared two ponies, and before I knew what was happening, Angus and Lily had schussed down too and leaped aboard.

'Come on, Henny!' I heard Marcus call as they galloped off into the distance. 'It's fun!'

I tried desperately to follow, but the sun was burning now and the snow getting slushy, turning to mud. My skis stuck horribly, and all I found, as I trudged wretchedly after them, were bits of Marcus's ski gear – his hat, gloves, boots, trousers, and even his underpants, littered in the snow. Finally, I came to a cottage in the woods with the horses tethered outside. As I staggered towards it, dripping with sweat, I saw a cradle, rocking on the porch. I peered inside. A pair of newborn identical twins gazed back . . .

The following morning I marched into work and greeted Laurie with a crisp, 'Good morning.'

'Morning,' he murmured, looking up surprised as I went straight to my room before coming in to chat to him as I usually did. I shut the door firmly behind me, shrugged my jacket off and arranged it neatly on the chair. Then I sat down to seize the phone. Penny answered immediately.

'Penny, you know that dinner-party you were having tomorrow?'

'Still tomorrow.'

'Still? It's still on?'

'Yes, why?'

'Can I come?'

'Of course you can,' she said, delighted. 'Oh Henny, I'm *so* pleased. You must be feeling a bit better. A bit stronger?'

'Much,' I said grimly. 'And Penny, can I bring someone?'

'Er, yes, all right. Who?'

'Just an old friend.'

She paused a moment. 'An old friend. By definition, Henny, any old friend of yours is an old friend of mine. We go back a long way.'

'So we do, my friend, so we do. And on that basis, trust me.'

There was another silence. 'So that's it then, is it?' she said slowly. 'No clues as to the mystery guest's identity?'

'No clues. Let me surprise you.'

'D'you know,' she said uncomfortably, 'I have a horrible feeling you will.'

297

# chapter sixteen

When I'd put down the phone to Penny, I glanced at my door. Laurie, I was sure, was deep in the sixteenth century, grappling with Lady Jane Grey's position on the monasteries, but I just wanted to make certain. Didn't want any ears wagging on this conversation. I tiptoed across and peered around. Ah. Even better. He'd adopted the Serious Business Position: horizontal on a sofa, laughing softly and murmuring into his mobile as he ran his hands through his curls. I'd hazard he had a more modern damsel than Lady Jane dangling on the line and was attempting to grapple with more than her monasteries. He spotted me and grinned and I smiled back, shutting the door softly. He'd be there for ages, I decided, padding back to my desk. Half the reason Laurie got in such a frantic muddle, I'd discovered, was that he was so fatally distracted by women. Poor love. Just like my husband, I thought grimly, reaching for the phone.

Keeping that thought firmly at the forefront of my mind, I tapped out a number. It felt so strange to be ringing it after all this time, and as it rang and rang, I felt a little less brisk. A little less certain. My heart was performing acrobatics and I was about to put it down in panic, when suddenly – he answered.

'Hello?'

'Rupert? It's Henny.'

There was a pause, then, 'Henny. How nice.'

And suddenly I was lost. Sunk. Marooned. Beached even. I didn't know what to say. My heart was banging away in my throat now, Finally, I found my voice. Ploughed on.

'How are you, Rupert?'

'I'm well. Very well.'

'Um, Rupert. Strange request.'

'Fire away.'

'I've been invited to a dinner-party on Friday. And I wondered if by any chance you'd like to come with me.'

I held my breath. And I suspect he tried to find his. His voice when it came was cautious.

'Well, I'd love to see you, you know I would. But a dinner-party? Is this the start of your London season? Seeing single girlfriends and going on theatre trips?'

'Something like that. Except she's not single, this girlfriend. It's at Penny and Tommy's.'

I heard him inhale sharply. 'Penny and Tommy's. Right.'

'And Benji will be there, along with his boyfriend, Francis.'

His voice grew fainter. 'Benji? With his . . . did you say *boy*friend, Francis?'

'That's it,' I agreed cheerfully, enjoying myself now. 'My brother's gay. You've missed out on quite a few years, Rupert. A whole stack of information.'

'Clearly.' He sounded bemused. 'Yes, I imagine I have.'

There was another silence. I smiled into it.

'Too much of a baptism by fire? Shall I take that as a no?'

He rallied. 'Certainly not. You can take it as a yes. Golly, dinner with my ex-fiancée's best friend and brother – not to mention his gay partner – who were last expecting to see me beside her at the altar in a morning-coat? Hell, who'd pass that up? Count me in. Next you'll be telling me Marcus is coming too. Make my evening.'

I laughed. 'No. Marcus is, um . . .'

'Still away on business?' he finished for me carefully.

'Still away on business,' I finished equally carefully. There was a pause.

'Right. Well, I'll see you on Friday then. D'you want me to pick you up?'

'Please. D'you know where?'

'I heard you tell the taxi driver. It's in my memory bank.'

'OK, fine. We'll have a drink first.'

'I have an idea I'll need one.'

I smiled and put the phone down. Yes, Rupert, you may

well need one. And yes, you can see me. But in public, with my friends and family around. I'm not sneaking about in parks or hiding in dark bars, wondering if anyone's watching. And no, Marcus, I am not sitting here crying my eyes out, either. You may be sleeping with your mistress and trying to assuage your conscience by saying to Perdita, 'Well, of course, she's sleeping with her boss so fair's fair . . .' But I'm not. And never was. Oh no, I'm doing something much more dignified. Much more acceptable. I'm being taken out to dinner-parties − maybe even to the theatre, perhaps − by an old friend. The fact that I once loved him more than life itself is neither here nor there. Playing dangerously? You don't know the meaning of it, Marcus. Put that in your pipe and choke on it.

By the time Friday evening arrived though, my bravado had evaporated as quickly as it had arrived. Suddenly I was as nervous as a kitten. What had I been thinking of, I wondered in horror, as I paced the flat, a glass of wine in hand. Taking Rupert? I must be mad! Well, I was mad, I reasoned as I stopped at the window. It had been a moment of pure insanity. A moment of *et tu, Brutus*, or *up yours, Marcus*, with Rupert and my friends and family as the fall guys. Because all I'd really been thinking about when I'd made that call, was my husband's face. Marcus's face when he found out, which I sorely hoped he would.

'She took *who*? To Penny's? And Benji and Francis were there?'

Oh, that would hurt. That would really hurt.

'But only for dinner, Marcus,' I'd say innocently. 'Not for a bunk-up. Not for sex, like you and Perdita.'

I lowered myself onto the sofa arm and gripped my wine glass tightly. Oh yes, we were really slugging at each other now, weren't we? I gazed out over the Kensington rooftops. Really in the ring.

When the doorbell went I jumped from the sofa arm and threw the remains of my drink – literally – down my throat. As I lunged for a cushion to mop frantically at my wet neck, I gazed in horror at my new pink cardi. A great lake had appeared over one bosom. Shit. I looked like I was lactating! I peeled the wet patch from my breast and shook it in a futile attempt to dry it, then ran to the bedroom ripping it off, buttons popping. With fluttery hands I seized a white shirt from the cupboard, threw it on then caught sight of myself in the mirror. Oh God, with my black skirt I looked like a waitress! *Something from the trolley, sir?* The doorbell went again. I panicked. *Old black top, old black top, where are you . . . ah.* I pounced on it, threw it on, but – oh God. I stared in horror at my reflection. A widow. Now I was a widow in weeds!

I finally ran out of the bedroom tugging down a rather low-cut red lacy number. The choice had been clear. Waitress, widow or tart, and I'd gone for tart. Didn't bode very well, did it? *Get your breath, Henny, get your breath. And for God's sake, smile.* I practised, but it twitched maniacally. The bell went again.

'Coming,' I called, in what I hoped was a light-hearted sing-song manner as I grabbed the door knob. I flung it open. 'Rupert.'

'Henny.'

Actually the smile wasn't hard. I felt it spread foolishly over my face as we gazed at each other. Naturally I was already panting from the exertion in the bedroom, but if I hadn't been – oh Lord, my hand shot to my throat to fiddle nervously with my necklace – I would be now. He looked divine. Quite . . . divine. His hair was recently washed and a bit damp at the edges, but the front was dry and flopped attractively in his eyes. Those familiar eyes, as blue as the sea and just as deep, all crinkly at the edges. I stared into them, hopefully without my mouth open.

'Thought you'd changed your mind.' He grinned. That lovely, lopsided grin.

'Hm? Oh no, I was – on the loo.'

'Ah,' he said politely.

Damn. Too graphic, Henny. Why *on*, not *in*? Why paint a picture?

His smile became quizzical. 'Er . . . shall I come in?'

'Oh! Oh yes. Good idea. Come in.' God, calm *down*, woman. He's the one who should be nervous, not you.

I led him into the drawing room, trying to sort of sashay elegantly across it, moving my hips a bit.

'Glass of wine?' I reached casually for the bottle I'd already opened on the side.

'I'll have a beer, if I may.'

Of course. He always drank beer. Damn.

'Right. Won't be a mo.'

I dropped the sashaying bit and hastened to the kitchen to get one from the fridge, my heart pounding. I nearly broke a nail getting the ring pull up, and as I poured it into a glass, I did it too quickly and got froth all over my hands. Suddenly he was beside me. He laughed.

'Here. Let me do that.'

'Oh. Thanks.'

He took it from me and our fingers touched briefly. I reached for a tea-towel to wipe the beer off, then wondered if he thought I was wiping where our hands had touched. Flustered, I exited swiftly and made for the drawing room again. As I propped myself up nonchalantly by the fireplace – tummy in, bottom in, shoulders back, heart racing – he came into the room slowly, pouring the rest of the beer. He glanced around, his face watchful, and made for the other end of the fireplace.

'Nice place,' he ventured politely. 'Girl done well.'

I flushed, realising I'd wanted him to register that, to see that my husband was successful and wealthy – that I had, indeed, 'done well' without him. Except it had backfired, hadn't it? Because suddenly I knew he knew I'd wanted to show off. And was it my imagination, or were his blue eyes slightly mocking as they took in the expensive antiques, the hastily purchased modern art on the walls, the stab at understated, classy opulence? This venue had been a mistake, I thought in a panic. Why hadn't I met him straight after work in a bar in Covent Garden? Where we'd have some atmosphere to rely on, some buzz to sink into? The expensive hush here was oppressive, and why were we perched at the mantelpiece like this? It was too high to rest my elbow on comfortably, and the angle was killing me, not to mention pushing my boobs out of this disastrous top. I felt like a barmaid. Probably looked like one. I dropped the arm. Now I looked as if I was waiting for a bus. Why hadn't I conducted this conversation curled up in a kittenish manner on the sofa? I looked at it longingly.

'Marcus still in Spain?' he asked conversationally, resting his elbow easily, but then he was over six foot tall. A large, Rococo-style clock loomed between us. I'd felt it was ostentatious when we bought it, but Marcus had insisted a marble fireplace needed a centrepiece. Suddenly I wanted to smash it. It seemed vulgar. And so *huge*. I had to practically crane my neck round it to see him. I cleared my throat.

'Rupert, I think we both know that Marcus isn't in Spain. Marcus and I have split up. We're living apart.'

He watched me across the clock. It ticked quietly between us.

'I'm sorry.'

I shrugged. 'So am I.' I roared on, no brakes now, 'The situation is all of his making, though. He's having an affair.'

Naturally I hadn't meant to tell him. Of *course* I hadn't meant to tell him, and certainly not the moment he'd walked in, but something had broken loose within me, worked free of its moorings and sailed defiantly out to sea, and suddenly – well, suddenly, Rupert seemed like the most natural person *to* tell. The *only* person, and yet, confusingly, probably the worst.

He put his glass down. 'I'm sorry again.'

I took a deep breath to steady myself. To steady whatever was out there, bobbing frantically on the waves. 'I'm sure it will resolve itself.'

'I'm sure,' he agreed quietly, his eyes not leaving mine. He was watching me as a panther would a gazelle.

'I'm sure it's just – well, you know . . .' I twisted my wine glass feverishly on the marble, 'a midlife crisis, or whatever it is you men are supposed to get at a certain age.'

'Women too, Henny.'

I flushed. 'Oh yes, women too. It's just a little blip, or whatever marriages as long as ours are expected to go through. It's well-known, isn't it? About fifteen years in, apparently.' I laughed nervously. 'A fifteen-year itch.'

'Are you saying you don't mind if Marcus has an affair?'

'Oh I mind, of course I mind. I wouldn't be human if I didn't. No, I'm just saying I'd be surprised if any marriage lasted as long as ours without some little hiccup along the way.'

'I wouldn't know,' he said carefully. 'But I'd like to think that "little hiccups" as you call them are not necessarily an occupational hazard. I'd like to think that when two people commit to each other for ever – that's it. For ever. Either that, or they shouldn't bother in the first place.'

I flushed. There were a couple of things being said here. Firstly, that Marcus had no excuse and I shouldn't be his apologist, and secondly, that Marcus, having made a commitment, should have stuck to it, and that if he, Rupert, had made it, he certainly would have. But that was easy to say, wasn't it? When he hadn't? When he'd bottled out? I was also aware that this was not the light friendly banter I'd envisaged before going out for the evening with an old friend. We hadn't even got beyond the décor before we'd embarked on affairs of the heart. My fault, naturally, but then . . . Rupert wasn't an old friend, was he? Who was I trying to kid? There were no dimmer switches in this relationship. It was full on or nothing.

'So,' I smiled. 'How's Army life? Still Changing the Guard at Buckingham Palace and socialising in the Officers' Mess at Jimmy's? Tough life.'

He laughed. 'Not any longer. I wish. No, now I'm no longer in the Guards, life is a bit more basic. Less refined.'

'Oh. Yes, of course.'

I listened abstractedly as he chatted on easily enough about the SAS, and I think I even managed to ask a couple of pertinent questions about secrecy and security and that sort of thing, and for the next ten minutes we achieved an acceptable level of conversation. I knew the damage had been done, though. Knew I'd said too much.

I tried to redeem the situation with yet more small talk in the taxi on the way to Penny's, but it was very small, and I was aware that Rupert was distracted. Deep in thought. You fool, Henny, I chided myself, my hands clenched on my suede skirt. How could you have given the game away so early on? On the other hand, I thought feverishly, all cards were on the table now, weren't they, so that was quite good. But in preparation for what, I wondered. What particular game was I about to play?

'Hi!' I greeted Penny nervously and extravagantly when she came to the door, horribly aware that I had quite a shock in store for her.

'Rupert.' She ignored me and bestowed a serene and practised smile on him, together with a peck on the cheek. He greeted her equally politely and I blinked as they exchanged a few words about how long it had been and how neither of them had changed very much, and then Rupert went through to the drawing room to see Tommy.

'Blimey. You don't seem very surprised,' I muttered, lingering to help her with the coats.

'If you weren't going to tell me,' she muttered back, 'it could only be one person. I hope you know what you're doing, Henny.'

'Haven't the faintest idea,' I informed her as I swept on through.

Tommy, who clearly hadn't believed his wife's prediction, looked staggered as he came up to shake Rupert's hand, and behind him, I saw Benji and Francis turn. They were standing over by the fire, and as Benji saw Rupert, he did a double-take. He shot me an astonished glance, then a wave of mirth swept over his face. He came up to kiss me.

'I know I said get out and about and make Marcus sit up, but this is ridiculous,' he said.

'I thought it was quite a trump card,' I murmured back.

'Oh, it's a trump card all right. Let's just hope Marcus hasn't got the Ace of Spades up his sleeve. Tread carefully, my love. You're on hallowed ground.'

'I shall. Francis, have you met Rupert?'

He hadn't, of course, and ostensibly was charm itself, but on hearing the name he exchanged a glance with Benji, whose nod confirmed his worst fears. Francis rolled theatrical eyes at me and I grinned brazenly back.

'And of course none of you have met the Thompsons, General and Mrs . . . er, well. Gerald and Pamela, perhaps.' Penny laughed nervously.

'Gerald and Pam will be fine,' growled the General.

'Tommy was the General's ADC in the Army,' Penny added, by way of explanation. 'Which is, kind of like being a servant, I think. Isn't it, darling? Er – no. Maybe not,' she tailed off helplessly as Tommy looked horrified.

We shook hands with a rather frightening-looking middle-aged couple, both of whom were tall with sleek grey hair swept back off high foreheads and thin, pinched noses. They were made for each other, I decided, as the doorbell went again.

'I thought we were eight?'

'Tommy's mother, plus latest squeeze,' Penny confided. 'When she heard there was a party going on, she wouldn't be dissuaded. I'm going to kill you later, incidentally.'

I grinned at this last aside, and as she went to answer the door, glanced across at Benji and Rupert, talking over by the fireplace. Some brothers might well have socked the cad who had jilted their sister squarely on the jaw, but not Benji. He had a few polite questions about Army life before landing his killer punch, which was where the hell had Rupert managed to find a cashmere pullover in such a divine shade of delphinium blue? If anyone could be relied upon to defuse a situation it was Benji, and as Mariella, Tommy's mother, gushed into the room on a whirl of costume jewellery jiggling in her over-tanned cleavage, her dyed blonde hair swirling around her shoulders, I decided she was a welcome addition too. I'd met her once or twice years ago, and remembered her as being good value in a louche, Merry Widow sort of way. She definitely liked the spotlight and was guaranteed to take the heat off me.

'Darling!' She kissed me enthusiastically in a wave of stale scent. 'Have we met?' She peered myopically, her pale blue eyes rheumy.

'Years ago,' I assured her. 'I'm Henriettta Levin, an old friend of Penny's.'

'Of course you are, of course,' she beamed, none the wiser. I detected whisky on her breath. 'And this is Juan, by the way.' She ushered a small, swarthy man into the circle. He had heavily lifted eyes and the most obvious black toupée I'd ever seen. 'Everyone, this is Juan. He's a Polynesian prince,' she declared proudly.

'That's a bit like being a Belgian chocolate,' Francis breathed in my ear. 'They're two a penny over there.'

I giggled and saw the Thompsons' eyes pop at the pair of them.

'He speaks no English, *mes enfants*,' warned Mariella, affecting a husky French accent as if that would help the communication, 'and I met him in Monte Carlo. Wasn't that lucky?' She turned wide eyes on her son.

Tommy, who couldn't have been more different from his mother, with his pale, consumptive good looks, very much the ex-Guards Officer with carefully parted hair and a sharp crease down his moleskins, managed to bare his teeth in an approximation of a smile.

'Terribly lucky,' he affirmed, clearly used to potential step-fathers of this ilk being foisted upon him. He shook hands politely.

'Hello, Juan.'

Juan accepted the hand gravely, did a dinky little bow, and clicked his heels. *'Enchanté,'* he informed the carpet. As his head came up, he found the mirror above the fireplace and soberly checked his toupée, giving it a little shift to the right.

'Champagne, everyone?' Tommy seized a bottle and wandered around waving it. I relaxed slightly and caught Rupert's eye as Tommy filled his glass. He winked. This is fine, I thought. This is going to be fine. And at least I was surrounded by people. Safety in numbers.

'I won't, thanks,' I said as Tommy attempted to fill my glass. 'I had a couple of glasses earlier. In fact, I might help myself to some water.'

'In the fridge, I'll get it for you.'

'No no, you're busy. I'll go.' I waved him back and disappeared out to the kitchen.

It would be a mistake, I decided, finding the Evian bottle in the fridge, to get disastrously drunk, and the wine I'd had at the flat was slightly edging up on me. I glugged down a couple of glasses of water, and as I shut the fridge door, heard a scuffle behind me. I turned to find Penny, Benji and Francis coming through the door in a huddle. Penny's eyes were huge.

312

'I cannot believe you've done this,' she whispered, gripping the edge of her kitchen table for support.

'Done what?' I asked foolishly, playing for time.

'Oh don't be ridiculous. Brought him – Rupert!' she hissed.

'Shh, he'll hear you.'

Francis quietly shut the door.

'Well, honestly Henny, how long have you been seeing him?' she demanded. 'Does Marcus know?'

'Since he followed me home from work, and no, Marcus doesn't know. But I don't mind if he does, because I'm not seeing him in that way. He's just an old friend.'

'Bollocks,' she snorted. 'You were going to marry him! How the hell did he track you down?'

'Through your uncle, if you must know. He was in the Army with him. Rang to speak to him at work and got me instead.'

'Laurie? Oh God, I might have known,' she moaned. She sank into a chair at the table and clutched her head. 'Might have known it would be *my* fault. But what's Marcus going to say? What are you *think*ing of, Henny?'

'Marcus can say what he likes,' I said stiffly. 'Christ, he's the love-rat. He's the one having an affair, so why shouldn't I—' I stopped. Three pairs of eyes looked accusingly at me.

'What?' demanded Penny. 'Have one too?'

'I wasn't going to say that. I was going to say, why shouldn't I catch up with an old mate. For old times' sake.'

'An old mate?' enquired Benji mildly. 'Well, only in the zoological sense, surely? Only as in Mr Orang-utan with the red bottom meets Mrs Orang-utan with the pink bottom. God, I can smell that cage of yours a mile off, it reeks of sex. And I can practically *see* the hormones hopping between you. Take care, my love.'

'Why does everyone keep telling me to take care?' I flared up. 'Why am I assumed to be so out of control?'

'Perhaps because you have the faintest whiff of the innocent about you?' offered Francis kindly. 'As if you've never seen quite so many sweeties in one shop before?'

'You mean I don't know how to handle myself,' I said crossly. 'A gauche, unsophisticated housewife who's up from the country and ripe for the picking because her heartstrings haven't been plucked in a while.'

Francis blinked. 'Couldn't have put it better myself.'

'And it's not just her heartstrings that are ripe for the plucking,' observed Benji. 'As the pheasant plucker said.'

'Oh don't be ridiculous,' I snapped. 'I know what you're all thinking, but you're wrong. I can handle myself perfectly well, thank you. Now let's get back to the party, shall we? We can't leave poor Tommy holding the fort.'

And raising my chin, I swept defiantly back to the drawing room. There was a great deal of eye-rolling and whispering behind me, but at length, they followed. Grudgingly.

Supper was interesting. Penny, a self-confessed domestic

# not that kind of girl

disaster, had strayed rather ambitiously from her usual fish pie to coq-au-vin. Or coq-oh-up, as she observed grimly to me in the kitchen, as we tried vainly to find some chicken amongst the bones in the pot.

'I've stewed it to distraction!' she wailed. 'Boiled it to broth!'

'So put it in bowls and give everyone spoons,' I suggested, rummaging in a drawer for a ladle. 'Here, scoop it out.'

'D'you think?'

'Why not? Very French.'

'But I've only got six soup spoons,' she said doubtfully.

'Give them to the Thompsons. The rest of us can have straws.'

She looked at me in horror. 'Joke, Pen,' I said hastily. 'Go rustle up some pudding spoons.'

'And keep pouring the wine down your end,' she muttered as we went back through to the dining room, balancing brimming bowls on trays. 'Then no one will notice.'

No one did seem to notice, the conversation being far too lively to worry about the food. Rupert and Francis, both amusing raconteurs, seemed to be getting on like a house on fire, whilst Benji, stuck at the other end with Mrs Thompson, strained jealously to hear what was being said, hating to be left out. Mariella, meanwhile, regaled the rest of us with the perils of dancing in Monaco's nightclubs when one had just had a bunion operation and was forced to wear carpet slippers.

'Perilous!' she exclaimed to a startled General Gerald. 'Those dance floors are like sheet ice. Lethal.'

It was a bit like an OAP complaining about getting to the Spa in the depths of winter.

'Something should be done about it,' she went on forcefully.

'Grit?' offered Benji.

'Poor Juan came a complete cropper the other night, and fell over during "The Locomotion". Had fluid on his knees for weeks.'

Visions of geriatric tax exiles being forced to shuffle around Monaco's nightclubs, complaining bitterly that the poles provided for pole dancing were too cold and slippery for their withered thighs and the flashing lights too hard on their cataracts sprang ludicrously to mind. I turned politely to Juan beside me to sympathise and quell the hysteria, but Juan, having planted himself firmly in the only chair facing a mirror gave a tight little smile – for tight was all it could be – and continued gazing at himself. From time to time he'd lean forward with a frown and adjust his toupée.

Mariella, meanwhile, had moved on from the perils of Monte Carlo's premier night spots and was up in the stars now, astrologically speaking.

'I haven't got Christmas presents for the children this year,' she was confiding in a low voice to her daughter-in-law. 'I've done their charts instead.'

'Splendid,' said Penny faintly. 'I'm sure that will go down a treat.'

'What is your brother?' Mariella hissed suddenly in my ear.

'Um, he's a fund manager.'

'No no,' she waved her spoon in Benji's direction. 'What star sign is he?'

'Oh. Er, Capricorn, I think.'

She leaned urgently across the table towards him. 'Young man,' she demanded imperiously. 'Are you a swimmer?'

Benji, keen to have a respite from Pamela Thompson's offsprings' education and the efficacy of her cleaner, brightened considerably. 'Not especially, but I like a bit of freestyle,' he quipped.

'Because if you are,' she swept on, 'you should know that Neptune is rising in your aura.'

'Is that a good thing?'

'Of course! Your energy is compounded twofold!'

'Excellent news,' grinned Benji. 'I shall get down to Putney Baths immediately. D'you think one of the lifeguards would like to share my energy? Slip in a length?'

'I thought the aura was the bit around the nipple,' muttered Francis in my ear, frowning at Benji to behave.

'Aureola,' I muttered back. 'D'you think Juan's are pierced?'

'Wouldn't surprise me. And not just his nipples, either.'

'Oh please.'

Pamela Thompson, meanwhile, in an effort to steer the

317

party back to more prosaic topics, had turned a bright smile on me.

'Have you and Rupert been married long?'

A horrible hush fell over the proceedings.

'Oh, er, we're not married,' I flushed. 'Just good friends.'

'Oh, I'm sorry. I heard you mention children, so I assumed . . .'

'Yes, yes, I have got children. From my first marriage. I mean – my m-marriage,' I stuttered, seeing quite a lot of people contemplate their plates. 'My husband and I are separated though,' I said defiantly, and saw Penny and Benji glance up at me, round-eyed.

'Well, how nice to have someone to take you to dinner parties,' Pamela rallied.

'Yes, isn't it?' I agreed, not daring to look at Rupert.

'Just what your sister could do with right now,' growled Gerald Thompson to his wife. 'A walker. Poor girl. Even a poofter would do. She was jilted a couple of weeks ago,' he explained.

Another hush descended on our little gathering.

'Well, not jilted exactly,' Pamela hastened to explain. 'Not actually at the altar. He broke it off just after the invitations had gone out. All the presents had arrived though, the dress had been bought . . . Poor Tilly, she was heartbroken.'

'I imagine she was,' said Benji quietly. 'I'm not sure even a poofter could help mend that.'

318

Gerald glanced from Francis to Benji, and as the penny slowly dropped, his eyes bulged.

'Didn't that happen to a gel you knew, Penny?' Mariella asked sharply. 'Years ago. Supposed to be marrying a chum of Tommy's in the Guards.'

Penny seemed unable to speak.

'Pretty little thing, with a very pushy mother. Quite *nouveau riche*. Definitely not top drawer. Tried to bag him too young, as I recall. Ended up marrying someone from the East End.'

'More soup, anyone?' enquired Penny, frantically plunging her ladle in again.

The evening deteriorated badly after that, with a lot of people finding succour in alcohol. The Thompsons didn't dally, murmuring nervous excuses about a long journey home, and Mariella and Juan left soon after, keen to test the boards at Annabel's. When they'd all gone, the rest of us collapsed in a giggling heap in front of the fire, and agreed that the evening had been an experience.

'Oh God, remind me never to entertain again,' moaned Penny, flopping down on a sofa and throwing a tea-towel over her face. 'Yes please, to the top,' she advised her husband as he went to fill her glass.

'Remind me never to accept an invitation again,' murmured Rupert, sinking weakly down beside her.

'You weren't invited,' she reminded him sharply, snatching

319

the tea-towel from her face and looking sideways at him, her mouth twitching.

'You're quite right,' he agreed, 'I wasn't.' He hesitated. 'And I shouldn't have come.'

'Oh *no!*' everyone chorused, inebriated beyond belief now. Of *course* he should have come, of course! He'd made the party! Also, insisted Benji, who was flying, it was marvellous to have closed the chapter like this. Seeing him again had given us all closure, as the Americans put it, and now we could all let bygones be bygones. And Francis wouldn't have missed meeting him for the world, would you, Francis? Francis, who didn't have a head for drink, opened one eye and agreed sleepily that he wouldn't.

When Penny finally showed us out at 2 a.m., she was adamant. Swaying, but adamant.

'Fine,' she slurred in a pissed whisper, eyelids drooping as Rupert went down the path ahead of me to find a cab. 'Fine. You brought him, and I don't mind.' She clutched the doorframe for balance. 'Helluva guy. Always liked him. Very sexy bottom. Very – you know. Pert.' She swayed a bit more, then lurched forwards suddenly and wagged a finger in my face. 'But whatever you do, don't have coffee. OK?'

I nodded gravely. 'OK,' I agreed in an equally pissed whisper. 'I won't.'

# chapter seventeen

'Coffee?' enquired Rupert casually as the cab rumbled back towards Piccadilly.

'Why not?' I agreed, equally casually. I flashed him a sexy smile. Unfortunately I was so dehydrated my top lip got stuck to my gums and I had to lick it free, which rather spoiled the effect.

Rupert leaned forward to speak to the driver. 'Pull up outside the Royal Academy, would you? We'll walk the rest.'

'Oh. Your place?' I said in alarm, clutching the door handle and lurching forward drunkenly as the cab came to a halt at the kerb.

Rupert swung the door open and glanced at me in surprise. 'Would you prefer one at yours? I thought this was more on the way.'

'Oh yeah, right,' I agreed casually. 'And I'll catch a cab back later. Just a quick cup, though,' I gabbled. 'It is pretty late.'

'Sure.' He got out and opened his wallet to pay. 'I can order you one,' he said, helping me out. 'I've got an account.'

'Oh, marvellous.'

Yes, marvellous. Splendid, in fact. I tried not to sway as he paid the driver; tried to look as if it was the most natural thing in the world for me to go back to Rupert's place at two-thirty in the morning. As the taxi trundled away we put our collars up against the wind and headed off. As we threaded our way around the back of the Royal Academy, the night air hit me; chilly now, with a hint of mist, it sobered me up. Just a quick cup, I decided nervously, and I'd throw it down my neck in seconds. Get back to Kensington. But we definitely *need*ed to chat, I reasoned. I'd been so on edge before in the flat, and we hadn't had a chance at Penny's to really – you know – catch up.

Our heels clattered up the stone steps and through the oak front door of Albany, then across the hallway and into the gilded lift. Rupert pulled the familiar, concertinaed door shut behind us. We stood in silence as it whirred into action and as it slowly picked up speed, purring up to the third floor, I felt the years drop off me. How many times had I heard that shudder, felt that lurch, as it overshot the floor – then shunted down an inch to the right level? Nostalgia washed over me as we walked out across the landing, and as Rupert put his key in the green door opposite, he saw my face. Grinned.

'Feel odd?'

'*Most* peculiar.'

He laughed. 'Wait till you get inside. When you realise no one's lifted a finger to improve the décor, you'll feel even more peculiar.'

He opened the door and I stepped in, glancing around. The pale, nondescript walls of the hall hung with sporting prints closed in on me instantly. 'God, you haven't, have you?' I said in surprise. 'Rupert, this is unreal. Like walking into a time-warp.'

He scratched his head sheepishly. 'I know. Can't seem to get round to it.'

I wandered through to the sitting room, which had been functional but tired in my day; now it looked downright exhausted. The pale brown sofa and chairs circa 1973 were still *in situ*, albeit with a few more holes and coffee stains on the arms, and the threadbare green carpet had even more bald spots in it, although I spotted a new rug by the fire.

'To hide the really monster holes,' Rupert informed me, flipping it back with his toe to reveal a barren patch.

The paintwork obviously hadn't been touched for fifteen years, but had deepened from a sad cream to a distressed beige, and was only enlivened by a wall full of military prints. Even in my youth I'd been itching to get my paintbrush out, but this was ridiculous.

'Rupert, why don't you sort this place out?' I said, the

drink emboldening me. 'It's like walking into Miss Havisham's patch, it's ridiculous!'

He grinned. 'You haven't seen the kitchen yet.'

'Well, I hope you've at least – oh good grief!'

I stepped into the familiar little room, to be confronted by the same peeling blue walls, yellow Formica surfaces, the old cork pinboard with a curling sporting calendar, the strip lighting on the ceiling, plus a few more holes in the black and white lino floor.

'I don't notice it,' he said simply, shrugging. 'Although I have to say, seeing it with your eyes now, I'm rather embarrassed. But it's purely somewhere to lay my head when I'm in London. And anyway, I don't like change.'

'And your father?' I said, astonished, moving from room to room. 'Doesn't he – well, no, of course he doesn't.' I corrected myself. 'We're talking Colonel Andrew Ferguson here.'

'Whose spiritual home,' Rupert remarked dryly, 'is probably the smoking room of Brooks's across the road. Home has never been a home for him. Anyway, he's never here.'

'Even when he's in London?'

'Not recently. He stays with his girlfriend. She's got a flat in London. That's where he is at the moment.'

'Oh, right. The new bird.'

I tried to imagine Andrew in some twenty-something's flat, possibly one she shared with a girlfriend; knickers and bras hanging from the shower rail over the bath, rock music blaring, girls chattering on the telephone or painting their nails, and in the midst of it, Andrew calmly doing the *Telegraph* cross-word on a bean bag, the fronds from a fibreoptic lamp occasionally rustling his paper.

'He takes his own Frank Cooper's marmalade and Gentleman's Relish,' Rupert informed me with a grin, following me down the passage as I peered in all the rooms in a totally pissed and nosy fashion.

'I'm surprised he doesn't take a hot-water bottle and a Teasmade, too. D'you mind me spying in all your rooms, Rupert?'

'Do I have any choice? You always were a nosy old bag – oh, now this one *has* changed,' he said, as I pushed open the door to his old room.

'I should hope so. If I find Airfix models of fighter planes still hanging from the ceiling . . . Oh, I see. Yes, it has a bit.'

I walked in and gazed around. Rupert's boyhood single bed had been replaced by a cream sofa, and shelves had been put up to accommodate hundreds of books. 'Golly.' I ran my hand along the spines. 'Something tells me you've taken up reading.'

'Less of the cheek. They were always here actually, in boxes, in that cupboard. Clearly your nosiness hadn't fully developed in those days and you failed to peer in.'

I grinned. 'All military history.' I cocked my head sideways to read the spines. It reminded me of home, somehow. My father's study. Just his subject. Someone else's, too. 'You've got the same literary tastes as Laurie,' I observed.

'Which is where the similarity ends.'

I turned at his tone. 'Oh really? What d'you mean? I thought you two were friends?'

He looked uncomfortable. 'Not exactly. We certainly know each other pretty well and we've served together in Northern Ireland, but I wouldn't say we were buddies.'

'Were you above him? I mean, rankwise?'

'I was his Commanding Officer. And if I hadn't been, I dare say he'd have been thrown out of the Battalion long before.'

'Oh? Why?'

He hesitated. 'Laurie's reputation goes before him, if you know what I mean. I've bailed him out of one too many scrapes.'

'You mean with women?' I blushed, suddenly remembering my own little scrape with him.

'Mostly with women. In fact – hell, what am I saying – always with women. And always at inopportune moments when he should have been on guard duty, or border patrol. We nearly lost a squaddie once, thanks to Laurie's negligence. He was supposed to be patrolling a farmhouse we knew the IRA had their eye on, but he was shacked up with a barmaid instead. His platoon went ahead to recce it without him, and one of them got a bullet in his head. Luckily it only took his ear off.'

'Oh.' I was silenced and sobered. Yes, it was a war these boys fought, wasn't it. In Iraq. The Gulf. Ireland. Not just dressing up in bearskins outside Buckingham Palace and knocking back the gin. It was so easy to forget that, particularly in Laurie's case, as he flashed his good looks all over the TV, using the glamour of having been a soldier to promote his media career.

'And no, I don't resent his success,' said Rupert, reading my thoughts. 'I wouldn't want the attention. He does seem to have done surprisingly well though, doesn't he?' He smiled. 'Any truth in the rumour that the books are ghost-written?'

'My lips are sealed,' I demurred, eyes lowered. I myself had been surprised to listen to a tape recently and discover that, although Laurie was reading the script, the text was actually credited to another historian.

'Anyway, he's so busy with the TV work now,' I added loyally. 'I think that's rather taken over from the books.'

'More lucrative too, I should imagine, and hey – why not? His face fits, he's got the credentials, the charm – let someone else provide the brainpower and do the legwork.' He smiled. 'It's always been Laurie's way.'

'So . . . why were you ringing him the other day? When I answered?'

He sighed. 'A while ago he was filming something in Ireland

and came to see us at our headquarters in Armagh. You know, famous TV personality pops into the Mess to have drinks with his old muckers – the boys loved it. Anyway, he went out afterwards with a few of the lads and managed to get a local girl pregnant.'

'Oh God.'

'Exactly. Oh God. He went home, and I ended up picking up the pieces. Since he'd been out with my boys at the time, I felt it was my responsibility. And solutions to such problems are still not readily available in rural Ireland. I was just going to leave a rather terse message with him, about the current state of affairs.'

'You mean . . . you arranged for an abortion? Over here?'

He looked uncomfortable. 'Let's just say he left a few loose ends. It wasn't going to be a social call.'

'Oh.' More of a bollocking call, clearly, from an irritated ex-Commanding Officer. There was obviously no love lost between them. 'He doesn't know I'm seeing you,' I said quickly.

'Good. Probably better that way.'

There was a silence as the implications of what I'd just said sneaked up on us both.

'Am I . . . seeing you?' I said boldly, raising my face to his.

His eyes radiated into mine, blue and steady. I gazed into them. Suddenly I lost my nerve. I turned away.

'So – is this where you sleep?' I faltered, going across to finger the curtains. I was happy fingering curtains.

'No,' he said, recovering quickly. 'Dad kips on the sofa if needs be, but since we're never here at the same time, I use his old room. I'll show you.'

He walked out, snapping off the light as he went and I followed. *Steady, Henny. Just . . . steady. Get that coffee down you quick, girl. Then go.*

'This is me.'

As the door swung open, I saw Andrew's old room. A blue and white checked duvet had replaced the sheets and blankets, and there was a new pine wardrobe, but otherwise, nothing had changed. Memories flooded back like the tide surging up the beach. I remembered when Andrew had gone away one weekend, and we'd spent pretty much forty-eight hours in this bed. Making love, making plans, eating breakfast, getting up only to wander around the Royal Academy and look at the pictures, then on to St James's Park to feed the ducks, then back to bed again. I felt the blood pulsate around my body. Did he remember? Of course he did. Of course. We stared at the bed in silence. A cat suddenly broke the moment, jumping from the top of the wardrobe to the bed, its black form stretched out gracefully – then curling to a ball on a pillow.

'Oh!' I jumped. 'Oh God, don't tell me that's FC. It *can't* be. Not unless he's twenty-five years old.'

Rupert grinned. 'Not FC, but son of.'

'Oh, sweet!' I went across to stroke the huge purring shape, marvelling at the similarity. FC had been a leaving present to Andrew from Peter, Rupert's brother, when he left for Australia. 'Something to remember me by,' he'd grinned, presenting his father with a kitten, wide-eyed and terrified. That went for Andrew, as well.

'A cat?' Andrew had yelped in horror, gazing at the ball of fluff in his hands. 'I don't want a fucking cat!' Thereafter it was known as FC, as in Fucking Cat, which was fine, until it went missing one night. Andrew, by this time and greatly against his better judgement, had become wildly attached to the wretched thing and was miserably trailing up and down Piccadilly in his dressing-gown looking for it in the small hours, when a couple of American tourists stopped, concerned.

'Oh Lord. What's his name?' the wife had enquired, glancing anxiously about.

'FC,' muttered Andrew, peering into a dustbin.

'Oh, how darling. What does it stand for?'

Andrew had turned and gazed at her for a long moment. 'Fanny Cradock,' he'd replied eventually.

We'd always joked — as much as you could with Andrew — that Freud would have had plenty to say about that.

The new cat rolled over in abandonment on the pillow, and I crouched to tickle his tummy.

'What's this one called?'

'AFC.'

'What's the A for?'

'Another.'

I giggled and rubbed under his chin, making him purr like a traction engine. Then I glanced up at Rupert standing beside me.

'Remember that time you put FC out on the landing in the middle of the night? That night I stayed when your father was away, and the front door shut behind you and you had nothing on?'

'And I was ringing the bell and yelling through the letter box, bollock naked while you were in the bath with the radio blaring? Vividly, Henny.'

'And the guy next door,' I snorted, 'what was his name?'

'Sir Henry Thorpe. The Honourable Sir Henry Thorpe.'

'That's it,' I giggled. 'He came back from a black-tie dinner with his wife and you were outside—'

'Shivering, hands over my privates, and Lady Thorpe, who wasn't quite the full sandwich, said excitedly, "Oh look, a corridor-creeper. Tell me, were you coming my way?"'

I laughed and straightened up. My eyes fell on the photographs on the chest of drawers. I stared.

'Oh!' I breathed. 'Is that your brother?'

'Peter,' he agreed. 'All grown up.'

It was a framed snap of Peter on a beach; a smiling, blonde girl beside him and three small children.

'That's his wife Kerry, and my nephews and niece. Kerry's a doctor.'

'Golly,' I boggled. 'Time marches on.' In my day, Peter was the reprobate Andrew worried about, the drop-out who bummed around Bondi Beach telling everyone he was going to be a cameraman.

'He's just shot the latest Scorsese movie. He was over here the other day, actually. Popped in on his way back from Hollywood for a few days. He's having a house built in Sydney. He brought the family. Dad was thrilled.'

'I bet,' I said softly. So Peter had turned out to be the white sheep after all. A steady job, building a house, a wife and kids. My eye roved over the other photographs: a black and white studio shot of his mother in an evening gown and pearls which I remembered of old, and a new one, a beautiful scenic shot of a lake, surrounded by rolling hills, a hint of mountains in the background.

'And this?'

'The view from my cottage in Ireland.'

I picked it up. 'It's beautiful.'

'Isn't it?'

'So how often do you – oh. Sorry.'

The frame had come to pieces in my hands, but before I could fix it, Rupert had taken it from me and was hastily bundling it back together, stuffing in a couple of old pictures which had fallen out of the back and which I didn't have time to see.

'Don't worry, it always does that.'

My eyes travelled back to Peter and his family.

'Rupert, do you ever think . . . I mean, d'you ever wonder . . .'

He put down the frame and his gaze followed mine. 'What, that if things had been different, that might have been me? Sitting on a beach with my wife and kids? A family, a proper home, rather than my dad's old apartment? A proper life? Of course. Not a day goes by when I don't regret it. Not a day goes by without me thinking of you, Henny. Thinking what might have been.'

I looked up at him. His eyes were blue and sincere. Focused on mine. I was unable to look away as I had in the other room. Unable even to blink.

'But . . . you've achieved so much,' I managed. 'So much more than you could have done with me. You've commanded your Battalion, joined the Special Forces, been out in the Gulf – you were even decorated out there.'

'Who told you that?'

'I read about it. It was in the paper.' I remembered Marcus spotting it in the *Telegraph*. Grunting as he read it over breakfast.

'Hmph. Seems your ex-lover has finally covered himself in some sort of glory. Bunged some explosives in the towelheads' direction and got himself a gong for his efforts.'

'Where? Show me.' And I'd avidly read the report.

'I gather you were a bit of a hero,' I murmured. We were

close now, inches apart. I could hear him breathing. 'Pulled an unconscious man back from enemy lines.'

'It's easy to be a hero when you're only looking out for number one. When you're not thinking of the widow, the children.'

'You see?' I said softly. 'I would have held you back.'

'You never held me back.' He lifted a finger and slowly traced a line down my cheek, to my chin. I didn't move. 'I held myself back. Held myself back from loving you, from jumping in feet first to what I instinctively knew to be right. I'm no hero. You were my life-force, Henny. My reason to be. Why I let you go, I'll never know. It was the single most cowardly thing I've ever done in my whole life. After that, I kept on having to prove myself. Prove that I wasn't a flunker. Wasn't windy. But every prize I won for my efforts seemed hollow after the one I'd lost. My rank swelled, and my life got thinner. I was the glory boy with a chest full of medals and an empty heart underneath.'

I felt my own heart pumping away as the blood coursed around my body, tingling in my fingertips, my toes. His face grew closer, our lips a hair's breadth apart.

'When are we going to have that coffee?' I whispered, futilely.

'I think we both know you don't drink the stuff, don't we? Unless your tastes have changed.'

'My tastes haven't changed,' I murmured.

## not that kind of girl

His lips closed on mine, and as he took me in his arms, the room rocked. I rocked with it, losing control of my senses as the years rolled away. As I kissed him, I felt as if I was shedding a skin – my older, middle-aged skin, the one I'd worn as a wife and a mother all these years, and now, standing here in his arms, I felt like the girl again. With the boy I'd loved so much.

And then there was no hesitation. Kissing me wildly, passionately, Rupert slipped my jacket off my shoulders. My hands fumbled for his shirt buttons as, still locked in an embrace, we stumbled towards the bed. His hands plunged into my hair, then cupped my face, as he paused a moment to break off and stare at me, as if he couldn't quite believe it. Then his lips found mine again and he relieved me of my top, struggling with it, rather inelegantly, over my head. We tumbled into bed, but not before my hand had hit the light switch. I wasn't twenty-one any more, and I didn't have the body he remembered, even if, I was astonished to discover, despite being broader and less skinny, he pretty much did. He rolled on top of me and kissed me from my ear down to the base of my neck and I felt my whole body turn to liquid.

'Get it off,' he whispered in my ear.

It was a long time since I'd been ordered to take my clothes off but I struggled obediently with my bra strap. His head jerked back.

'No,' he gasped. 'Bloody cat! It's on my head!'

I glanced up. In the gloom it did look rather as if he had two heads, but that could have been the drink.

'Go *on*!' I gave it a shove. The cat squealed indignantly and landed lightly on the floor, feet first. A second later, he was back, nestling in the crook of my neck.

'Ouch!' I squealed. 'It's got claws!'

'It'll have to go,' muttered Rupert. 'This isn't quite how I envisaged this moment.'

'Chuck it out,' I panted, sitting up and marvelling at the urgency in my voice, at the un-characteristic waves of desire crashing over me, at the longing for his body to be back next to mine as he leaped from the bed. As the blood stormed around me, I was astonished. Delighted, too. After all, I usually regarded this as something of a spectator sport, didn't I? Didn't always join in. With Marcus, that is. *Marcus.* The storming blood froze in my veins.

'I'll shove him out of the kitchen window onto the fire escape,' Rupert promised as he hastened from the room. 'Back in a mo.'

I didn't answer. Stayed sitting bolt upright, my blood still frozen. After a moment, it thawed and my heart began to beat again. I flopped back miserably on my pillows.

Yes, but – think what Marcus has done, I reasoned, desperately trying to claw back ground. What he's probably doing right now! I tried to imagine it, frantically summoning up the requisite images. Ah – Perdita's cottage, that was it, in the picturesque bedroom under the eaves . . . her lithe tanned limbs wrapped around him with – ooh yes, riding boots on, and spurs too. 'Come on, Marcus, faster, gallop!' 'Bastard,' I muttered. Yes. It was sort of working. Oh – and the whip. Don't forget the whip. Go on, Perdita – hit him hard.

'Shit!' came Rupert's voice from the kitchen, along with the sound of breaking glass.

'What's happened?' I called. There was an angry feline squeal.

'Bloody thing jumped back in and knocked a glass off the draining board. Be with you in a minute.'

I heard more swearing and banging around as he doubt-less tried to sweep up the glass. I pulled the duvet up to my chin and stared at the ceiling. Oh come on, come *on*. My nerve was slipping away like mercury now, I could feel it sliding right out of the door and down the street, and summoning up more visions of Marcus on the job didn't seem to be helping. I could see *her* all right, but not him. Every time I tried, I could only see his face, white with anger and contempt, even though he was flat on his back with Perdita astride him riding for England – hard hat on, whip clenched between her teeth . . .

I rolled onto my side and brought up my knees in a foetal position. Would it help, I wondered, if I imagined them in our marital bed? At home? After all, that's what she'd suggested in her email, so perhaps that's where they were now. In our sumptuous cream bedroom, between my Egyptian cotton sheets. I ground my teeth at the thought. Yes, that was doing the trick. How dare they! How dare she slide out of bed and slip into my silk robe? Well, grubby towelling robe, actually, so perhaps she wouldn't, but padding naked into my bathroom, picking up my cleansers and toners and putting them down with a sniffy air, admiring her flushed, post-coital cheeks in my mirror. A warm feeling – could be anger, could be desire, either way it was hot and I was going with it – spread back around my body like a hot spring. Oh, come on, Rupert, come *on*, I've got it now, I thought, fists clenched in triumph. We're getting somewhere! I felt like an impotent man, marvelling at something he didn't see very often and jolly well wanting to run with it before it disappeared.

Finally I heard a door slam shut and Rupert's firm, familiar tread came down the passage. Too firm, perhaps, and rather slow for one intent on his red-hot lover. The door opened. By now, as I'd wrestled with images of Marcus and Perdita, I'd wrestled out of the rest of my clothes too – thrown them aside in a liberated, inebriated fashion. I was sure it would help the nerve, and the libido – and anyway, suddenly I wanted him to see me. Naked. I kicked the duvet aside too. Yes, suddenly I didn't want to hide the Caesarean scar, the fuller bosom, the stretchmarks. I wasn't the girl he'd known, but I was very definitely a woman. I raised my chin as he turned on the light, and let a seductive smile play on my lips. It froze there. For standing framed in the doorway, in his pinstriped suit and Brigade tie, an *Evening Standard* tucked under one arm, was Andrew Ferguson.

# chapter eighteen

I snatched up the duvet and clutched it to my chin, horrified.

'Andrew!'

He stood there, mute with astonishment. Then it dawned.

'Henrietta.'

We stared at each other for a brief, appalled moment, and then he came to. Snapped off the light, went out and quickly shut the door.

'Dad? What the hell are you doing here?' I heard Rupert's voice in the passage.

'Looking for a bed for the night if that's not an unreasonable request.' Andrew's voice was level, but tense. 'I just put my head round your door to see if you were here, but it seems you have company.' He lowered his voice. 'What the hell are you up to, Rupert? She's married, for Christ's sake!'

I lay there, rigid with shock and embarrassment, and didn't

hear Rupert's response, but there was a furious, hissed exchange culminating with Rupert snapping, 'I'll do as I bloody well like!'

Having momentarily lost the will to live, I was suddenly galvanised into action. I leaped out of bed and ran around the room, snatching up my clothes abandoned on the floor. My skirt, my bra – where? Ah, at the foot of the bed – oh God, the shame! With trembling fingers I threw it all on. I was just doing up my shirt, when Rupert came in, pale-faced, a muscle twitching in his cheek.

'You don't have to go, Henny.'

'Of course I do!' I gasped, struggling with my shoes. 'Oh my God, Rupert, I thought you said he was at his girlfriend's!'

'He was, but a relative of hers was taken ill. She had to go, that's why he came back here, but I will *not* have you turfed out in the middle of the night.' He was white with anger. 'Stay, I'll sleep on the sofa.'

'Don't be ridiculous,' I spluttered, 'of course I'm going. I'm married, Rupert, as we keep so conveniently forgetting and as your father has so thoughtfully reminded us.'

'And so is Marcus.' He came in and shut the door.

'So an eye for an eye?' I regarded him steadily.

'But it's not just that, is it?' He came across and put his hands on my shoulders. 'This would have happened anyway. It would have happened regardless of his infidelity, you know that, Henny. In your heart you know this was meant to be.'

I gazed into his clear, confident blue eyes. So sure. So convinced we were meant to be together. I glanced down.

'Maybe.'

He lifted my chin with his finger so I had to look at him.

'I don't know,' I whispered. 'I feel so confused. And so ashamed, right now. Oh God, Rupert, your father . . . He saw me—'

'In bed, so what?'

I gulped. Yes, well, slightly more than just in bed, actually, but we wouldn't go into that right now. I reached for my handbag.

'I'll get a taxi,' I said.

'I'll ring for one for you.'

'No, I'll go out and get it.' I didn't want to hang around here any longer than was necessary.

'I'll come with you.'

'Rupert, you don't have to—'

'Henny, of *course* I'll get you a taxi. What – you think I'd let you wander around on your own at two o'clock in the morning? I'll get my coat.'

My own coat, I recalled, was still in the sitting room where I'd left it. Without thinking, I nipped across the landing and through the open door to get it. It was dark, but I knew it was on the far side, on the window seat. I went quickly across and picked it up, but as I turned, I saw Andrew sitting facing me on the sofa opposite the window, still in his suit, a glass of whisky in his hand. Just – sitting in the dark. The moon from the uncurtained window washed palely over his face. I stopped still. Our eyes met for the second time that night.

'This is no place for you, Henny.'

It was said softly. Kindly, almost. It was also the first time he'd ever called me Henny. I swallowed. Nodded.

'I know.' Then I put my head down and hurried from the room.

Rupert was waiting for me by the front door. He let me out.

'He was in there,' I muttered.

He swung around. 'Oh God. Sorry.'

I shook my head. We clattered downstairs.

'When I heard a door close,' I gabbled, 'I thought it was you, putting the cat out.'

'No, I was still trying to shove him out the kitchen window, but every time I tried, he shot back in again. Dirty little voyeur.'

'The cat, or your father?' I said grimly as we marched through the hall to the front door.

He grinned as we reached the street. It was raining now.

'Forget it, Henny. God, we're practically middle-aged – who cares what my father thinks?'

'I know,' I said miserably. 'But he makes me feel about seventeen again. I always was terrified of him. Felt he didn't think I was good enough for you.'

343

'Did you?' He turned from scanning the road for a taxi to look at me, astonished.

'Didn't you know that?' I shook my head, bemused. 'How little you know, Rupert. He knew it. I knew it. My mother knew it. Everyone knew it. And yet, just now . . .'

'What?' Rupert's hand shot out as he spotted a cab.

'Well, he was almost nice to me. Almost . . . gentle. He just said, "This is no place for you, Henny".' I remembered his eyes. Filling up, almost.

'God, he can talk,' snorted Rupert. 'As if a bimbo's flat is any place for *him*. Here we go.'

A taxi swished wetly to a halt beside us, the rain dripping from its hubcaps. Rupert turned and took me in his arms. The rain was coming down steadily now, soaking our hair, my upturned face. He cupped my face in his hands and kissed me very thoroughly on the lips. I felt my legs turn to jelly as one long kiss unfurled after another. Deep down in the engine room all mechanisms purred, well-oiled, ticking over very nicely, thank you. Lack of real opportunity in the sodden street made me braver, more brazen, and as I came up for air my hands were inside his coat, up his jumper on his warm skin. I was breathing heavily too. Practically looking for a convenient bus shelter.

'In yer own time,' said a bored voice.

We drew apart and I gazed at Rupert wantonly. I couldn't believe I was being so shameless. Such a hussy. At nearly three in the morning, in the middle of Central London. But it felt so good. So right. And I was loving every minute of it. Desperate for more.

'I'll ring you,' he whispered. 'Tomorrow.'

'Right!' I gasped, for gasp was all I could do. Aside from shoo the taxi away and kiss him again. Rupert bundled me in.

'Twenty-four Campden Hill Grove, Kensington,' he informed the driver, and I sank into its black depths with a sigh.

As we accelerated down towards Hyde Park Corner, I turned round to look at Rupert, standing there in that familiar lopsided stance, his hands in his pockets, head cocked to one side, the rain streaming off his blond head. I waited till he was out of sight, then twisted to the front again.

'*I love him,*' I said to myself. Then aloud, in surprise: 'I love him.'

'Pleased to hear it,' grunted the driver, whose partition window, I hadn't realised, was open. 'I'd hate to think you'd kiss a man like that if you didn't. Don't look like that kind of a girl.'

'I'm not,' I said in surprise, blushing. 'No, I'm not.' Suddenly I had one of those awful moments when you want to bare your soul to a complete stranger.

'I knew him years ago, you see. Almost married him.'

'Ah.'

'And now . . . well, now I've found him again after all these years – fifteen actually – it's quite bizarre. I feel exactly the same, as if we're just picking up from where we left off, without skipping a beat. Isn't that extraordinary?'

'Yeah, it is,' he agreed, but he shot me a wary look and fiddled with his radio, trying to tune it in.

'And although I know it can't be right,' I ploughed on, 'I'm married, you see, two children, so all terribly complicated . . . I know it's not entirely *wrong*, either, if you know what I mean. I feel so happy. So *alive*. Surely that can't be wrong?'

The driver, alarmed, turned his music up.

'I feel like a new woman,' I said in surprise, inching forward excitedly in my seat, keen to share. 'I feel stirrings in my soul,' I raised my voice over the music, 'that I didn't know were possible. And not just in my soul, either. Physically, too. Deep down.'

He reached behind him and gingerly shut the partition.

'And d'you know, I don't even wonder where this will go, what will become of us, what they'll say about us – family, friends, society, the Church,' I ranted, temporarily forgetting in my fervour that I didn't even go to church, unless you counted carol concerts and Christingles. 'I just feel . . . well.' I sank back in the seat and smiled, a beatific smile, anointing the wet streets . . . those heavenly streets. And those heavenly lamp-posts, too. 'Well, I feel blessed.'

346

# not that kind of girl

When I got to the flat, still grinning foolishly, I rewarded my man handsomely for sharing my spiritual experience. He pocketed his tip with a weary nod as his due for having to escort yet another loved-up inebriate home in the small hours, and departed. Except, I stopped still on the path as I went to the door, I wasn't inebriated. Not now. I had been before, at Penny's, and possibly at Rupert's too, but it was wearing off, and I was sure the magical glow that surrounded me, this lovely, warm aura that I felt so keenly, was not alcohol, but love. True love.

Exhilarated, I bounded up the stairs, and with joy in my heart and excitement fizzing in every vein, let myself in. The flat was dark and cold, the heating having gone off long ago, so I put a match to the gas-effect fire in the drawing room. Just for two minutes, I decided, shivering, while I made myself a hot milky drink and drank it in front of the flames, before tumbling into bed. I wouldn't sleep immediately anyway, I reasoned, being too much on fire myself.

The flames leaped instantly to life, and as they did, I spotted another light flashing across the other side of the room. En route to the kitchen I pressed the button and, as I was waiting for the kettle to boil, listened with one ear to the messages. First to my mother telling me that Barkers were having a sale and she'd managed to secure a whole *heap* of towels at rock-bottom prices – very good quality and far too many for her, so would I like some for the farm (no prizes for guessing where she was pushing me and nearly dislocating her elbow in the process), and then to Benji, saying something in a rather strained voice that I almost didn't recognise. I frowned, put the cocoa tin down and went back to the drawing room. Erasing Mum, I pressed play again and squatted down, noting that the time of the message was 1 a.m. Only a couple of hours or so ago.

'Henny, it's Benji. Um, bad news, I'm afraid. Dad's had a minor heart attack. It's nothing serious, they assure us, but they've moved him from the Nursing Home to the Royal Free for monitoring. I'm here now with Mum, but there's no need for you to dash out. We just felt you ought to know. You can reach me here, on my mobile, or ring in the morning. They'll probably move him back tomorrow, anyway.'

I stared at the machine. Played the message again. Felt the gaiety of two minutes ago drip off me like the rain down the darkened windows. Dad had had a heart attack. They'd said he might, a few years ago, when he'd had twinges in his upper arm, plus pins and needles. A warning, they'd called it. And he'd taken pills to thin the blood. But somehow, one had never really expected it. He was always so fighting fit in the Home – fighting being the operative word – and one always felt too that with senile dementia, he couldn't have another illness, could he? To compound it? One was enough. It simply wasn't fair. He had enough on his plate. Or more to the point, Mum did.

Mum. I straightened up. Thought of her worn, brave face in the cafeteria last week, her single-minded doggedness to get through this come what may. I knew that she was by his bed right now, that same, anxious, won't-let-go expression on her face, her hands tightly clasped, as if the tighter she clenched them, the better things would get, the rings he'd given her for marriage, for two children, for eternity, biting into her hands.

I picked up the phone and punched out Benji's mobile number, but it was turned off. I tried Francis's, but that was off, too. Damn.

Still in my coat, I snatched up the door keys and went across the room to shut the gas supply off from the fire. Then I let myself out of the flat and locked the door. Yes, it was nearly morning by now and yes, he'd said not to bother, but if Benji was there, I could be too. Could be there for Mum. Good heavens, the three of us had sat in enough hospital cafeterias together over the last four years – one more wouldn't hurt. And anyway, I thought, clattering down the stairs, the coffee at the Royal Free had yet to be sampled. I couldn't let them savour that experience on their own.

Naturally there wasn't a taxi to be seen in residential Kensington at that time in the morning, so naturally I had to walk, or rather trot, through the gridwork of streets. The grand white townhouses towered over me and the rarefied pavements practically squeaked with indignation as I jogged all the way down Church Street to the main road. A fair dollop of my adrenaline, I knew, came courtesy of my evening with Rupert, and I was shocked to realise I was relieved to have a channel for it; an excuse not to go to bed. I was quite sure I wouldn't have slept. Would have lain there, wide-eyed, my heart racing all night.

I jogged on past Barkers, scene of my mother's triumph this morning: piles of discounted linen sat in darkened windows now, their slashed prices less urgent in the gloom. I thought of Mum, happily battling away in there today, an experienced sale-goer, a bargain-hunter *par excellence*, unaware, as she muscled professionally through the scrum, intent on her battle to secure at least 50 per cent off the recommended retail price, where she would end her day.

A lone taxi cruised up a side street towards me minus its yellow light, but I flagged it down anyway. It purred to a halt beside me. A tired, elderly face peered out.

'I was goin' home, but if it's on the way to Kilburn?'

'The Royal Free?'

'Yer in luck.'

Off we trundled. I perched on the edge of the seat and gripped the handrail hard. I hoped Dad wasn't being too beastly to Mum. Wasn't telling her in a loud, carrying voice not to darken his sickbed door since he didn't even know who she was, for crying out loud, and that even if he did, he certainly wouldn't have married her. Let alone procreated with her. I saw her lips, compressed and brave, her chin raised as he flirted with the nurses, enquiring, with a louche wink, if he'd be lucky enough to have the pleasure of that particular little blonde's company tonight, fiddling with his tubes? Monitoring his heartbeat, giving him a bedbath, perhaps . . . ? Finally I imagined him dropping off to sleep; a drug-induced sleep probably, and Mum still not stirring. Looking down on his sleeping form; his face, softened by slumber to resemble the husband she'd once known, the more kindly, gentle one. I imagined her face softening too, as she reached out and took his hand, without his knowledge, without fear of reproach.

As the taxi pulled up in Pond Street, I jumped out and paid the fare. The Royal Free was a huge place, and one I was unfamiliar with, which was a rarity. Benji had once considered writing a Good Hospital Guide, with entries such as: *Chelsea and Westminster: lovely minimalist décor, but disappointing public conveniences, and at all costs avoid the bootfaced Sister on the fifth floor. Charing Cross: heavenly nurses, good shop in foyer that sells Walnut Whips and Curly Wurlies, but has a lunatic doctor in the psychiatric ward who should probably be sectioned himself, etc.* This one, though, we didn't know.

As ever, I found the main reception with difficulty – another topic to be tackled in Benji's book – but happily there was a girl on the desk. I was about to ask her for the cardiac ward when I spotted a familiar figure sitting by the coffee-machine. His head was bowed and his elbows rested on his knees. His clasped hands drooped between them.

351

'Francis?'

He looked up. Saw me. And in that instant, as our eyes met, I knew. I stopped in my tracks.

Francis got up and came towards me, his face grey. He lifted his arms up from his sides, then dropped them again in a helpless gesture. It was all there. All of it. But still I wanted to hear the words.

'He's dead?' I whispered, almost gagging on the words.

He nodded. His eyes were full of love and sorrow.

'Yes. I'm so sorry, Henny. He's dead.'

# chapter nineteen

Francis held me for a long time. I didn't cry, didn't sob, just stayed frozen and mute in his arms, my head on his chest. My eyes were wide and disbelieving as I gazed at the small checked pattern on his shirt. He smelled of soap powder, clean skin, a hot iron. In my peripheral vision, I could see the girl on reception, head down, studiously ignoring us, finding some paperwork to do. How many grieving families must she have seen, I wondered. How many times had she had to turn delicately away? Go home to her husband and say, 'Oh God, another one today, Ted. Another poor family in floods.' And Ted, from his slumped position in front of the television would grunt, 'Well, if you will work in the same building as the Grim Reaper. Cup of tea?' 'Please.' And she'd take off her shoes and rub her sore toes, and that would be it. As much as it would impinge on her consciousness. And why should it? And why should I be thinking of her, of her life, I thought, shocked. When my father . . .

'Where's Mum?' I raised my head.

'Upstairs.'

'With Benji?'

'Yes.'

'So when . . . ?'

'About half an hour ago.'

I inhaled sharply. Gritted my teeth. 'Francis, he shouldn't have died.' My voice, when it came, was low and shaky. 'It was only a minor heart attack, Benji said—'

'I know.' He squeezed my rigid, wooden shoulder. 'I know what he said. This shouldn't have happened. It wasn't in the script.'

After a while, I stepped back from him. 'I'll go up,' I told him.

'Sure?'

'Sure.'

Together we found the lifts and made our way up to the cardiac wards. As Francis led me down one bleak grey corridor after another, the lino floor squeaky underfoot, I felt numb, unreal, as if I was walking through this hospital in someone else's body. We passed a couple of open wards, then Francis stopped at a little side room and opened the door. Mum and Benji were sitting on the far side of the room, Benji holding Mum's clenched fist in his lap. Two untouched cups of tea were cooling in front of them. I instantly recognised the venue from all my hours of hospital drama viewing as The Room Where They Tell The Relatives. Mum's face was grey, the colour of the ashtray in front of her which had been emptied but not washed. I swooped to hug her. She didn't hug me back, but remained impassive, leaden. Benji got up and held out his arms. I walked into them. He held me close. I could tell he'd been crying.

'Benj.'

'Henny Penny,' he whispered, using my childhood name.

'Daddy!' I sobbed suddenly, tears scuttling up my throat like a high-speed lift.

'I know.'

And I knew he knew. As I broke down and wept, great shoulder-shaking sobs that wracked my body, making me hiccup and shudder and catch my breath in pain, I knew he knew. I wasn't crying for the Dad we'd known for the last few years, who we'd only seen in Homes and hospitals, sliding further and further into dementia, into someone we didn't recognise, but for the Daddy we'd had when we were little. The kind, reflective, calming influence that our family had relied on. The Daddy who'd taken us to the Baths at Swiss Cottage on a Sunday morning and taught us to swim, then on to the library to choose books, or up to the Heath to fly kites. The Daddy who would settle us outside the Smugglers Inn with a bottle of Coke and a packet of crisps while he calmly smoked his pipe and read the *Observer* and Mum flapped around at home in her Marigolds, engulfed in steam as she got the Sunday lunch. Daddy the peacemaker, the diplomat, the voice of reason when my mother's voice grew shriller and shriller. The one we'd go to in a crisis, shutting the study door softly behind us, creeping in. 'Um, Daddy, you know Mum says I can't go to Lizzie's party because we have to see Gran . . .' That Daddy. The one who found a way round Mum for us. The one who'd gripped my hand so tightly on the way back from that church in Hanover Square. The one who'd said he'd rather stick needles in his eyes than have a son who was a queer – his words – and then, the following year, had included Francis in the family holiday. And driven miles in the searing Provençal heat to find a doctor when Francis reacted badly to mosquito bites. That Daddy.

Benji held me close as I sobbed on and on. I never knew I had so many tears. At length though, the deluge subsided and I grew calmer. I drew away from him: blew my nose, exhausted. I looked down at Mum, still inert in her chair. Silent.

'She's in shock,' said Benji softly.

'I'm not in shock, actually,' she said quietly. 'I'm thinking very clearly.'

Benji and I waited. I wiped my eyes with the heels of my hands. They were shaking, I noticed. Mum sat there, hands clasped, not looking at us but staring straight ahead, her eyes over-bright. She was wearing a houndstooth jacket and skirt and black patent shoes, and her honey-blonde hair was swept back from her face and around her ears, immaculate as ever. Benji sat beside her.

'What are you thinking, Mum?'

'What neither of you are saying. That in a way it's a blessed relief. A release from a life that was so dire. So awful. That all he did was sit in plastic chairs in geriatric Homes, that the man we knew would rather be dead than be in the places he's been over the last few years. Would rather be dead than suffer the indignities, the bedbaths, the over-familiarity, the patronising and the institutionalising. That the Daddy you and Henny are mourning would have taken this way out years ago. Like a shot.'

I sat down on the other side of her, shocked. 'But that doesn't make it any easier surely, Mum?'

'Oh, I think it does. I've grieved so much over the years for the Gordon I knew, the man I married, and now . . . I almost feel I've got him back again.' She turned to me. 'Have you seen him?'

I stared at her, horrified. 'No. I . . .' I shrank away.

'Don't you want to?'

'Well . . .'

'Henny, do,' she insisted, taking my hand. 'Benji and I were there when he died, and we held his hands. Both of us. I'm so grateful for that.'

I glanced up at Benji. He nodded soberly.

'I'd like you to see him too,' she urged. 'He's so peaceful. So calm. So like your daddy.'

Still holding my hand she stood up, nodding at me encouragingly. I swallowed and looked appealingly at Benji. He shrugged, miserably, helplessly. At length I took a deep breath and let her lead me out of the room and down the corridor. Benji followed. Mum stopped opposite another side room, and Benji went to have a word with a nurse. She glanced at me; nodded, and came across to open the door. Benji put a hand on my arm as I was about to go in. Searched my face anxiously.

'Do you want to do this, Henny?'

I looked at Mum. I wasn't at all sure I did, but she wanted me to, and actually, I thought as I went in, gripping Mum's hand, she had a point. I approached slowly. A white sheet was tucked right up around Dad's chin. I looked down at his face.

He looked dead: that was the first thing that struck me. He didn't look as if he was asleep, as some people say: people don't sleep like that, so – abandoned, the flesh falling away down the side of his face; so waxy pale. But on the other hand, Mum was right. It was Daddy. My Daddy. Not the hideous caricature we'd come to know. I wanted to bend down and kiss his forehead, knew that was the sort of thing I should do, had seen grieving families do it in films. But I'd never kissed his forehead before.

After a moment, I turned and walked away. I headed out of the room and across the corridor to the window opposite; clutched the sill, taking in deep breaths. Great gulps of air filled my lungs which felt squeezed of oxygen. Benji and Mum followed.

'All right?'

I nodded quickly. 'Yes. You were right, Mum. I'm glad I've seen him. That's how I remember him. How he was before he was ill.'

The glue that had somehow held me together in that room suddenly came unstuck, and as I cracked, tears streamed down my cheeks. Benji's too. We clung to each other for a long time. When we parted, Mum was over by the window, staring out at the night. Mute, drawn into herself. I went to go to her, but Benji held my arm, shook his head.

'She *is* in shock,' he murmured. 'She doesn't know it, but she is. Leave her.'

After a bit, a doctor materialised from somewhere and spoke to Benji in a low voice about administrative details, I don't know what. When he'd gone, we stayed for a while, the three of us, huddled in that corridor. I had an awful sense that if we went, Daddy would be moved. That he'd be taken out of the hospital where he'd only just crossed the line, was only just dead, and into the world of the really dead: the land of slabs and mortuaries. I wanted to keep him here, in limbo land, for a little bit longer.

Eventually, though, Francis appeared. I realised he'd tact-fully absented himself, having delivered me to my family. He raised kind eyes at Benji.

'Home?'

Benji nodded. 'Home.'

I turned. 'But where's Mum going to—'

'With us,' he said firmly. 'She's staying with us. For a few nights. Henny, if you want to . . .'

'No.' I shook my head. 'No, I'm going home too.'

There didn't seem much point in going to bed when I got back to the flat, so I turned an armchair around to face the window and sat with my feet up on the sill, my head lolling back, looking up at the moon. And then I went a long way away. I covered a lot of ground that night, a lot of miles: trawled through a good many years. At first I wished I had my photograph albums with me, but actually, I didn't need them. I shut my eyes and all the best pictures came to me. I saw him coming into the flat on a gust of cold wind, a package in his hands, excitement in his eyes as he slipped into his study to open it in private, this precious find, a new book about the D-Day landings. I saw him after the fathers' race at sports day, coolly accepting his prize of After Eights, my friends' eyes popping as they clapped my bookish father who could also shift. I saw him showing me how to trace with greaseproof paper, how to make glue with flour, how to whistle through a blade of grass. I saw him running for a bus at Swiss Cottage with Benji on his shoulders, Benji shrieking with laughter as they caught it. I saw him playing French cricket with us in the communal gardens behind the flats, bat in both hands, pipe in mouth. Mostly though, I saw the wry humour and intelligence in his face; the quizzical gleam in his eye as he asked me, casually, if Custer was staging a last stand in the Finchley Road I had so much war-paint on my face.

Eventually, a cold light crept up on the sky and the darkness shrank away. I was glad. Glad it was no longer the day my father had died.

At a reasonable hour, I rang Marcus. He was silent on the other end. Shocked. Eventually, his voice came, slightly taut. He'd loved him too.

'Henny, I'm so sorry.'

'Thank you,' I managed.

Another silence. Then: 'I hadn't realised . . . well, the last attack he'd had was so minor, only a twinge. I hadn't realised . . .'

'None of us had, Marcus.'

'No. Poor Gordon.'

'Poor Dad.' I put the receiver against my stomach. Squeezed my eyes tight shut. Then I wiped my face with the back of my hand.

'Still there?' he said softly, when I replaced it to my ear.

'Still here.' I took a deep breath to steady myself. Let it out shakily.

'Marcus, I'm going to see the children at school today. Going to go and tell them. Then, if they want to come to the funeral, they can.'

'Oh.' He was quiet. Thoughtful. But he knew I had the upper hand. Knew that whatever I said, went. They say love changes everything: but death does, too.

'And I'll be there at the farm for them if they want to come home.'

'Right.' I could hear the cogs of his mind whirring.

'Not for ever, Marcus, just for a few days. It's just I don't think this is quite the moment to also tell them their parents are splitting up, do you?'

'No,' he said shortly. Embarrassed, perhaps. 'No, it's not.'

'Let's let them get over this little hurdle, and then choose another exeat for your Savoy Grill surprise, agreed?'

He caught his breath. It was said with unnecessary venom, but I couldn't help it.

'Agreed,' he said meekly.

Another silence hung between us.

'Give them my love, Henny,' he said eventually. 'And to you, too. Look after yourself.'

I nodded. Couldn't speak, so instead put down the phone.

After a few moments, when I'd blown my nose and made myself a cup of strong black coffee, I rang the schools and arranged to go down that afternoon. I also asked for a day off for each of the children to attend the funeral. Then I rang Laurie. I'd hoped to leave a message on his machine, but he answered in person.

'Poor you,' he murmured. 'How awful. And it comes in waves, doesn't it? Great, head-crushing waves. One moment you think you're perfectly all right, and the next, you've hit the deck.'

'Yes. Yes, that's it,' I said, surprised. 'Who . . . ?'

'My sister. Four years ago. Cancer.'

'I'm sorry.'

We were silent. It seemed everyone was touched. No one was immune. Everyone had their story.

'Take as long as you like, Henny. Only come back when you're ready.'

'Thank you.'

The last thing I did was to send Rupert an email, telling him what had happened and why he wouldn't find me at home. Why I was turning my mobile off for the day.

Since I didn't have a car in London, I borrowed Benji's to get to the schools, picking it up in Chelsea.

'Where's Mum?' I asked as I followed him through to his kitchen to collect the keys.

'In bed.'

'Ah. Has she cried?'

'All morning.'

I nodded. 'Good.'

He walked me back to the car, gave me a hug goodbye, then stood on the pavement, watching as I drove away. He'd never reminded me of Dad, I thought, as I watched him in the rearview mirror, but actually, there was something in his stillness today. His composure. He bent his head and went back inside.

As I cruised easily out of London and down to the country in Benji's sleek BMW, I felt faintly soothed by its expensive purring, its classical music, its leather and chrome. It insulated me from the outside world, from the horrors of last night, and I began to feel a bit better. It came as a surprise then, when Elgar's *Nimrod* came on the radio and I had to pull over to howl. I couldn't see, I was crying so much. It was a piece that sawed through me at the best of times, but now, at the worst of times, it opened me up. How right you are, Laurie, I thought, stuffing a sodden tissue back in my bag in a layby and blinking madly. One moment you're fine, the next, you're on the floor. I turned the engine over again. How right you are.

Angus's school was my first port of call. Set in acres of rolling Northamptonshire countryside, it was looming, Gothic and grey, with plenty of arrogant turrets and sneering gargoyles set at the end of a long drive. The main body of it was grouped around a quadrangle, which was accessed through a stone archway. I parked just outside the arch and walked through, making my way to one of the more modern houses behind the ancient façade. As I passed by a ground-floor window, I spotted Angus's house master behind his desk in his study. He instantly got to his feet as he saw me and I realised he'd been waiting. I couldn't help smiling. He was a tiny man, terribly formal and correct, and as he came to the front door to greet me, his Brylcreemed head was bowed low. It wouldn't have surprised me if he'd been sporting a black armband. He took my hand in both of his, like a vicar, and gazed respectfully at my shoes.

'My sincere condolences, Mrs Levin,' he murmured.

'Thank you.'

'It must have been a terrible shock.'

'Yes. It was rather sudden. Does Angus . . . ?'

He raised his head a fraction. 'I'm afraid I took the liberty of telling him, because once he knew you were coming, he imagined the worst. His father, perhaps, or his sister. Divorce on the cards, maybe . . . you know how an adolescent mind works.'

'Er, yes.' So divorce was worse. Heavens. I swallowed and followed him inside to his study.

'But I have to warn you, Mrs Levin,' he shut the study door behind us and laid a sombre hand on my arm, 'he has yet to emote.'

'Oh, right.' I tried not to smile. The idea of Angus 'emoting' in front of this stiff little man was unimaginable.

'Perhaps he has in private,' I suggested. 'You know, in his room. And the thing is, Mr Cartwright, for the last six years my father was an invalid. He was in a Home. He had senile dementia, and didn't recognise his grandchildren. We stopped taking them to see him when it became upsetting.'

This much was true, although on one occasion recently, Angus had come with me. I'd been getting ready to go to London to see Dad, and had been surprised when Angus had said he'd like to come. He'd played whist in the day room with him and Dad kept glaring at him and asking him who the devil he was. When Angus won the game, he called him a flaming cheat. I smiled, remembering Angus calmly dealing the cards out again and letting him win the next game. Dad eyed him suspiciously. 'Flaming yobbo.'

'Ah! The lad himself.'

Angus, looking awkward, was ushered into the room. His hair needed washing and his shirt was hanging out.

'Hi, Mum.'

'Hi, darling.' I pecked his cheek quickly.

'Now. I'll leave you.' Mr Cartwright bowed again, almost in half this time, and seemed to shuffle out backwards, wringing his hands like Uriah Heep.

I gave Angus a proper hug and we sank down on the sofa, relieved to be alone.

'He wants me to burst into tears, Mum, and I can't,' Angus said despairingly.

I smiled. 'I know.' I patted his hand.

'I mean, the thing is,' he struggled to explain. 'It's awful for you and everything, and I'm really sad for you, Mum,' I squeezed his hand, grateful, 'but to be honest, I didn't really know Grandpa. Except when he was normal, when he was younger, and that was ages ago. And I can't help thinking . . . well, I know it's an awful thing to say 'cos he's your dad . . .'

'No, say it, Angus.'

'Well, wouldn't he rather it was this way?' He twisted to look at me; honest, fifteen-year-old eyes. 'Rather than going on like that in that awful Home? I know I would,' he said with feeling.

I thought of Mum's similar sentiments. 'If you mean, would the man I knew six years ago . . .'

'The real grandpa,' he put in.

'Would he have wanted to die? Then yes.'

Yes. I could just hear him. Could just see him too, in the flat in the Finchley Road, glancing up from the *Independent* at breakfast, over his glasses – 'What? Go ga-ga? In some nuthouse? Jesus, shoot me, would you?' Leaning back in his chair to call around the kitchen door, 'Audrey, slip me a cyanide sandwich if it ever comes to that, all right?'

'But the thing is, Angus,' I struggled on, 'as the man he'd become . . . well, he was very happy. Content.'

'Bollocks,' Angus said angrily, getting up and going to the

window. He thrust his hands in his pockets and stared out. 'He'd have been horrified if he could have seen himself. Seen what he'd become.' He glared defiantly at the cricket pitch, the autumn leaves billowing across it from the oaks over-hanging the boundary.

I smiled down at my hands. The arrogance of youth. There was only one way to be, and that was strong, vital, fit and most definitely *compos mentis*. No half-measures. Anything else, any compromise, was a waste of time.

'Well, whatever,' I said softly. 'You may be right, darling.' I eyed his straight back as he stayed at the window, watching the groundsman rake the leaves away from the wicket.

'I'd like to come to the funeral, though,' he said, turning. 'Like to say goodbye properly.'

I nodded. 'Good. I'd like you to come.' Hadn't wanted to force it, though.

'Anyway,' he added thoughtfully, 'I've never been to a funeral before.'

I smiled. It was said rather as if he'd never been to an ice-hockey match. Or a bar mitzvah. A life experience to be ticked.

We chatted some more, and then we went for a wander outside. Angus took me down to the lower playing-fields and we watched a bit of a football match that he would have been in if I hadn't been coming. When the games master came across and asked if he wanted to go on for the second half,

Angus looked momentarily delighted, then glanced nervously at me.

'Of course, darling.' I hugged him. 'I'd much rather you were scoring goals. Go on, go and get changed. I've got to go and see Lily, anyway.'

'OK. Give her my love, by the way.'

'I will.'

Now that was a first.

He shot off to get changed and I folded my arms against the wind and headed slowly back to the car. As I walked up the gravel path, Mr Cartwright emerged from his house to say goodbye.

'And rest assured, Mrs Levin,' he purred, bustling me to the car, 'Angus is in good hands. As you know, we pride ourselves on our pastoral care here at Shelbourne. We'll give him all the counselling he requires.'

'Er . . . right. Thank you.' Out of the corner of my eye, I saw Angus, already changed into his strip, racing down the lower lawn to unceremoniously hoof the reserve off and take up his rightful position at left back. 'Although I'm not entirely convinced that counselling will be necessary . . .'

Lily's school was a different story. When I arrived at the rambling Victorian pile in Berkshire with its pointy red-tiled roofs and crumbling green paintwork, the front door appeared to be locked. No one came when I rang the bell, so I went round the back, pushed through a side door and wandered up and down some empty corridors until I found a pretty sixth-former with long soft hair and beautiful manners, painting her nails in a science lab.

'Oh, they're all in prep,' she assured me, slipping off the desk. She showed me into the Headmistress's study, which was also empty, then disappeared, promising to find her for me.

I sat down facing the leather-topped desk, and after a while, the door flew open and in bustled Miss Whitehorn, the Deputy Head.

'Sorry! Sorry!' she gasped. A newly appointed member of staff, she was very large and very breathless. On our first meeting with her last term, Marcus had whispered confidently in my ear, 'Lesbian.' Her spectacular bust was heaving now and her gown flapping as she flew to greet me, wreathed in smiles as I got up.

'*Mrs* Levin.' She shook my hand warmly, and rather painfully, actually, her rings were so numerous. 'What a *lovely* surprise.'

'Er, well. Not too much of a surprise, surely? Only I did telephone . . .'

'Oh yes, yes, I believe we did get the message, but still, lovely of you to come in person. Sit! Sit!'

She waved a commanding, chubby hand and bustled around to the other side of the desk to take up Mrs Hargreave's rightful position. She lowered her enormous bottom carefully as if anticipating a creak, then safely installed, beamed widely.

'Mrs Hargreave sends *sincere* apologies, but she's still hammering away at the Duke of Edinburgh, I'm afraid.'

I blinked, taken aback. Gracious. Mrs Hargreaves and Prince Philip? 'Oh?'

'The Fourths are taking their award this term. Need to brush up on their sheepshanks. So – will I do?' She twinkled across the desk at me.

'Of course. Um, is Lily . . . ?'

'*So* excited, dear girl. Because you know,' she leaned forward and winked, 'they do love a day off.'

'Oh. Yes.'

'Saturday week, isn't it?'

'Um, no. Next Thursday, probably.'

'Thursday? Really?' She sat back and looked surprised. 'Unusual day. Tell me,' she leaned forward eagerly again and clasped her hands, 'what's she going to wear?' She hissed excitedly.

'Um, w-well,' I faltered, 'I'm not sure. Haven't really thought. Not black, I don't think.'

'Oh no no!' She threw up her hands in mock horror. 'That wouldn't do at all. Mind you, these young girls,' she twinkled at me conspiratorially, 'wouldn't put it past them. They do love their grunge. Their,' she posted quotation marks in the air, 'Goth! So – where's it to be?'

'Oh, er, a little chapel in North London.' My palms felt a bit sweaty on my skirt.

'Lovely! A low-key affair?'

'Well, yes. I think so.'

'Super! And a party afterwards?'

I shifted uncomfortably in my seat. 'A glass of sherry and a sandwich perhaps. At my mother's.'

'Splendid.' She beamed. 'Your mother must be very excited, I imagine?'

I stared. 'I'm sorry?'

'Your mother – seeing her first granddaughter married?' she prompted.

I stared some more. Miss Whitehorn's head tilted to one side. 'Lily's older sister?' she said encouragingly, widening her eyes as if perhaps I were educationally subnormal. 'Getting married?'

I licked my lips. 'Lily doesn't have a sister. I'm here because her grandfather's died.'

She gazed at me across the desk, her eyes uncomprehending. Then she straightened up and looked down at her notes. Shuffled through them.

'I'm so sorry,' she murmured at length. 'That's another girl – Amelia Wade-Walker. Her mother's coming to see me, wanting to take her out for a . . . yes. Yes, I do see now.' She peered nervously at her notes. 'Got in a bit of a muddle. I'm so sorry. Yes, Lily.' She removed her glasses. Folded her hands and lowered her head decorously.

'Sincere condolences, Mrs Levin.'

By the time Lily was eventually found and ushered into the room I was feeling faintly giggly and having to breathe hard through my teeth. Miss Whitehorn muttered her apologies and exited swiftly, gown flying.

'Why are you smiling, Mummy?' cried Lily, launching herself into my arms. 'It's so sad. Poor Grandpa!'

'I know, poor Grandpa,' I agreed, hugging her close and kissing the top of her head fiercely. 'I'm sorry, Lily, I think I'm getting faintly hysterical. Grief and hysteria appear to be very closely linked.'

Lily had a good cry which made me cry too, but then she cheered up enormously when I said Miss Whitehorn had given me permission to take her out to tea. Miss Whitehorn would have let me take her to the moon, if I'd wanted.

'With Rosie?' she asked, wiping her face and turning wet, appealing eyes on me. 'Can Rosie come too?'

'I don't see why not.'

And off she ran, sniffing, to inform her best friend.

Tea was a great success. Rosie, whose family were staunch Roman Catholics with their own private chapel at their pile in Ireland, went into ghoulish detail over the chocolate cake about her own grandfather's funeral, and how Lily had to be prepared to see him laid out at the altar *with the lid off*.

'Will I?' Lily asked later, eyes wide with fear as I hugged her goodbye in the drive. 'Will I really have to do that?'

'Of course not, darling. The lid will be firmly on, and you don't have to come at all if you don't want to.'

She gave this some thought. 'Is Angus coming?'

'He is, but he's two years older than you.'

She paused. 'No, I do want to come. I definitely want to.'

I smiled, gave her another hug, and then got in the car. She knocked on the window and I buzzed it down.

'Daddy will be coming, won't he?' she asked anxiously.

My heart stopped for a moment. 'Of course. Why d'you say that?'

She shrugged. Lowered her eyes and scuffed her toe in the gravel. 'Dunno. It's just . . . you came on your own today.'

'Because Daddy's working,' I said quickly.

She glanced up. Nodded, then grinned. 'Yeah, OK. Bye then, Mum. See you next week.'

I let the hand-brake out and purred slowly off down the drive. As I watched her wave me off in the rearview mirror, standing alone in the middle of the drive in her maroon school uniform, my stomach lurched with fear. How young she looked. How small. How vulnerable.

# chapter twenty

In the event, the funeral happened sooner than expected. Three days later, in fact, due to a cancellation,

'A cancellation?' I said to Benji when he rang and told me. 'What – someone's decided better of it? Decided to live after all? This isn't the hairdresser's, Benj, you can't just cancel your appointment with St Peter.'

He laughed. 'No, they've gone to a different venue. Decided the chapel at Golders Green wasn't big enough. And if we don't take this slot, Henny, we won't get another one until Friday week.'

I blanched at the vocabulary, but wasn't too shaken. Having worked alongside Mum and Benji these past few days and chosen coffins and brass handles and silk linings, I knew the spade-calling nature of the funeral world. And perhaps it was as well that another moral dilemma had been taken out of our hands. That along with deciding what was an appropriate amount of money to spend on our loved one and whether to go for pine or oak, we didn't also have to decide whether an appropriate amount of time had lapsed and we were ready for burial. Perhaps it was as well one 'muscled into one's slot'.

The chapel was indeed small though, I thought nervously, as I walked down the aisle with Angus on Wednesday morning and sat next to him in the front pew. Tiny. I couldn't help wondering where the other family had gone that was more spacious? More superior? And had they chosen better handles than ours? Still, it suited our needs, I decided firmly, crossing my legs and smoothing down my black skirt. We were a small family.

I glanced about and smiled politely at the few relatives whom I'd already greeted outside: a couple of aged aunts, Great-uncle Matthew, Cousin Alfred and his wife Valerie, and their unmarried son with that funny nervous tic. Presumably he was my second cousin, but I could never remember his name. Mum was in the front pew on the other side of the aisle with Benji and Francis, and I was keeping the space beside me for Marcus and the children. There was no sign of Marcus, but then he was collecting Lily from school and the M25 could be bloody. When the door opened behind me, I glanced around, nervous about seeing him after so long, but it was just a clutch of old family friends, neighbours from the Finchley Road. As they came in, windswept and huddled in overcoats, I smiled gratefully. In the past, one or two had tried to visit Dad in the

Home, but he hadn't remembered any of them. He'd been openly rude, in fact, so gradually they'd drifted away. These few then had come for Mum: the Spiras, the Carters from upstairs, and I recognised Howard Greenburg too, who lived in the flat below. I gave him an especially grateful smile. Good. I'd hoped he'd come, for Mum's sake. Moral support. Other than that, the chapel was empty: aside from the vicar, busying himself with the order of service sheets, and, of course, my father, in front of the altar. In his middle-of-the-range oak coffin, with its middle-of-the-range brass handles. I took a deep breath. Let it out slowly. Soon be over.

A blast of cold air sent the hymnsheets flying and I turned, relieved to see Marcus and Lily bustling down the aisle; Lily, in her school uniform, Marcus in his dark overcoat. He'd performed that particular school run, whilst I'd met Angus off a train from Northampton. I smiled warmly at Lily and looked across at Marcus, wondering what sort of expression to have on my face. He came right down the aisle before his eyes cut to mine and he gave me a curt nod. I nodded back. I see, I thought grimly, facing front. That sort of expression. I gripped my hymnbook hard.

'All right?' I whispered to Lily as she sat down beside me. I gave her a kiss.

'Yes.'

She looked a bit pale though, and I slipped an arm round her shoulders. Marcus slid in next to Angus. I wondered if he'd been quizzed by Lily on the way down as to why he was picking her up alone. I hoped so. Stupid, *stupid* man, I thought angrily. Perhaps being here together in church would concentrate his mind, make him realise what he was throwing away?

At that moment the organ struck a decisive chord and we got to our feet. I caught Benji's eye and we glanced at Mum, but she was staring straight ahead, looking stoical and elegant in her navy Jaeger coat, her chin high and eyes dry, having done all her crying, she'd assured me as I'd hugged her outside, these past few days.

I'd done mine, too. Mostly in the evenings, when I was tired. Sometimes I'd pick up the phone and chat to Benji; mostly, though, I'd been grateful for the quiet of the flat. Needed it. I hadn't been entirely alone, either. I'd also spent time with Rupert.

Naturally, our love affair had had to be put on hold – we were both tacitly aware that this was not the time to rekindle it – but we were also aware that the world has a curious way of turning, irrespective of personal tragedy, and that in time, rekindle it we would. Meanwhile, however, we'd met in my lunch-hour. Despite Laurie's assurances that I needn't, I'd gone straight back to work, preferring the routine and discipline of the office to the solitude of the flat. Rupert met me in the Piazza, and we'd walk across to St James's Park, kicking up the leaves, getting hot dogs from a stand and eating them

on cold, damp benches, much as we'd done years ago. I'd
occasionally talk about Dad, and Rupert would listen, sometimes chipping in, and sometimes coming up with some
memories of his own.

When we'd parted yesterday at the park gates, he to go
back to the Ministry of Defence in Whitehall and I to Covent
Garden, he'd taken my face in his hands and kissed my lips
gently, the first time he'd kissed me since that night in his
flat. I'd felt the heat wash over me.

'I have to go away for a bit,' he said. 'But I'll be back.'

My stomach rocked. 'For a bit? Really? How long?'

'Only a few days.'

'Where?'

He made a face and looked away.

'You can't say?'

'I'm not supposed to.'

I nodded, knowing better than to press it, and wondered
fleetingly what his real life was like: where he was flown to,
which battle arenas he was dropped into, and then a few days
later, suddenly spirited away from again. I knew I'd never find
out. Knew that although some individuals, as he'd wryly
commented, not only told but wrote lucrative accounts, he
never would. For him, the Official Secrets Act remained just
that – secret. I'd watched as he'd walked away from me, and
wondered just how dangerous it was. I knew from quizzing
Laurie that the SAS didn't just work in war zones one read

about in the papers, but in places we weren't even aware had troubles concerning us.

'What business is it of ours what happens in Nigeria?' I'd asked Laurie casually, putting a cup of coffee in front of him and re-starting a conversation we'd had earlier. Laurie had shrugged noncommittally.

'Governments sometimes ask for our help, and depending on the circumstances, we go in.'

'Like mercenaries?'

'In a way, but in a slightly different capacity. For the government, rather than personal gain.' He looked round from his screen. 'Why, Henny? Why d'you want to know?'

'No reason,' I'd blushed, going back to my room.

He knew though, I was sure of it. Recently, Rupert had walked me back to the office, and when I'd instinctively glanced up at the second-floor window, I'd seen Laurie's face looking down. He hadn't said anything as I'd come in, but his expression was troubled. I remembered Rupert's scathing condemnation of him. Was my boss wondering if I was learning too much about him, perhaps?

As Rupert had disappeared down towards Whitehall yesterday, a tall, thin figure in a Covert coat, his blond head melting into the crowd, I wondered how I would feel if he never came back. My stomach lurched with such velocity, I had to turn around quickly and walk away, astonished at the force of my feelings.

# not that kind of girl

Standing here now, in this tiny North London chapel, all that seemed a world away. Like a different life. Someone else's, not mine. That woman in the blue cashmere coat, meeting her lover in parks, feeling the wind in her hair, the years drip off her as she laughed and kicked up leaves – it was like a clip from a film. For here I was, the real me, a middle-aged woman with my estranged husband and my two teenaged children, my hair in need of highlights, burying my father.

The vicar cleared his throat and lifted his heels from the floor. 'May I start by requesting that all hymnsheets remain in the pews after the service. Time and again they disappear, and replacing them is so irksome. A collection for the new organ will be taken on your way out.'

'And good morning to you too,' muttered Angus beside me.

'Let us stand and sing together hymn number 245.'

As the organ vibrated noisily in the limited space, our little congregation made a valiant stab at 'Jerusalem'. We'd just embarked on the second verse when the church door opened again, this time with something of a clatter. We all turned, still singing thinly, to see the door being propped open by Barbara, the Jamaican nurse, whilst behind her, a motley collection of geriatrics from the Home piled out of a mini-bus. With the help of Grace, the other nurse, they negotiated the steps and shuffled in, talking loudly.

Some had dressed soberly for the occasion in back-to-front

hats and wrongly buttoned overcoats, but one, I noticed, still had her slippers on. Another had deemed an angora bedjacket and Wellingtons more appropriate. They shuffled flakily through the door, gazing around with mouths open, like children. Two particularly vocal old women wanted to know why it was so bloody cold? They were shushed by Barbara as they shuffled into the back pew, quarrelling over where to sit and snatching hymnbooks from each other. I saw one pinch the other hard on the arm. One old boy came in ramrod straight with a chest full of medals, and another, bent double in a dusty old smoking jacket and tartan trousers, smiled vacantly, waving a cigar.

As they squashed noisily into the back pews, elbowing each other and staring around, the vicar eyed my mother in alarm. She gave a resigned shrug and carried on singing. Benji caught my eye and winked delightedly; I smiled back. Benji always liked a party, and actually, he was right. Of course these people should be here. They'd been Dad's life for the last six years, for heaven's sake.

As one old dear with a very hunched back took a feather boa from a carrier bag and whipped it defiantly around her horizontal neck, I was reminded of that poem 'When I Am an Old Woman, I Shall Wear Purple'. Mum's constant refrain was that Dad had lost all dignity in the Home, but it seemed to me that these people possessed, if not dignity, then some sort of superiority. It was as if they'd unzipped themselves and stepped out of their skins onto a higher, giddier plane, where no one could touch them. They were flouting convention, dressing and behaving as they liked, making up for lost time, for the sobriety of their younger days – and too bad if no one else saw it like that.

Their singing was robust but erratic, and one or two even had a stab at the descant which wasn't terribly relaxing. It was a bit of a relief when the dark Satanic mills faded into the background and we all sat down again. The vicar then began his address, attempting to sum up the life of one Gordon Arthur Tate. He talked about Dad's early life, his time at Oxford, his period of National Service, and then his career as a structural engineer. As he listed the projects Dad had worked on, I saw Lily stifle a yawn. I smiled. Mum hadn't wanted a family member to make this address for fear of it being too emotional. Well, there was certainly no danger of that. The vicar talked on and on, and when he got to Dad's passion for history, I heard a commotion behind me. Glancing round, I saw that the back two rows of the congregation had got to their feet and begun to shuffle out. The old boy in medals was sliding open the mini-bus door and shepherding the Twilight inmates efficiently aboard. Benji shot me a frown. I shrugged, bewildered, and after a moment, Benji slipped out too. A few minutes later, while the vicar was still talking, the Twilight Home inmates shuffled back in again and resumed their seats.

'They thought they were at the wrong funeral,' whispered Benji in my ear before he sat down. 'Dad had told them he was a trapeze artist in a circus, not an engineer. Apparently his stage name was Renaldo.'

'Oh!' I blinked.

Afterwards, we trooped outside, squinting in the low sunlight and walking in huddled clutches to the cemetery at the back. As we sheepishly assembled around a gaping hole in the ground, I held Lily's hand tightly. Angus, who was over six foot now, had taken Mum's arm, which made my eyes fill up. It took a few minutes for the Nursing Home inmates to join us, speed not being their forte, but sure enough, they were soon pushing their way to the front, jostling and arguing.

'Awfully crowded,' commented Barbara, sidling up beside me. I moved, hastily.

'Oh, sorry. Lily, move along, darling.'

'No no.' Barbara put a hand on my arm. 'The accommodation.'

'Oh.' I gulped and stared at the hole. It certainly was a bit hugger-mugger. Dad was apparently being squeezed between two parallel graves, with another right at his head, and one at his feet.

'Yes, well, I suppose space is limited,' I said nervously, wondering if polite graveside chat was the norm.

'It's better than the one in Highgate – that's absolutely

heaving – but you should have tried to get him into Kilburn. It's lovely, Kilburn. Lovely views.'

'Right,' I said faintly, although it occurred to me to wonder of what benefit that would be to the occupants. 'You're . . . au fait with most London cemeteries, I take it?'

'Can't think of one I haven't been to,' she chuckled proudly. 'Shh now, dear, the vicar's going to do his bit. He won't want you gassing on.'

As the coffin was lowered into the ground Lily squeezed my hand and I squeezed back. The vicar spoke of dust and ashes, and Mum, when invited to, tentatively sprinkled some earth. So did the man with the medals. And the lady with the feather boa. Then everyone, it seemed, wanted a go. I shut my eyes as Angora Bedjacket went back for her second throw. *Keep breathing, keep breathing.* I was also dimly aware of a commotion behind me, some panting and arguing. When I turned, I saw that the two old ladies who'd been pinching each other in the back row of the chapel were bent double and wrestling to pull a wooden crate through the throng.

'You don't mind the doves, do you, dear?' whispered Barbara in my ear.

'Doves?'

'Released at the graveside. Two of them, usually. It symbolises the deceased's spirit, soaring up to heaven. Gloria and Vera always do it.'

'Oh! Um, well, I'm not sure.' Good God. Whatever next?

'Oh yes, Mummy, it'll be lovely,' enthused Lily.

'Oh Lord,' I muttered. I hesitated. 'Well quickly, go and see what Granny says.'

Lily hastened over and whispered in Mum's ear. I saw her raise her eyebrows a fraction and move her lips just perceptibly.

'Granny says – whatever,' Lily reported back breathlessly.

Gloria and Vera duly manoeuvred the crate to the head of the grave. I glanced at the vicar, but he'd clearly seen it all before. No doubt if a pair of randy dogs had been released to roger away amongst the graves, he'd still have had that same faraway, beatific expression on his face. He rocked back on his heels, cassock billowing in the wind, dreaming of lunch.

As Gloria struggled with the catch on the box there was a nasty moment when it looked like Dad's soul was going to be trapped for ever in an orange box. Happily though, she worked it free, and a pair of grey pigeons soared up into the sky.

'Doves?' muttered Benji in my ear.

'Pigeons are cheaper,' Barbara explained. 'Free, as a matter of fact. Vera's brother breeds them for racing. We usually dye them white, but we didn't have time, I'm afraid. Nice touch though, don't you think?'

'Very,' agreed Benji drolly, as we watched the birds circle overhead then zoom off determinedly. 'And where, exactly, does Vera's brother live?'

'Hendon way, I think.'

'Twenty-two, Stonecroft Road,' put in Vera helpfully, straightening up from the crate and dusting down her hands on her bobbly cardigan.

'Excellent.' Benji nodded as the birds duly homed off in that direction. 'Nice to know where my father's soul is. Where his final resting-place is.'

Back in my mother's flat, it quickly transpired that we'd seriously under-catered for our new friends.

'I had no idea they were all coming,' Mum hissed to me in the kitchen as we peered through the hatch, watching the sitting room fill up.

They instantly made for the table she'd laid with plates of food and glasses of sherry, stuffing in two sandwiches at a time and draining the glasses.

'Clearly funerals are the highlight of the geriatrics' social calendar,' Francis observed as he came in with a couple of empty plates. 'Come on.' He reached into the bread bin and passed a sliced loaf to Angus. 'Get buttering.'

'Actually, I'd go easy on the sherry,' said Marcus, coming back with a tray of empty glasses. 'We don't know what medication they're on, for God's sake. We don't want another funeral on our hands. Boil the kettle, Lily.'

In the event, our visitors made the party go with a bit of a zing. They were refreshingly unfazed by the nature of the occasion, even putting bets on who would be next, and were clearly out to have a good time.

'Marvellous man, your father,' Tartan Trousers confided to me as I joined what seemed to be a permanent queue for the loo. 'Talented too. Imagine being able to ride a monocycle and kick a pile of cups and saucers onto your head at the same time. And then put a lump of sugar in the last cup!'

I swallowed. 'Quite.' Perhaps I'd come back to the loo later.

They all remembered Dad very fondly, though.

'A very funny man, your father,' observed the hunchbacked lady with the feather boa, laying a cool, dry hand on my arm. 'If a little smutty.'

I smiled and after a chat with her, drifted on. I was moved to hear the more alert members of the group – those who weren't slumped staring into space or fast asleep in armchairs – say much the same. Clearly Dad had been the Home's clown: not a side of him we'd seen at home, although the humour had always been there. They'd seen it in the raw, I suppose, stripped of its subtlety and intelligence. Nature without the nurture.

At one point, the old boy with the medals proposed a toast. They all got rather chaotically to their feet – zimmer frames clanking and walking sticks flying – and raised their glasses.

'The Great Renaldo!' went up the cry.

The rest of us, who'd muttered 'Dad', or 'Gordon' froze,

wide-eyed. I couldn't look at Mum, but saw Benji choking with laughter into his sherry.

The party resumed, but after a while I glanced across at Mum. She was standing over by the window with both hands in the small of her back looking tired and talking quietly to Howard Greenburg. I'd noticed him earlier, seeing to people's drinks and handing round cakes, and been pleased that he was making an effort. I looked around for the children. They were perched on a sofa, trying vainly to make polite conversation with elderly people who didn't know what day it was, let alone what a GCSE or a lacrosse match was. One desiccated old lady, gazing enchanted as Lily chatted on, reached out a bony hand to stroke her hair. I felt proud of them, but enough was enough. I caught Marcus's eye, something I'd avoided most of the afternoon, and he nodded. We might be conducting simultaneous affairs and be ready to lynch each other, but we'd been married for fifteen years and could still tell each other across a crowded room that the party was over. I went into the bedroom to get the coats, whereupon a few neighbours quickly followed suit. Hopefully Barbara and Grace would take the hint.

'Sure you don't want me to stay behind and help tidy up?' I asked anxiously as I kissed Mum goodbye at the door.

'No, dear, I've got masses of help as it is.'

I smiled and wrapped my scarf round my neck. 'Howard?'

'No, no. Howard and Angela have been marvellous already.

389

They made the vol-au-vents. I wouldn't dream of letting them do any more. No, Benji and Francis are staying on to help clear up. Now you get off, my darlings. I'm worried about your long drive.'

'Angela?'

'Howard's girlfriend. You met her, over there by the Hostess trolley. Nice woman.'

I glanced through the door at an auburn-haired woman in a smart navy suit. 'Oh. I thought that was his sister!'

'No, he met her at the Parkers' whist-drive last month. She's a widow. Now off you go, love.'

'But . . . don't you mind?'

'Mind?' She looked confused. 'Why should I mind?'

'Well, I thought . . .'

She stared. Then her mouth fell open. 'What – me and Howard Greenburg? Oh, don't be ridiculous, Henny. I've known him forty years! Bertha was my best friend! Anyway,' she grinned, 'he's got terrible halitosis.'

'But I thought—'

'Go on, away with you. I'll be glad when today's over, I can tell you. Thank you for your support, my loves,' she kissed the children. Then she squeezed Marcus's hand. 'And thank you, for coming.' She eyed him gratefully, then went back inside.

I trailed blankly down the stairs as my family clattered on ahead. As they piled into the car parked just down the road,

# not that kind of girl

Marcus, in the driving seat, leaned across and opened the door for me. I got in.

'Got that wrong, didn't you?' he observed dryly as I sat down.

I leaned back in my seat. 'Clearly.'

# chapter twenty-one

'Can I put a CD on?' asked Angus from the back seat.

'Yes,' Marcus and I both said together.

We glanced nervously at one another. Normally it was an emphatic 'No!' but clearly we both felt Def Leppard, or whatever it was Angus was about to subject us to, was preferable to stony silence.

Eardrums reverberating, we set off towards Kent and I thought how odd it was to be back in the family car: the children on the back seat bickering as usual, Marcus beside me, his familiar hands on the steering-wheel guiding us home. Home. Well, it had to be home, obviously, because the children were with us. We couldn't possibly go our separate ways. Had to keep up appearances. Yes, that was what we were doing, I thought, as a lump came to my throat. I gazed out of the window. Keeping up appearances. I took a deep breath. I was bound to feel emotional, I reasoned.

Of course I was. It had been a very emotional day.

Once we reached the farm though, it was worse. While I'd been away, the trees had changed colour to dazzling effect, and the house, tucked in the soft fold of the valley with the stream glistening beyond, looked magical. It was caught in one of those last, sudden blazes of golden light that only happens at this time of year and makes everything look like a film set. Home, I thought, as I got out of the car and shut the door. My home. And what would become of it now, in this new, fractured family? Who would it belong to? Marcus presumably, I thought, crunching across the gravel drive, since I'd never contributed a penny.

I opened the back door and gazed around at my farm-house kitchen, Farrow & Balled to within an inch of its life. But then again . . . didn't wives usually stay in the family home with the children? I was sure the law was weighted that way. But could I really chuck Marcus out and live here with Rupert? I put my bag on the table and stared at the navy-blue Aga. LIVE with Rupert? Is that what I was planning? My pulse began to race. In my heart I already knew it was what he wanted, longterm commitment, but . . . I bit my lip. Through the window I could see Fabrice, Marcus's horse, rugged up for the winter, grazing peacefully in the meadow. No, I certainly couldn't live here with Rupert. What – see him out in the yard every day feeding the chickens? Strolling around Marcus's orchard? Have the children come home to someone who wasn't their daddy, Rupert at the head of the table? No. So obviously I'd leave it to Marcus. And Perdita. I swallowed. And instead, *she'd* walk around *my* garden, feed *my* chickens, and take *my* dog for a walk. I felt the blood surge to my cheeks. Would she hell. Bugger *that*.

Dilly was scratching at the bootroom door and I let her out, pausing only briefly to acknowledge her. I felt hot, clammy. I walked through to the sitting room, holding myself tightly and flicking on lights as I went. No, it would have to be sold. Definitely sold. Neither of us could live here without the other, it was our home, Marcus's and mine. Too many decisions had been made together, from the colour of the walls to the position of the light sockets, to having flagstones or terracotta tiles in the hall . . . It had been our project, our baby, and if we weren't here together, it would have to go.

Perfect, I thought miserably as I mounted the wide oak staircase, my hand dragging on the rail. Just perfect. So the real losers here would be the children. No home to come back to any more, no familiar bedrooms, no playroom, no ping-pong table, just a flint cottage with Daddy and Perdita and a flat in London with Mummy and Rupert. Panic rising and having to breathe really quite hard now to control myself, I went down the corridor to the bedroom.

I could hear them in the playroom below me, squabbling about who got to lie on the most comfortable sofa, who got command of the remote control. Another battle ensued about who went to get the crisps, and then I heard Angus's voice in the kitchen, outraged that there wasn't the usual supply of smoky-bacon flavour in the larder, or any chocolate digestives in the tin. Well, of course there weren't, I thought. I hadn't been here.

In my room I pulled out jeans and an old jumper and started to take off my dark-grey suit. I'd bought it specially for today, but at the back of my mind had known it would do for work; that it was an investment. For work I was surely going to have to do, I thought grimly, only on a more serious basis now. Not as a joke, a laugh, a few days away from the mud and the simple country folk – no, as a fulltime occupation. As a single mum. I sat down on the bed in my bra and pants feeling cold and numb as the ramifications were rammed home, one after another. The door handle turned as I peeled off my stockings, and Marcus came in.

'Oh. Sorry.'

Our eyes met in confusion and he backed out again.

So. It had come to that. I dropped the nylons in a heap on the floor. My husband, on seeing me in my underwear and feeling so uncomfortable, being so unfamiliar with my body, had had to back away. Too used to seeing a different girl in the buff, I thought, bile rising. And even Marcus wasn't shameless enough to view two women in one week in a state of undress. I got angrily to my feet, pulled on my jeans and went to find him. He was in the bathroom having a poo.

'Oh. Sorry.' I shut the door quickly.

I stood outside and covered my face. Christ. Now I was doing it. And we were a couple who had happily done anything in the same room. Had always barged in on each other. Although I must admit, I always quite liked a private poo. Wasn't very good at straining with an audience. I waited until he came out. His face was inscrutable.

'Marcus, we must talk.'

'Fire away.'

'Well, obviously it's going to be quite awkward, the next couple of days. You know, being in the same house. But for the children's sake, we must get on with it. Just for now.'

'I agree.' He folded his arms.

I swallowed. It was so odd talking to him like this. He was so cold. So remote. Like a stranger.

'Clearly we can't sleep in the same bed.'

'Clearly.'

'So you can sleep in your dressing room.'

'Thank you so much.'

'And tomorrow,' I ploughed on, ignoring the sarcasm, 'well, tomorrow we'll just keep out of each other's way, I think.'

'If that's what you want.'

A silence hung between us.

'I – I shall probably go shopping,' I faltered on, filling the gap.

'And I shall go hunting. Lily wants to come too.'

I blinked. 'Lily? She's never been out before, has she? Oh Marcus, do be careful. Look after her, won't you?'

He did not deign to reply to this, just gave me a withering look.

I pressed on. 'Right. Well, no doubt Angus will want to see Tom, if he's around, so that's all organised.'

'Isn't it just?' he said bitterly.

I stared at him, appalled at his tone. Shocked at his newfound contempt for me. Tears welling, I turned and went back to the bedroom. I stood still and held myself tight, staring bleakly at the bed. I stayed there a few moments, just holding myself. Then I noticed something. The way the bed had been made. Not the way Linda or I made it, with the lace cushions in a neat little stack, largest at the back, smallest at the front – the lace cushions which, if Marcus had anything to do with it, would be in a heap on the floor. No. They were in an unfamiliar circle. A sort of . . . tasteless clutch. And on my bedside table was a little vase of flowers, which someone had picked from my garden to have by her side when she woke up. Perdita's side.

I caught my breath in fury, then flew out of the room. I cornered Marcus on the landing, fists balled.

'And Perdita's going too, is she?' I shrieked. 'Hunting?'

He blanched. 'Of course.'

'Oh, of *course*,' I mimicked. 'Of *course* she is. Whinnying away in her skintight jodhpurs and her leather boots – giddy-up!' I trotted on the spot holding imaginary reins. *'Of course!'*

Angus came to the bottom of the stairs. He frowned. 'Mum?'

I dropped the trotting and glared at my husband standing there so impassively, so seemingly full of moral superiority. If Angus hadn't been at the bottom of the stairs I'd have slapped his stupid face. Instead, I pushed him bodily into the spare room behind us and shut the door.

'There's been a change of plan,' I hissed. 'I will not be sleeping in the marital bed tonight, I'll be sleeping in here, because for reasons which I'm sure you'll appreciate, I won't feel comfortable in there. Savvy?' I shoved my face close to his. 'Savvy, Mister Booted and Spurred and Tally-ho Over the Fences We Go? Oh, wait a minute, let me whip your back-side first, darling.' I turned and gave mine a mock slap. 'Mmm, ooh – harder!'

He frowned. 'Henny, are you on drugs?'

'Oh, drugs! Oh yes, that's a good one, isn't it? Sex *and* drugs, ooh splendid, let's accuse her of that too, shall we? That would make you feel better, wouldn't it? You'd love that, wouldn't you, Marcus? Then you could say, "Not only is my wife having an affair, she's snorting cocaine too!"' I sniffed up an imaginary line from my hand. 'Mm, yummy! And why stop there? Why not say – say I'd been giving blow jobs in Waitrose car park?' I said wildly. 'Behind the shopping trolleys? Why not make it *all* up? Say it was *all* my fault?'

'You're insane.'

'And you're looking for excuses!' I spat. 'Excuses for your appalling behaviour – well, I won't give you any. *You* started this mess, Marcus,' I prodded him in the chest with my finger, 'this is all of *your* making and I am not going to be the scapegoat. You will not hang your grubby little misdemeanours on me! Now get out of my bloody bedroom!'

He didn't. Just stood there regarding me with disdain.

'All right!' I panted eventually, fists clenched. '*I* will!'

I barged past him and stalked out. Unfortunately I tripped over the rug at the top of the stairs which rather spoiled the effect, but nevertheless, I thought as I tottered away, it was a magnificent exit.

The following morning I got out of bed and drew back the spare-room curtains. It was a beautiful bright morning, the sun just making it over the top of the trees to the east, coldly lighting up the valley. Down below in the stableyard I could see Marcus and Lily grooming their horses: radio on, a cup of tea apiece, chatting quietly as they plaited and brushed and picked out feet. Not my idea of fun, but Lily loved it and adored the fact that her father now did it with her. They could endlessly discuss Dutch gags and laminitis and bog spavins, with Angus and I rolling our eyes in horror, and would spend hours in the stables hosing down and mucking out. I turned and reached for my dressing-gown. No. I couldn't take her away from here. Of course I couldn't. This was her home, and she must stay here with Angus and her Daddy. I couldn't be that selfish. So it would be me, then. I'd be the one on my own. In London.

Tears filling my eyes, I sat at the dressing-table and brushed my hair hard until my head hurt. I gazed at my reflection in the mirror that Marcus and I had found in a little antique market in Paris. Everywhere I looked, everything I touched, I thought in panic – the little cross-stitched mat Lily had sewn in reception class, the clay pot Angus had made – shrieked *family, family, family!* And he was the one destroying it all, wasn't he? I paused in my brushing and looked out of the window again as, bottom raised, he picked out Fabrice's hind hoof. He was the one cleverly disguising it as All My Fault and breaking up the happy home with his – his tart! I swung around in fury and hurled the hairbrush across the room, narrowly missing Lily as she came bursting through the door.

'Christ!' She ducked as it hit the wall behind her.

'Oh – sorry, darling.'

'Why did you do that!' she squeaked, regarding me with horror.

I licked my lips. 'Saw a wasp. Thought I'd – you know. Nail it. Missed.'

'Oh.' Then she frowned. 'What are you doing in here, anyway, Mum? Why didn't you sleep in your room?'

'Your father was snoring for England,' I said smoothly,

turning back to the mirror to avoid her eyes. 'Thought I'd sleep better in here.' I picked up my comb. *Your father*. I'd heard ex-wives refer to their husbands like that, when talking to the children. Not 'Daddy' any more, but 'your father', as if he was nothing to do with her. All the fault of the unfortunate offspring.

'Mummy, will you come to the meet? Follow the hunt?' Lily was behind me now in the mirror, her blue eyes huge.

'Oh darling, I was going to go shopping.'

'But Mummy, I'm so nervous, please come. You could follow on foot. I'll be much better if you're there.' Tears were close, I could tell.

I turned on the stool to hug her. 'Daddy's going – you'll be fine.'

'I know, but he might go fast, and the thing is, Jemima Montague says the fences are going to be really high today. And Freckles is so small and—'

'Then don't go, darling!'

She drew back, shocked. 'Oh no, Mummy, I must. Most of the Pony Club are going. Molly's going. That would be wussy. Oh no, I'm *going*, but I'd be so much better if you were there. Please!'

I sighed and turned back to the mirror. Going to the meet would, of course, involve coming face-to-face with Perdita. Have her lord it over me as she sat high on her mighty steed. I saw her arrogant, pale face sneering down at me. Right now though, there was another little face, pleading with me in the mirror. I turned. Smiled.

'Of course I'll come. Maybe Angus will too. Yes, we'll follow on foot.'

She swooped and hugged me. 'Oh thank you, Mummy – it would make all the difference! I'll go and tell Daddy.'

She ran back out again. Well, that would be an interesting exchange, I thought, getting up and sidling over to the window – Lily telling Daddy I was coming to meet the mistress. I waited, half-hidden behind the curtain. Marcus was facing me now, crouched down and intent on painting a front hoof with some sort of black nail varnish. Wasn't it all a bit poofy, I wondered? All this plaiting and manicuring? A bit – you know – girly? Lily ran out into the yard excitedly. He listened and then nodded curtly, but his expression didn't change. Cool. Very cool, Marcus, I thought, gazing down. He hadn't rocked back on his heels, spilled his nail polish and exclaimed, 'Ye gods, the game's up!' But then he wouldn't, would he? After all, he hadn't got where he was today without a certain *sang froid*. Yes, well I've got *sang froid* too, I thought as his eyes suddenly flickered up to mine in the window. I didn't duck away, didn't flinch, but stared down. Oh yes, I can be icy cool.

The meet was in the village, just outside the pub, and as Angus and I drew up, we could quite easily have just driven onto a biscuit tin lid. The hounds had been mustered on the village green and were winding excitedly around the horses' legs as they stamped and whinnied, their riders, in pink or black coats and hunting stocks, knocking back glasses of port passed around by a smiling publican. It was a fair-sized field and mostly adults, but with a good smattering of children too, on Thelwell ponies. The rest of the village was out in force, on foot, in Barbours and wellies. There were young mothers with children in pushchairs, pensioners with dogs on leads, all chatting and laughing, enjoying the spectacle and bathed in glorious sunshine.

I parked outside the village shop, watching as an elegant blonde woman, very much in the Camilla Parker-Bowles mould, trotted up the lane towards us on her mare. Known locally as Perfect Pippa since she never had a hair out of place, she was followed by her husband, Timid Timmie, a little man on a huge black horse, wearing spectacles. (Timmie, not the horse.) The *on dit* was that she ruled the roost, and he was so besotted he just trotted along behind her, rather as he was doing now. Pippa, lipgloss shining and hair carefully netted, recognised me and raised what I was sure was a friendly hand, but somehow, up there on her mount, it couldn't help but look imperious. I nodded back.

'Come on, Angus,' I muttered. 'Let's go.'

My son was making strange convulsive movements beside me in the car, which to the uninitiated might suggest some sort of fit, but to the mother of a teenage boy, the wires gave it away.

I lifted the earpiece. 'Let's go!'

'Wha'?' He jerked around, annoyed.

'Come on, we're going.' I turned his iPod off.

'I think I'll stay here,' he grumbled, sliding down into his seat and pulling the hood of his sweatshirt up. He looked around nervously. 'This isn't really my sort of thing.'

I'd had to practically drag him out of the house to accompany me in the first place.

'But Mum,' he'd whined from his prone, Roman-Emperor-At-Home position on the sofa, 'Kilroy's got a woman on who's married her adopted son. And they've had Siamese twins!'

'Angus, you're supposed to be a flaming scholar,' I'd snapped. 'What would your house master say if he knew you spent your entire exeat with your eyes glued to the television? You're supposed to have your father's brains!' See? 'Your father' again.

'Well, I obviously got your eyes then, didn't I?' he'd retorted, quite cheekily, I'd thought.

Eventually though, he'd raised himself up to a vertical position, pushed his bare feet into soggy grey trainers and dragged yards of frayed denim across to the back door.

'Oh look,' I said brightly as I got out of the car now and shut the door behind me. 'Laura Montague's here. And she's brought Jemima.'

'Where?' Angus whipped his hood off.

Jemima Montague was a rather fetching nymphet of fourteen whom Angus had something of a crush on: although you wouldn't know she was a nymphet today, I thought, camouflaged as she was, almost identically to Angus, in sinister hoodie, ripped jeans and trainers.

'Might just go and say hello,' he grunted, and was out of the car and mooching moodily across the road really quite rapidly for him. I followed to greet Laura. Laura was a mate I'd hit on early upon moving here. I'd liked the fact that she always seemed to have egg down her jumper and looked a bit chaotic. She, too, was an uprooted Londoner, one of the few here today, I noticed, not in regulation lovat green but wearing a fuchsia-pink jacket and tight yellow jeans. She'd endeared herself to me early on by sneaking out of her house late one night, very pissed, to paint the speed camera in the village which had snapped her three times. Her husband, Giles, had been appalled, but on slinking furtively into a crowded village shop the following morning for some paint-stripper, she'd been surprised to find herself hailed as something of a local hero. There'd been much cheering and back-slapping. The Montagues lived in the prettiest pink rectory on the edge of the village, and Marcus and I often had supper with her and Giles in the pub. On the most recent occasion, Laura – up to nine points now on her licence – had spent the evening trying to get Giles, a barrister, to share some of her points.

405

'And be done for fraud?' he'd replied laconically. 'Not necessarily the career move I'm looking for, darling.'

We'd had a lot of fun with them, and it was with a pang that I realised we wouldn't, in future. As I approached, I noticed one of her legs was darker than the other.

'Bloody dog peed on me!' she cried, shaking it in horror.

'Oh God, poor you,' I commiserated.

'And there's a lot of it. Those dogs are bloody big you know. Got huge bladders.'

'Hounds,' I corrected, handing her a tissue.

'Whatever. Thanks. God, I haven't seen you for *ages*, Henny. Where have you been hiding?'

'Working,' I said shortly as she mopped away. I didn't want to go into my father. Not right now. 'Up in London.'

'Oh, of course.' She straightened up. 'Eleanor Strang told me you're working for that dishy TV historian. God, lucky you! Gosh, aren't you frightfully tempted, Henny? I wouldn't kick him out of bed.'

I blushed. 'Er, well. I do my best to resist, obviously.'

'What on earth for? God, I wouldn't. D'you know, the closest I got to some excitement this week was winning a prize in the village show, and then that awful Mabel Turner complained about my entry. "That's never a courgette, that's a marrow!" she hissed spitefully to her husband, Bert. So I eyed Bert and said loudly, "Just because you've never seen such a big one, Mabel!"'

I giggled. 'Yes, you've got to take your thrills where you can, round here.'

She grimaced. 'Tell me about it. Speaking of which, let's at least get ourselves a glass of free port while we're standing around freezing our arses off, shall we?'

We squeezed nervously past a couple of snorting, stamping horses to grab a drink from a passing tray. Laura glanced around.

'You can see why this is considered a toffs' game. Perched up high in their red coats with their whips and spurs, they look like gods. The fact that that's Gary the mechanic is neither here nor there; he looks like Lord Many-Acres.'

'Except that there *is* Lord Many-Acres,' I murmured as the local nob swept by, florid of face on a frisky bay. I looked around anxiously for Lily.

'Jemima not riding today?' I said as I scanned the field and saw her standing with Angus.

'No, she's a bit windy about hunting, ever since she fell off at that ditch. Molly is, though, she's bold as brass. She's with Giles, over there.'

Giles, atop a very solid-looking cob, waved as I turned. His horse shook its head and the bridle jangled noisily.

'Got a lot of iron in its mouth, hasn't it?' I murmured. 'The horse, not Giles.'

She laughed. 'Oh, Giles likes good brakes. He's a very cautious chap. If we're asked out to dinner on a very windy night, he puts a chainsaw in the boot.'

I giggled. 'I don't believe you.'

'I kid you not. Ooh look, Perfect Pippa.'

'I know, I spotted her earlier. With Timid Timmie.'

'Can't think what she sees in him,' Laura said sotto voce. 'He's so cringing – and that dreadful stammer! The other day he summoned up the courage to ask me if he could "p-pop ahead of me" in Waitrose, as he only had "one thing in his b-basket". Came out in a complete muck sweat. I can just imagine him in bed. "Um, P-Pippa, oh p-perfect one, would it be all right if I p-popped my p-plonker in now?"'

I laughed. 'She probably swats him away like a dirty old fly and goes back to painting her perfect nails. Come on, I want to find Lily.'

We muscled our way further into the stamping, snorting throng and I glanced around anxiously.

'There she is,' said Laura suddenly, pointing.

Lily, looking white-faced and nervous, but very smart in her tweed jacket and Pony Club tie, was standing up in her stirrups on Freckles, searching for me. I waved madly, and when she finally saw me, relief flooded her face. She waved delightedly back, and poked Marcus in the ribs beside her with her whip. He was deep in conversation with someone on a grey horse, but broke off when he saw me, nodded, then went straight back. He said something to his companion, and after a moment, the girl turned to look too. It took me a moment to realise it was Perdita. She said something to

Marcus, and the pair of them roared with laughter.

I felt my face flush with embarrassment and fury. God, the *nerve* of the man! Not even attempting to be coy and careful, to shield me from her, but parading around with her in front of half the village! And with our daughter beside him!

'Isn't that Perdita Fennel?' Laura said in a low whisper.

'I believe so,' I spat.

'God, she's a goer. I didn't go to the Hunt Ball in the summer because Molly was ill, but apparently she was all over the men.'

The Hunt Ball. No, I didn't go either, because Mum had been staying that night. Marcus had gone though, said he had to. To support the hunt.

'Apparently she went off with some chap at the end of the evening. Took him back to that cottage of hers for a jolly good seeing-to. No one knows who it was, except that he's very definitely married and very definitely local. It's all a bit hush-hush. I tried to get it out of Eleanor Strang who was there, but she wouldn't tell.'

My heart began to race. Was this Laura's way of telling me that she knew – that everyone knew? The entire village? And that, as ever, the wife was the last to find out? Was she telling me to look to my laurels? To watch out? I glanced at her. She was watching Molly now, her face impassive. I fumed quietly. So. He'd gone back with her that night, had he? While I'd been at home with Mum. I watched Perdita now, talking loudly to someone else on a huge chestnut, looking admittedly very slim and glamorous in her navy coat with mustard collar.

'Anyway, apparently she's dead nervous today,' Laura confided.

'Why?' I could hardly speak. Nervous? I'd never seen anyone so brazen and cocksure in my life.

'This is her first time out as joint master. She's leading the field. Come on, they're off, let's go and wish the girls luck.'

Horns were blown and the hounds lifted their heads. Excitement filled the air as the whipper-ins, ruddy-faced boys in mustard coats, called them expertly to heel – 'Bounder, Lurcher, Tizer!' – each known individually by name. They rounded them up with their long hunting whips, then trotted smartly off down the lane, the pack of hounds ahead, the field mustering and jostling for position behind. We just managed to squeeze through and reach Molly and Lily as they were setting off.

'Mummy! We're going!'

'I know – good luck!' we called. And: 'Stick at the back!' 'Don't jump anything too big – go round it!'

I looked at Marcus as he shadowed Lily on Fabrice. *Jump as high as you like and break your bloody neck*, was what I wanted to say, but instead I gave him a tight, public smile. He touched his hat back. Pillock. Who did he think he was, Harvey-bleeding-Smith?

The sound of hooves pounding on tarmac filled the air, and everyone who wasn't already on the village green came to their garden gates to watch them go by and wave.

'They might be going over your way first, now that Marcus has lifted the ban,' Laura called to me over the din.

'What ban?'

'Apparently the previous owner of your place banned hunting over the land. Bit of a townie. It's been lifted now. Didn't you know?'

'He never tells me anything,' I said crisply. 'Is that where they're heading for, then? Our place?'

'No, they'll be goin' over Top Common way first,' said a wizened old boy in a flat cap in my ear. 'See if they can flush anythin' out up there.'

'Oh God, that's quite a hike,' groaned Laura. 'Not sure I'm up to that. Shall we follow in the car?'

'Definitely. I'm all for cheating. Let's take mine, it's got four-wheel drive.'

'Jemima and I are going to follow on foot,' said Angus, suddenly materialising beside me.

'Fine, darling,' I said, surprised. Angus didn't walk to the television if he could help it. Left it for his parents to turn off. I'd never known him so keen to take a five-mile hike, but then he didn't usually have the lovely Jemima beside him. Laura and I watched them go, shoulders hunched, hoods up, hands thrust in pockets, denim trailing in the mud.

'Look like they're off to do some mugging,' Laura said.

I giggled. 'I know. We pay a lot of money for deportment like that. Come on, let's go.'

We piled into my jeep and set off. Laura, who seemed to know the terrain, barked instructions bossily, making me race round lanes and then take the occasional short-cut through a field.

'Through here!' she yelled as we shot through a farm, then, 'Sorry!' flashing a winning smile out of the window to the astonished farmer as we scattered ducks and chickens in our wake.

'Are you sure this is the way?' I gasped as we bounced down a pot-holed track, our heads practically hitting the roof.

'Positive. This is much the quickest way to Top Common. Here, swing a left here through this gate, then go right along the track. Oh, and have a swig of this.' She produced a hip-flask from her pocket whilst attempting to light a cigarette with the other. The flame jiggled as we rattled along.

'I won't, thanks,' I told her. 'Not actually while I'm driving. Might have a swig when we stop, though.'

'It's the only bit of hunting I can participate in,' she said, knocking it back. 'And you can bet your life *they're* all quaffing away from their stirrup cups. Giles usually comes back pissed as a fart. Oh look, there they are!'

Sure enough, up on the brow of the hill in the distance, the hunt came into view. The hounds were streaking out of a covert baying loudly, and then the rest of the field followed, galloping at full tilt, riders crouched forward in their black and pink coats, in stark relief against the emerald green of the meadow.

'Quite a sight,' I said, shading my eyes with my hand.

'They're heading up towards Bellingdon End now. Come on, across here. I'm pretty sure this is Ed and Sophie Carter's land, they won't mind.'

She pointed me through an open gate and we roared across the field, bouncing over ruts and flying through ditches, Laura spilling ash and sloe gin with every bounce.

'Bit different to London life, eh Henny?' she bawled above the engine noise.

I grinned. 'I'll say.'

She shifted around in her seat to face me. 'So what exactly are you doing up there? I mean, apart from work?'

I took a deep breath. Stared straight ahead. 'Actually, I met up with an old boyfriend,' I said brazenly. At that moment we lurched out of the field and hit tarmac, swinging sharply round into the lane. Laura righted herself as she fell against the door, then clutched my arm, her eyes huge. 'No! God, how *exciting*! And?'

'And . . . well. You know – just lunch, that kind of thing,' I said lamely.

'Just lunch? Blimey, I haven't had lunch with a man who wasn't my husband since about 1982.'

I blushed, slightly less brazen now. She gazed delightedly at my pink cheeks.

'Ooh, and you still fancy him!' she squealed. 'Henny, how thrilling! Does he make your heart beat faster as you gaze across the table at him? I know if I had lunch with a certain Paddy McAllen of the Fourth Seventh Dragoon Guards I'd go weak at the knees, be chewing the table leg! Should have married him, of course.'

I glanced at her quickly. 'Really?'

'Well,' she considered this. 'Maybe not. He *was* a bit of a shit. Led me a very merry dance. But if his name crops up at a dinner party I still blush like mad and drop my napkin on the floor to give my face time to cool down as I eyeball the carpet. Giles thinks it's hysterical. Hang a right here, Henny.'

I felt her eyes on me as I swung the wheel around and we dived down a woodland track. If the pack were headed for Bellingdon End, they'd come through here. We found a clearing a bit further along and parked. When we'd got out and were leaning on the bonnet, Laura passed me the hip-flask.

'*Just* lunch?' she probed lightly.

I hesitated. 'Well, obviously we had to walk it off. Had to take a walk in the park.' I smiled.

She stared. 'Well well,' she said softly. 'You sly old dog.'

We were silent a moment. The wind rustled the leaves in the trees above us.

'Be careful though, won't you, my friend?' she said eventually. 'Got a lot to lose.'

I narrowed my eyes into the beechwood. 'Have I?' I said quietly. 'Not sure I haven't lost it already. And anyway, what's sauce for the goose and all that . . .'

She gave me a puzzled look, but at that moment, heralded by haunting cries, the hounds appeared from nowhere – masses of them, in fact, howling and scrabbling and sniffing frantically around the very clearing we were in.

'They've lost the scent,' said an old boy, running up on foot with his terrier on a lead.

'Obviously,' agreed Laura as we backed nervously into the bushes.

A moment later, the rest of the field appeared on horseback. As they cantered up looking none too pleased and gathered to stand for a breather, the horses stamping and snorting, I was relieved to spot Lily, still on board, right at the back. She didn't see me, but was looking around anxiously. I waved. Still she didn't see me. Taking my life in my hands I squeezed bravely through the steaming horseflesh towards her, wincing as I got sweat on my jacket, but I couldn't get past a huge dun-coloured horse, planted squarely in my way.

'Whip, please,' said a curt voice from above. A ruddy-faced man in hunting pink glowered down at me. I gazed up at him, uncomprehending.

'Sorry?'

'Whip, please!' he repeated, more urgently this time.

I glanced around. Everyone was watching me. Did he want me to whip him?

'WHIP, PLEASE!' he roared, making me jump. Heavens. Was this a peculiar hunting custom? I hesitated, then tentatively took his whip from his hand, and gave him a little tap on the leg.

'There.' I smiled and handed it back.

He stared down at me, horrified. Then, kicking his horse, he barged past me, jolly nearly knocking me over.

'Well!' I gasped, staggering to stay upright. Laura pulled me back roughly into the bushes.

'"Whip, please," means get out of the way the Whipper-in's coming,' she hissed, as sure enough, a man in a mustard coat on a vast black horse shot by at a gallop. He surely would have mown me down. Flattened me.

As I got my breath back, a cry went up behind us. Then a hunting horn sounded, and suddenly – the whole field was away again, careering off, it seemed, from a standstill. Perdita was in the lead, I noticed, bottom raised provocatively – very taut, very sexy. She smiled down as she cantered past. I glared back.

'Come on, we've done our bit,' said Laura, hastening back to the car. 'Molly and Lily have seen us now, so we can just pretend we saw the rest of it. Pretend we were out for hours. Anyway, I've got a leg wax booked in half an hour.'

# not that kind of girl

We piled back in, and she didn't question me further. I knew I'd said too much, though. Gone too far. But I'd wanted her to know. Wanted her to know that I wasn't the long-suffering wife, the last to hear about her adulterous husband and the village tart; that I already knew. And I wasn't stupid, either. Much as I liked Laura, I knew she was a terrific gossip and that she'd be straight on the phone to Eleanor Strang after her leg wax.

'Eleanor, you'll *never* guess . . .'

'What?'

'Well, you know Henny Levin has been staying in London . . .'

Good. *Good*, I thought firmly as we drove back down the lanes, both deep in thought. I wanted them to know. Wanted them to know that if they'd spent the last few months – no, *six* months, if it had started at the Hunt Ball – feeling sorry for me – 'Poor Henny, how ghastly' – they needn't. Because I had a life of my own. A love of my own. And not just a quick legover in a crummy flint cottage, either. No, I had the real thing. The love of a man who didn't just fancy me, didn't just lust after me, but worshipped the ground I jolly well—

'Henny, look out!'

THWACK!!

I hadn't, though. Hadn't looked out. And as I screeched to a halt, I knew I'd hit something. Something brown and fast-moving that had shot out from nowhere, right in front of me.

'Shit!' I gasped as we both lurched towards the windscreen, then back into our seats. 'What was that?'

But Laura was already out of the car, running round the back. I got out shakily and went to join her. She was standing in the middle of the road, her hands shooting up through her hair. She gazed down in horror.

'Oh Christ, Henny,' she breathed. 'It's the fox. You've hit the bloody fox!'

# chapter twenty-two

'Oh my Christ.' I scurried, horrified, across the tarmac to where she was standing. Sure enough, a large furry creature lay motionless in the middle of the road, eyes shut, mouth gaping, tail spread out in a russet fan behind. My hands shot to my mouth.

'Oh, how awful. I feel dreadful!'

'Well don't, it's called pest control. Only I'm not convinced it's quite the control those guys had in mind.' She glanced nervously over her shoulder as, far away in the distance, we heard the sound of horns and baying hounds getting closer.

'Shit — the hunt!' I squeaked. 'What'll they say?'

'Well, they won't be too thrilled at having their sport curtailed so abruptly, I can tell you. I think they'd rather planned on making a day of it.'

I gazed at her as it dawned. 'Oh my God,' I breathed. 'Marcus will kill me.'

She shot me a look as if to say, 'What, more than he would if he knew the sport you were having in London?' Then swung around as a horn sounded again.

'Yes, well they're sodding well coming now, Henny, and they'll have our guts for garters!'

She shaded her eyes into the distance, as on the brow of the hill, lolloping hounds were followed by streaming pink and black coats, galloping out of a copse into view. They were still a good half-mile away from us, but getting closer all the time. Even at this distance, I could make out Marcus, up in his stirrups on Fabrice, and Lily close behind him.

'Oh Lord.' I began to tremble. 'The hounds are on the scent. They'll be down here soon. What'll we do?'

'Get back in the car,' Laura said in panic. 'We'll just drive on.'

'Don't be silly, Marcus will have seen it's us!' I swung back to look. 'There aren't many purple Discoverys in Flaxton, for God's sake, we can't just drive off and leave it! Can't we hide the body? Chuck it in a ditch and cover it with leaves?' I looked around desperately for a handy ditch and some spare leaves.

'Don't be ridiculous, the hounds will find it in seconds, and then everyone will know we did a hit and run. Our names will be mud in the village. No. I know.' Her eyes narrowed dangerously. 'We'll take it with us. Got a dog blanket?'

I stared. 'What?'

But she'd already flung open the back of the jeep and was dragging Dilly's blanket out.

'Here, take one end and slide it under him.'

I gazed down aghast. 'Oh yuk!'

'Come *on*, Henny. They're getting closer, and if they find us we'll be lynched. Probably on the village green!'

This terrifying image, complete with Marcus and Lily in the front row, arms folded, eyebrows raised accusingly, seemed to galvanise me, and I flew to Laura's side. Together we slid the blanket under the very large, very hairy, very dead fox.

'And then take two corners each,' Laura panted as I tried not breathe in the horrific stench which was filtering up my nose, '. . . and lift . . . like a hammock . . .'

'He's enormous!' I gasped, staggering under the weight.

'Full of my chickens, no doubt. Hope he hasn't got rabies.'

I nearly dropped my corners. 'Shit!'

'Not in this country, Henny, now come *on*! They're nearly here!'

Sure enough, over the brow of the hill, the hunt, in full flight, was galloping towards us, full pelt down the valley, hounds to the fore, but closely followed by Perdita and the field.

'Won't they wonder what we're doing?' I trembled as we hurried the body to the car.

'They won't know at this distance,' she panted. 'They'll just see the car. If they ask, we'll say we had to stop so you could be sick.'

'Why me?' I yelped, as with a mammoth effort, we heaved the smelly bundle into the jeep, although actually, I paused to clutch my mouth as the stench rocketed up my nose, I might just heave at any moment.

'Because you hit the bloody thing, now come on!'

We ran around, jumped back in and lurched off down the road, just as the hounds jumped the gate two fields away. By the time they'd jumped the next hedge into the lane and reached the extremely smelly patch where the fox had lain, we were out of sight and around the next bend. Unfortunately for us, so was a tractor – going very slowly, at about five miles an hour, its trailer rattling, laden with bales of hay. It stopped at a five-bar gate to turn in. The farmer got out of his cab, waved an apology, and with all the time in the world, went to fumble with the padlock.

Laura and I sat there, frozen in horror, staring straight ahead, not speaking, barely breathing in fact, as behind us, back around the bend, we heard the sound of hounds howling, no doubt circling in confusion as they came to a complete stand-still in the road. Presumably, though, they wouldn't stay there for long. Presumably, soon, they'd pick a route. I gripped the wheel, shut my eyes tight, and prayed. Dear Lord, please *please* don't let them pick ours. Please! Sadly though, my prayer fell on deaf ears, and moments later, we heard the sound of hammering hooves behind us.

Oh fucky fuck.

Eyes still tightly shut, I slid down in my seat and prepared to die. Prepared to be stranded there, with no possible means of escape, as the hounds, catching a whiff of the fox, surrounded the car, leaped up at the windows, and howled to be let in. It would be like that Stephen King movie where that poor woman spent the entire film locked in a car with a mad dog – Kujo, or something – going berserk outside, except it wouldn't just be one dog, there'd be hundreds of them: swarming like locusts, baying for our blood, and riders too, all bending down and peering in – Marcus's face, Perdita's – all wondering what on earth was going on and why the hounds were so interested in our car and, actually, what on *earth* that mound was under the blanket . . . with the red tail sticking out . . .

'Oh thank Christ!' Laura squealed.

I snapped my eyes open as the tractor disappeared through the gate. Dry-mouthed and badly in need of the lavatory I plunged into first and roared off with a screech of tyres, just as a pair of mustard-coated hunt servants appeared at a smart trot at my window, hounds at their heels. We raced up the lane in silence, not daring to speak until we'd reached the junction with the main road which led back to the village.

'For a moment there I thought we'd had it!' croaked Laura.

She reached for her hip-flask and knocked it back. I nearly snatched it from her hand as she passed it to me. Held it to greedy lips.

'Me too. Thought our number was up.' My voice was trembling. 'Thought any minute now they'd be pounding round that bend . . .'

'Giles, pink with fury . . .'

'Marcus, absolutely livid . . .'

'And imagine the girls!' Laura squeaked, as we got faintly giggly now, hurtling down the road, passing the flask to each other, high on our narrow escape. 'Molly and Lily! God, they'd never *speak* to us again. We'd be on tack-cleaning duty for months. Imagine the shame we'd heap on our families. Caught in the act! Off to dump the body in the nearest lake! I take it that's where we're going, incidentally?'

'Haven't the faintest idea. D'you think that's best?'

'Definitely. Go left here, it's quicker. And we'll weigh it down. Put stones in the blanket and tie it up. Don't want him coming back to haunt us, appearing in the stream in the village, a bit of Dilly's blanket stuck to his tail, paw pointing accusingly. God, it would be like something out of *Midsomer Murders* – *left*, I said, Henny!'

But I'd skidded to a halt on the open road, white-faced and speechless because, on preparing to take the aforementioned left turn I had, like any good motorist, glanced in my rearview mirror. Only to see, sitting up very straight in the back, and looking me right in the eye – Monsieur Reynard, with a small cut on his forehead. I couldn't speak. Just . . . couldn't speak. Pointed mutely over my shoulder. Laura turned to look. She screeched in terror, and in seconds flat we were out of that car.

'Open the boot, open the boot!' I gibbered, as we both ran away as one, up the verge towards London which, with hindsight, of course we should never have left.

'No fear!' she shrieked. 'What if it bites!'

By now though we'd stopped and turned back, clutching each other on the roadside, staring in frozen terror at the car.

'You go,' she breathed.

'No, you.'

Happily though, neither of us had to as, moments later, the fox, having calmly negotiated the dog guard between the boot and the seats – a mere trifle to a professional chicken-house breaker – and pausing only to give us a look of withering magnitude, slipped, like a streak of red, out of the open passenger door, through the hedgerow, and away across a field of stubble.

Laura and I watched in stunned silence, still holding onto each other, as he disappeared.

'Bloody hell,' she murmured at length.

'Bloody *bloody* hell,' I agreed.

'Not dead.'

'No, not dead. Just stunned.'

Laura reached into her pink jacket. Between us, we silently drained her hip-flask before tottering back to the car on jelly legs.

We drove on for a bit in silence.

'Well, I think we made it much more sporting, actually,' Laura declared finally, tucking her blonde hair decisively behind her ear. 'The pack were far too close. We just gave it a sporting chance.'

'Absolutely,' I agreed staunchly as we purred back towards the village. 'And he did look terribly old. Infirm, even. All we did was behave like caring citizens. Gave him a lift.'

'Exactly.' Her mouth twitched. 'Into the next county,' she snorted.

We were still giggling uncontrollably, shaking with laughter in fact, as I dropped her off at her leg wax appointment a few minutes later.

'Oh God,' she gasped, wiping tears from her face as she stumbled weakly from the car. 'I haven't enjoyed a day out in the country so much for ages. We must do this more often, Henny, you're a tonic. A real tonic. I'll bring more gin next time, though.'

'Good idea!' I agreed.

I waved goodbye, and feeling rather light-headed now, weaved slowly back to the farm. Every so often I sniggered, in a rather pissed fashion, into the steering-wheel.

Marcus, of course, couldn't see it in quite the same humorous light. He strode back in a few hours later, all booted and spurred and soaking wet after a fall in a river – looking nothing, I promise you, like Mr Darcy in that wet-shirt moment – and flung himself into the Windsor chair by the Aga.

'How was it?' I asked innocently, stirring a white sauce.

'Bloody farce!' He flung down his whip. 'We had a marvellous run and were hot on its heels, then all of a sudden the scent went completely dead – right where we saw your car, actually. We raced round in circles like idiots for the rest of the day, trying to pick it up again.' He eyed me suspiciously. 'You wouldn't know anything about that, would you, Henny?'

'Not a thing,' I said lightly, pouring the sauce over some gammon and popping it back in the oven to brown. My face, when I turned, was naturally flushed from the heat of the Aga. 'How very boring for you. Now, Angus, lay the table, would you? And Lily, when you've had a bath you can mash the potatoes. We'll have supper at eight.'

The following day was Sunday: a wet and drizzly one, and the children were both due back at school that afternoon. The school run was always a two-man job since we'd cunningly chosen schools in completely different directions to ensure that nothing so simple as dropping them off simultaneously occurred. It was politely agreed over lunch, which might be the last I ever cooked in this house, I thought as I took it out of the oven, that Marcus would take Lily, who needed to be back at six for a play rehearsal, and since Angus had been offered a lift with a boy in the neighbouring village, I'd wait here and see him into the car that was picking him up, before going back to London myself.

'Why are you going back to London tonight?' asked Lily, spearing a Brussels sprout.

I glanced at Marcus, realising we'd slipped up. 'Because I have to go to work tomorrow, darling.'

'Yes, but you usually go from here.'

'I know, but I've got to be in early. Laurie's very busy. I may as well stay at the flat.'

There was a silence as she digested this.

'D'you stay in the flat a lot?'

I paused. This would, of course, be a very good moment. A moment when all four of us were gathered around the kitchen table, to say, 'Yes, actually I do, and the thing is, Lily, I'll be staying there a whole lot more in future.' A good moment to tell them that their lives, as they knew them, were coming to an end. I glanced at Marcus, wondering whether he'd seize this opportunity. Whether he'd clear his throat, put his knife and fork down portentously. Instead, he calmly popped a roast potato the size of a house into his mouth, and I breathed again.

'Now and again, darling. I stay now and again,' I told Lily. 'It is, after all, jolly convenient.'

'Tom's mum says a flat in Town is the slippery slope,' said Angus with a grin. A piece of carrot flew out of my mouth and right across the table. 'Says she wouldn't let Tom's dad have one in a million years.'

'What's the slippery slope?' asked Lily anxiously, looking from my choking face to her father's.

'Nothing, love,' I muttered, sinking into a glass of water. Marcus chewed on, jaws rotating methodically, eyeing me bovinely as I hastily cleared the plates. 'Now, come on. Help me put these in the dishwasher.'

In the event I was pleased it was Marcus taking Lily back and not me. If there were any more awkward questions he could jolly well field them, I thought, as I hugged her tight in the drive and said goodbye.

'Will you come and take me out to lunch before the next exeat?' she asked. 'You're allowed to. Becky Mason's parents came last term.'

'Of course I will.'

'And will you come with Daddy?'

I looked over her fair head at Marcus, standing waiting by the car door. He nodded curtly.

'Of course,' I said, hugging her again, a lump in my throat. 'We'll both come.'

As I waved them off I wondered how, after that heart-wrenching moment, Marcus could still want to go through with it. But that curt little nod had said it all. *Yes, we'll take her out to lunch together, but the next exeat . . . The next one, Henny, we'll have to tell them.*

He's a hard man, I thought, holding myself tight as I went slowly back into the house. I never knew how hard. He, who purports to be so principled, so virtuous, but all the time . . . ooh, it made my blood boil!

I slammed around the kitchen for a bit, clearing up, then snatched my Barbour from the back of the door. I needed some air. The afternoon had turned damp and chilly, but I'd walk along the river and up the hill to clear my head. Angus had drifted back to his bedroom, and I could hear music reverberating down through the ceiling. I attempted to yell up and tell him where I was going, but the volume was against me, so instead, I left him a note. Then I called to Dilly and went out of the back door.

The wind had dropped now, and a mist was beginning to settle over our valley. The air was soft and damp, and as I walked through the sodden fields and down to the river, it wafted gently against my face, settling on my hair. The river was full and limpid, swollen by the recent rain and lapping at the banks where the chestnut trees were clumped darkly on the other side. I crossed the river at its narrowest point, picking my way over the stepping stones that Marcus and Angus had sunk last summer, threading my way through the trees, then up the hill towards the little stone wall, right at the top.

Don't think, I told myself sternly as I strode through the damp grass, gazing down at my glossy Wellingtons. Just – don't think. Don't think, Is this the last time I climb this hill, or thread through the woods with Dilly as she scampers after rabbits? Don't wonder, Is this the last time I'll stop at the top, catch my breath and turn and look at the house below, nestling in the fold of the valley? Just concentrate on moving.

I did turn though, and sat too, on the stone wall, looking at the lights from the kitchen twinkling below. It was that special time of day, when the evening is trying to close in, spreading darkly against the sky, but the day seems determined to hang on for dear life, to every scrap of light it can muster.

From this vantage point, I could see the whole of the valley: the cottage to the right of us, the farm to the left. A proper, working farm that one, not a tarted-up farmhouse like ours. And it was still moving. Cows were coming into sheds, doors were clanging, dogs were barking, ducks were being shut up for the night. It was one of the reasons we'd liked this spot, Marcus and I. It had authenticity, we felt. Wasn't just a valley full of ex-Londoners, people like us, who'd moved out of Town to claim their slice of a rural idyll, having shinned up the greasy urban pole.

And, of course, our house had once been a working farm too: had been in the same family, apparently, for several generations. The Sewells, they were called, those farmers who'd sold to the Pipers, the people who'd had it before us, who'd got divorced. The three Ds, our estate agent had called it: Divorce, Death and Debt. The latter had forced the Sewells out, and the former, the Pipers. And now us, too. And we'd never thought we'd be contenders for that particular D. Had thought we'd be much more like the Sewells, here for the duration, for the next couple of generations, passing it on to Angus or Lily, then their children. As I sat, gazing at my house slumbering in the valley below me, I wondered what those hardworking Sewells would have thought of us. Of our affairs, our fast cars, our flats in Town. Whether they'd feel we'd let the house down. Let ourselves down. Of course we had. Of course.

Not to mention the children. A lump came to my throat. All right, they weren't little children any more, they were teenagers, away at school, with their own lives, but they were still very impressionable. How would it affect them? Everyone knew children from broken homes behaved differently, it was well documented. What would happen to mine? Would Lily become attention-seeking, grasping? Angus, quiet and withdrawn? Tears flooded suddenly down my cheeks as I sat there, gripping the stone wall.

I wiped them away with the back of my hand. Turned my wet face up to the darkening sky. And then I wondered, as I watched the black clouds scudding across the firmament, if I wouldn't wait for him. For Marcus. When Angus had gone, and he came back from dropping Lily. Not go straight back to London, but give it one last shot. Maybe I'd light the fire in the sitting room. The one we'd reclaimed together, exclaiming delightedly as blow by blow, the builders had revealed the original hearth. Maybe we'd sit there opposite each other with a glass of wine, the fire between us, and maybe I'd persuade him to give her up. Tell him I knew. That I forgave him. Ask him never to see her again. For the sake of our children. Our marriage. Please, Marcus.

At length, I dredged a deep sigh up from my boots and heaved myself off the wall. I called to Dilly, and with my head bent, went back down the hill again. I glanced at my watch. Half past five. Angus's lift would be here in half an hour. I had to get back to make sure he'd got everything he needed for school. Make him a sandwich before he went, fill a cardboard box full of cereal packets for him to take to the Common Room and wolf down with his mates. He ate so much these days. As I went back through the dark chestnut wood, quickening my pace a bit – the trees were closing in now, slightly spooky in the gathering gloom – and emerged, relieved, into the open meadow, it suddenly occurred to me that Angus's lift was already here. There was a car in the drive, and in the light from the window, I could see two figures moving around the kitchen. Oh Lord, had I got the time wrong? Was it five o'clock they were coming to pick him up?

I hastened on, leaping across the stepping stones and hurrying through the horses' field. I could see through the kitchen window that Angus had the lid of the Aga up, and was putting on the kettle. Well, that was a relief. They couldn't be in too much of a hurry if they were stopping for a cup of tea. And then, just before I got to the garden gate – I stopped. Stared at the car in the drive, then back again through the window in sheer disbelief. The car, I now recognised. And the other person moving around the kitchen, the one perched on the table as Angus measured the Earl Grey into the pot, throwing back his head and laughing at something Angus had said – I recognised him too. Oh God. It was Rupert.

# chapter twenty-three

I stayed still at the gate and stared. The rain was pelting down now, but I barely noticed. My heart was pounding at the base of my throat. I watched as he levered himself away from the table and went to the fridge. He took the milk out, handed it to Angus, then jumped back onto the table again and sat there, legs swinging. He was wearing brown corduroys and a red pullover, his blond hair flopping forwards. I saw Angus hand him a cup of tea and lean against the Aga, smiling shyly and nodding at something the older man said.

I walked on quickly, my pulse racing. Rupert. In my house. With my son. What the hell . . . ? I started to run. My legs felt like two bits of rubber though, stumbling unsteadily along. As I approached the house, I slowed again. Walked, with as decisive a tread as I could manage, up the path. Then my hand closed on the back-door handle – and I burst in.

'Oh hi, Mum.' Angus turned, unconcerned.

435

I stood still in the doorway in my dripping Barbour and boots. Could hear my breath coming in shallow bursts. Dilly slid past me and made for her water bowl. She began to drink noisily, sloshing it everywhere.

'Rupert.' I trembled. 'What on earth . . .'

'I was passing,' he said easily, jumping down from the table and pecking my cheek sociably. 'Thought I'd drop by and see if you wanted a lift back to London.'

I glanced at Angus, but he didn't seem to find this strange. Dumb with horror, I played for time. Took my Barbour off for something to do and hung it on the back of the door, while all the time, questions crowded my mind. What had he told Angus? How had he introduced himself? 'Hi, I'm an old friend of your mum's and I was just passing? Knew she worked in London and since I'm going that way . . .' Or, 'Hi, I'm your mum's brand new lover, but actually, an old one too, since we once very nearly got married'?

'I didn't know he was *the* Rupert,' said Angus with a grin. 'The one you went out with years ago. Lily's going to be really jealous I've met you and she hasn't,' he advised him.

Right. Clearly a mixture of the two.

'Yes – well, that was all a long time ago,' I said quickly, my mouth drying as it tried to form words, my brain not quite knowing what it was going to say. 'But goodness, how extraordinary you were passing, Rupert. And that you even knew where I lived.' I fumbled with some papers on the island.

436

'Oh, I remembered from that change of address you sent in your Christmas card.'

'Oh!' Christmas card. Yes, that was good. Exchanging Christmas cards was fine.

'We were just talking about Bosnia and stuff,' said Angus. 'Sounds really cool. I might join the Army, Mum.'

I didn't reply. Went to refill Dilly's water bowl, hiding my face in the sink. 'I thought you were based in Hereford?' I said into the stream of running water.

'We are, but for complicated reasons we were flown back to Andover yesterday, which is only up the road. This is kind of on my way back to London.'

Kind of? Hardly. And Andover was not up the road. It was a good thirty miles away.

I switched off the tap. 'Angus, run up and get your rucksack, would you? I want to check you've got everything ready before the Barkers get here.'

'I haven't packed yet.'

'Well, go and do it now, please. They'll be here in a minute.'

Grumbling, he peeled himself off the Aga rail and dragged his denim flares upstairs. The kitchen clock ticked loudly in the silence as he mounted the back stairs. The moment he was out of earshot, I rounded on Rupert, horrified.

'What the hell are you doing here!' I gasped. 'And what did you tell him?'

He shrugged. 'Exactly what I said – that I was your old

437

boyfriend who you bumped into recently in London. He's a nice lad.'

I stared at him, speechless. 'But – you're in my house, Rupert. My family home! What if Marcus had been here?'

'Oh, I saw Marcus drive off with Lily about half an hour ago. Figured he was taking her back to school. I knew it was in Berkshire, so I imagined he'd be gone a while.'

I gaped at him, aghast. Stunned into silence. God, the nerve of the guy. So he'd been watching, had he? Watching the house. Watching me, even? He was tanned, I noticed suddenly. Quite brown from his few days away. Where had he been? In Iraq? Running covert operations? Jumping out of helicopters and lying in sand-dunes with his men, waiting to storm an Iraqi stronghold? So sitting in a lane in rural Kent and assessing when the coast would be clear to stroll into his girlfriend's marital home was not going to be too taxing, was it?

Functioning on automatic, I went to put the milk back in the fridge. My hands were shaking. I was scared.

'Well you must go,' I whispered. 'I have my son to see off to school, and Marcus will be back soon.'

Just then a car tooted in the drive and headlamps lit up the kitchen. I dropped the milk bottle in fright.

'Looks like they're here,' Rupert said casually, strolling over to peer out of the window. He stooped to pick up the rolling, but happily not broken bottle en route. 'Angus's lift. Blue BMW?'

438

'Yes. Yes, that's it.' I ran my hands through my hair and watched blankly as Rupert plucked a dish-cloth from the sink and deftly wiped the milky floor. Well, at least Angus would be out of the way. That was something.

'Angus!' I hastened to the foot of the stairs, but he was already coming down.

'I heard. And it's Mrs B. driving, which is a real bummer. We'll have opera all the way.'

I forced a smile. 'Got everything?' I said, walking quickly with him to the back door.

'Yep. And you don't have to check. I only brought home a couple of files.'

'And you've got the new socks I put out for you?'

'Yeah, they're in the bag.' He turned and grinned at Rupert. 'Nice to meet you.'

'You too.' Rupert stuck out his hand and Angus shook it as I watched, frozen.

I walked out with him to the car, bending to greet Mary Barker in the driver's seat, thanking her profusely and prom-ising it was my turn next. Then I hugged Angus hard.

'Bye, darling.'

'Bye, Mum. God, your heart's going like a bongo drum!'

'Is it?' I stepped back quickly. 'Must be climbing to the top of that hill. Not used to the exercise.'

'Getting old.' He grinned. 'You should go to Pilates like Tom's mum.'

'I should,' I agreed as he got in the car. There are a lot of things I should do, I thought nervously, biting my thumbnail as I waved him off, but going to Pilates with Tom's extremely fit young mother was not top of my list. Right now, up there at number one, was getting my lover out of the marital home.

'Rupert, you must go,' I breathed as soon as I'd shut the back door behind me. I flew to the window and drew the curtain. As I did so, I caught a glimpse of Bill, shutting up the chickens. He saw me and winked. Bugger! I swung around.

'Bill's seen you!' I exclaimed.

He frowned. 'Bill?'

'Our gardener. Oh God.' My hand shot to my mouth. 'He'll tell Marcus.'

'Tell Marcus what – that someone dropped by? A stranger? He doesn't know who I am, Henny.' He came towards me. 'And anyway, why are you worrying about what Marcus thinks when we all know what Marcus is up to?' He stopped. Looked down at me and smiled. 'It's lovely to see you, incidentally.'

He was close to me. Very close. His blue eyes vivid. Intense. 'It's lovely to see you, too,' I whispered.

It was. And as our eyes feasted greedily, suddenly I knew it didn't matter. Nothing mattered. As he took me in his arms and found my lips, I gave way against him. His mouth opened on mine and I responded eagerly. The spotlights were bright above us, and after a moment, he reached out for the dimmer switch by the back door. Turned them right down. Turned them off. Only the light from the hall shone through, bathing us in a soft, rosy glow. He pulled me hard against him, then pushed me up against the counter, pressing himself on me. I felt desire wash through my body like a high-pressure shower, only the force was coming from below. I went weak with longing as he ran his hands over my body in the dark. How long we might have stayed like that I don't know, had Dilly not barked suddenly, hearing the dog at the neighbouring farm. I came to my senses.

'Rupert, not here,' I said breathlessly, pushing him away. 'This is my home – Marcus's home, for God's sake.'

'Fair enough,' he said quietly, but his breath was coming in bursts like mine. His eyes burning. 'So let's go.'

'Both of us?' I said fearfully.

'Of course, both of us. Pack a bag.' It was said reasonably, but nevertheless with some force.

'But what will Marcus think, if I'm not here when he gets back?' I was thinking aloud now.

'Were you supposed to be here?'

'No, but . . .'

'So how were you going to get to London?'

'Take a taxi to the station, I suppose. Then a train . . .'

'Exactly. So leave a note to that effect. Why d'you need to see him to tell him that?'

I twisted my hands in agitation as I paced the kitchen. I flicked up the lights again. He was right – I didn't need to see Marcus. But I had wanted to wait, to talk to him. Just to see . . .

'And anyway, how d'you know he'll be coming straight back? The chances are he'll assume you'll go when you've seen Angus off, won't he? Maybe he won't come straight home.'

I swung around. 'You mean . . .'

He shrugged. 'Sunday night. Why come back to an empty house? Why not go to Perdita's?'

I went cold at her name. Stopped at the sink and hung on, gazing into the white porcelain. 'Yes. Yes, you're probably right. It's on the way back.' I imagined him driving slowly past the riding stables, seeing a light on in her cottage. Pausing in the lane, turning into the yard. Parking under her bedroom window, a smile playing on his lips as he got out of the car and went to ring the bell. And who was the fool? Waiting here all alone? I turned. Licked my lips.

'Wait there, I'll pack a bag.'

Ten minutes later I was sitting beside him in his car as we purred smoothly back down the dark lanes that threaded through the valley. It was raining heavily now, and I watched as the windscreen wipers hypnotically swiped away sheets of silver-black water. I looked beyond them into the dark night, into the black fields and the dripping trees. Silence floated between us. My mind was spinning. I didn't speak until we'd reached the motorway.

'You've put me in an invidious position, Rupert,' I said, my voice quavering. 'By meeting Angus. He's bound to mention it to Marcus at some stage. You're forcing my hand. Pushing things along. I don't like that. Don't like being manip-ulated.'

I was shocked at hearing myself say those words, at the force of my feeling. But it was true. I didn't like it.

'I'm sorry,' he said quietly after a moment's thought. 'You're quite right. I've comprehensively let the cat out of the bag, but the truth is, I didn't know he was there. Angus, I mean. I saw Marcus pack the car, and Lily and Angus come out. I assumed he was taking them both back to school. I wasn't aware that Angus didn't get in the car, he must just have been seeing them off. I saw you go for a walk with the dog, and got the shock of my life when I rang the doorbell ten minutes later and Angus answered. I'd only rung to check the house was empty.'

My mind whirled at the scenario. 'Right. So then what were you going to do — break in and wait for me?'

'Not break in, no. The key's under a brick by the back door.'

I inhaled sharply. 'Is it indeed.'

'And I would have waited until Bill had shut up the chickens and gone back to his cottage.'

His cottage. He knew where Bill lived. Really knew the lie of the land. I turned to look at him, at his straight nose

443

and full lips, his strong profile against the dark, rain-spattered window.

'You mean business, don't you?'

He paused. Gave this some thought. 'I don't want to lose you again, Henny, if that's what you mean. And I don't think you mean to lose me.'

We came to a halt at some lights. He reached out and put his hand on my leg in the dark. Slid it further up my thigh. I felt my insides melt at his touch.

As the lights changed, he put his hand back on the wheel. I shifted position. Extraordinary, the way he just had to touch me . . . I stared out of the window as rows of black houses under a phosphorescent glow rushed by. I felt foolish. Naive. Vulnerable even. This was quite a carnal awakening, something I hadn't expected at this stage of my life. Was this how it was for Marcus and Perdita, I wondered? Tingling with longing whenever they touched? I'd felt contemptuous of that, always had done, but . . . surely this was different. After all, I had once loved Rupert very much. Even so . . . I licked my lips.

'Rupert, when we get back to London, could we go out? You know, have supper somewhere?'

'Sure,' he said easily. 'I'd rather planned on us eating. I haven't had much today. But I thought we might eat in. Bought a couple of steaks.'

'Oh. Oh, fine. I just didn't want . . .'

'What, to fall into bed?' He smiled. 'To be dragged back to my lair, caveman-style by your hair? I do have a few subtle moves, Henny. Don't do everything SAS-style. And listen, no pressure, OK? None at all. When we've eaten, I can drop you back to Kensington if you like.'

I nodded, relieved. But we both knew that wouldn't happen. Somehow, though, I felt better having the option in place. If the intent wasn't there, if nothing was premeditated . . . well then, somehow that absolved me of guilt, didn't it?

Who was I trying to kid.

An hour or so later we were climbing the stairs to the Albany flat. I'd decided en route that I was cooking, and would make a sauce to go with the steaks, and Rupert was reminding me of the last time I'd cooked for him, about fifteen years ago, in my parents' flat. Chicken in a cream sauce, apparently, which my mother did a lot, but that night, I couldn't find the recipe for it. My parents had gone to the cinema so I'd cooked it for Rupert and Benji: three chicken breasts with a carton of cream, heated and poured over the top.

'You ate it,' I giggled as we climbed the stairs. 'You actually ate it!'

'God, it must have been love,' he groaned. 'I felt as sick as a dog, I remember that. Benji gave his to the cat, as I recall.'

'And then tried to spy on us when I sent him to bed. We were snogging on the sofa in front of *Fawlty Towers*, remember?'

'I do. And his head kept popping round the door with those beady brown eyes. He was frightfully interested for one whose predilection was so clearly in the other direction.'

'Oh.' I paused on the landing. 'You mean you always knew?'

He shrugged as he put the key in the door. 'Well, I was pretty sure he wasn't interested in women. You had that incredibly pneumatic young neighbour, remember—'

'Tammy.'

'Tammy! Exactly. She kept making passes at Benji in the corridor, squeezing past him wearing next to nothing, tits hanging out, and then ringing the doorbell in a towel to borrow a pint of milk. I remember Benji passing it to her with weary indifference, glancing over her shoulder to see if she'd brought brother Michael along, wondering if he needed an extra pinta too.'

I giggled as he shut the door behind us. 'Yes, you're right. How funny that you remember that.' I flung my handbag on the hall chair, feeling lighter now, easier. 'Yes, I suppose he made no secret of his sexuality really. It's a wonder it took us all so long to click. One just assumes one's brother is straight, I suppose.'

'And he's happy?'

I followed him into the sitting room. 'Oh very. He found Francis pretty quickly. They've been together for years. Francis lives with him. In the house you—'

'I know,' he said quickly.

I was about to say, 'in the house you saw me go into, in Chelsea,' but perhaps he didn't want to be reminded of another undercover operation. Another time he'd watched me, loitering this time under a Chelsea lamp-post, having followed me home from work. I tried not to, but had a quick mental picture of him on the Tube, watching me from down the other end of the carriage perhaps, behind a newspaper. Well, nothing wrong with that, I thought staunchly. I should be flattered. How many middle-aged women could boast a gorgeous man like Rupert watching their every move? I shivered. The flat was dark, and on the chilly side. I could do with a drink.

'Gin and tonic?' Rupert read my mind as he raced around turning lights on.

'Please.'

'Bum-freezing in here, sorry.' He put a match to the gas-effect fire, then turned and caught me in his arms. Gave me a quick excited kiss, before moving on. 'Now, to the kitchen, since you're determined to redeem yourself. Although what you'll find to make a sauce with I've no idea.'

I followed as he opened the fridge door with a flourish and brought out some rather tired-looking mushrooms. Made a face.

'Oops. Sorry.'

'Nothing wrong with them. I'll fry them up and add – I don't know . . . tomato purée?'

'Now that I have got.' He reached up and passed it to me from a cupboard.

'And wine?'

'Wine.' He lunged and seized a half-empty bottle. 'Which'll be fine for cooking, but I'm going to go round the corner to get a decent bottle for us to drink.'

'And the steaks?'

'In that plastic bag. You're not going to start cooking them yet, are you?'

'Why not? I thought about twenty minutes on each side?' I grinned as his face fell. 'Relax. I'll pass them quickly round a hot pan when you get back. I have acquired a few culinary skills along the way, you know. No, I just thought I might season them, that's all.'

'Ah.' He grinned. 'Had me worried there. Thought I'd be chewing leather. Right – I'll be back in a jiffy, the off-licence is only round the corner.' He grabbed his wallet, then hesitated.

I smiled. 'Go on then,' I said softly. 'And don't worry. I won't be gone before you get back.'

Our eyes met in recognition. He gave a rueful smile and then, with a backward wave, he went.

I took the steaks out of the bag. Yes. Odd that we could read each other so comprehensively. That he knew I was nervous about being here. That he felt he had to reassure me. I could feel him willing me to realise that once we'd been to

448

bed together, all would be well. I sensed we both knew that, and that was why he was so anxious to get that hurdle out of the way. For us to officially be lovers. No question about it. To lie in bed all day if we felt like it, stroll hand-in-hand along Piccadilly. He wanted to put his marker down, say, 'There, mission accomplished.' And why was I so nervous all of a sudden? Why was I holding back?

I wasn't, I reasoned, as I chopped the mushrooms and let them soften in some butter in a pan. I watched as they fizzed. I wasn't holding back. I just hadn't, in my mind, figured on being here with him tonight, that's all. A couple of hours ago I was in the bosom of my family, wondering whether to attempt a reconciliation with Marcus – doomed, I realised now, as he was doubtless at Perdita's – and now, here I was in Rupert's flat. I didn't like surprises. I'd somehow assumed I'd go back to work for a few days, and then – well, maybe he'd contact me next week. By which time, I'd be dying to see him. And by which time Marcus, in all probability, would have left a cold little message on my answer machine about arrangements for our next meeting with the children, details of where and when we were to break the news of our split to them, and I'd be feeling rejected and unloved.

Yes, that was it, I thought, glancing up from the pan. I wanted to feel like the victim, not the aggressor. Wanted to be able to justify my actions, but Rupert was forcing the pace. Our pace. I took a huge slug of my gin. You're just nervous,

I told myself. It's a long time since you've been with another man, that's all it is. I gripped my drink and wandered into the bedroom as the mushrooms fried. And you know very well, that once he takes you in his arms, brings you in here, you'll be lost. I held myself tightly, gazing down at the bed, feeling that warm glow already. Then my eyes fell on the chest of drawers, the photographs. Suddenly I darted across. Oh yes, those photos.

I picked up the one taken from his cottage in Ireland, the view of the hills, and quickly took the back off. It wasn't hard, it almost fell apart in my hands, as it had done when Rupert had first shown it to me, when some photos had fallen out which he'd stuffed back in rather too quickly. I sifted through them. Well, how odd. There was the one of his mother that I'd spotted, and an old one of him and Peter as children, but not the one I'd felt he hadn't wanted me to see. There had definitely been three in here, and one was missing. Was it of me, I wondered? And had he been embarrassed still to have it, to be carrying my likeness around when I'd married, had children, moved on?

I put the pictures back swiftly, just as the telephone rang by the bed, making me jump. I stared at it. Should I answer it? No, of course not. This wasn't my house. Just let it ring. As it happened, after two rings, an answer machine clicked in. I listened to Rupert's voice advising the caller to leave a message, and then after the tone:

'Rupert, it's me, Dad. Listen, can you give me a ring when you get back? There's something I want to talk to you about. I know we both hate Sunday-night callers, but it's important. Thanks, bye.'

I frowned. Andrew. What could be so important? Well, just about anything, Henny; you don't know all there is to know about their family life, do you? Maybe someone was ill, maybe anything. I jumped as it rang again, but this time it was a different ring. A charge of the light brigade summons. A mobile one. The one that Lily insisted I had. I darted to my bag in the hall and fished it out.

'Hello?'

As I answered, Rupert came back through the front door. He raised enquiring eyebrows at seeing me on my phone.

'Darling? It's me.'

'Oh hi, Mum,' I said publicly, letting Rupert know.

He grinned and moved past me to put the bottles on the side in the kitchen. Two, I noticed, as I followed him through, and some Cointreau, to which I was particularly partial, and which he no doubt remembered.

'Darling, is this a good time? I'm not disturbing you?'

I picked up my wooden spoon and turned the mushrooms. 'No, it's fine, Mum. I was just, um, getting some supper.' I blushed and saw Rupert smile as he prepared to pull a cork.

'Oh, but I tried the flat. Your machine's on.'

'Er, yes, sorry. I put it on because I was going to have a

quiet night in. You know, just watching telly.' There was a silence. I frowned into it. 'Mum? Are you OK?'

She sighed. 'Not great, my love.'

My stomach flipped. 'Oh Mum, why?' I left the mushrooms and turned round in alarm. Heard her swallow hard.

'I don't know. I suppose it's only just hit me. Your father and everything. I'm just . . . well, I'm having a bad moment, that's all.'

I gulped. 'Oh Mum. Poor you.'

I felt sick suddenly. Poor Mum. Golly, we'd all assumed so much. Taken so much for granted. Her strength at the funeral, her seeming imperviousness to Dad's death. Of course, it was bound to take its toll. I was frightened by her silence on the other end, though. Usually you couldn't get a word in edgeways.

'Mum?'

No answer.

'Mum, are you all right?' I felt panicky suddenly. 'D'you want me to come over?'

'Would you, my love?' Her voice wavered.

'Of course I will. Of *course*.'

# chapter twenty-four

I saw Rupert's eyes cloud over as I clicked off the phone.

'You're going over there?'

'I have to, Rupert, she's upset. God, my father only died a week ago, we're all upset. I have to go to her.' My voice broke as I said it.

'Of course,' he said quickly, recovering himself as I dashed around scooping up my bag, my coat. 'Why don't I drop you?'

'No, I'll get a taxi. Why should you?'

'Because I want to.'

I turned at his voice. Suddenly I saw how forlorn he looked, standing in his kitchen, arms limp and helpless by his sides, his steaks and wine on the table, his romantic evening evaporating before his eyes. I went across and hugged him hard. Kissed him on the lips.

'I'm sorry. I'll be back,' I promised.

'Tonight?' he said hopefully.

I smiled. 'If I can. If she's not too upset. But Rupert, if not, well then tomorrow, or the next day. Or even next week. We've got so much time. We've got all the time in the world, haven't we?' I gave him a little shake, forcing a smile out of him. 'What's the rush?'

He grinned sheepishly. Scratched his head. 'You're right. There is no rush. It's just . . . well, now I've got you, Henny, I so badly don't want to let you go.'

'I know. And I understand that. But Rupert, I'm not going anywhere, OK?'

'OK,' he agreed.

We kissed again, and then again, a bit more passionately this time, dangerously so. Laughing, we untangled ourselves.

But as I ran lightly down the stairs to the front door, shutting it behind me, why all the while, did I feel a curious sense of freedom stealing over my soul? Why so liberated, as I ran out into the rain-soaked street, as if I'd escaped? No, that was just my imagination, I reasoned, hurrying along. That was ridiculous.

I could easily have got a taxi in Piccadilly, but the traffic was heavy for a Sunday night, so I dived down into the Tube. Quicker, I reasoned, and somehow, being amongst all these anonymous Sunday-night people rattling along to their various destinations – their homes, their families – suited my mood.

As I emerged into the dank night air, I fished in my bag and rang Benji. Francis answered.

'Benji's in the bath. D'you want me to get him?'

'No, no, it's not urgent. It's just – well, Mum rang and asked me to come over. She seemed quite upset, and I wondered if you'd seen her?'

'Today, of course,' said Francis, surprised. 'We always have her to lunch on a Sunday, and no, she seemed fine. A bit quiet, obviously, but no tears. I think it's . . . well, not exactly a relief, but a release for her. I'm surprised she's having a downer. D'you want Benji to pop over as well?'

'No, don't worry, I'm sure she's fine. Maybe just having a glum moment. Sunday nights can be a bit depressing, whether you've just lost your husband or not.'

'Well, quite. *Songs of Praise* can have me in floods, and when they get to "Fight the Good Fight" I'm reaching for the nearest sharp knife. Ring us if you need us, sweetheart.'

'Will do.'

When I'd walked up the Finchley Road and got to Mum's road – my old road, its redbrick mansion blocks with their distinctive white trim marching smartly up the hill towards Hampstead like a row of soldiers, I thought how strange it was that Dad would never come back here. We'd always said, when he was in the Nursing Home, 'when Dad comes back', even though we knew he probably wouldn't. We'd always pretend he'd mend that window lock, or see to the fuzzy television, when he was better. Now, of course, he never would. Would never walk up these stairs in his tweed overcoat and tie, raising his hat with one hand to Mrs Spira as she popped nosily out of her ground-floor flat to see who was going upstairs, holding junk mail in the other having picked it up from the mat to throw away whilst everyone else just ignored it, and glancing appreciatively at the water colours he'd put in the stairwell for everyone's benefit, to brighten it up.

A lump came to my throat as I climbed. Good, I thought. Good, I was remembering that father. The one who'd lived here. And it was a comfort. I'd tell Mum that, when I saw her; encourage her to do the same. Maybe we'd get some photo albums out? Remember all those family holidays in Northern France, making sandcastles on Omaha Beach whilst Dad stood on the cliffs above us, amongst rows of war graves, tears in his eyes, Benji and I trying not to show our impatience as he pored over war records in yet another cemetery. And then there was that funny bed and breakfast we always stayed in, where Dad was convinced the landlady was a transvestite.

'Look at the size of her feet!' he'd hiss as she brought in the croissants. 'Must be!' Mum, frowning as Benji and I corpsed into our jus d'orange.

Yes, there were plenty of funny moments and happy snaps from those days, and we'd get them out, I determined, as she opened the door. Have a laugh, and then a cry, and then blow our noses and eat scrambled eggs in front of *Monarch of the Glen*. Perfect.

'Hello, darling.' She leaned forward to kiss me.

'Hi, Mum.'

I was relieved to see she looked absolutely fine. Her hair was immaculate, perhaps with even a few more blonde streaks at the front, her make-up full on, and she was wearing a beige rollneck sweater, camel skirt and black patent heels. She smelled subtly of Chanel No 5.

'How are you?' I asked anxiously, standing back to survey her face for a moment when I'd kissed her. 'I have to say, you look terrific.'

'Oh yes, I'm fine actually. It comes over me in waves, obviously, but I've been there and done that earlier this morning. Had my usual weep, and very therapeutic it was too. Do remember that, darling, if you're feeling sad about Daddy. Have a little cry, it works wonders. Don't hold it in. Find some old photos or something, and let it out.' She ushered me into the hallway.

'Yes, I . . . I know. I was going to tell you to do the same, but— hang on, Mum. I thought you were depressed?' I followed her down the passage into the drawing room.

'No, that was a bit of a ruse,' she said carefully. 'I'm afraid I got you over here on false pretences. But I was worried you might not come, otherwise.'

'What d'you mean, I might not come otherwise? Of course I'd have come.' I followed her, blankly, into the drawing room.

'Well, would you, dear? Bearing in mind where I dragged you away from?'

She turned to look at me and I caught her eye, horrified. How the hell . . . but as I was taking this in, I was also taking in the reflection of the man standing with his back to me, facing the fire at the other end of the drawing room. Even if I didn't know that pale-green cashmere jumper and that greying swept-back hair, I'd know that familiar, ramrod-straight back anywhere. Apart from anything else, I could see his reflection in the overmantel mirror.

'Andrew.'

He turned. 'Hello, Henny.'

I stopped midway into the room. Turned to Mum, bewildered. 'What's going on? What's *he* doing here?'

'Andrew's come for a drink, that's all,' Mum said easily, crossing to the drinks tray on the sideboard and freshening his whisky glass as he passed it to her. 'Although he might stay to beat me at cribbage later, as is his wont.'

'Nonsense, your mother's a mean card-sharper as I'm sure you know, Henny. I'll be lucky if I get a game off her.'

Mum smiled as she passed his drink to him. Turned to me. 'Drink, darling?'

I perched, slack-jawed, on the arm of a convenient chair, neglecting to answer or to take my coat off.

'Cribbage?' I echoed.

'Or a film,' put in my mother calmly. 'If the mood takes us. And if I can persuade Andrew to see something slushy. I'm not as keen as he is on scary thrillers.'

'I can't think how you know that,' he said, 'since we've only been allowed to see one of those. Everything else has to have a huge dose of saccharine poured over it, and preferably with Jack Nicholson rejecting the younger dolly bird for the older woman of substance.'

Mum laughed. '*As Good As It Gets.*'

'*Something's Gotta Give*, actually.'

Mum's eyes widened in surprise and she laughed again. 'You're quite right,' she said. As the laughter faded, they both turned to look at me.

I stared. Realised my mouth was open. Shut it, and licked my lips.

'I don't believe this,' I said.

'Why not?' asked Mum gently. 'It's surely more believable than Howard Greenburg downstairs, with his incontinent dog and dental hygiene problem.'

'The dog has a dental problem?' enquired Andrew mildly.

'No no, Howard does.'

'Ah.'

There was a silence. I remained speechless.

'Sorry,' commented Andrew, at length. 'Am I so very unsuitable?'

I opened my mouth. Shut it. Tried again. 'No, you're not,' I croaked. 'But I never in a million years would have thought . . .'

'That I was his type?' put in my mother smoothly.

I flushed. 'I didn't mean that. It's just so unexpected, that's all. Rupert said –' there, I'd said his name. But then we all knew, didn't we? Of course we did. 'He said you'd met someone in Annabel's,' I said in a rush, turning to Andrew almost accusingly.

'And so I did. Your mother.'

I turned, aghast. 'What! What the hell were you doing in Annabel's? Dancing round your handbag?'

She laughed. 'Hardly. No, the Pipers had their sixtieth there. Just a dinner-party for ten – you can eat in there, you know, it's not all dancing the night away. But it was a ridiculous venue, we'd have been much better off in a quiet restaurant, but Donald Piper's always flaunted the fact that he's a member, so there we were. And there was Andrew, too, skulking in a corner as I came out of the Ladies.'

'I was at some terrible military stag-party. A mate of mine in the Battalion was getting married for the third time, to the latest in a succession of increasingly younger wives. A pathetic attempt to recapture his youth – hence Annabel's. It was a relief to see your mother, I must say.'

'A relief? But – hang on.' I clutched my head. 'Because of a certain family feud fifteen years ago, a certain Montague

and Capulet situation with pistols at dawn, one might reasonably assume you couldn't stand the sight of each other!
Wouldn't cross the road to spit at each other, or so I presumed.'

'That's not quite true,' Andrew said carefully. He cradled
his crystal glass in his hand. Gazed down as he swirled the
amber liquid. 'After you and Rupert . . .' He paused. 'Well.
After Rupert left you in the lurch like that, I felt very badly.
Whatever I might have felt about you both being too
young—'

'Or too unsuitable.'

'I never thought you were unsuitable, Henny.' He looked
up. 'Although I was aware you felt that.'

'Whatever,' I muttered, biting my thumbnail savagely.

'Whatever I might have thought, I still felt his treatment
of you very keenly. Thought it was shameful.'

I nodded, accepting that. 'Yes, I know. Dad told me you
wrote to him. Came to see him.'

'I did, in this very flat. In that study through there. A very
long talk we had. He was an extremely sympathetic, intelligent man, your father.'

'Yes, he was,' I said, surprised. Not surprised that he was,
but that Andrew should have been alive to that.

'After I'd gone, he wrote to me, thanking me for coming
to see him. Said it was a decent thing to do, and I needn't
have, and he was sure some men wouldn't. Said he appreciated the gesture.'

I nodded cautiously again. Yes, Dad would have done that too.

'I wrote back and said it was the least I could do under the circumstances, and I apologised again for the hurt caused. I also enclosed a little known publication by Edgar Morrison on the Normandy landings; I could tell from the books which lined his study walls that it would interest him. Said that I didn't want it back. He did send it back a couple of months later though, saying he'd found it fascinating and wouldn't dream of keeping it, and did I know, incidentally, that Edgar Morrison was lecturing on the very subject at the British Museum a few weeks hence. I didn't, but was pleased to be informed. I went along. Your father was there. He raised his hat to me from one side of the room, and I raised mine from the other. That was all.'

I looked at Mum. Her face was impassive.

'Six months later,' Andrew went on, 'there was another lecture. This time in Boulogne, which I attended with a group of military friends. Your father was there too, with a party of North London ex-servicemen. Naturally we couldn't avoid talking then, and anyway, a year had passed since the wedding fiasco. He said you'd met someone else, someone at work. Said you were getting married. I was relieved, and told him Rupert was throwing himself into his work, was serving abroad. We parted, both slightly encouraged, I think. Then there was a dinner at the Mansion House, to which wives were invited. Audrey came to that one.' He nodded at Mum.

'That's right,' she said. 'And you came here the following Sunday to look at some documents Gordon had found that he thought might relate to Waterloo. You stayed to lunch.'

'I think I do need that drink,' I said, getting up and moving to the sideboard. I poured myself a gin and tonic with a shaky hand. 'What – you're saying you became friends? With Mum and Dad?' I turned to look at Andrew, then at my mother, astonished. 'Why didn't you tell me?'

'Because you would have looked at me with the same mixture of horror and disbelief you have on your face now. You were so hurt, Henny. So – demeaned. Naturally. It would have seemed like such a betrayal of trust to admit we liked Andrew and saw him occasionally. That your father, in particular, got on very well with him. Shared interests. We decided not to mention it.'

'Did Benji know?'

'I'm not sure. There wasn't really anything *to* know. No big secret.'

'No.' I nodded. 'I suppose not. And I suppose . . .' I hesitated. 'I might have been hurt.' I looked at her guardedly.

'Exactly. And then,' she sighed, 'well, then we rather lost touch. Andrew travelled so much in the Army and Dad became ill, so . . .' she tailed off. 'We sent Christmas cards, of course, and when Andrew found out about your father's condition,

463

he was kind enough to write to me and tell me how sad he was. How sad that such a fine, academic man should lose the faculty he most valued, and was valued for. I remember the letter very well,' she said quietly. '"A pernicious disease", you called dementia. A cruel one, but one that Gordon would want me to spit in the eye of and march on regardless, as if he were still beside me.'

I glanced down at my drink.

'And I did,' Mum went on. 'Spit at it. I really did – for years. I wouldn't accept that it had taken my husband. Wouldn't give in to it. Until he just wasn't there any more. Wasn't the Gordon I knew.'

There was a silence. Mum regarded the bottom of her glass. Then she glanced up. 'Andrew and I only met again a few months ago,' she said, almost defiantly. 'This isn't something that's been going on for a while.'

'But that night in Annabel's,' Andrew conceded with a wry smile, 'we were both extremely pleased to happen upon each other. We both decided our respective evenings were disastrous. A classic case of sixty-somethings trying to be thirty-somethings and failing dismally. We talked for a while, and your mother kindly agreed to make up a bridge four the following evening at the Chelsea Arts Club. Someone had dropped out with flu.'

'That was a lovely evening, wasn't it?' She turned to him and I saw a light in her eyes I hadn't seen for years. I was aware too that she was trying to mask it, in front of me.

Andrew smiled. 'It was. We sat in the garden and played cards. It was so hot inside, and then when Martin and Pamela had gone, we went for a walk down by the river.'

'That's right,' Mum agreed. 'Past Albert Bridge . . .'

'And on past Cleopatra's Needle.'

'Almost to the Temple.'

For a moment, it was as if I wasn't there. They were both far away, remembering some magical evening when they'd walked together under a velvet sky, the lights from the bridges reflecting in the water, the river lapping darkly at the shore, the soft night air enveloping them. An evening when they'd discovered one another, and thought, Yes, he's a nice man, a good man, underneath that chilly, pompous façade. And likewise, Yes, actually she's a very brave, resilient woman, whose initial silliness has been tempered by the cards life has dealt her. And she's become a finer woman because of it, although no one wants to be told that. No one wants to be told that the slings and arrows are the making of one in the end, and that, as Nietzsche said, whatever doesn't kill you, makes you stronger. But it was true of Mum. A jilted daughter, a gay son and a very sick husband had turned her into the sort of woman she was today. The sort of woman Andrew could not only respect, but could fall in love with, too.

I got off the arm of the chair and went to sit on the sofa, in front of the fire. I slipped out of my coat, and Mum and

Andrew sat opposite me. I stared at their feet. Andrew's cashmere socks and shiny brown brogues appeared from his moleskin trousers, crossed at the knee, one foot bobbling slightly: Mum's particularly good legs in their sheer stockings, neat ankles tapering into expensive Italian shoes. And suddenly, it didn't seem so extraordinary. Why, after all, would someone of Andrew's intelligence and standing, a well-respected Brigadier in command of a Battalion, want a twenty-something nymphet beside him? Why did one automatically assume the worst of men? Why not a companion of his own age who could still turn heads, was still irrefutably elegant, dressed as she was from head to toe in Bond Street's finest, and who was still regarded as a very good-looking woman?

I wasn't surprised at Mum though, I thought guiltily. Hell no. Andrew Ferguson was a strikingly attractive man, but I was surprised . . . that he'd considered our family again. That he'd come back for more. Hadn't we given him enough grief? And hadn't we once, despite his protestation just now, been not quite good enough for his son? At least, that was the impression I'd got. But was that me, being over-sensitive at the time? Too busy wondering if I'd gone to the right schools? The right house-parties?

I remembered our first meeting in the Albany flat all those years ago: Andrew's chilly reticence at the breakfast-table. Was he shy? Shy, because his son had brought home a pretty girl and he was unused to female company at his breakfast-table,

466

in that exclusively male flat? And had he covered his shyness with pomp, and I'd mistaken it for disapproval? Were we both so full of our own insecurities that we'd failed to rumble each other?

I glanced up. Andrew was watching me carefully. My mother's hands were clasped tightly in her lap, her rings gleaming, her knuckles white. Suddenly I realised with a jolt that the tables had turned. That this was a couple sitting before me, hoping for *my* permission. For my approval. I smiled nervously. Made a helpless gesture with my hands.

'Well, what can I say? Of course I'm delighted you've found each other. Of course.'

Mum smiled faintly. Leaned back against the sofa cushions. Andrew nodded briefly, and a glimmer of a smile reached his lips too.

I got up quickly. Walked to the window and gazed out. But where does this leave me, I wondered nervously, running my finger along the white gloss paint. Me and Rupert? In a foursome, for heaven's sake? With parents as gooey-eyed about each other as their children? Golly, Benji would have a field day. I could see us being the butt of endless jokes, except . . . no. No jokes. I saw Benji's face, suddenly. Appalled. And not at this union. At mine.

'So is this why you asked me over here, Mum?' I turned, defiantly. 'Was this the point of the ruse? To let me know you were seeing Andrew? Ask me to sanction your private life?'

'No, it wasn't. It was to talk about *you*, my love. Because for obvious reasons, I know a certain amount about your private life, too.'

I blushed, and turned back to the window to hide my burning face. It hadn't escaped me when I'd walked into the room, that the last time I'd seen this man I'd been naked in his son's bed. But I'd managed to blank that for the last ten minutes. Managed to blank that night, when Andrew had appeared unexpectedly from his girlfriend's flat. *From Mum's flat.* This flat, I thought with a jolt. When a relative of the girlfriend had been taken ill. Of course – it was Dad. Dad, who'd been taken ill. And Andrew would have been here when my mother was telephoned by the Nursing Home to say Dad had been rushed to hospital, had suffered a heart attack. I remembered Andrew's words to me in that sitting room as I dashed through to retrieve my coat, turning to see him sitting there in the dark, on the other side of the room. Words that I'd thought had resounded with disapproval.

*'This is no place for you, Henny. You shouldn't be here.'*

But he'd been trying to tell me something: to get to my father's bedside. And again, I'd read him wrongly. Had felt only guilt, shame and inadequacy in the face of what I'd believed was his moral superiority.

And then later, of course, Andrew would have told Mum that he'd seen me in the flat. Hopefully sparing my blushes – and hers too – by glossing over my flagrantly undressed state,

468

but nonetheless outlining the situation. And that must be why she wanted to speak to me now. She'd presumably guessed where I was.

I gazed out through dark window panes into the garden I knew so well, the one we shared with the neighbours; it was illuminated slightly now by the light from Mrs Spira's ground-floor flat. The heavy branches of the yew tree spread out like skirts over damp grass, whilst glossy laurels and rhododendrons crowded the edge. Yes, she'd got me here to advise me against it. To tell me I was playing with fire, remind me of my responsibilities. I remembered her tone in the Nursing Home when she first heard Marcus and I had separated. 'Get straight home now, my love. Mend those fences.' Except — she didn't know they were beyond repair. Irredeemably broken. I turned and folded my arms tightly. Looked her in the eye.

'Rupert and I are adults, Mum. We're out of your jurisdiction. I know you mean well but we were once very much in love, and now we've found each other again. This is not a flash in the pan, some grubby affair to feel ashamed of; this is something we both feel very strongly about. It's a rekindling of something that was once very real, and still is. Something neither of us will deny this time around.' I raised my chin.

'I'm not questioning your strength of feeling, Henny, or your commitment to Rupert. I never did. I'm questioning his.'

I blinked, wrong-footed. 'What d'you mean, you're questioning his?'

Andrew looked up from the bottom of his whisky glass. His pale blue eyes regarded me gently, but squarely.

'He's married, Henny,' he said.

# chapter twenty-five

I felt the world, as I knew it, tilt beneath me. My stomach lurched and I began to breathe very fast. I stared at Andrew's narrow, fine-boned face, so redolent of Rupert's, with those blue eyes above high cheekbones. Blue eyes steady and true.

'Married?' I breathed. Even as I said it, the idea became preposterous. 'Oh, don't be ridiculous,' I burst out. 'He can't be!'

'He is.'

'But – he can't be! He'd have told me!'

'Would he?'

I stared at him, horrified, brought up short. Suddenly I couldn't look at those penetrating eyes any more. I turned sharply and went to the window once again. My mind was racing like a speeded-up film, my heart pumping as I gazed out at the dark night. A thick fog was settling over the spreading yew tree now: I could smell it seeping across the damp North London garden.

'He can't be,' I said again, but softer, with less conviction this time. There was no answer from Andrew behind me. Worse than a contradiction almost. But . . . I struggled. How? How could he be? He lived in Albany, for heaven's sake, and there was no sign of a wife there. No evidence of a female presence, no pretty cushions, old lipstick ends in the bathroom. Or *did* he live there? Did he perhaps live elsewhere, and that was the London pad? The very much man-about-town pad, to be used – as far as she was concerned – only in emergencies, *in extremis* . . . Jesus. *Married.*

I turned. 'Children?' I heard myself say.

'Three.'

'Three!' I nearly choked.

He nodded. I licked my lips, trying desperately to assimilate this new information, my eyes roaming wildly about the room as I wrestled to comprehend. Rupert. A father of three.

'How – how long has he been married?' It was my voice, but it didn't sound like mine. It was high and shrill, as if someone was squeezing my throat from below.

'Five – maybe six years.'

I saw my mother watching me, her face anxious, distressed: her hands clenching and unclenching. I moved across to the bookcase at the side of the room, holding onto a shelf with my fingertips to steady myself, gazing at the spines. It was the overflow from Dad's study when he ran out of room in there. The books looked dusty through lack of use.

Six years. With three children. Which meant three under the age of five. One of just school age, then a toddler, and then a baby. Hard work. Very hard work. For Rupert's wife. I breathed in sharply, hearing the quick suck of air through my lips, still getting used to the idea, still assimilating the information. Trying to imagine it. Where was she, I wondered. In London? No. No, probably not. Not if Rupert was conducting another life here. She must be up in Hereford, on an Army base. A friend at school had lived on one – modern houses in a friendly cul-de-sac, semis for squaddies, detached for officers, with a patch of green at the front and swings at the back. There wasn't a lot of money in the military, and inside, they were basic, functional. I saw her now, on a Sunday night, struggling with bathtime. A fractious baby, desperate for a bottle in her arms as she knelt on the bathroom floor, two toddlers stamping in the bath, shrieking with glee, the water going in their eyes and the laughter turning to tears as she struggled to placate them, her arms already full of squirming baby.

I remembered those years. The tedium, the frustration, the exhaustion, the rattiness, the lack of stimulation, the burning desire to talk to anyone over the age of five. And Marcus had been so good about coming home early, giving a hand with bathtime, reading stories. And where was her husband? What

473

had he told her? 'Sorry, darling, I'm still in Basra,' or Faluja, or some other sensitive, war-torn somewhere, on a highly dangerous important mission, naturally. And naturally it would take precedence over three small children and a wet bathroom floor. And all the time, all the time, he was cooking fillet steaks in his cashmere pullover, for me, his mistress. Nipping out to the offy for some claret, for his floozie. Who was also married. I swallowed. Regarded the leather spines with their gold embossed lettering before me. Did that make a difference, I wondered? Make it better? I turned.

'So he's married,' I said hoarsely. 'Well, I'm married too,' I countered.

'You are,' Mum agreed.

'And – and sometimes – well, sometimes marriages don't work out. Not all marriages are made in heaven, you know. And anyway, people only go looking for someone else if they're unhappy.'

Even as I said it, I knew it wasn't true. I hadn't been unhappy with Marcus. I'd been bored at times, but not with him. Just with my empty nest. With my monied, stockbroker-belt life, where my housework was done for me and I tried hard to fill my days. I'd wanted to spice it up a bit. Well, I'd certainly done that.

'And sometimes marriages need to be worked at,' said Mum quietly. 'Need to be fought for. Many are worth fighting for. But of course, it's much easier to throw in the towel.'

'Or perhaps not even bother to throw in the towel,' put in Andrew. 'To run two lives at the same time.'

Like Rupert, he meant. Rupert, running two women, two houses, two lives. Why hadn't he told me? He must have known I'd find out. And after all, I had a marriage, for heaven's sake – children, a home – why not tell me about his? Why hide it? Lie? I thought of her tucking her children in at night. Desperate for a drink as she went downstairs, for that magical, white-wine reward when she'd finally got them all down.

'What's her name?' I said to the dark window.

'Sinead.'

'Sinead?' I turned. 'That's Irish, isn't it?'

'Yes, she is Irish. Lives in Ireland.'

My mind spun. 'So – so that little cottage, the one in the photo on Rupert's dresser, is that their home? Where they live?'

'That, I believe,' Andrew picked his words carefully, 'is Rupert's holiday cottage. A very basic little place near Dundalk, on a river. A retreat.'

'Rupert's cottage? Not theirs? And – you *believe*? Why don't you know?' I gazed at him. He didn't answer. I looked at Mum. She glanced down at her hands.

I licked my lips. 'Andrew, what's going on here? Have you met Sinead? Been to their house?'

He gave himself a moment. 'Yes,' he replied eventually. 'Yes to both those questions. But only once.'

'Only once!' I was staggered. 'But, hang on – they've been married for six years!'

He struggled for the right words. 'Henny, Rupert's very private, as you know.'

'Is he?' I flushed angrily. 'No, I didn't know that. He was never private, or secretive, with me!'

'No, you're right,' he conceded. 'He wasn't. And when he brought you home that first time, when you stayed the night after the ball – well, you could have knocked me for six. I nearly fell off the chair at the breakfast-table. You were the first girlfriend he'd ever brought back, unlike Peter who'd had them traipsing in and out since he was sixteen. And the last.'

'The last? You mean . . .'

'The next one I met was already his wife. Sinead. He got married without my knowledge. Without telling anyone, in fact. To a girl he'd known for some time, apparently. But there was no big wedding. No ceremony. They just quietly went ahead with it one day in Dundalk. Even Peter didn't know.'

'Good heavens.' I sat down abruptly on the arm of a chair. 'How extraordinary.'

'He leads an extraordinary kind of life, Henny. The nature of his work dictates a degree of secrecy, of privacy.'

'Well a degree, yes – but surely other SAS officers lead relatively normal family lives? Just don't blab too much when they come home. Presumably they still mow the lawn though, go to the pub, have Sunday lunch . . .' Unlike Rupert, I thought suddenly, whose whole life, it seemed, was shrouded in mystery. And shrouded from me, too.

My gaze skimmed the top of Andrew's head for a moment, then I found his eyes. 'He wasn't going to tell me, was he? I mean, at all?'

Andrew made a hopeless, embarrassed face. 'I doubt it.'

'And – and yet, he appeared to want to commit to me, Andrew. I mean, in a deadly serious, permanent way that I couldn't even begin to contemplate. That I felt was far too scary, too over the top.' It was true, I'd repeatedly shied away and pushed it to the back of my mind, but in Rupert's eyes – oh no. This relationship was utterly serious.

'Oh, I don't doubt that for one minute,' said Andrew vehemently. It was the first thing he'd said with any real conviction since we'd started this conversation. 'I don't doubt that at all. He wanted you very much.'

'Yes, but . . .' How could he? I wanted to say. How could he have me, and still have another life in Ireland? With Sinead? Was he going to have his cake and eat it? Except . . . no. That didn't ring true either. My head was spinning.

'And you, Henny?' said Mum, coming forward and sitting on the opposite arm of the chair, breaking into my thoughts. 'Are you deadly serious? How do you feel now you know he's married?'

I got up and turned back to the window. 'The same,' I

wanted to say. 'This hasn't changed a thing. Not a thing.' But it had. It had changed everything. I stared out. The fog had turned to rain now; that fine, insidious rain that drenches everything, quietly and stealthily. I gazed down at the sodden black grass and wondered when he'd been planning on going home. When he'd been planning on walking through the door in Dundalk, scooping up the four year old running excitedly towards him –

'Daddy!'

Kissing his tired wife as she came down the hall to meet him, a baby in her arms, a toddler clutching her skirt, a weary smile. 'Good trip?'

Oh no, it changed everything.

'And she, I take it, is unaware of me?' I swung back to Andrew. 'Unaware of my existence?'

'Oh no, she's very aware of you. Has been for years.'

I stared at him. 'What d'you mean? How d'you know?'

'Because I've talked to her. When I say I've only met her once, it's true. But that once was last weekend, for the first time. I went to Ireland to see her, at Peter's insistence. I had a long telephone conversation with him and he persuaded me to go. He's been convinced for years that Rupert had some sort of other life going on, but he's too far-flung in Australia to do anything about it. But he said if there were children involved, which he was convinced there were, then I, as their grandfather, should find out. So I went.'

'But where? How did you know where to go? And why Ireland?'

'Laurie tipped me off.'

'Laurie?'

'Yes, Laurence De Havilland, your employer,' he said patiently.

I shot my fingers up through my hair, bewildered now. 'Hang on – why would Laurie know?'

'Because he served with Rupert in Northern Ireland, years ago. They did a tour of Armagh together. Towards the end of it, Rupert joined the Special Forces and worked under-cover in Dublin, but even though he'd left the Regiment they still came across each other militarily. And I know Laurie through the Brigade, you see. See him at regimental dinners, that sort of thing.'

'And . . . he knew about this? About Rupert's other life out there? How come?'

'A few years back, there was a bit of a scandal. Laurie had left the Army but had gone back to Armagh to see some of his mates who were still serving there. You know, the big hot-shot TV presenter drinking in the Mess with his old Army buddies, good PR. Anyway, while he was there, he got a local girl pregnant. She came over here to have an abortion, and because of who he was, it got into the papers. It was nothing very much, just a few lines on page nine of the *Daily Mail* – "History man in paternity scare", or something, but in the report, it said that Donna O'Sullivan left the abortion clinic in London with her brother-in-law. The picture was of her and Rupert.'

'Oh!'

'Exactly. Oh. Peter was over from Australia at the time, and he spotted it. Pointed it out to me. We rang Rupert in Ireland who laughed. Completely poo-pooed it. Said – how ridiculous, the paper had got it wrong. He *had* darted over from Ireland and met the girl at the clinic, but as a favour to her brother, who was working with him in Dublin. *Friend* of the brother, he maintained, not brother-in-law. Honestly, these hacks.'

'But it was, in fact . . .'

'Sinead's sister who Laurie had got up the spout.'

I remembered Rupert's scathing condemnation of Laurie. No morals, no sense of responsibility. Leaves his mess for other people to clear up. But it was a mess slightly closer to home.

'Right. So Rupert's rumbled . . .'

'But laughs it off. But for ages it's rankled and I've wondered. And then the other day, after I saw you in the flat, I got to thinking. Thinking that if my son *did* have a life I didn't know about in Ireland, then you probably didn't know about it either. And that maybe you should. Maybe we should all know. And maybe I should take my head out of the sand and find out what was going on before a bloody great can of worms erupted.'

# not that kind of girl

'So you rang Laurie.'

'Exactly. I rang Laurie, who was loth to tell me initially, but eventually confirmed my worst fears. He said that the girl he'd got pregnant did have a sister, and that the sister lived in a tiny community on a remote part of the east coast. She had small children, and lived close to Dundalk – in Dromiskin, in fact. The same village as Rupert.'

'Right.' My breathing was getting shallower. 'So you went out there.'

'Two days ago, I went out there. I found the village, and then I went to the pub. I showed the barman a picture of Rupert. Asked where his wife lived. It didn't take long.'

'And it's true.'

'Oh yes, it's true. She's his wife all right.'

'But – why keep it a secret? Why not bring her home to England, or – or live openly with her in Ireland? *Does* he live with her?'

'A bit, apparently. But not much. He visits.'

'He *visits*!' I yelped. 'Why?'

Andrew shrugged in a despairing gesture, palms up, fingers splayed 'I don't know yet, Henny. I'm still new to the situation. There's so much I still don't know, so much that's between Rupert and Sinead, but I have my theories, of course I do.'

I got up and turned back to the window. Watched as the rain, heavier now, splattered against the dark pane, beating out a tattoo. Suddenly I didn't want to know his theories.

Didn't want the explanation. An owl screeched high up in the yew tree then flew off into the night. I exhaled onto the glass and as condensation formed, rested my forehead on the window. Down below me, in the first-floor flat, a child cried out, then there was the muffled sound of a mother, quietening it. Must be Howard Greenburg's daughter-in-law, I thought. Brought the grandchildren for a visit. The child persisted.

'But I want it now!'

And then suddenly, I realised that the voices were much more proximate. Not down below at all. The hairs stood up on the back of my neck as I lifted my head off the glass and listened. They were too clear to be coming from Howard's flat; they were here, in this flat. The child called out again. The sounds were coming from the bedroom at the far end of the corridor. I spun around.

'Who's here?'

Mum got up and came towards me, her hands outstretched in a desperate, soothing gesture, her eyes huge and troubled.

'Oh darling, we weren't going to do this, Andrew and I, we agreed.' Her eyes darted anxiously down the corridor. 'Agreed it was too much for you to take in all at once, and they were tired, anyway, they were going to sleep. Sinead agreed, we talked to her about it.'

My eyes widened in horror. My stomach tipped. 'She's here? Sinead's here, with her children, is that what you're saying?'

# not that kind of girl

Footsteps padded quickly down the passageway, and in another moment, the door burst open. A girl of about ten shot into the room wearing pink jeans and a white T-shirt, her long dark hair flying.

'I *can* have a drink, can't I?' She ran across to Mum. 'Mam says I can't, but I can get one by myself from the kitchen. I've done it before!' Her voice was high, lilting, unmistakably Irish. Her eyes very blue. Unmistakably Rupert's.

'I'll get it for you,' said Mum, quickly taking her shoulders and ushering her out as the child, with round eyes like blue marbles, twisted around to stare at me, at the stranger she'd been hurried away from.

'Now,' I heard Mum say as she ran the tap, 'drink up, and then straight back to Mummy.'

She tried to hurry her back, but then there were more footsteps, firmer this time, and then another voice joined her in the kitchen.

'I'm sorry, Audrey, I couldn't stop her.'

My heart seemed to halt for a moment. I looked at Andrew. He met my eyes, then glanced away, down at the carpet. I held my breath. The seconds ticked by. There was a whispered discussion in the kitchen, then moments later, she appeared.

She came through the doorway holding her child's hand. She was tall, slim and very pale, with thick dark hair to her shoulders which hung in her eyes in a heavy fringe. Attractive, but not in a pretty, fluffy way. This was a strong face, a direct

483

pair of hazel eyes under dark brows, and a square jaw. As she came into the room, I noticed she had a slight limp. Another child darted into the room behind her, a boy of about seven, and she held out a hand to steady him, to stop him careering ahead. He saw me and darted shyly behind his mother, peeking out.

'I'm Sinead,' she said simply, stopping just inside the room.

I nodded. Tried to speak, but the words wouldn't come. Instead, blood rushed up my neck to my face, staining my cheeks. An awful, shaming blush.

'It's all right, I know who you are.' She regarded me a moment longer, then bent to see to her children.

'Go on now, Tom, get your coat. You know where it is, we're going now.'

'We're going?' His voice was high and reedy. 'You didn't say we were going out.'

'Well, I'm saying now, so go on with you. Don't touch that,' she admonished as the girl darted across the room to the bureau to pick up a china rabbit of Mum's. Sinead followed and took it from her hands. 'Go on now, Hetta, get your coat.'

'Hetta?' I said, despite myself. I'd been called that on occasion. My mind whirled. 'Short for . . .'

'Henrietta, that's right. But we call her Hetta.' She looked at me defiantly. I met her eyes. Clear and direct. I nodded mutely. Jesus. Henrietta.

She turned to Mum. 'The children have rested now, Audrey. Tom slept for over an hour, so thank you for that. We'll be going to see their father now.'

'Daddy!' The girl jumped up and down on the spot. 'We're going to see Daddy?'

'Is that wise?' asked Andrew, stepping forward anxiously. 'Without, you know. Letting him know?'

I was conscious that everyone was very aware of me. Standing, listening.

Sinead gave a wry smile. 'If I were wise, Andrew, I wouldn't have let you persuade me to come over in the first place. But now we're here, yes. I must.' She kept her eyes on him. 'And I'd like to go when I know for sure he's alone.'

I inhaled sharply.

'Will you be back?' asked Andrew. 'I mean, will you be coming back here, or . . .'

'I don't know,' she said simply. 'I'll have to see how it goes.'

Her voice, which up to now she'd kept steady, was slightly strained, aware of her audience. I watched dumbly as this scene was enacted before me, like a play I was watching but not participating in.

'There's always a bed for you and the children here, dear,' said my mother softly.

I turned to look at her, astonished. She met my eye, and suddenly, I felt humbled. She was right. Of course she was right.

'Thank you,' said Sinead. 'You've been very kind.'

My heart still hammering, I watched as she chivvied her children into their coats. They were older than I'd imagined, and where was the youngest, the baby? Must have left it behind. She made her son pull his anorak zip up before he went out, and told her daughter to find her trainers.

'Now, please, Hetta.'

'I don't know where they are.'

'Back in the bedroom, I expect,' said Mum, bustling away.

'Well, go on with you, child,' chided the mother. 'Don't let Audrey get them, go look.'

'Take my car,' said Andrew suddenly, fishing in his pocket and holding out his keys. 'I don't need it, and at this time of night you can park anywhere, even on a yellow line.'

'Thanks.' She looked up from struggling with her son's zipper and smiled. Grateful that this stiff, formal man, her father-in-law, was going out of his way for her. He hadn't met his grandchildren before, but through no fault of his own. Now he was making up for it. Making up for lost time. She straightened and took the keys.

'Goodbye, Hetta,' Andrew said as the child ran back into the room in her trainers. 'Tom.' He nodded at them awkwardly, as was his way, but they were demonstrative children, delighted, no doubt, to have found a brand new grandfather they didn't know they had, and Hetta ran to him and put her arms up for a hug, a kiss. Tom too.

I saw Andrew flush, delighted, as he bent to return their embrace.

'And you know where you're going?' he said over their heads to their mother. 'You know Albany? It's off Piccadilly, you can't go wrong.'

Sinead laughed. A light, musical sound. 'Andrew, I've never set foot in England before, let alone London, but don't worry. I've got Audrey's *A to Z*. I'll find it.'

Andrew looked troubled. 'Why don't you let me drive you? I can do that. And I can wait, if needs be. Bring you back later.'

'You will not,' she said. 'Jeez, in Rupert's eyes you'll have interfered enough just by getting me here. He won't thank you for driving me to the door and loitering outside his flat. No, I'll find it.'

My being, which up until this point seemed to have been frozen in time whilst this scene was being played out, crackled into life at this moment. Something uncoiled within me at his name. I opened my mouth.

'I'll show you,' I heard my voice saying. 'I'm going that way. I'll come with you and show you where it is.'

# chapter twenty-six

Sinead had crouched down again to tie her son's laces. She glanced up at me. I was aware of my mother's and Andrew's eyes on me too. She rose slowly in the silence. Regarded me a moment.

'OK,' she said softly.

Another highly charged silence followed. Even the children seemed aware of some development and were quiet. The air felt thick, heavy. I swallowed and moved into it, going purposefully across to a chair to pick up my coat. My hands were shaking as I did up the buttons, and I bent my head in studied contemplation of them to avoid my mother's eyes. A moment later, the children began their chattering and clamouring as Sinead ushered them towards the door, and the atmosphere was broken.

Mum found my ear as she opened the door. 'Is this wise?' she murmured anxiously.

# not that kind of girl

'I don't know,' I muttered back. I caught a glimpse of Andrew's face as we left, tense and worried, but moments later – it was too late. I was in that familiar stairwell with the flat door shut behind me, walking downstairs with Sinead by my side.

Hetta ran ahead of us, but Tom, a live wire, waited behind to slide down the banisters. His mother turned, exasperated as he shifted his bottom onto the rail and slid towards us.

'Off, Tom. Now!'

She hoiked him off and he laughed. She admonished him again, but it was something to do, I felt, to chide the child, to hold his arm and march him down, and we were both glad of the distraction. Hetta waited at the bottom for us to catch up.

'Who are you?' she asked, falling into step beside me and turning round eyes up.

'I'm . . .' I faltered.

'This is Audrey's daughter,' said Sinead easily. 'She's going to show us the way to Daddy's.'

'Will we see Buckingham Palace?' asked Tom.

'No, I don't think so,' his mother replied. 'But I'll show you tomorrow. We'll go see it then.'

'With Daddy?'

I felt my throat tighten again. *Daddy.*

'Maybe.'

'We haven't seen him for six months,' volunteered the girl beside me as I reached up for the doorknob.

'Seven,' corrected her mother.

I felt my head bow. I seemed to be getting smaller by the minute. I opened the door for them.

'I thought you had three children?' I said as she went through. 'I'm sure Andrew said three.'

'Rupert has three children. I have two,' she said. I watched her back as she exited. Felt frozen with shock.

'You mean . . .'

She turned to look at me, outside in the dark now: a shadowy figure in the front garden.

'He has another daughter in Kosovo. She's about eleven, I believe. Also called Henrietta.'

I felt the blood leave my face as I let the door go. I forced myself to walk on after her, down the path to the pavement, my heart pumping. I was aware of her just ahead of me; aware of the shocks she knew she was calmly delivering. Zap. Zap. Zap.

'Right,' I breathed as she paused beside a blue Audi.

'Rupert was out there for a year or so. He struck up a relationship. These things happen.'

She eyed me as she opened the Audi door. What things? I thought. Her husband having relationships, or him having two daughters called Henrietta? The children scrambled in the back and Sinead showed them how to put on their belts, then made to get in herself.

'D'you want me to drive?' I asked, still reeling. Three children. Different mothers.

# not that kind of girl

I saw her hesitate. An unfamiliar car in an unfamiliar city.

'No, I'll drive,' she said firmly.

And I would have done the same. Would have wanted to be in the driving seat for this particular excursion. This particular *tête-à-tête*.

I directed her down the hill to the Finchley Road, my head still spinning. What was this, *Soldier Soldier*? A girl in every port? And were there more children she didn't know about? More bloody Henriettas?

'That's it,' she said, reading my thoughts. 'No other children.'

'And you believe him?'

'Oh, he's always been honest. Scrupulously. He's never lied to me once.'

Well, he has to me, I thought. Or had he? I tried to remember if I'd ever asked? Asked if he was married with kids? Or just assumed he wasn't?

'But . . .' I struggled to comprehend. 'Andrew said you'd been married for six years. I thought your children would be younger.'

'Did you?' She turned to look at me from behind the wheel. Eyes clear, challenging.

'Well . . .' I faltered.

'We have been married for six years. But I've known Rupert for fourteen.'

491

'Fourteen!' I looked at her, astonished. Fourteen. I'd known him for fifteen.

'So . . .'

'I know all about you, Henny,' she said softly, her eyes trained on the road now as she navigated the car around the Swiss Cottage to Avenue Road. 'I picked up the pieces.'

I remembered Tommy saying that Rupert had been posted to Ireland soon after the wedding. That he'd gone to Hong Kong as planned, but after a few months, had been promoted, got an attachment somewhere grittier.

'The pieces were of his making,' I said steadily. 'He left me. At the altar.'

'I know. And he never got over it.'

'Well, funnily enough, it took me a while too,' I said tersely.

'But you met someone quite quickly, didn't you? Fell in love and got married within a year.'

'Yes, I fell in love and got married. And he met you!'

'Yes, he met me. Except . . . I could never quite match up. Never quite be what he wanted. Because he always wanted you.'

'He could have had me!' I said angrily. 'But he jilted me.'

'I know. He flunked it – lost his nerve. And that's shaped his life. That's why his life is as it is. Dangerous, uncertain, unsettled – he's tested himself ever since, to make sure it never happens again. He's been blown up twice, got the VC in Iraq – he's desperate to make sure he doesn't flunk again. And he

492

didn't want to tie himself to me, either – and not in case anything happened to him, nothing so altruistic as that – but in case you ever came back. But I made him, after Tom was born, and when Hetta was about five. She was starting school, and doing that without a father's surname in a small, rural Catholic community is not easy. There was shame in it. It wasn't fair on her. Wasn't fair to have her taunted, teased.'

'So . . . that's why he married you?' I was shocked by her candour.

'That's why he married me. For the children.' She gave a wry half-smile. Looked straight ahead. 'Oh, he was fond of me all right, I'm sure of that, but I'm under no illusions either. He always hoped you'd come back. Leave Marcus. Always mentally kept me in reserve.'

'He told you that?' I said, aghast.

'Not in so many words, but in the way . . . in the way that he never completely gave himself to me. Couldn't. I told you, he's honest. And you have to be true to yourself, to your own heart. You can't live a lie. Right here?'

'What? Oh yes. Right here, then left at the top. But . . . you accepted that?'

'I loved him,' she said simply. 'That was enough for me. That was being true to *my* heart. I even let him call my daughter after you, although I drew the line at Henny.' She glanced at my shocked face as we sat at the lights at Baker Street. She sighed. Went on in a slightly gentler tone. 'Many

493

people "settle" for a marriage, Henny, don't you know that? Settle for a partner who's not their ideal. We can't always have what we want. But not many are as honest about it as Rupert.'

Or as cruel, I thought privately, my heart pounding.

'Henrietta Tate,' she said quietly as we moved off from the lights. 'Sitting here beside me in this car.' She shook her head in wonder. 'Who'd have thought?'

I shifted uncomfortably.

'I've lived in your shadow for fourteen years,' she said, a slight smile playing on her face. 'Lived with your ghost, and always wondered . . . well, if I'd ever meet you one day. What you'd be like.'

'Nothing special,' I muttered awkwardly.

She shrugged. 'Special to Rupert. He never got over you.'

'Or perhaps . . .' I gazed into the lights of Oxford Street ahead. 'Perhaps he never got over what he did to me. What it meant to be a man who leaves a girl shattered and distressed at the altar. What that made him. In his eyes. In other people's eyes. In the Army's eyes. Perhaps this is more about him, than me.'

She considered this. 'Maybe.'

We cruised quietly down the wet black streets towards Piccadilly, each lost in our own thoughts. On a Sunday night the traffic was relatively light. At length, I cleared my throat.

'If you go left down here it takes you to the back of Albany. You can park and walk round to the front.'

I glanced into the back seat. The children were quiet now, heads lolling back, eyes round and glazed as they stared out of their respective windows at the lights, their unfamiliar surroundings. Slightly different from the fields of Dundalk, I imagined.

'Here will do,' I said, indicating a space behind a lorry in a side street. She tucked the car in and switched off the engine. I turned to her.

'Will you find your way now?'

'I will, but I want you to do something for me.'

My heart jumped. 'What?'

'I want you to go on ahead and tell him we're here. That we're coming. I'll wait in the car.'

My mouth dried as I looked at her. 'Why?'

'Because he hasn't seen us for seven months. And I figure you've seen quite a lot of him lately.'

I held her eyes for a minute, then buckled and looked away.

'I'm guessing,' she went on quietly, 'that you might have unfinished business here, too. I'm asking you to resolve it. Either take him, or leave him. But resolve it.'

I looked back at her. Swallowed. 'And if I take him?'

'Well, then I'll know for sure. Finally. My story is resolved too.' She gave a half-smile, a hint of a shrug. 'And all is not lost. My children still have a surname; they still have a father. Rural Ireland we may be, but there are plenty of children of divorced parents. There's no shame in that. Obviously I'd prefer it to be different, but I don't have the whip-hand here. Never have had. You do.' She paused. 'It's up to you, Henny, and let me tell you, I'm relieved. I've wanted this day for a long time. Looked forward to it. I'm glad I've met you.'

I regarded her in the driver's seat, dimly lit from the street-lamps. Her hazel eyes were steady, clear. This was a strong woman. A resilient woman. A woman who'd done her best with the life she'd been offered. Who'd tried to mould it, shape it into something she could be proud of. I thought of her in her cottage in Dromiskin, prowling around downstairs when the children were asleep, wondering where he was, what he was doing. Wondering, more recently, if he was with me. Hoping in a way that he was. That she could have her day of reckoning.

'I'm glad too.'

I got out of the car, and stood still for a moment, steadying myself. Then I walked quickly in the direction of Albany. It had stopped raining, and the air was damp and still. I went around the corner and turned into Piccadilly, my clicking heels contrasting sharply with the relaxed stance of a clutch of tourists peering at a poster outside the Royal Academy. I turned left into the forecourt, pushed through the main front door, then inside the lobby – stopped, and took a deep breath. I stared at the row of bells. Then I raised my hand, and rang Rupert's.

'Hello?'

'Rupert, it's me again.'

# not that kind of girl

'Henny!'

The surprise and delight in his voice made me shut my eyes for a moment. Rock back on my heels. Then the buzzer went to admit me, and I pushed through the heavy inner door. I ignored the lift and took the stairs, needing the time to gather my thoughts, prepare a few words, but of course, I was there in moments, and when he opened the door, my thoughts were in tatters. There he was, this handsome man with this extraordinary life; tanned from the Gulf, from leaping out of armoured cars in the desert, his men fanning out behind him with machine guns, a girl in every port, but all the time, with only one woman on his mind. One girl in his heart. Me. His blond hair flopped over his forehead and he pushed it back, grinning delightedly in his bright red jumper.

'You made it!'

As he stepped aside to let me in, I knew I was about to be taken in his arms. Knew that in a matter of moments his lips would be on mine, full of love and passion as he ran his hands hungrily over my body, backed me up against the wall. I thrust my hands in my coat pockets and stepped aside from him in a deliberate gesture. Glanced up, and saw his eyes fill with confusion.

'Rupert, Sinead's downstairs.'

His face went blank for a moment.

'Sinead,' I said again, my voice unsteady. 'She's downstairs. With the children.'

I watched as this filtered through. As the penny visibly dropped. He stared at me wordlessly.

'Your father went to find them in Ireland,' I ploughed on. 'He and Peter realised they were out there somewhere, and he brought them back with him. I met them just now in Mum's flat. She and your father, it transpires,' I gave a hollow laugh, 'have been friends for years. Ever since we parted. Ironic, isn't it? And now it seems they may become more than friends.'

'He brought her here?' he breathed incredulously, ignoring my last remark. 'Brought Sinead here?'

'Because he was keen to do the right thing. Introduce himself to his family. To his grandchildren. Welcome them to England. How about you, Rupert? Are you keen to do the right thing? Were you even going to tell me they existed? Or were you going to let me find out a year or two down the line, when I was in too deep, and it was too late to worry about them?'

He shut the door carefully behind me. His eyes flickered momentarily to the ceiling, then down at the floor as he gave himself a moment to think. To collect himself. He nodded. 'Yes, I was going to tell you. But—'

'When?' I demanded. 'When were you going to tell me?'

'In time.'

'What, when you'd bedded me?' I flung my arm down the corridor towards the bedroom. 'Is that what all the unseemly haste was about? When you'd comprehensively hooked me? When you knew I couldn't go back to Marcus, or at least, when you knew it would be much, much harder?'

'Henny,' he sighed, 'this is different. This isn't the wife and kids. This isn't like you and Marcus, your children.'

'Why? Why isn't it?' My voice rose shrilly.

'Because, unless she hasn't told you the truth, you'll already know that I never wanted it.' His voice went up a notch too. 'Never wanted the shackles of a wife and children, always wanted to be free in case you came back. I never wanted to tie myself to anything – a steady job, a country, a woman, a home – nothing!'

'But you have! You have all that – a wife, a home—'

'I don't have it *here*.' He thumped his chest with a clenched fist. Brought his face closer to mine. His eyes burned into me. 'I don't feel it here, in my heart. She knows that.'

I stared into his eyes. 'But that's so unfair, Rupert,' I whispered eventually. 'How can you do that? And the children, what about them? All of them?' I eyed him knowingly.

The light went from his eyes and he gave a tight little smile. 'Ah. So she's spilled *all* the beans, has she?'

'Your father told me that. Sinead just confirmed it.'

He shrugged. 'Yes, OK, I have three children. So what?'

'Two girls called Henrietta.'

'Yes.'

I stared at him. He held my gaze defiantly.

'*Both* of them, Rupert?' I yelped.

'Well, they were hardly going to meet, were they?' he said almost angrily. 'What difference does it make what they're called?'

'A difference to you, surely! Don't you care? Your *off*spring! Christ!'

He thought for a moment. 'No, I don't. I mean . . .' he struggled with the truth. 'I care more now, now that they're older, and yes, I'm very fond of them. But at the time – no. I was a soldier, and it was just . . . oh God, a baby. Then: "What d'you want to call her, Rupert?" A dewy-eyed mother in bed, gazing at a bundle. "Oh God, I don't know." "Well, what name do you like?" "What name do I like? I like Henrietta."'

We stared at one another.

'I didn't care, Henny, no. Not really. Not like a proud father should. These were girls I'd slept with, not partners I'd picked out for life. I was young, I was careless, they got pregnant – Jesus, it happens. Particularly in my line of work.'

'Shagging around.'

'Well, I wasn't going to stay celibate, for Christ's sake! Not for fifteen years!'

There was a highly charged silence. We stared at each other in the gloom of the hall.

'You lied to me, Rupert.' My voice shook.

'No, I didn't.'

500

'Yes, you did. When we met in the street, outside Benji's house—'

'You didn't ask me if I was married. You asked me if I'd ever met anyone. The answer's no. It's still no. It's only ever been you, Henny.'

'But you married Sinead.'

'Yes, I married her,' he said impatiently.

'Why?'

'Because she wanted me to. For the children.'

'Simple as that?'

'No. Nothing in Ireland is as simple as that.'

I stared at him. 'What d'you mean?'

'I owed it to her.'

'Owed it to her? Why?'

He hesitated. Then he turned away from me and walked down the hall a few paces. When he turned back, his eyes were stony. His face pale. 'Henny, fourteen years ago, when I met Sinead, I'd just finished a six-month tour of Northern Ireland. I was known in the Province as an Officer in the Guards. After that, I was seconded to the SAS and worked undercover in the South. I was in plain clothes, civvies, and I was gleaning information about the IRA. Using it against them. I worked in Dublin, mostly. Plenty of Englishmen do. My identity was changed, and I became Charles Parker, Civil Servant with the High Commission.'

'Oh. Did they know?'

'Who?'

'The High Commission.'

'Of course. That's the point.'

'You were a spy.'

'Of sorts.'

I waited.

'At the weekends, I went to Dundalk. The Army bought me a cottage on a river there. A country retreat, ostensibly, somewhere to fish. It's also where an awful lot of terrorists come from.'

'Right. So you were spying there, too.'

'Doing surveillance work, yes.'

'There's a picture of it on your chest of drawers.'

'Exactly.'

I thought for a moment. 'The one underneath, the one you didn't want me to see, being of Sinead and the children.'

He flinched at this remark, but let it go. Swept on. 'Sinead worked in a bar that I drank in nearby. I had an English accent. People wondered about me. Have you any idea how brave it was of her to see me?'

'You told her who you were? Who you really were?'

'Not at first, but eventually, yes. It wouldn't have been fair not to.'

'Brave of you, too. She might have betrayed you.'

'She might, but danger's an occupational hazard for me. And I'm armed. I'm a soldier – she's not.'

'So . . . even braver of her to bear your children. To want to marry you.' I was brought up short with the realisation.

'Exactly. And after Hetta was born, she was questioned about me.'

'You mean, they were on to you? The IRA?'

'They had their suspicions, but nothing tangible. I was, after all, Charles Parker, working in Dublin, remember. Then, a few years later, after Tom was born, someone followed her out of the supermarket one day. She was aware of a man behind her in the car park, and she tightened her grip on the buggy, on Hetta's hand. As she walked quickly to the car and opened the boot to unload the groceries, he approached her. Asked if she'd like a hand. She declined, but he stretched down nonetheless, ostensibly to pick up a heavy carrier bag, but instead, he fired a pistol into the back of her knee.'

'Oh my God.' Both hands shot to my mouth.

'He shattered her kneecap. Left her lying in the street. Hetta screaming, Tom in the buggy. Blood everywhere.'

I kept my hands cupped over my mouth. 'How awful!' I breathed.

He shrugged. 'Quite common in Ireland. In those days, anyway.'

I lowered my hands slowly. 'She limps,' I whispered.

'Yes, she does. And she always will. It's something she'll carry with her for the rest of her life. A stigma. And that's the intent. It's supposed to be a badge of shame, to let everyone know you've collaborated. It's one up from being tarred and feathered – which still happens, incidentally.'

'My God.' My stomach tipped.

'I was in Bosnia at the time, but when I got back . . . when I opened the front door of her cottage and she came towards me, carrying the baby, limping . . .' He swallowed.

I waited. Yes, I thought. Yes, you're a tough man, Rupert. But no one's that tough.

'We talked, and she said that since everyone knew, since the whole community knew, and since she was going to bear the stigma for the rest of her life, she wanted to bear my name, too.' His eyes misted over for a moment. 'I remember her so clearly, sitting at that kitchen table. Her leg still bandaged.' His eyes came back to me. 'What could I do?'

I leaned back against the wall, my hands clenched now in my coat pockets. I took a deep breath.

'Is she still in danger?'

He shrugged. 'Yes. No. Maybe. Things have calmed down a bit in Ireland. Ostensibly there's been a ceasefire. But still, people disappear. Bodies are found in lakes. I certainly can't live with her in her cottage in Dromiskin in the conventional sense. I have to be very circumspect.'

'But she could live here, with you, in London.'

'She could.'

'Or on the base, in Hereford.'

'Yes.'

'She'd be safer.'

'Undoubtedly.'

'And – would she come?'

'I don't know. I've never asked her. And she's too proud to ask.'

'You owe it to her,' I whispered.

He smiled sadly. Nodded. 'And there's the rub. Do we live out our lives with people we owe, those we're indebted to, those who've borne our children, those who, through our own carelessness, we find ourselves shackled to, or do we keep searching for what our heart tells us is right?'

I gave this some thought. 'I think,' I said, choosing my words carefully, 'that sometimes what our heart tells us is right, is overblown. Exaggerated, because it's unattainable. And therefore, all the more attractive.'

He considered this. Then: 'Do you? I don't.'

My heart began to thump. 'It's not going to be, Rupert. Not after all of this. We can't just carry on, regardless of everyone. Regardless of whose dreams we're trampling on, whose lives we're wrecking.'

'*You* can't, you mean.'

'No. *I* can't.'

'So that's a no then, is it?'

I clenched my jaw. 'It's a no.'

Our eyes locked as we absorbed the ramifications of this. This was the final demarcation line for us, and we'd reached it sooner than either of us imagined. This was never again. No going back. A dead end for ever. A wave of shock and sadness swept over me. Rocked me, almost. It dawned on me that I'd never see that passion seep through his body again, through his muscles, his skin, his eyes, feel that incredible heat that emanated from him, so spontaneous, and so absolute, it took my breath away. I'd never feel my own body respond in kind, either. Never feel my bones turn to liquid, my stomach lurch so beautifully, never feel – so alive. So young. The brave soul in me, some would say reckless, mourned that. Mourned that passing. Yet another part of me – and, I believe, the greater part – gave a quiet sigh. Of relief. Relief that I was stepping back from those fathomless depths which, in no time at all, would have closed over my head as I went down, never to surface, at least in any recognisable way, again. And this was what Sinead had wanted, I thought with a jolt. For me to choose. To go with whichever was the greater part of me. The better part of me. To tell him to his face. To say no.

I raised my chin. Kept my gaze steady. 'Goodbye, Rupert.'

He kept his eyes on mine, but I saw a shadow pass over them. He opened his mouth to speak. Shut it again.

I had an overwhelming feeling that if I spoke, or prompted him to speak, cajoled him not to be so very sad, so very devastated, all would be lost. That any ground I'd gained would fall away under me. Crumble. And that I would be lost, too.

# not that kind of girl

Falling down into that chasm. Instead I turned, reached for the doorknob, and with a shaky hand, let myself out.

I went down quickly, my steps echoing in the empty stairwell. At the bottom, I pushed open the heavy oak door. Outside, the drizzle had returned. I put the collar of my coat up against it, then retraced my steps back past the Royal Academy, and around to the car.

Sinead had got out of the car. The children, from this distance, appeared to be asleep inside, and she was leaning against it, her arms folded, her back to me. As I approached, she turned. Her pose was deliberately nonchalant, but her eyes gave her away. I walked up to her and stopped.

'He's all yours.'

She looked at me for a long moment, then nodded briefly in recognition. Despite her efforts at opaqueness, something flickered in her eyes. It looked suspiciously like hope, to me.

And then I turned and walked away.

# chapter twenty-seven

I walked and walked, in a westerly direction, underneath Hyde Park Corner, left into Belgravia, around Wilton Crescent and on. My hands were thrust in the pockets of my navy coat, my chin tucked into my collar against the rain, and my eyes trained on the wet pavements, only occasionally raised to assess where I was going, like a captain on his bridge, looking into the eye of a storm.

Gradually, the rain abated and the cool air dried my wet cheeks. I strode on, clinging to motion, knowing if I stopped, I might be overwhelmed: not by sadness or regret, but by a guilty knowledge that I was running away. That with every stride I was distancing myself from Rupert, from his passion, which when I'd been with him had felt so right, but now that I'd escaped it, horrified me in its intensity.

Yes, that was it, I thought with a jolt: I'd escaped. Had had a narrow escape. Rupert had always known that once he'd got me back, there'd be no return to any other life. I'd have joined him, on his nomadic odyssey through life – not physically, of course, I couldn't quite see myself running around the streets of Basra in a flak-jacket – but nevertheless, his lot would have been mine. I'd have been swept along on the tide of his passion, right out to sea, my hand raised feebly, not waving, but drowning.

And it frightened me, that sort of passion. It thrilled me and excited me, but it frightened me more. To be elevated to such an iconic level, to be so relentlessly important, to be the Henrietta Tate Sinead had referred to with ironic awe, to be so profoundly significant . . . it would be suffocating. And yet vanity made it hard to let it go. To say, 'Look, I don't really want that sort of adoration. I'm quite happy sorting the socks in the washing-basket, thanks very much.' And it was particularly hard when the adoration came from a man who was so profoundly significant himself.

I kept on walking, the wet leaves turning to slime underfoot as I passed one embassy after another in rarefied Belgravia, then on past the deserted flower-seller's barrow in Pont Street towards Chelsea. As I crossed Sloane Square I thought of Sinead, still leaning on the car perhaps, deep in thought, but preparing now to wake her children, to hold their hands as they stumbled sleepily along the London pavements to their father. I thought of her getting to the imposing portals of Albany, stopping in the lobby, taking a moment to compose herself. I thought of her making her way slowly up the stairs to his flat, a child on each hand. I hadn't shut the door completely when I'd left, hadn't quite had the nerve for that degree of finality, so – would it still be open? Ajar, so she wouldn't have to knock?

The children would be excited now, as they mounted the stairs, and would tumble noisily into the flat, and he'd hear them, stationed as he was, perhaps by a window in the sitting room, his back to the door, hands thrust in his pockets, staring out over the rooftops of London, the streets into which I'd vanished. And then he'd know a decision had to be made. Know, that the expression he had on his face as he turned to greet her would speak volumes. Would shape the rest of their lives. It would tell her whether, now that all was lost, he'd be moving on again alone, or whether, now that he knew I wasn't an option, he could love her instead. Love her for her bravery, her devotion, her quiet steadfastness – something she'd already indicated to me she would find acceptable. Whether his restlessness had stopped with losing me. I hoped it had. I really did. Because I truly believed what I'd told him earlier, that the image he'd carried of me all these years was a distorted one. One he'd taken out of his memory bank from time to time and airbrushed to a perfection that didn't exist, and I hoped he'd feel, not that Sinead had won, but that reality had won. That what was truly tangible and ready and available to make him happy was right there under his nose, and had been

all along. That he'd no longer hanker after a rose-tinted image
of another life with me.

I made my way down the King's Road, and then threaded
left amongst a tangle of pretty, whitewashed houses and garden
squares. And what of me? I thought with a sudden lurch.
Where did this leave me? Panic rose within me but I pushed
it down and walked faster, hoping speed would quell the
dread. One thing was certain, I decided, as my heels clipped
hastily along the sodden pavements, alone I might be – eventually – but I didn't want to be alone right now. I didn't want
to go back to the flat in Kensington, walk up the stairs into
a cold, dark drawing room and face reality, face the mess I'd
made, if I could possibly help it. It was no surprise then,
when I found myself taking the street that went past the
Sporting Page.

This late on a Sunday night, the pub was closed. The
drinkers Benji and Francis grew weary of would have long
since gone home. 'We know we bought a house near a pub,'
Benji would grumble, 'so we try not to rail like a couple of
old queens, but "Ay Zigger Zumber" night after night *is* a
little wearing . . .'

I knew they liked to be tucked up in bed early on a Sunday,
so would they still be up? I glanced at my watch. Half past
eleven. Had I left it too late?

When I rang the bell, Francis appeared at the door looking
like a matinee idol in a Noël Coward play. He was wearing

a gold Paisley dressing-gown and his blond hair was brushed neatly off his forehead.

'Henny!' He stepped back in surprise. 'Good Lord. I wondered who on earth could be ringing our bell at this time of night. We've had a few early trick-or-treaters, so Benji's busy filling up the water pistols.'

'Do I need to deploy them?' came a gleeful voice from the kitchen.

'Not unless you want to start a family feud,' Francis called back. 'And anyway, I have a feeling you've got it the wrong way round, Benj. I believe the hob goblins get to play tricks on us, not vice versa.'

A red plastic gun and a bristling moustache appeared around the kitchen door. 'So I'm breaking the rules. Wouldn't be the first – oh.' He stopped. 'Hello, dear heart, it's you. What's up?'

As I crossed the threshold, my eyes filled up, and by the time he'd got to me, I was overcome by tears. I hadn't felt at all like crying on the way over, had felt my resolve strengthen with every step, but somehow, as his impish face turned to one of concern, I was lost. All the pent-up emotions I'd been keeping tightly under wraps these last few hours burst their constraints, as I sobbed woefully on his shoulder. He held me close, making comforting noises in my ear, waiting for me to stop.

'Benji,' I gasped at last, coming up for air. 'Your pistol's in my back.'

'Oh, sorry, hon.' He put it hastily aside and led me in.

I felt faintly ridiculous now, as I sat down on the sofa in the sitting room, Benji perched beside me peering anxiously up under my fringe, Francis, equally concerned, opposite.

'Sorry about that,' I muttered, stuffing a hanky up my sleeve. 'Don't know what came over me.'

'Children?' ventured Francis tentatively.

I shook my head. 'No. They're fine.'

'Marcus?'

I shook it again. 'No.'

'Boy trouble?' enquired Benji gently.

I inhaled sharply. Boy trouble. God, didn't it sound trite. I nodded, my head full of snot and tears. 'Boy trouble,' I breathed.

Benji crossed his legs and wriggled delightedly into the sofa, his hands clasped on his knees. 'Marvellous. I love a bit of hetero drama. Tell Uncle Benji all.'

And so I did. Haltingly at first, but my voice steadying as I got under way. And they listened avidly. When I got to the bit about the revolver being emptied into Sinead's leg in a supermarket car park, Benji stood up quickly. He went to the window and gripped the sill hard. He couldn't take cruelty in any denomination. Couldn't read the newspapers if they were too dreadful, Francis had to hide them. There was a silence.

'And I suppose,' I said, letting out a shaky breath, 'that in some warped kind of way, I feel responsible for that. Feel that if it hadn't been for me, it wouldn't have happened. That if he hadn't met me first, Rupert would have whisked her to England and married her, or not been with her in the first place. Found someone else – I don't know.'

'And if your aunt had balls, she'd be your uncle,' Francis snorted derisively.

I blinked. 'Sorry?'

'I mean that you can conjecture anything out of anything, if you want to. It's nothing to do with you, Henny,' he said. 'The situation is all of their making. Rupert and Sinead's.'

I sighed. 'Maybe.'

'And Rupert?' Benji turned from the window to face me. 'How d'you feel about him now? Now that this grand *affaire du coeur* is finally over?'

There was something faintly mocking in his tone that I didn't like. 'Upset, obviously,' I said defensively. 'And sad. This has been a huge thing for me, Benji.'

'Sad bereft, or sad regretful?'

I frowned, confused. 'Both. I think.'

He came across the room, his dark eyes beady as he looked down at me. He tapped his chest. 'Does it hurt here?'

I nodded. 'Yes.'

'You're sure?' He put his head on one side.

'Yes, of course,' I sniffed, wiping my nose with the back of my hand. 'What d'you mean?' I added doubtfully.

'What I mean is, now that you're away from him, are you longing for him constantly? Hankering after him? And has your heart secretly been heavy without him all these years?'

'No, of course not,' I said, feeling uncomfortable. 'I haven't really given him a second thought. But I've had Marcus.'

'And you didn't ever feel you'd settled for second best with Marcus? Ever wondered what could have been?'

'No. Never.'

'And yet when you're with him, when you're with Rupert now . . .'

'Oh, now, Benji, I just melt.' I felt my damp eyes shine as I looked up at him. 'Golly, when he takes me in his arms . . .'

'Runs his fingers through your hair?'

'Breathes on your neck,' put in Francis.

'Glides his hands up your back,' added Benji.

'Yes, yes.' I shivered, remembering. 'All of that. I – I just dissolve!'

Benji pursed his lips. Exchanged a knowing glance with Francis, who nodded sagely.

'What d'you think, Dr Francis?'

'Ah yes, I'm afraid so, Dr Benji.'

'What?' I frowned. 'Why are you afraid so?'

Benji made a face. 'That's sex talking, buddy.'

I blinked. 'Sex?'

'Quite a different thing from love,' Francis informed me gently.

'Oh!' I was shocked. 'D'you think?'

They nodded in unison, like a couple of wise old owls.

'Most definitely.'

'So—'

'Seven-year itch,' Benji diagnosed crisply, folding his arms. He began to pace around the room like a professor, pontificating to his tutorial group. 'Except in your case, fifteen and a half, but then you always were a late developer.'

'Thanks!'

'And of course, it was very easy for you to mistake it for the real thing, because you loved him once before.'

'Quite,' agreed Francis soberly.

'So when he came back into your life, back from his battles, his crusades . . .'

'All broad-shouldered and masterful . . .'

'Tanned from the desert, six-pack rippling . . . Ooh, heavens.' Benji touched his forehead lightly with his fingertips.

'Easy, tiger,' advised Francis.

'When he came back,' resumed Benji, 'like the proverbial knight in shining armour after all this time, you thought, This must be it! You felt something stirring, something blossoming—'

'I did, I did!' I insisted.

'In your loins, dear heart. Your loins.'

'Oh.' I was shocked. 'Really?'

Francis smiled kindly. 'Don't be too hard on yourself, Hen, sweet. It's an easy mistake to make.'

516

'Is it?' I swallowed doubtfully. 'But . . . what about Rupert? Was it the real thing for him, do you think? Love?'

'Without a shadow of a doubt,' Benji stated. 'That's why he waited so long.'

'But . . . *why* did he wait so long? He knew I was married, for heaven's sake, why did he think I'd become available at some point? Why put his life on hold?'

'Because, as I said to you before,' he repeated patiently, 'every relationship has a sensitive moment. Goes through a vulnerable time.' He spread his hands expansively. 'When you know each other inside out like you and Marcus do, marriage becomes like a comfortable old cardigan. And then, one day, you wake up and think, Is this it? My life? What next? What else? And if you're not careful, the What becomes Who. Rupert was waiting for that moment, biding his time. It took fifteen years, but he got it. He knew the time was right, he knew it was his big moment. Unfortunately, he blew it.' Benji sniffed and inspected his fingernails. 'Jolly bad luck on him, but a narrow escape for you.'

Francis nodded grimly. 'I'll say.'

I gazed at the pair of them, my mouth slightly open. A contemplative silence fell over our little gathering.

At length, I licked my lips. 'D'you know,' I said slowly, 'I sort of knew all of this, all along. Sort of knew it, but . . . couldn't articulate it.' I gazed down at my knees, horrified. Good Lord. Sex. Just sex.

Benji sat down beside me and patted my leg. 'Oh well, look on the bright side.' He winked. 'Nice to know there's life in the old girl yet. That you're not entirely ready to hang up your basque and suspender belt.'

I flushed. 'Thanks. But I'll have you know that nothing actually happened, anyway. Well, no more than a few snogs.'

Benji pulled a face. 'Shame. Might have been just what you needed.'

'Benji!' I swatted him with the back of my hand. 'And anyway, how come you pair of learned old sex therapists know all this?'

'Because as I told you once before, Henny, it comes our way too. With knobs on – if you'll excuse the pun. But we have to forget—'

'Gerald,' said Francis meaningfully.

'Or Tarquin,' rejoindered Benji menacingly.

'Ooh. I *never* fancied Tarquin,' said Francis hotly.

'Not much. I heard you admiring his new washing-machine the other day. Asking winsomely about its turbo action, its nice big tub.'

'Because you admired his kitchen drawers! "*Love* the way they glide in and out so smoothly, Tarqui",' he mimicked. 'In, out, in, out . . .' He thrust his hips back and forward.

'Boys, boys,' I said wearily. 'I get the point. So . . .' I hesitated. 'You think I'll live?'

'Of course you'll live,' said Benji, straightening his back.

He clasped his hands primly on his knees. 'Just go home to Marcus and—'

'Marcus is having an affair,' I reminded him bitterly.

'Just as *you* were near as dammit having one, petal! So what? *Fight* for him, dear heart – see her off! Unleash some of those latent terrier instincts I know you inherited from our dear mama, snap at her heels, bite her buxom behind and chase her off down the lane! Go *get* your man and muscle back into your marriage, your house, your hearth. You *do* love him really, you know that. You're just being pig-headed.'

Inexplicably, I felt my eyes fill again. 'I do, don't I?' I turned to him, ridiculously shocked.

'Of course!'

'So . . . should I go now?' I asked doubtfully.

'Well, not *right* now – it's gone midnight, for heaven's sake. Stay the night and go tomorrow.'

'It's Monday. He'll be at work.'

'And so will you,' he reminded me. 'So go after work.'

'Oh. Yes.'

'Don't give up your day job,' he nudged me playfully. 'Just in case.'

'In case what?' I said, alarmed.

'Sorry, tasteless joke,' he said hastily as Francis glared at him. But I knew what he meant. In case Marcus said no.

'So!' Benji got up quickly, gliding over that little *faux pas*.

519

'That's settled then. It's the spare room for you, my pet, off you go. I'll bring you a hot-water bottle and a cup of cocoa. Francis was just making some, weren't you? You've changed the sheets, haven't you, hon?'

'No, because you changed them on Thursday.'

'No, I didn't. We decided we'd wait until Consuela had ironed the white Christian Dior with naif flower motif, remember?'

'Oh Lord.' Francis looked shocked. 'So we did. In that case they haven't been changed since your mother stayed. I'll do it now.'

'Don't be silly, I'll crawl into Mum's sheets.'

They turned to me, horrified. 'We wouldn't *hear* of it,' said Benji, appalled. 'No no, Francis will do the necessary.'

They bustled out of the room, Benji gently bossing Francis as they went upstairs. 'At the top of the airing cupboard, hon . . . no no, far right, further along . . .'

'Got them.'

'And the matching pillowcases?'

'Yup.'

'Oh, and some Evian water too. Pop it by the bed, lover.'

I was about to shout up and protest that I could stagger to the bathroom tap, but realised they were enjoying themselves. They didn't often have people to stay, and this had turned into a bit of an occasion. Personally, at the prospect of unexpected guests I'd been known to flip the duvet over, inspect the bottom sheet for watch springs and just change the pillow cases, but I didn't tell the boys this, they'd be horrified. They were fastidious creatures, and I remembered Benji, at the farm once, wandering from bathroom to bathroom saying in a bemused tone, 'I can't seem to find a nailbrush.' I didn't have the heart to tell him we didn't possess one. No, they were happy in their rituals, and I realised with a pang, this was what I missed. The rubbing along together, the teamwork, the closeness. I wanted to sling on that comfortable old cardigan. Wanted Marcus.

I got wearily to my feet, feeling faintly foolish. As if I'd narrowly avoided a bad car accident. As if I'd only swerved out of the way of the blaring horns at the very last minute, just in time.

I mounted the stairs to find Benji and Francis in the spare room, still fussing over the sheets.

'And don't forget to spray the bottom sheet.' Benji handed him some lavender water. 'But *spray*, hon, don't tinkle. Remember Toby.'

Francis giggled.

'Toby?' I asked.

'Francis got carried away with the lavender once, and our house guest, a certain Toby Wetherby – a very camp piss artist who'd tumbled into the spare room *quite* the worse for wear – appeared at the breakfast-table the following morning looking very red-faced. "I've got good news and bad news," he announced portentously. "The bad news is, I appear to have wet the bed. The good news is, I have very fragrant piss".'

They clutched each other as they remembered, and I managed to raise a smile. Benji noticed. Patted my arm.

'See, dear heart? Can't be too badly broken, can it, the old ticker? Now, a couple of fresh towels . . . oh – and some clean pants for the morning. Never been worn.' He fished into the back of the airing cupboard and produced a pair of cellophane-wrapped, Christmas novelty Y-fronts.

'What?' he demanded, seeing my face. 'You haven't got any others, have you? And they're fine, look.' He whipped them out of their pack. Dangled them from his pinkies. 'Just a bit airy at the front. You won't be used to that around your privates, but otherwise, they're perfect.'

'If I can get into them,' I said, taking them from him. 'You've got hips like a snake, Benji.'

'Ooh, and a clean pink shirt,' he said, delving back in excitedly. 'In case yours is a bit whiffy from all that snogging.'

'Benji,' I warned, knowing he was enjoying himself now. Showing off.

'Sorry,' he grinned, passing me the pile of clean laundry. 'But you do see, dear heart, don't you?' He looked at me searchingly. 'That all is not lost? That tomorrow, as our blessed Scarlett so succinctly put it, is indeed another day?'

I smiled sheepishly. Nodded. 'Yes, I do see. And tomorrow *is* another day.'

And with that, I pecked his cheek gratefully, and went wearily off to the very fragrant spare room, feeling as if I could sleep for a hundred years.

# chapter twenty-eight

At breakfast the following morning, I eyed Benji over my cappuccino.

'So what d'you think about Mum's news?' In the course of revealing Sinead's identity I had, of course, revealed Andrew's. 'You didn't say much.'

'Because I already knew.' Benji glanced up from his *Financial Times*. 'Francis told me.'

'Francis?' I turned astonished eyes on Francis as, immaculate in a grey flannel suit, he took some croissants out of the oven.

'I was passing your mum's flat the other day and stopped by to drop off some bumf about that Venice art course she was interested in,' he said, tossing the croissants quickly in a basket. 'Ouch. Hot. At least, I was about to, when I realised who I was following up the stairs. I stopped and listened in the stairwell as your mother answered the door. She greeted her visitor extremely affectionately. I'd never met him before, but she called him Andrew and from the brief glimpse I got downstairs I recognised his son's blue eyes and razor-sharp cheekbones. Something of a dish.'

'Clearly Mum thinks so too,' murmured Benji, going back to his paper.

I blinked. 'You're not surprised?'

'Not really. I knew they were friends, and friends, at that age, when they're both single and a bit lonely, have a habit of making a very happy union out of convenience. Certainly an improvement on Howard Greenburg, don't you think?'

'Oh definitely. But why didn't you tell me?'

'What, that they were friends?'

'Yes! God, everyone seemed to know except me.'

He shrugged. 'Same reason Mum didn't, I suspect. Wasn't sure how you'd feel about it.' He closed his *Financial Times*, folded it carefully and gave me a sideways look. 'How *do* you feel about it?' he enquired lightly.

I put my coffee cup down. 'Fine. I mean . . .' I hesitated. 'No, fine. Definitely pleased for Mum. Pleased she's got some-thing of a life at last, and actually . . . pleased it's him. He's a nice chap.'

'That's exactly what he is,' Benji grinned. He stood up and tucked his paper under his arm, clicking his heels sharply to attention. 'A nice, old-fashioned, thoroughly decent chap, who buys his marmalade at Fortnum's and his titfers at Locke's.

Sir!' He saluted smartly. Then he wagged his paper at me. 'And you don't get many of those to the pound these days.'

'And it's not as if Rupert leads a conventional family life,' I mused, gazing past him abstractedly, thinking aloud. 'I mean, I don't suppose I'll have to see him, just because of Andrew.'

'What, you mean you don't suppose you'll be basting the turkey with Marcus this Christmas and look up to see Mum, Andrew and Rupert, sailing through the back door bearing gifts?' Benji grinned wickedly.

I dropped my coffee cup with a clatter. Went cold. 'Don't,' I whispered, horrified. 'Benji, don't!'

Yes, it was strange, I thought an hour or so later, as I walked up the stairs to my office in Covent Garden, how permanently horrified I was at the moment. How terribly, terribly, aghast, after the event. How, the thought of Rupert made me drop my coffee cup, quicken my step in alarm up these stairs, clutch my handbag to my chest. Was recoil really so close to passion, I wondered guiltily? Perhaps it was. After all, passions did cool, didn't they? It was well documented in countless romantic novels, and after they'd cooled – did they go stone cold? Congeal? Perhaps they did. And perhaps they cooled quicker, I thought uncomfortably, if, as Benji had commented, they'd been masquerading as something else all along. Something more basic. I bowed my head and scuttled to my room.

# not that kind of girl

The day passed all too quickly. Laurie was out at meetings for most of it, just ringing in occasionally to rattle off a few instructions, and in no time at all, it seemed to me, it was five o'clock, and I was going back down that familiar staircase again. Going home. To face my husband. Face the music.

I took deep breaths as I tottered along to the station, horribly nervous now. Despite what Benji had said about unleashing my terrier instincts and chasing Perdita off down the lane, I'd had nasty visions all day of her unleashing her own Rottweiler ones. Of turning tail and sinking her perfect white teeth into my bottom as she saw *me* off, with Marcus urging her on behind. In fact that, coupled with the less violent but equally nightmarish vision of her and Marcus glancing up from their M&S lasagnes as I walked through the back door in an hour or so's time – forks frozen, cosy chat halted – almost had me coming to a standstill as I approached Charing Cross.

But . . . perhaps he'd be alone, I thought hopefully, as I bought my ticket. And perhaps he'd be delighted to see me? Perhaps he'd jump up from the table, from his *Evening Standard* and his lonely jar of pickled onions, knock over his solitary glass of wine in his haste to get to me and take me in his arms? I had a little trouble imagining that last scenario, so I plunged quickly down the platform – keen, for once, to lose both mind and body in the scrum of humanity; to join the perpetual struggle to get home.

The train was delayed – signals apparently – and I had to wait ages for it to leave the platform. As I sat in the stationary carriage, it occurred to me that I might see him. Marcus, I mean. I glanced about nervously. This was pretty much his normal train, surely? But unless he was hiding behind a newspaper, there was no sign.

By the time I'd got to the little station in Kent, after a stop en route for some troublesome autumn leaves, it was getting late. Naturally, it took Simon twenty minutes to accomplish what any other taxi driver could do in five, by which time, night had well and truly fallen. I stood, really quite terrified now, at the end of the pot-holed drive, gazing at my house. All was dark, all was quiet. I could hear a muntjac calling to its mate in the beechwood behind. A moment later, the call was returned. A good omen, surely? I gulped and set off down the drive. As I got to the end of it and began cautiously crossing the gravel, the outside light came on, making me jump. From nowhere – but actually from behind the chicken-house – Bill appeared. Bill. Bloody *Bill*, I thought, clutching my heart and breathing again. He gave me his toothless grin as he measured out the Layers Pellets for the evening feed, his face yellow in the halogen light.

'Bin away?' he called, scattering the grain and still grinning foolishly.

'That's right, Bill. On business,' I muttered, quickening my pace.

'Ah. Business. That'll be with the tall feller with the red jumper then, will it?'

I stopped. Stared straight ahead. I'd forgotten he'd seen Rupert come to the house. Seen him spirit me away. I could never quite work out whether Bill was devious or just plain stupid.

'That's it,' I said evenly, walking on. I rooted in my bag for my keys. 'My boss.'

'Oh aye.'

There was no sign of Marcus's car in the drive, and the house was in darkness. Presumably I'd beaten him back. Well, that was a relief.

''E has bin back,' Bill informed me, not leaning on the gate as usual, but rather worryingly opening it and coming through. 'But 'e's gone out now.'

'Has he,' I said tersely, still rummaging for my keys. God, where were they? That would be typical, wouldn't it, if I couldn't bloody find them and had to ask bloody Bill to let me in.

'Yes, 'e's bin doin' that a lot lately,' Bill observed, slowly advancing towards me, hands in pockets, jingling change. 'What with you bein' away an' that. Comin' in, then goin' out again, like. Reckon 'e's bin goin' elsewhere.' He stopped, quite close to me now. Grinned.

'Obviously,' I snapped, knowing exactly what he was trying to tell me. I felt panicky, suddenly, backed up against the door like this. I didn't like being so close to Bill at the best of times: why couldn't he sod off? Ah, here were the keys. Thank God.

'Yeah. 'E has a shower like – always has a shower – and then changes. Very dapper 'e looks in 'is smart clothes. An' then 'e's off out.'

I let myself in quickly. '*Thank* you, Bill,' I seethed.

'Like as not 'e's bin at the aftershave too. Smells like the dog's bollocks.'

I spun round furiously from the relative safety of the doormat. 'I said *thank* you, Bill. I do not require any information about my husband's whereabouts, I know exactly where he's been going night after night and what he's been doing, so you don't need to fill in the gaps. Now kindly attend to my poultry which is what you're employed to do here and keep your nose out of my private life.' I made to go in, then turned. 'And, incidentally, your hands out of my knicker drawer!'

He stared at me. Frowned. 'Knicker drawer?'

'Oh, don't come the innocent yokel with me,' I spat. 'I know all about your nasty little fetish. In fact, if I explored the forensic evidence I'm convinced I'd find traces of chicken poo in my underwear. Unfortunately that route is not open to me, but rest assured, I will get to the bottom of this. I will have your guts for fingering my garters!'

And with that I slammed the door in his face. Unfortunately,

I did it just a bit too hard, and after an ominous rattle, the pane of glass shattered – and fell to the floor.

Bill and I stared at each other through the fresh air.

'Shit!' I squeaked, fists clenched. I turned on my heel, flicked on the light, and strode to the broom cupboard, seizing the dustpan and brush.

Damn. *Damn.* All I bloody needed, I fumed as I swept up with shaky hands. I was still in my coat, and my handbag was swinging off my shoulder and getting mixed up in all the bits of glass. I tossed it angrily aside. Fine homecoming this was turning out to be.

When I'd cleared up, I raised my head warily. Bill had gone. Disappeared into the darkness. Well, that had seen him off, I thought, slightly guiltily. I straightened up and regarded the gaping hole bleakly. Clingfilm? I plucked it doubtfully from the kitchen drawer. No, probably not. What would Marcus do about it? Ask Bill to knock something up until he got the glazier out, probably. And then give me a withering look and a piece of his mind for slamming a glass door. Oh *would* he, I thought, fury mounting. What, all dressed up with clean underpants on and smelling like the dog's bollocks – *would* he indeed. And how long had I been washing those bloody under-pants for? How many years? And all during his affair too, for what – six months? Nine months? Ironing them carefully just so Perdita could peel them off with her French polished nails or her bleached teeth? And then he had the nerve to stride

531

back in here, fresh from her designer sheets, complaining like some bloody domestic tyrant that no one ever changed a light bulb or replenished the bog rolls! Ooh. We'd soon see about that!

Grabbing my keys and bag, I marched smartly out of the back door again. Poor Dilly was going berserk in the boot-room at hearing and smelling me but not being let out, although she'd gone a bit quiet, I'd noticed, when the glass had shattered – fine guard dog she'd turned out to be – but she'd just have to stay there a bit longer. Right now, I had an errant husband to recover. A few bleached teeth to knock out. I strode outside.

My choice of transport was limited and I was reduced to taking the MG, so I nipped back inside for a plastic bag to cover the seat. I didn't want a soggy backside and old-ladies'-undies smell to scupper my dignity. I also applied lashings of lipstick and mascara as I drove madly down the winding lanes. Didn't want the woman-scorned-through-lack-of-skincare-regime look either, oh no. I must not appear like the old-bag-traded-in-for-younger-model. Although I probably was, I thought with a lurch, nearly driving into a ditch. How old *was* Perdita, I wondered nervously. Thirty-something, like me? Or still late twenties?

Although I'd beetled furiously down the lanes, I turned very carefully into the riding stables, very quietly. I didn't go right into her drive either, but came to a halt a good distance from the little flint cottage, all the while looking out for Marcus's car. It wasn't in the drive, but then he was hardly likely to leave it lying around for all to see, was he? No, he'd probably popped it in there, I thought, spotting a little timbered barn. I got out, and shutting my car door softly so as not to alert them, stole on tiptoe across the gravel. I tried the handle. Locked. Well, of course it was. Marcus locked everything. I could hardly get out of the house sometimes he was so bloody safety-conscious. And no doubt he had keys to this house too, so he could just let himself in and out when he felt like it. Just as if it were his own home.

My courage momentarily deserted me as I thought of him strolling in as if he lived here, dumping his briefcase on a chair – 'Hi, darling!' Kissing her, just as he'd peck me on the cheek as I stood at the Aga, only she wouldn't be dressed in a filthy old dressing-gown and Wellingtons, but a skimpy cardi and tight jeans. Encircling her waist from behind, nuzzling her ear . . . getting eau de parfum rather than unwashed hair, and then a tongue in his mouth, rather than a flea in his ear about being late. Helping himself to a beer from the fridge, looking over her shoulder to see what was for supper – which wouldn't be Sunday's cold lamb and a defiant baked potato, but something she'd lovingly prepared earlier: a tender chicken leg in a creamy sauce perhaps? Or a fillet steak wrapped in puff pastry. She'd take it from the oven and put it on the table, then light the candles, her eyes meeting his seductively over the flame. He'd pour her a glass of red wine, and then before she sat down, she'd murmur something about how hot she was from the oven and slip off her cardi, to reveal, not a dirty bra, but a pretty camisole top. Pretending not to notice that Marcus could hardly hold his wine glass he was quivering so much, she'd seat herself opposite him, soft music wafting atmospherically from the sitting room, where no doubt they'd retire later: by the fire with their brandies . . . before legging it upstairs.

My heart began to race now and my breathing was unsteady. Great gusts of air seemed to be shuddering furiously up and down my nostrils. I went quietly towards the downstairs window of the cottage, picking my way across the flowerbed, snagging my coat on a climbing rose, and peered in. The curtains were drawn and I was limited to a tiny carrot of light at the top, but if I stretched on tiptoes . . . No. Still couldn't see. Had they legged it upstairs already, I wondered? Skipped the first course – chicken leg in the kitchen – and moved onto the main course – leg-over in the master bedroom? Or were they at it even now, on the rug in front of the fire? I pressed my ear to the glass and listened. I certainly couldn't hear any signs of life downstairs . . . no saucepans clattering, no cutlery clanking on plates, no muffled chatter or music, but what I *could* hear, distinctly I thought, stepping back abruptly into a clump of *alchemilla mollis*, was movement from upstairs.

Standing stock still, I listened intently in the darkness, the chilly night air sharp and crisp around me. Yes, there were definitely sounds coming from up there. Sounds of . . . what *were* those noises? Those regular tapping sounds, like a wood-pecker . . . getting louder and more urgent, with – yes, a bouncing noise too. Like a children's trampoline. Springs going. And the tapping noise was banging now, against a wall, accompanied by groans and moans of –

'Yes. YES! Yes, THERE. Oh GOD!'

I froze, horrified, in the mud. Christ! They *were* at it. Right above me. Only yards, probably *feet* away from my head!

The shrieks intensified. 'Yes. YES. Oh, you bastard. YOU BEAUTIFUL BEAUTIFUL BASTARD!'

Bug-eyed with shock, I stood rooted to the spot in the *alchemilla mollis*. Then I came to. The blood washed hotly up through my body like chip oil surging to the boil, and in a trice I'd hastened round to the back door. It was a stable door, unfortunately, and I nearly knocked myself out on the top half as I only opened the bottom. For a moment I saw stars, then clutching my head and swearing violently I flung it aside and bowled on through to the kitchen. Sure enough, it was empty, aside from some yapping terriers in their basket, and sure enough, there were signs of a half-finished meal on the table. Two chicken breasts sat cooling in a creamy sauce, a dish of mashed potatoes and courgettes lay forgotten in their tureens, a bottle of claret was half-empty. A kitchen chair had been knocked over, no doubt in a hasty scuffle for the stairs. Or perhaps they'd attempted some sexual gymnastics on it? Some erotic tussle? But whatever ecstatic heights they'd reached down here, it was nothing to the dizzy summit they were reaching upstairs, judging by the shouts of pleasure and pain coming from above.

'Christ, you . . . Ahh. AHH! AHHH! Oh my God. Oh my GOD!'

Ignoring Perdita's yappy terriers who were barking frenziedly at my heels – keen to join in, no doubt, probably as frisky as their mistress – I strode through the kitchen and found the stairs. I took them two at a time. How *dare* she, I fumed. How *dare* she ravage my husband? And how dare *he!* How *dare* he bonk the living daylights out of one of our neighbours – a shrieker, no less – for all the village to hear. I was surprised I hadn't heard them from the car. From my own farmhouse!

She was howling like a dog now, like one of those hunting dogs on the scent. 'ARROOO! AROOOO!'

Christ alive.

I flew across the landing and kicked open the door to the *salle d'amour*, like Clint entering the OK Corral. The room was dimly lit and in chaos: clothes were strewn everywhere and coils of winding bedlinen lay all over the floor. But there, sure enough, on the creaking brass bed, naked and on all fours and facing away from me, was Perdita, in what is probably known in the horsy world as 'the hound position'. Behind her was a familiar bare bottom, rising-trot muscles clenched, thrusting away furiously.

'MARCUS, HOW DARE YOU!' I screeched at the top of my voice, fists balled, face puce with fury.

The action stopped instantly. Perdita's head whipped around, her pink face startled, blonde hair mussed. It was followed, only a split second later, by the bare bottom's head, which was equally flushed and astonished, but clearly did not belong to the bottom. For it was not my husband.

'Oh!' I gasped.

My hand shot to my mouth. Timid Timmie and I gazed at one another in abject horror.

'Oh! I'm so sorry. I thought you were my husband!'

# chapter twenty-nine

The pair of them de-coupled in a flash, and Timmie swung around, monstrously priapic. My eyes popped. Heavens. He didn't look so timid now, did he? Positively plucky. In fact, my eyes fairly watered at the magnitude of his pluck.

'What the hell do you think you're doing?' shrieked Perdita. She grabbed the duvet and dived under it. Timmie hastily pogo-sticked to join her.

'So sorry. Looking for my husband. Not here,' I breathed, transfixed it seemed, with disbelief, to the spot.

'P-piss off!' spluttered Timmie, his eyes wide with horror. His hands clutched the duvet, right up at his chin. 'Go on, p-piss off!'

My wits returned smartly. 'Right. Will do.'

I shut the door quickly. Gazed at it incredulously a moment, before movement from inside – someone leaping off the bed and diving into a dressing-gown, perhaps – galvanised me.

538

'I do apologise!' I yelped, backing away.

'I'll have the police on you!' Perdita roared. 'How *dare* you just barge into my house?'

'I – I did knock,' I lied. 'But – there was no answer. Sorry!' At which point, sensibly, I turned and fled downstairs.

'It's outrageous!' she stormed, flinging open the door and appearing, a furious vision in white towelling, at the top of the stairs.

'Sorry!' I shrilled again over my shoulder, but by this stage, I was well and truly at the bottom: well and truly nipping through the kitchen, athletically side-stepping the fallen chair and the yapping terriers, and out of the back door. As I ran across the drive to the stables, my hands fluttering about in my bag for my keys, eyes still like saucers, I caught my breath. Lordy, as Benji would say. Lordy! Not Marcus at *all*. Not *my* husband at all, somebody else's husband – Perfect Pippa's, to be precise. Timid Timmie of all people and – good gracious. I gulped as I scrambled around frantically in my bag. Now we knew what Pippa saw in him. Perdita too, clearly!

The kitchen door flew open and Perdita appeared like an avenging angel, just as I'd found the keys and thrown myself into the driving seat. My mind spun and my tyres too, spraying up gravel as I took off, desperate to escape. As I shot off out of the drive I glanced up and saw the bedroom curtains twitch. Timmie's terrified face appeared for a split second, then disappeared again. Probably scrambling into his boxer shorts;

probably hopping round the room on one leg as he struggled into his trousers, buttoning his shirt up wrong and grabbing his shoes, desperate to rush off home. Either that or leave the country.

Perdita was striding across the driveway now, brown legs flashing, dressing-gown flying. I gave an apologetic little wave and mouthed, 'Sorry!' out of the window, but she flicked two furious fingers back. Right. I swallowed. Might keep out of her way for a bit. Might go to Tescos rather than Waitrose from now on.

I drove off down the lanes, wiping a bead of sweat from my nose, my mind in turmoil. I was horribly, horribly confused. Because if Marcus wasn't there, where was he? Was he shagging Perdita on some kind of timeshare basis, I wondered wildly? Bagging Tuesdays and Thursdays while Timmie got Mondays and Wednesdays? I floated the idea for a moment, then dismissed it. No. Quite apart from it being a monstrous idea it was inconceivable that Perdita would even consider Marcus after . . . well. I swallowed. Not that Marcus was under-endowed, you understand, but he certainly couldn't compete with – with *that*. I roared on.

But if he wasn't having a ding-dong with Perdita, who was he having one with? My mind roved around the village, trawling through all the single women's houses. Was it Emma Tilding, perhaps, whose husband had left her and gone off with his secretary? Or Amanda Lewis, whose husband had come out of the closet – literally – wearing her nightie and suspenders? Or, and this really shook me, really floored me, was he not having an affair at all? At this point I nearly lost control of the car, only hauling it clear of the hedge at the last moment. But – no. No, nonsense, of course he was, there was definitely *something* going on, I could smell it, but – damn. I gripped the steering-wheel hard. I'd been so sure it was Perdita. *So* sure. But why? I wracked my brains as I swung the car round the final bend and into our pot-holed drive. Why had I been so convinced?

Unfortunately there was no time to get to the bottom of this conundrum, because as I bounced along the track, wrecking the suspension but past caring, I realised, with a jolt, that there was something of a reception committee awaiting me at the other end.

The house was lit up like Crystal Palace. All the lights were on, upstairs and down, and none of the curtains had been drawn. The outside lights were blazing too, and in the gravel sweep that graced the front of the house, sat a police car, lights flashing, driver's door flung wide. Beside it was Marcus's Range Rover looking equally temporary, and Marcus was standing between the two cars looking white-faced and worried as he talked to a policeman. My heart stopped for a moment. Oh Lord, I thought in horror. What now? Was it one of the children?

Parking erratically in a spray of gravel and forgetting in my panic that Marcus and I were barely on speaking terms, I rushed across.

'What is it? What's happened?' I gasped.

Marcus turned and regarded me coldly. If he was surprised to see me, he managed to hide it. I recognised the burly, ginger-haired policeman beside him as our local bobby.

'We've been burgled,' he said curtly. 'Or at least, broken into. I haven't established yet whether anything's been taken.'

I followed his eyes around to the side of the house: to the huge, gaping hole in the back door.

'Oh! Oh no. That was me.'

He frowned. 'Sorry?'

'Yes, I came back about half an hour ago. Got in a bit of a bait about something and accidentally slammed the back door. The glass fell out. Sorry.'

He looked at me for a long moment, as if he wasn't quite sure which hole I'd crawled out of. At length, he turned back to his companion. 'Sorry, Ray,' he said quietly. 'It seems I've got you out on a wild-goose chase. My wife has been relieving her stress by indulging in some energetic door-slamming.'

Ray chuckled and put his notebook away. ''S'all right. My wife indulges in much the same, normally followed by a frying pan aimed at the back of my head. I thought it was a tidy burglar though. Couldn't see much glass.'

'Yes. No. I swept it up,' I gabbled. 'Sorry, Ray. Sorry to have dragged you out.'

'No problem.' He grinned, then took his cap off and scratched his head. Frowned. 'Have to make a note of something in my book though, I'm afraid. Won't put down burglary, of course. How about domestic dispute?'

Marcus smiled thinly. 'Why not?'

I swallowed. 'Um, yes. Fine, Ray.'

He grinned and gave Marcus a knowing look as he got back in his car. Then, with a cheery salute he turned around and drove off. When his police car was safely bumping over the horizon in a cloud of dust, Marcus turned to me.

'What the hell are you doing here?' he enquired coldly.

'This is still my house, Marcus,' I said defiantly. Although not so defiantly perhaps, as I might have done had I just caught him in a compromising position.

'Yes, well next time you forget your key and decide to just break in, leave me a note to that effect, would you?' He stalked off towards the back door.

'I didn't break in.' I scurried after him. 'I told you, I slammed it too hard. Bill was annoying me. He—'

'Where *is* Bill?' He stopped abruptly and looked around. 'I tried to find him earlier, see if he knew what was going on when I saw the door, but he's not here. He's not in his cottage, either.'

'Er, pass,' I said nervously, hovering on the doorstep while Marcus strode in ahead of me and began clearing the kitchen table. He threw what looked like the remains of his breakfast toast in the bin and chucked the plates in the dishwasher. Not so tidy now, I thought, glancing around. Sunday's newspapers were still in a heap on the table. Cereal packets, too.

'Linda not been coming in?' I ventured, still on the doorstep. Odd, to feel like a visitor in your own home.

'She's ill,' he said shortly. 'Well, come in, damn you. Stop dithering.'

'Thanks,' I muttered meekly, stepping inside. Yes, meek. Conciliatory. Much better under the circumstances, Henny.

'I suppose you've come for more clothes, have you?' he said irritably, turning the taps on full blast, splashing some greasy pans in the sink. 'Help yourself.' He jerked his head upstairs. 'Meanwhile I'm going to get my supper if you don't mind. I was about to have some in the pub when Jack Portwin came in. Said he'd been walking his dog past our house and spotted a hole the size of a crater in the back door.'

'Oh! Is that where you've been then? The pub?'

'Of course it's where I've been. It's where I've been every bloody night, and I have to tell you, it's wearing a little thin. Their menu is limited.' He retrieved a wet pan from the sink, gave it a cursory wipe with a tea-towel and banged it down on the hob. 'I'm sick of chilli-bleeding-con-carne night after night, they need to ring the changes. I must speak to Vi.'

I perched gingerly on a kitchen stool. 'Every night? I mean on your own?'

He took some rather ancient-looking sausages from the

fridge and tossed them in the pan. 'Every night except tonight, not that it's any of your business. Tonight I had some company, until Jack walked in and spoiled my evening. Is that all right by you?' He turned to me, eyebrows raised enquiringly. 'While you're playing the field in London? All right if I have a drink with someone?'

'I'm not playing the field, Marcus,' I said quietly.

'Ha!' he snorted derisively. He turned back and shook the sausages boisterously in the pan. 'That's your story.'

I cleared my throat. 'Who were you having a drink with?'

'Pippa Hall, as it happens. Timmie's away on business, and she came in for some cigarettes. I invited her to have supper with me.'

'Oh!' I inhaled sharply. 'Oh no, Timmie's not away on business. He's at Perdita's house. In the bedroom, in fact. I've just been there. Caught them at it.'

He glanced at me over his shoulder. 'Timmie Hall? With Perdita Fennel?' He took the pan off the heat and turned. 'Good Lord.'

I watched him closely, gauging his reaction.

'Surprised?' I asked keenly.

'Well – of course,' he blustered. 'Timmie Hall, with Perdita . . . Christ, the old dog. Who would have thought he had it in him.'

'Oh, he's definitely got it in him. I had a bird's-eye view. Jealous?'

He frowned. 'Sorry?'

'Are you jealous, Marcus? That it's him and not you?'

He looked at me blankly. 'Why should I be jealous? That a shrinking violet like Timmie is getting his leg over on a regular basis and I'm not – sure, absolutely green, but it stops there. What are you on about, Henny?'

Was he bluffing? I couldn't tell. I felt a bit unsure of my ground. 'Because that's where I assumed *you* were, Marcus. At Perdita's. That's why I went there.'

He folded his arms. Squinted incredulously at me. 'You thought *I* was there?'

'Yes.'

'What . . . in her bed?'

'Yes!' I could feel myself going pink.

He gazed at me, stupefied for a moment. Then suddenly, he threw back his head and roared with laughter. He hooted up to the ceiling, bellowing into the rafters. Then he clutched his sides, and turned and gripped the Aga rail, wheezing. Finally he had to sit down, he was laughing so much.

'Oh, so it's funny, is it?' I stormed. I got up and flew to my bag, hanging on the back of a chair. 'So what about this?' I took the email she'd sent him from my purse and slapped it down on the table in front of him, fuming as I stood over him. 'Explain this away and keep laughing, Marcus!'

He wiped his eyes and contained his mirth enough to pick up the piece of paper.

'"Why shouldn't I be the mistress?"' I quoted, my voice shrill with fury. '"I anticipate some action!"' I screeched. '"Why shouldn't we meet at your place!"' I stabbed my finger at the words. 'See? It's all there in black and white!'

He stopped laughing. Blinked. 'Where did you get this?'

'I found it in the pocket of your briefcase. Carefully stashed away, eh Marcus!'

He was clearly bemused. I folded my arms, triumphant.

'I wondered what I'd done with it,' he murmured. 'I needed her email address the other day to give to someone who wanted to pay a hunt subscription. Couldn't find it.'

'Aha! Well, *I* found it.' I nodded grimly.

He cleared his throat. 'Yes, it's the email she sent me after I wrote to her—'

'Well, clearly, Marcus! You've clearly already written to her, this is a reply to some sort of romantic missive from *you*!'

'After I wrote to her,' he repeated carefully, 'and congratulated her on becoming Master.'

I frowned. 'What?'

'On becoming Master. Of the hunt. MFH. I quipped that in these emancipated times, perhaps she should be called Mistress.'

I stared at him. Lowered my bottom slowly onto a convenient chair. 'Oh.'

'I also expressed a hope that with her at the helm, we'd have some sport. She's known to enjoy a gallop, and she agreed, predicting there would indeed be some action.' He glanced down at the email again. 'She also suggests that since I've lifted the ban the Pipers put on our land, we have a meet here. On the front lawn. You know, like a scene from *Horse and Hound*, with you handing round the port and the sausage rolls. Doing the Lady of the Manor bit, like you've always wanted.'

'Oh.' It appeared to be all I could say. I sat there staring at him blankly. He returned my gaze. At length I licked my lips. 'But, hang on. Laura said that after the Hunt Ball, which you went to on your own, Marcus, Perdita took someone back to her cottage. Someone's husband . . .'

'Pippa's, clearly. And everyone's terrified of her, so they kept schtum. Oh no, if it had been your husband it would have been all round the village in no time. No one's frightened of you.'

'So . . .' I got up slowly. Walked carefully round the table, trailing my fingers on the wood, my mind racing. 'No, wait.' I stopped suddenly. 'There was something else. Oh yes – in your diary.' I swung round accusingly. '*Out with P*, it kept saying. Out with Perdita!'

'Yes, because she's my riding instructor, for God's sake, and I've been out hacking with her. Going up to the cross-country course at Westgate. You *know* that, Henny.'

I stared at him, my mouth hanging open. I shut it. 'So you're not having an affair with her?'

'Jesus, woman. You've just seen Timmie Hall in her bed. What d'you think she is, insatiable or something?'

'And . . . you're not having an affair with anyone else?'

'Oh right, let's cast around, shall we? Who did you have in mind?'

'Well, I don't know,' I blustered. 'Someone at work, someone in the village—'

'Someone I picked up on the train? Someone I found in Tescos as I was buying my Lasagne For One?'

'Well . . .'

'Someone I pulled in the village shop perhaps, when I got really desperate? Old Mrs Hawkins with the moustache? Or Miss Piper, with two fingers on one hand, the rest having been caught in the bacon-slicing machine?'

'Well, I—'

'No, Henny. Sorry to disappoint, but no, I'm not having an affair with anyone.'

He got up from the table and moved slowly around it. I gazed at him, stupefied and, I have to say, a mite put out.

'So. That's me then, isn't it,' he said, his eyes trained steadily on mine like a panther's. He came to a halt opposite. 'That's me in the clear.' He rested the heels of his hands on the table and leaned across it, his face darkening. 'How about you though, Henny? What have you been up to recently, hm? Who have *you* been having an affair with?'

# chapter thirty

His dark eyes glittered as they bored into mine.

'N-no one!' I yelped, snatching up his cigarette packet from the table. 'No one. Of course not!'

I lit one with a shaky hand and nearly choked to death. I hadn't smoked for ages. He took it from me as I spluttered and wheezed. Took a drag himself as he watched me, then blew the smoke out in a thin blue line.

'Really? No adultery to speak of?'

'No!' I gasped. 'Of course not, Marcus.'

'No sport? No . . . action? No clandestine meetings? No back to his place? No walks in parks at lunchtime?'

I stared at him, aghast. Felt my whole body flush. Oh God. What did he know?

'Marcus, I swear,' I whispered. 'There was nothing serious. I mean, we – I didn't – you know.'

'Sleep with him?'

'No!'

'Rip his kit off?'

'No!'

'Bonk his brains out?'

'No! No!' I was horrified. Scared, too.

'It was just that kiss?'

My mind whirled. Kiss? Oh God, which kiss? Which particular kiss had he seen? One in the park? Or had he been at the window of Albany flat as I'd lain there, naked but for a come-hither smile? Had he been posing as a window-cleaner, perhaps? Buffing the glass?

'Which kiss?' I croaked, ready to sign the decree nisi right now, ready to totter to my grave.

'The one I saw, Henny. With my own eyes. When I surprised you in the flat.'

I stared, utterly lost. Then it dawned. 'Oh – *that* kiss!'

'Yes, *that* kiss. Which one did you think I meant?'

'The one with Laurie!'

'Well, of course the one with Laurie. Christ, who else would I mean?'

'Oh no one.'

I shook my head furiously, got up quickly and went to the Aga. Began frantically rearranging the tea-towels hanging over the rail. My hands were trembling and my heart was beating fast.

'No, you're right.' I gulped. 'That was . . . the only kiss. With Laurie, Marcus.'

'And you were very drunk.'

'Very drunk,' I repeated numbly. 'Drugged, too,' I muttered bleakly, remembering.

He nodded. 'I know.' He scratched his head. Looked sheepish. 'And I feel, in retrospect, that . . . well. That I might have over-reacted.'

My heart, still hammering away in my ribcage at my narrow escape, stopped suddenly. What? Marcus had over-reacted? Marcus was . . . *wrong*? This was ground-breaking stuff. Revolutionary. Next thing you know, he'd be apologising.

'And I'm sorry.' He hung his head.

I swooned and reached back to clutch the work surface. Suddenly I felt awful.

'Oh no, Marcus. It wasn't your fault!'

'Well, maybe not,' he agreed quickly, clearly unused to such unfamiliar apologetic waters.

Heady with relief at not having my other, more heinous crimes discovered, I swam to meet him.

'You were upset,' I said supportively.

'Of course I was upset. My wife was in bed with a strange man!'

'On bed.'

'Sorry?'

'On, not in.'

'OK,' he agreed. 'On.'

'And *non compos mentis*,' I reminded him.

'Exactly,' he conceded. 'Which is why, on mature reflection . . .' He hesitated. 'If that's *really* all it was . . .'

'Of course that's all it was!'

'And you haven't seen him since?'

'Well, I've *seen* him since – I work for him, Marcus. But
I haven't seen him socially, if that's what you mean.'

'Haven't had lunch? A drink after work?'

'Marcus, he's shagging a TV producer at Channel Four.
This week. Last week it could have been someone different,
but it was never me. Never would or *could* have been me,
even if I'd wanted it to be, which I didn't. I'm far too old
for him,' I added generously.

He nodded soberly. 'Yes, I can see that.'

I blinked. Blimey.

He scuffed his toe and gazed down at the floor. When he
looked up, his eyes were full. His voice cracked when he
spoke.

'I'm sorry, darling.'

I boggled. Sorry again? *Sorry twice.*

'Oh no, darling.' I stumbled towards him. 'No, *I'm* sorry.
I'm the one who should be sorry.'

I fell into his arms and we clutched each other tight. I
could hear his heart beating against mine. He smelled of lambs-
wool, of shaving cream, of alpha male. Of Marcus.

'I've been such a fool,' he whispered. 'So full of stupid,
ridiculous pride.'

My heart lurched, full of guilt.

'No, *I've* been a fool,' I cried, anguished. 'It's me! I've been so stupid!'

He shrugged. 'You got drunk. It happens.'

'Yes, but . . .' I bit my lip, stared guiltily into his blue sweater. Tears filled my eyes.

'I've missed you,' he said huskily in my ear.

'And I've missed you too,' I sobbed, and in another instant, as our heads whipped round and his lips found mine, we were kissing madly.

'Oh Marcus,' I gasped, when we finally came up for air, holding each other tight, 'haven't we been ridiculous?'

'Puerile,' he agreed. 'So much we nearly threw away. So much. What a waste that would have been. What a stupid, ridiculous waste.'

'And actually,' I sniffed, reaching for a tea-towel to mop my eyes, blow my nose too, 'I only realised how much I loved you when all this happened. I mean – I always knew, obviously, but nearly losing you, nearly having it all taken away . . .'

'I always knew,' he said softly. He took a step back and regarded me steadily at arm's length, his hands on my shoulders. 'Have always known you were the only one. I think that's why I reacted so childishly.'

I gazed into his honest dark eyes, so full of love, full of warmth, and felt humbled. He'd always known. He'd never wavered, as I had, so very recently. He'd never considered an affair; considered someone else. It was my turn to hang my head. After a moment though, I raised it.

'Let's go to bed,' I said decisively.

His eyes widened. 'Good Lord. Are you instigating sex?'

I giggled. 'When was the last time I did that?'

'1991, according to my records. Every night for a month, but that was only because you were keen to conceive Lily and you'd read somewhere that blanket-bombing the eggs changed the nature of the sperm and would result in a girl-child.'

'Well, it obviously worked.'

'Clearly. And I have very fond memories of that time. It's the only time I can remember gasping, "No! No more! Not again!" as you shimmied into the bedroom wearing nothing but a baby-hungry look in your eyes.'

'No stamina, that's your trouble.'

He took my face in his hands and kissed my mouth hard. 'Don't bank on it,' he murmured.

For a moment there, as his eyes blazed hotly into mine, I was transported back in time. Back to his Holland Park flat, in fact, just after the split from Rupert, when he used to cook me supper after work. Only, on that occasion, on that particular evening, the kitchen table had been used for something else . . . I felt the pit of my tummy turn to liquid. Felt a degree of heat generate through my body. Why, of course, I thought in surprise. Lust. Benji would be proud of me. Although I wasn't sure I was up to the kitchen table these days.

'Come on,' I murmured, leading him stairwards. 'Let's go.'

'Have you shut the chickens up?'

'Oh, *Marcus!*' I stopped.

'Only asking – it's just the fox is about and I don't think Bill's done it. Where *is* bloody Bill?' He frowned. 'Tell you what, you go up and warm the bed, darling. I'll be up in a jiffy.'

He hastened out of the back door, leaving me smiling fondly after him, and then, with a lovely warm feeling inside, I mounted the stairs. My stairs. In my house. With my hand brushing the shiny oak banister I'd stripped myself and then had French polished at vast expense. I paused at the landing window; gazed out at the inky night with its sprinkling of stars. I could just make out the post and rails at the bottom of the garden: the stream, the horses beyond. My view. My horses. My home. And it was so good to be back.

In the bedroom, I slowly got undressed, pausing occasionally to rearrange objects on my dressing-table which hadn't been put back in quite the right place – photos, ornaments – still smiling foolishly the while. As I was peeling off my bra, the phone rang. I plucked it from the bedside table.

'Hello?'

'Mummy? It's me.'

'Lily! Darling, how lovely.' I turned as Marcus came in behind me. *Lily,* I mouthed.

He nodded. Smiled as he began to undress, his eyes travelling down my bare back.

'Mummy, it's our school play on Friday, had you remembered?'

'I had, my love, and you're Friar Tuck.'

'No, Maid Marion now, because Daisy Forbes is in the san, which is *so* much better. Except I have to kiss Lizzie Stanley.'

'Robin Hood?'

'Yes, but only an air kiss. Are you coming down?'

'Of course I am.'

'With Daddy?' Her voice sounded a bit strained. I stood up straight.

'Of course with Daddy. Why not?'

'Oh good.' She sounded relieved. 'Oh Mummy, I'm so pleased.'

'Why, my love?'

'Well, I'm probably just being stupid and maybe it was Grandpa dying and everything, but you both seemed . . . I don't know. A bit strange. And then Celia Parker's parents split up and she was crying in the dorm and – oh, I don't know. I've just had awful thoughts about you and Daddy recently.'

'What nonsense,' I declared roundly. 'You read too much, Lily. Either that or too much television.'

'Yes,' she agreed happily. 'Yes, you're probably right. See you both on Friday then? I'll reserve two seats.'

'On Friday, my darling. Night night.' I put down the phone. 'That was Lil,' I said fondly. No response from behind me. I turned. 'Marcus?' His face was like stone. 'What is it?'

'The pants,' he said, nodding down.

'Pants?' I glanced down. Sprigs of holly twinkled back at me. 'Oh, they're Benji's. I stayed there last night. He lent them to me.'

'Ah.' His face cleared. He slipped into bed. 'That would explain the festive motto on the bottom. I thought you'd been telling me porkies, Henny. Thought you'd got mixed up in some vile sex ring while you'd been in London.'

'Why?' I frowned over my shoulder, trying to read it. 'What does it say?'

*'Santa's little humper.'*

'Oh!' I giggled and slipped in beside him.

'I was about to hotfoot it to Santa's grotto,' he murmured in my ear, 'and give him a piece of my mind.'

I chuckled as he took me in his arms. 'Chickens all tucked up?'

He kissed my nose. 'They are, but I had to do it myself. Bill's nowhere to be seen. Hope he hasn't finally gone to Clacton like he's always threatened, to live with that widowed sister of his.'

Oh Lord, I thought guiltily. Maybe he has. But actually, I had other things on my mind. It had occurred to me just now that I didn't want my heart lurching every two seconds as it had over the pants incident. Didn't want continually to be wondering what Marcus knew, or imagined, or was about to find out. As he snuggled up to me, I took a deep breath.

'Marcus, I ran into Rupert Ferguson while I was in London.'

He moved his head back on the pillow, the better to see me. 'Oh? That sad loser. What did he want?'

'Oh just – you know, to chat. Catch up. Why loser? Why d'you say that?'

'Well, anyone who cocks up his life as comprehensively as he has isn't what you might call a winner, is he? He hasn't exactly come first in life's lottery, has he?'

'You mean because he ditched me at the church door?'

'Well, I wouldn't imagine that's coloured his life for the better,' he said with a snort. 'You make a prat of yourself in front of your family, your friends, your Commanding Officer, all your colleagues – doesn't do much for your reputation, does it?' He turned and reached for his alarm clock. Began to set it for the morning.

'So . . . you don't mind that I've seen him?' I propped myself up on one elbow and stared at his profile as he frowned into the clock's dials. 'We spent quite some time together . . . catching up,' I said bravely.

559

He laughed and checked the time with his watch. 'Henny, if you're wondering whether I'm going to go off the deep end about you meeting up with that guy, you can relax. I've got a bit more faith in your judgement. An obvious charmer like Laurie had me worried, I'll admit, but a man who's never recovered from losing his bottle – no. Rest assured, I won't be losing any sleep over him. I haven't spent the last fifteen years wondering if you secretly wish he'd pitched up at that church, if that's what you're thinking.' He sighed, put the clock back on the table and rubbed his eyes. 'Six o'clock start tomorrow I'm afraid. Got a meeting at eight.'

'Right,' I muttered.

'I imagine that decision has wrecked his life?' He turned back to me, pulling the duvet over his shoulder.

'A bit,' I admitted.

'And he never married?'

I hesitated. 'He did, but . . . oh, it's complicated.'

'Bound to be,' he grinned, taking me in his arms again. 'And frankly, I couldn't be less interested, but what I'd really like to know is why you insist on doing so much talking, when you promised so much action?'

Some time later, as I was lying back on my pillows, gazing at the ceiling and listening to Marcus's rhythmic breathing beside me, I turned my head and looked out of the window into the velvety night. I hadn't bothered to draw the curtains since the only peepers on our marital bed would be the night owls and the bats as they flew their dark corridor back and forth along the river.

As I lay there, relishing the peace and quiet after London, something deep within me uncoiled. Relaxed. My soul was definitely at peace, I thought happily. But my mind . . . I frowned up at the ceiling. If only . . . Suddenly, on an impulse, and after a sideways glance at Marcus to make sure he was really asleep, I slipped out of bed. I reached for my dressing-gown and stole downstairs.

Once in the kitchen, having reassured Dilly it was only me and she could go back to her basket, I shut the door softly behind me. Wrapping my dressing-gown around me I crept across the room, plucked the phone from its cradle and dragged a chair up to the Aga. Then I pulled up my knees and stared at the numbers. I started to dial, then realising the door to the back stairs was open behind me, got up and softly shut it. I sat down again and dialled his number. It rang and rang, and for a moment I thought he wasn't there.

Then: 'Hello?'

'Benji? It's me, Henny.'

'Henny, my flower. How are you? Marriage intact?'

'Oh yes, it's all going marvellously,' I purred happily. 'And you were quite right, it was absolutely the right thing to do, to come back. But Benj, as the married woman's agony aunt, I have one more question for you.'

'Fire away, dear reader.'

'Well, I rather bravely told Marcus I'd run into Rupert in London. And he was incredibly relaxed about it.'

'Really?'

'Yes, extraordinarily so. But then, thinking about it, I didn't exactly . . .' I licked my lips. 'Well, I didn't exactly give him the whole story. I mean, I didn't totally come clean and tell him I'd – I'd –'

'What?' he said sharply. 'Slept with him?'

'Oh no! No, because I didn't, Benji. But there was quite a bit of – you know, hanky panky. And the thing is, Marcus was so sweet about everything and I'd like to tell him the *whole* truth, so there are no secrets between us. So that we're absolutely back where we used to be before all of this happened. D'you think I should? Should I tell him there was a teeny bit more than I admitted to? More than just chatting?'

There was a silence.

'Do you even have to ask?'

I nodded soberly. 'I should, shouldn't I?'

'NO!' he screeched. The receiver nearly jumped out of my hand. 'You bloody shouldn't! Henny, there are some things you *can't* unburden yourself of just to make you feel better, because believe me, *he* won't feel better, and he won't be sweet and relaxed about it either. Jesus!'

'Really?'

'Really! Take it from me, some secrets are worth keeping,

particularly if they protect the fabric of a relationship. Christ. Elementary!'

'Is it?' I blinked.

He sighed. Went on in a gentler tone, 'You're a new girl to such deceptions, aren't you, Hen?'

I frowned. 'And you're not?'

There was a pause.

'Ah, my sweet.' His voice, when it came, was distant. 'Ask me no questions, and I'll tell you no lies. We all make mistakes. But it doesn't alter my commitment. Doesn't alter my love and devotion. Not in any way, shape or form. That's rock solid, buddy. As yours is, too.'

I smiled into the receiver. We were silent a moment.

Then: 'Thanks, Benji. You're right. I'll keep schtum.'

'I would, dear heart.'

I was about to say goodbye, when I remembered. 'Oh, and incidentally, your pants nearly got me into very hot water. The message on the back took a bit of explaining to Marcus.'

He laughed. 'Ah, you discovered that, did you? Yes, well, fair's fair. Your undies nearly got *me* into trouble once, too.'

'They did?'

'Remember I borrowed a pair when Francis and I last stayed at your gaff? I hadn't brought enough and snitched some from your room. Francis spotted their unfamiliarity that same night. Questioned me *very* closely.'

563

'Oh God, you're such a perv,' I giggled. 'And you probably went for pink frilly ones. Serves you right.'

'Certainly not. Brand new M&S white, still in their packet. Nothing kinky about me. I did tidy your knicker drawer while I was about it, though. It was a disgrace.'

Somewhere in the distance, across the fields, I heard a car engine start up throatily. After a moment, a car came down the track from the cottage, heading for the front drive. As it roared past the house, I recognised it as Bill's Fiesta, stuffed to the gunnels with cases and boxes. A table was strapped to the roof, a grim-faced driver crouched over the wheel.

'What?' I croaked.

'Well I had to, petal. There aren't many knicker drawers I'd presume to knock into shape, but yours was one of them. Now. Any more questions, or can I get into my jim-jams and have my cocoa?'

'No,' I said abstractedly. 'I mean, yes. You have your cocoa. And thanks, Benji.'

'My pleasure, flower.'

I put the phone down and stole back upstairs, pausing briefly at the landing window to watch the car roar down the lane, its tail-lights disappearing in a cloud of dust. I crept back to bed and lay there, my heart racing. Heavens. Marcus would freak. Completely freak. After a while though, my beating heart stilled. Yes, of course. Benji was right. There were some secrets that couldn't be unburdened. Some secrets which preserved the very fabric of a marriage, and without whose necessary ballast, the whole edifice would collapse. Some secrets which had to be kept. And anyway, I smiled into the darkness. How would he ever find out? And with that reassuring thought in mind, I turned over and went straight to sleep.

# The Wedding Day

## Catherine Alliott

Annie O'Harran is the wrong side of thirty. A harassed single mother (of almost teen-aged Flora), she's escaped her faithless first husband, and against all expectations met her hero. She has a blissful summer ahead to plan her wedding.

But first Annie must escape London and surround herself with calm in order to meet the horrible deadline set by the only publisher ever to have expressed interest in her writing. Giving mad Aunt-to-be Gertrude a cameo role in her novel is surely a small price to pay for the loan of a fabulous writer's retreat with its own private beach?

But no sooner has she arrived in Cornwall, than the doorbell starts ringing. Everyone, it seems, from her competitive sister and her noisy brood, to her louche ex-husband and his nubile young girlfriend, has had the same idea for their summer holidays. And then there's the houseguest who doesn't even bother to knock . . . Just as long as none of them affects her big day at the end of the summer . . .

0 7472 6723 5

## headline

# A Married Man

## Catherine Alliott

When Lucy Fellowes is offered a dream house in the country she leaps at the chance. It's hard enough living in London on an uncertain income, but when you're widowed with two small boys it's even harder. And anyway, a rural retreat will bring her closer to Charlie. Charlie? The only man in four years to make her heart beat faster. Perfect. Or it would be. If only he didn't belong to someone else . . .

A wickedly witty new novel about how complicated relationships get when you grow up, from the best-selling author of *Rosie Meadows regrets . . .* and *Olivia's Luck*.

'Alliott's skilled handling of such delicate, difficult and deep material marvellously counterpoints the Cotswolds comic archetypes and provides psychological depth and shadow to the sparky surface action. Sensitive, funny and wonderfully well written.' Wendy Holden, *Daily Express*

0 7472 6722 7

**headline**

# Rosie Meadows regrets . . .

## Catherine Alliott

*Well, what could I say? If he was smitten then I could be too, and I sank back into the whole cosy relationship with a monumental sigh of relief. I didn't have to try too hard, didn't have to be too witty, too amusing, too beautiful . . . It was like landing on a feather mattress after all those years of being Out There.*

Three years down the line, however, Rosie's beginning to think that 'cosy' isn't all it's cracked up to be. Bridge parties have never really been her thing, and it would be nice to feel beautiful just once in a while. Enough is enough. It's time to get her life back.

'Alliott's *joie de vivre* is irresistible' *Daily Mail*

'Hilarious and full of surprises' *Daily Telegraph*

'A joy . . . you're in for a treat' *Express*